The
Cottage
in the
Woods

The Cottage in the Woods

Katherine Coville

A YEARLING BOOK

Text copyright © 2015 by Katherine Coville
Cover art copyright © 2016 by Petur Atli Antonsson
All rights reserved. Published in the United States by Yearling, an imprint of Random House Children's Books, a division of Penguin Random House LLC, New York. Originally published in hardcover in the United States by Alfred A. Knopf, an imprint of Random House Children's Books, New York, in 2015. Yearling and the jumping horse design are registered trademarks of Penguin Random House LLC.

Visit us on the Web! randomhousekids.com
Educators and librarians, for a variety of teaching tools, visit us at RHTeachersLibrarians.com

The Library of Congress has cataloged the hardcover edition of this work as follows:
Coville, Katherine.
The cottage in the woods / Katherine Coville.
pages cm
Summary: Presents the story of "Goldilocks and the Three Bears" as told by young Teddy's governess, who came to work at the Vaughn family "cottage" shortly before a golden-haired girl, ragged and dirty, entered the home and soon became a beloved foster child, until evil characters tried to take her away.
ISBN 978-0-385-75573-3 (trade) — ISBN 978-0-385-75574-0 (lib. bdg.) — ISBN 978-0-385-75575-7 (ebook)
[1. Fairy tales. 2. Bears—Fiction. 3. Governesses—Fiction. 4. Foster home care—Fiction. 5. Characters in literature—Fiction.] I. Title.
PZ8.C834413Cot 2015
[Fic]—dc23
2014015872

ISBN 978-0-385-75576-4 (pbk.)
Printed in the United States of America
10 9 8 7 6 5 4 3
First Yearling Edition 2016
Random House Children's Books supports the First Amendment and celebrates the right to read.

To my writers' group, MFL,
without whom this book would not exist:

Mary Jane Auch
Patience Brewster
Cynthia DeFelice
Robin Pulver
Vivian Vande Velde
Ellen Stoll Walsh

And especially Bruce Coville, Helper Extraordinaire.

Contents

1

Errare Humanum Est

The Cottage in the Woods, they called it. Later on that became the gatekeeper's lodge, yet they had been so happy there that they kept the name for their grand new manor house. Mr. Vaughn couldn't have been any prouder if he had built that place with his own two paws. It was his vision, his will behind it all, as if he'd wrestled it from rock and timber himself. It was no cottage either. The very thought is laughable.

Eight bedrooms it had in the east wing alone, with balconies, and hot and cold running water no less. And the huge nursery, of course. They had such hopes, such dreams! And then there was the great hall itself, so grand, with the parquet floor and the carved mantelpiece; the den, for him, and the solarium, for her; and the drawing room with the crystal chandelier. And out through the French doors were the terrace and the gardens. Those French doors that the servants said never did shut right. The one flaw. That whole great house just sitting there, and a child could have opened those doors.

And did.

But rustic? No, nothing rustic about it, not even my own quarters. Yet they talk about the three bowls, three chairs, three beds as if that were all there was. No one seems to realize that that was as far as the girl could count then. There was so much she didn't know. A regular little savage she was in the beginning. But I'm getting ahead of myself. Master Teddy would've stopped me with a look, and insisted that I start over. Nothing pleased him half so much as a story well told.

I was an eager young bear that fall when I first came to live at the Cottage. I had been taken on as governess to Master Teddy, my first position. Fresh out of school and desperately anxious to please, I was determined to prove myself and make my dear papa proud. Papa had raised me from a cub after Mama died, and he'd showered as much love on me as any two parents could have. "Ursula," he would say to me, "you're the apple of my eye and the beat of my heart!" And so it was with great ambition and pride that I set off to join the Vaughns' household. Indeed, my father and Mr. Vaughn had been friends in their university days, and I knew that Father greatly prized Mr. Vaughn's good opinion. My own parents had married young—married for love—and I had come along shortly thereafter. Mr. Vaughn had married much later, after he had made his fortune in lumber and speculation. He had prospered brilliantly, while Father struggled by as headmaster of a small school. But their friendship still thrived.

Papa was a great believer in education, and so, despite our slim resources, he had managed to send me to the fine private seminary for young ladies that had lately been the center of my life. At Miss Pinchkin's Academy for Young Ladies, I received instruction in literature, history, art, music, French, science, nat-

ural history, geography, algebra, and comportment, including
how to serve tea, and how to properly respond to a young man
proposing matrimony. Feeling keenly the faith that Papa placed
in me, and wanting so to please him, I had worked my hardest
and graduated in three years, the youngest in my class. Upon my
graduation, Papa presented me with the most precious gift I had
ever received, my mama's silver locket. A lovely piece of jewelry,
it opened to reveal a miniature portrait of Mama and Papa on
their wedding day. I wore it always from that day forward. That
and Mama's wedding dress were the only things I had of hers,
and they were my prized possessions.

I believe it was due to Mr. Vaughn's friendship with Papa
that he was willing to take me on as governess despite my young
age, but Papa expressed his confidence in me, and rather than
cause him a moment's disappointment or anxiety, I would have
aspired to anything, or suffered any manner of hardship in silence. I often felt my dear mother's presence too, watching over
me and encouraging me always to do my utmost.

Such was my frame of mind as I made my way for the first
time up the winding drive through the Forest to the Cottage in
the Woods, expecting to see around each bend the spires of the
fairy-tale palace I had built up in my imagination. The reality
proved more enchanting than any fantasy. I still can recall the
effect on my senses when the vista opened up and I beheld the
Cottage in all its comeliness and perfection. It was a thing of
beauty, surely the largest, grandest, most impressive home I had
ever seen, yet still somehow cozy and welcoming. As I stopped to
take it in, I had no premonition of the trials that lay in wait for
me there. I only knew how appealing it looked as I came toward
it, and how it seemed to draw me in.

The big double doors were opened by a gray-haired gentle-man of ferociously erect posture. He was human, as was so often the case, conventional wisdom holding that humans made the best butlers. We sentient creatures of the Enchanted Forest had traditionally prided ourselves on our open-mindedness about humans. (Whether the humans were as open-minded about us was another matter.) Indeed, it was impossible to predict in the Forest which creature, from a spider to a donkey, might begin speaking to you. Some of us had been enchanted by witches or wizards, some had eaten fairy food or stumbled on some place that was under a spell, and some, like me, had inherited their enchantment from Enchanted parents. I had come from a long line of Enchanted bears, the proud Brown family, and could not imagine life otherwise, but there were wild bears in the Forest, and other animals as well, living in their natural state. It was not always easy to tell who in the Forest was Enchanted and who was not, and so it was best to be very polite and consider-ate to all. This, at least, was the philosophy of most inhabitants of the Enchanted Forest. Occasionally, prejudice would rear its ugly head somewhere, and create divisions between humans and the Enchanted, but I had never experienced this. There were even rumors of places far beyond the Forest where all beasts were wild, and humans hunted them, for food or for sport, but these were cautionary tales to scare miscreant youngsters with; no thinking beast could credit such anecdotes.

But back to my story. I went straight to the front door, rapping lightly with the knocker, and upon its being opened, I produced a bright smile and gave the butler my name. He nodded solemnly and showed me into the library to await the master, making a slight bow as he left the room. Somehow, despite his courtesy, I felt certain that he had judged me as terribly young and gauche. I had to quell a flash of resentment, for I had worn my most sober outfit and forced myself not to stare openmouthed at the grandeur around me, but purposely adopted an expression that I hoped would look profoundly serious and mature. Despite my feigned sophistication, I felt my eyes widen as I took in the vast collection of books: row upon row of finely bound volumes lined up from floor to ceiling. I drew closer, surveying the titles. Here were all the classics; the writings of the ancient philosophers, including some humans; volumes of mythology, religion, and poetry; and a procession of thick encyclopedias. Several books lay open on a wide table, and I peered into them, feeling as if I were invading someone's privacy, but I was in love with books and could not help myself. I picked up one thick volume, bound in red, holding the place carefully while scanning through the pages. It consisted of phrases written in a language foreign to me, with English translations. I chose a phrase and tried to sound out the words under my breath.

"Scisne latine?" rumbled a deep bass voice behind me. I jumped, the book slipping from my paws and landing open, facedown on my shoes. I was mortified, frozen to the spot. I looked up at the forbidding countenance of he who must surely be Mr. Vaughn, my employer, and stammered my apologies. Dark eyes flashed back at me from under a broad brow. The effect was quite forceful. Everything about his manner and dress announced that this was a bear of consequence, not to be trifled with. I swallowed hard.

"Miss Brown, I presume?" he said.

"Yes, sir," I answered. "It's Ursula, sir."

"Well, Miss Brown, are you going to pick up that book, or must I?"

"Oh yes, sir," I breathed. My power of movement came back to me with a sudden jolt, and I bent over and scooped up the book, noticing as I did that several pages were wrinkled. "I am so sorry, sir," I said. "I'll replace the book, of course. I shouldn't have touched it. I don't know what came over me. It was an accident, sir. I'm afraid your voice startled me. I'm really very good with books. I'm an avid reader. I've always loved books. I . . ." My voice trailed off as I realized I was saying too much. I set the book down gently on the table and was silent.

"*Errare humanum est,* Miss Brown. From the ancients. 'To err is human.' One may philosophize that it is also ursine. We shall dismiss this incident as unimportant. In the future you will, I am sure, learn to overcome this unwarranted nervousness in order to avoid any more such accidents. I have confidence that you will live up to the same level of virtuous character and professional excellence that I've always respected in your father. Is my faith justified?"

"Oh yes, sir," I answered.

"Good. *Vincit qui se vincit,* Miss Brown. 'She conquers who conquers herself.'"

"Yes, sir."

"Then we understand one another?"

"*Je comprends très bien, m'sieur,*" I replied, hoping to impress him.

"Ah, yes. Listed among your many accomplishments, you speak French. Very good. You will instruct young Theodore in both Latin and French."

I swallowed hard. "But, sir, I barely recognize Latin."

"Your references greatly praise your ability to learn quickly, Miss Brown. Take the book of Latin phrases, and here, this Latin dictionary and grammar book, and this history of Rome, and yes, of course, the legend of Romulus and Remus." This he said as he drew the books from their shelves and piled them in my arms. "If you begin studying at once, you'll be conjugating Latin verbs in a fortnight. You should be able within the month to commence teaching beginning Latin along with the French. French is derived from Latin, you realize; they are closely related."

"Forgive me, sir, but a month?"

"All right, then. Let us say before the winter snows. Surely you can handle that assignment?"

"But won't that be a lot for the youngster to take in?"

"Nonsense. The young mind is like a sponge. We must put it to good use. I will not have my son idling away his time. You are his teacher. Teach! *Audaces fortuna iuvat.* 'Fortune favors the brave.'"

"Yes, sir. I will do my best," I responded, trying to hide the quaver in my voice.

"Good. I expect nothing less of you," he said, ringing the servants' bell and taking a gold timepiece out of his vest pocket. "Fairchild will show you to your quarters. You will join the family tonight for supper, where you will meet my wife and Master Theodore. We sit down at table in half an hour. Don't be late."

2

The Echo

&

I followed Fairchild through a maze of corridors, up a back stairway, and down a long, wide hall hung with paintings. Some were portraits, and some were representations of celebrated moments in history, like Tom Thumb's famous horse ride, and the running of the great race between the Tortoise and the Hare.

The many family portraits were easily recognized by one unmistakable trait that had apparently been handed down from generation to generation: a distinctive, aristocratic snout. One portrait stood out in harsh contrast to the rest, a depiction that could easily have been Mr. Vaughn himself were it not for the queer, ugly smile, and something repellent about the eyes. The figure wore a long black coat from another era, with an incongruous bunch of lace at his throat, and a wide black plumed hat. I thought perhaps he was a pirate, certainly some variety of scoundrel. As I stood pondering, Fairchild suddenly cleared his throat, bringing me back to reality. He had been waiting with pained forbearance, holding the heavy stack of books I had just been given.

"Who is this?" I asked, indicating the portrait.

"Perhaps the head housekeeper, Mrs. Gudge, will give you the tour, later," he said. "Perhaps after supper," he said more pointedly, "or tomorrow."

"Oh yes. Yes, of course," I answered, recalling the master's admonition to be on time for the meal. After a few more turns, we reached my quarters, which consisted of a sizable, simply furnished bedchamber and double doors leading to a balcony that looked out over the kitchen garden. It was appointed in pale blue, with a blue counterpane on the four-poster bed and shiny new chintz covers on the chairs. A mirror was propped up on the bureau, and I wondered briefly if it might be a magic mirror. A household like this one would doubtless have many magic mirrors, but I hardly dared hope one might be provided for the governess.

Certainly someone had taken pains to ensure my comfort. Fresh water had been left in a pitcher, and a vase of cut flowers adorned the mantelpiece. Simple as it was, it was quite the most elegant and charming place I had ever inhabited, and I was grateful for the Vaughns' generosity, but I was also faced with the fact that I had been dreading since I first applied for the position: I would have no roommate. One might suppose that I would be thankful for the newfound privacy, but I only felt a cold stab of apprehension at the idea of sleeping utterly alone. I tried to imagine what this room would be like in darkness. Would moonlight come in the window? Would there be creaks and bumps in the night? Adrift in a sea of childish fears, I suddenly realized that time was passing. I quickly washed my face and paws, put on my clean black stuff gown and my best lace collar. Checking my reflection in the mirror, I considered asking it for directions back down to the dining room, but I thought that I could retrace my steps and so I didn't take the time. I stepped out my door, took a left turn and a right, and found my way back to the portrait gallery. That much was easy. I hurried past the disturbing portrait of the pirate, trying not to look at it. After that, I was not certain which way to go. Stairways led in two directions. One direction was darker, so I took the other. This brought me before long to a narrow hallway, which I followed to a large parlor. From there I took several turns, none of which yielded anything familiar. By this time, I knew I must already be late for the meal, and I felt my heart beating a little faster. As I searched in vain for the wide hallway I remembered, I regretted miserably that I had not tried to get directions from the mirror before I set out. Finally, I retraced my steps to the first stairway and braved its shadows, nearly colliding with the tall figure of Fairchild, who had apparently been sent to find me. I thought I saw a flicker of amusement cross his features, but human faces were notoriously hard to read. He accompanied me to the dining room, where I found myself once again explaining and apologizing and trailing off into an awkward silence.

"Miss Brown," said Mr. Vaughn with awful courtesy, "how very good of you to join us. No doubt you will be seated in your own good time."

Perceiving that this was to be the end of the matter, I sat down, and the introductions were made, first to Mrs. Vaughn, as was proper, and then to little Teddy, my charge. (Only his father called him Theodore.)

"I'm staying up late tonight!" Teddy immediately announced. "Because you're here. I get to eat supper with Mama and Papa! And—"

"Remember what we discussed, Teddy," said his mother, not unkindly.

"Oh!" said Teddy, and the cub covered his mouth with both paws and was quiet. I suppressed my laughter, and gazed at Mrs. Vaughn, who made an indelible first impression. She was a great beauty, with wide, gentle eyes and a reddish tint to her fur, but there was a hint of melancholy about her too, as if she carried some deep secret sorrow. She was dressed in lilac silk, with elegant accents of lace and ribbon, the very picture of genteel prosperity, yet she was genial and did not put on airs. I was touched by her concern for me, and gratified when she asked whether I had liked my quarters, and whether I would like a servant to guide me when it was time to return to them. I, who had grown up without a mother's affection, found myself now on the receiving end of Mrs. Vaughn's warm caring. It was a new, but not unwelcome, sensation.

"Really, my dear," she said, full of solicitude, "why don't we assign one of the servants to guide you about the house until you can find your way around?"

"I'm afraid that would be an awful imposition," I said, trying to be polite, but hoping she would override my objection. Daylight was fading even as we ate, and I already dreaded the idea of traveling the darkening hallways by myself.

"I'll do it!" chimed in Teddy eagerly. "I can show her around, can't I, Mama?" The cub sat bolt upright, radiating enthusiasm. He took after his mother in looks, with soft brown eyes and reddish fur, offset nicely by his royal-blue sailor suit. I looked at the bright-eyed cub and smiled broadly, and was rewarded with a toothy smile of his own. How charmed I was by this buoyant little soul! I remember that moment as the beginning of a natural sympathy between the two of us. As his teacher, I knew I must maintain the dignity of my position, but with my child's heart I fully enjoyed Teddy's company from the very beginning—his generous impulses, and his natural curiosity and ebullience.

The meal passed, with a bounty of good food: fresh fish, bread, and three kinds of berries, followed by sweetmeats made with honey. I noticed that the cub used excellent table manners, as if he had been warned ahead of time to be on his best behavior. I thought it almost abnormal for a youngster to behave so well, and I looked forward to finding out if this was usual for him.

When it came time to retire, Teddy and I were sent forth with a bright candle to find the nursery, which was adjacent to my room. His parents promised to come up for Teddy's bedtime, but apparently wanted to encourage his urge to be helpful by letting him guide me there himself. They must have assumed that I would provide an adequate sense of security for the youngster, should he need it. Little did they suspect that I looked to the cub for my own security.

As we set off through the gloomy passages, Teddy kept up a steady flow of childish banter, which served to distract me from my fears. Before we even reached the stairs, I had learned that his vocabulary was quite large. I also learned the number of toy boats in his collection (ten) and the identity of his favorite toy (a stuffed badger named Freddy). As we climbed the staircase, his conversation started to flag. I began to notice the stairs creaking beneath our feet, and to listen for other noises. I held my candle higher and looked behind us, where the stairwell seemed to fall away into oblivion. Was it just the echo of our footsteps I heard? Ahead loomed the picture gallery, and I was suddenly seized with a wish not to walk past that menacing portrait with the half-mad eyes again. I held tightly to Teddy's paw and took a deep breath. There was no help for it; through the gallery we must go. I focused on the floor in front of my feet and walked as fast as I could without actually dragging Teddy in my wake, but he stopped, just in front of the portrait, and seemingly attempting to bury himself in the folds of my skirts, he said, "Look!"

"What is it?" I said, not wanting to hear the answer.

"His eyes!" said Teddy tremulously. "Do you see? They follow you."

I cringed as I looked up at the painting. The eyes had taken on a lifelike glow in the candlelight, and they did indeed seem to be looking right at me. I took another deep breath, trying not to show my fear in front of the cub, and said calmly, "Oh yes, that wicked-looking old rascal. And who is he?"

Teddy looked up at me with awed sincerity and dread, and whispered, "It's Great-Uncle Ruprecht. Nurse told me a secret, but it's secret, so don't tell anyone. She says Uncle Ruprecht has a restless spirit. She says he walks the hallways at night. Do you think he does?"

"Absolutely not!" I replied, in my best no-nonsense voice— not because I felt so certain at that moment, but from outrage that his own nanny would try to scare the impressionable cub. After all the years I had suffered with my own nighttime fears, I would not have inflicted them on this youngster for the world. "Let's just make a face right back at him, shall we?" I said brightly, and proceeded to do so. Teddy covered his face with his paws, as if fearing some retribution from the old pirate, but, since the retribution never came, he began to be amused too. Soon he was making faces at the portrait as well, and dissolving into laughter. "Come now," I said. "It's off to bed with you." I gripped his paw firmly and marched determinedly onward. It was only as we reached the far end of the gallery that I became aware again of the echo of our footsteps behind us. I stopped short, bringing Teddy to a halt beside me, but the soft, swishing footsteps continued—too long. Too long to be an echo. Teddy and I looked at one another, and then, as of one accord, we ran.

3

Nurse

How long we scrambled in headlong flight, I do not know. Time plays tricks on us when we are in our extremities and makes a single minute stretch into eternity. I only know that at the end of such an eternity Teddy charged into the nursery with me half a heartbeat behind. We slammed the door, and I leaned against it, breathing hard, while Teddy peered intently through the keyhole to see if anything had followed us. As I struggled to collect myself, I gained my initial impression of the nursery. First the size—easily twice as big as my chamber. It seemed nearly empty, excepting one corner near the fireplace where there was a small cluster of furniture, a rocking horse, and some shelves full of toys. On the other side of the fireplace was a big, overstuffed chair, and sitting in the chair was a grizzled old lady badger of generous proportions, dressed in a cacophony of hideous patterns and colors from her skirts to her ruffled dustcap. But what arrested my attention was that her head was thrown back, and she was guzzling from a small flask. I took in all of this in an instant, and in the next instant she gave a surprised squeak, and, wiping her mouth with the back of one paw, quickly hid away the flask with the other. This, I realized, must be Nurse, and her guilty gesture left me in no doubt about the contents of the flask.

My fright from the hallway faded as I reacted to this development. I could not immediately settle on what course to take. Surely if the master knew of this offense, Nurse would be summarily dismissed. For my own part I was innocent enough to be shocked by her behavior. Was she drunk? Though her eyes were red-rimmed and, I thought, slightly unfocused, she seemed self-possessed, and glared at me with unmistakable loathing. Not knowing what else to do, I decided to behave as if everything were normal. Accordingly, I approached her, extending a polite paw, and introduced myself.

"Ah, yes," she responded, making no move toward me. "The new chickie. The governess. Isn't that just grand, though? Isn't it a privilege to meet you? A privilege, I'm sure. And aren't we just in awe? Awestruck, that's what it is." And her shoulders shook as she laughed a dry, wheezy laugh. It sounded like "Heesh heesh hee. Heesh heesh heesh hee."

Taken aback, I withdrew my paw. While her words seemed grandiloquent, her manner was sneering and caustic. I could think of no response but stood there dumbly.

"Oh!" she cried. "Was that too sarcastic? *Do* excuse me! Y'see, that wasn't really sarcasm, chickie," she said, climbing down out of the chair and drawing herself up to her full two feet of height. "That was just a bit of IRONY. Life's full of irony, don't you know." And she began the dry laugh again, putting her whole body into it.

I felt myself stiffening. Her contempt was almost palpable. Miss Pinchkin's Academy had not prepared me to deal with such abominable rudeness. Papa had taught me to use good manners to my elders, no matter what, and so I tried again. "My name is Ursula Brown," I repeated, as politely as I could.

"Well, well, Miss Chickie Brown," she responded. "Chickie, chickie, chickie. Heesh heesh hee." She turned her back on me and waddled unsteadily over to the wardrobe, pulling out a nightshirt. Then her whole manner changed as she faced about and called Teddy over to her. "Come here, dearie," she coaxed, her voice all sweetness and honey. "Time for bed now. There's a good cub."

Teddy, who was still peering out through the keyhole, said, "Wait! Wait! I think I see something!"

Her response was swift and implacable. In a voice harsh enough to peel paint, Nurse barked one brief order for him to come "AT ONCE!" Teddy flew to her side. Despite her small size, he meekly accepted her ministrations. In a few efficient moves, she had him out of his clothes and into his nightshirt, his teeth brushed and face washed, and tucked into his little bed. I noticed a smaller, badger-sized bed nearby as Teddy babbled on, unstopping, about Great-Uncle Ruprecht and the footsteps in the hallway.

"Oh yes, dearie," Nurse agreed. "He's a bad one, old Uncle is. We'd best not be walking about the halls at night, had we, now?" Teddy's sensitive little face looked nearly terrified, and he burrowed under his covers.

I drew in my breath, hot anger rising in my breast. Already I felt a bond with the cub, and the thought that Nurse would play on his fears and undermine his confidence incensed me to the point where I felt I must do something, but what? Nurse was clearly in authority here, and I dared not challenge her. Sitting on Teddy's bed, I bent over and, lifting the covers slightly, whispered softly to him, "Don't you believe that for a minute, Teddy. It's just an old picture with scary eyes!"

Two big brown eyes peered over the edge of the counterpane, and I thought he would respond, but he quickly covered his head again.

I turned to see Nurse, paws on hips, giving me an evil glare. Had she overheard me?

"Some people ought to mind their own business!" she growled. I immediately thought that Teddy *was* my business, but could not summon the nerve to say so. I stood up, and though I towered over her, I felt much the smaller of the two of us.

Swaying slightly, she announced, "This is *my* nursery! I'm the nurse! You should call me *Nurse*! That's not to say I'll answer to you, of course, but life's full of disappointments, isn't it, now, chickie?" She sauntered over to the far side of the room, out of Teddy's earshot, and I followed after her.

"Just you keep your snout out of my affairs, chickie," she hissed, "and stay on my *good* side."

I was struck by the thought that she had a side worse than this. The silence stretched out. Was she waiting for me to agree to this? Surely she understood that Teddy was my charge too? I wanted to say as much, but her little black eyes seemed to bore into my skull, and I said nothing.

"Good, then," she barked. "That's settled!"

"Wait!" I blurted. Thinking of Teddy's haunted look, and feeling that I owed it to him to say something, I screwed up my courage. "I just wanted to ask you . . . don't you worry about making the cub fearful?"

"Me?" she jeered. "Me make him fearful? Why, it wasn't me came running in here as if the hounds of Hell was on my tail, was it? And what a sight that was!" she snickered. "What a sight!"

Here she began the "Heesh heesh hee" again, her paws clapping together, her head and shoulders bobbing up and down with each breath.

I endured her insufferable laughter in silence, and was mentally casting about for a suitable response when I realized that there was none. She was right. I had allowed Teddy to see me giving in to fear. The knowledge stung, but it only served to make me even angrier. What had I done, compared with her drinking spirits and purposely trying to scare Teddy? What would the master think of her conduct? I'm sure my expression was mutinous, and, as if she had somehow read my mind, she drew the flask from her pocket and wiggled it back and forth in front of me, a look of cunning in her eyes. "And don't you be getting any ideas about telling tales on me, chickie, or I might have to tell the master about this little flask I had to take away from you!"

"You had to take away from *me*? What can you mean?"

"Why, your flask." She smirked. "Right here. The one I caught you drinking from."

I bit my lip, fighting back the tears of rage and frustration that threatened to appear. "That's a lie!" I cried.

"A lie, is it? Supposing you tell the master your story and I tell him mine. Who do you think will be believed? The new young chickie, or the trusted old family retainer? Eh? Who do you think will be sent packing?"

Her question hung in the air like the blade of a guillotine. I could feel the bite of the cold metal as I silently faced the answer.

There was no one here to speak for me. Even Teddy had been busy looking through the keyhole, and had not seen her with the flask. I was the stranger. I would not be believed. I would be, as she said, the one sent packing. Perhaps if I had been older, less diffident, I would not have been so easily intimidated, but having never personally encountered such villainy, I was unprepared to deal with it. While my spirit rebelled at the gross injustice of the situation, I exclaimed, "I had no intention of going to the master!"

"Oh, well, ain't that a MARVEL? Very big of you, I'm sure. Very SMART too, if ye take my meaning. I wonder if I can be so generous? Perhaps I owe it to the master to shed light on the character of his new employee!" Nurse wiggled the flask again and laughed her hateful laugh.

The door clicked open, and the flask was whisked into Nurse's pocket just as Teddy's father walked in. The badger's expression changed in a trice from malicious glee to the most agreeable tranquillity. "Good evening, Mr. Vaughn," she intoned sweetly. "I was just talking to the new governess. Tryin' to get her off on the right foot, you know."

My own thoughts were turbulent, and I was afraid it must show on my face. What were her intentions? Would she carry out her threat? Before I could think of a word to say, little Teddy piped up from the other side of the room. "Papa! There were FOOTSTEPS in the hall! Real ones! Uncle Ruprecht was after us! So we RAN. We ran all the way. Did you hear them?"

Mr. Vaughn picked Teddy up and held him close. His countenance grew dark and serious. "Who has been filling your head with such nonsense?" he asked.

"But it was REAL, Papa. Miss Brown heard them too. We heard them behind us in the gallery. So we ran."

"That they did, sir," drawled Nurse. "I didn't like to tell you, but they did come running in here mighty wild, sir. I was just having a bit of a talk with Miss Brown about scaring the child, sir." She turned to me with a little half smirk, as if daring me to contradict her, and I knew I was caught. If I exposed her for telling Teddy stories about Uncle Ruprecht, I was sure she would use her lie about the flask to get me dismissed. I stood mute, waiting to see how things would fall out. Mr. Vaughn's eyes turned intently on me. "If I might have a word with you in the hallway, Miss Brown?"

I nodded and picked up my candle. On my way out of the room, I glanced at Nurse, who was still smiling demurely. She caught my gaze and purposefully patted the pocket where she had hidden the flask. Then she winked and snickered, covering her laugh with a cough.

4

The Magic Mirror

Mr. Vaughn followed me into the corridor and shut the door behind us. "I want to make it perfectly clear, Miss Brown, that Theodore is not to be fed any fanciful or superstitious notions, most particularly not those that can only be designed to make him nervous and fearful. I must have your full agreement on this or I'm afraid your position here will be very short-lived."

I felt the sting of tears at the corners of my eyes. How could everything have gone so wrong so quickly?

"What do you have to say for yourself?" he asked.

"Well, sir," I began, searching for the right words, "we did hear something in the hallway, but I see now that it was very foolish of me to run. I'm afraid my nerves were a little over-wrought, and I didn't stop to think of the effect it might have on Teddy. It won't happen again, sir."

"And what of Uncle Ruprecht?"

I paused, wondering how to clear myself without incriminating Nurse. "I did not even know who he was until Teddy told me. I told no stories of him or of anyone. Please believe me, sir. I would never try to frighten Teddy in any way."

Here Mr. Vaughn subjected me to his penetrating stare, as if he were dissecting the whole of my character, testing its steadfastness, and gauging where it came up short. I trembled at this examination, but I hoped he would see my sincerity.

"I believe you would not, Miss Brown," he said at length, "but perhaps your own fearfulness is still a threat to Theodore's peace of mind. Need I point out that you are in a position of authority, and must be ever mindful of your example to the young? Theodore cannot learn rationality or courage from one who has not these qualities in herself. *Vincit qui se vincit.* 'She conquers who conquers herself,' Miss Brown. I suggest you take it as your motto. My eye will be upon you."

"Yes, sir." I exhaled, realizing that I had been holding my breath.

"Now, then, do you require accompaniment to your door? It's the next one on the right."

"No, sir. I will be fine, sir," I said, nearly choking on the words. I raised my candle high and stepped off into the darkness, hoping my stride looked confident and purposeful even though I inwardly quailed. I ran my free paw along the wall, as if following a lifeline, all the way to my door, then sighed with relief. My chamber, while dark, seemed a few degrees safer than the inky hallway. I shut the door tightly, then began a careful exploration of every nook and cranny, checking behind the heavy drapes, inside the tall wardrobe, even under the furniture. All I could see was that someone had brought up my trunk and valise. Satisfied at last that nothing lurked in the shadows, I unpacked my few belongings in the dim candlelight, prepared myself for bed, and climbed between the sheets on the overstuffed mattress. I left the candle burning on the bedside stand, unable to bring myself to extinguish it.

As I lay there, the troubles of the day crowded in on me like birds of prey. I had ruined Mr. Vaughn's book, gotten lost, been late to dinner, abandoned self-control and run through the hallway with Teddy, made an enemy of Nurse, and come close to losing my job before it started. How could I ever face Papa if I was dismissed? What a disappointment it would be to him, and an embarrassment, if his old friend were forced to let me go. One phrase kept repeating itself in my mind, that dire warning: "My eye will be upon you." This, taken with the knowledge that Nurse would use anything, be it truth or falsehood, to harm me, left me feeling more alone and friendless than I ever had been in my life. I covered my face with my paws and gave in to bitter tears.

Even so, I knew that I would never hear a word of reproach from Papa. What would he say to me if I could tell him my troubles tonight? The smallest of smiles started on my lips. I could almost hear his voice, deep, jovial, soothing, telling me that all was not lost; that Mr. Vaughn had not yet given up on me; that morning would bring a fresh start and I would surely do better tomorrow. I pictured him in his rocker by the fireplace, his lap robe over his knees, and it seemed to me as if I smelled the sweet, pungent smoke of his pipe. I felt myself tearing up again.

I could not let Papa down. There must be a way—a way I could earn a place of trust with the Vaughns, a way to win out against Nurse's nefarious accusations. What would it take? I wondered. Probably a long time, if they were going to accept my word over Nurse's. A long time of doing well and not making mistakes. It seemed impossible, and yet Papa would want me to try. He'd want me to do my best no matter what. And then I thought of Teddy's poor, frightened little face, of him being persecuted by Nurse and his parents not even knowing it. Maybe I could be his friend as well as his teacher, and maybe there would be something I could do for him.

And though in this house I had not a single soul to confide in, I did have one place to unburden myself. I wiped away my tears with the back of my paw, and got out of bed. There on the writing desk lay my new journal, a parting gift from Papa, bound in plain brown cloth and locked with a small brass padlock.

I got the tiny key from my shoe and unlocked it, opening it to the first page, blank and patiently waiting for me. Picking up the pen, and dipping it in the ink, I began the habit that has served me so well to this day, lightening my burdens and preserving my memories, that of writing nightly in my journal, my best, and often my only, confidant. It assists me even now as I tell this story, which has since become so clouded by gossip and myth. I have only to reach into my trunk and open one of the old volumes, covers worn and pages curling, to make the years fall away.

I wrote late into that night, until my eyelids drooped, and my heart felt emptied of all its burdens. Then I knelt beside the bed, keeping my eyes open for fear of whatever might be lurking in the dark, and said my prayers. I was faced with the uncomfortable thought of that which I had been taught from cubhood: that one must pray for one's enemies. I had never had an enemy until now, but with Nurse's sneering image fresh in my mind, a prayer for her seemed a very bitter pill to swallow. I grappled with my feelings until my lips grudgingly formed the words "God bless Nurse," and I mentally choked them down. My mind at peace, I was soon sleeping the sleep of the innocent. I can picture myself now, lying there peacefully, eyes closed, and all unknowing. Little could I have imagined then what challenges lay ahead for me, or what tears I would shed in the times to come.

∂

Despite the fact that I had stayed up so late, I awoke early to the song of a wren outside my window, an anthem of such hopefulness and buoyancy that I immediately threw back the drapes and opened the doors to my little balcony. The air was alive with birdsong. The sun's golden rays glimmered through the laced tree branches, creating a filigree of blue shadows on the lawn. I breathed in the essence of countless delightful scents borne on the breeze. I began to hum a little tune as I performed my toilet, and was still humming when one of the maids arrived to tell me my breakfast was served in the kitchen. She was a young bear about my size, only very attractive, with a pleasingly pear-shaped frame, and I couldn't help but compare her to my own flat figure. I thought I would try to make some friendly overture, but she was gone as quickly as she came—before I could ask her to show me to the kitchen. I did not want to venture out again without some guidance, and so I turned to the mirror on the bureau and gave an experimental knock on the corner. "Hello, Mirror?" I asked. "Is anyone there?" I rubbed its surface with my handkerchief, wondering if it could have grown indolent with disuse. "Hello?" I knocked again.

My reflection in the mirror turned to roiling dark clouds, but no other face appeared. Only a disembodied voice croaked, "Go away!" and the mirror went black. I rapped harder on the shiny surface, and said forcefully, "Mirror, I'm afraid I must insist. Wake up."

"What is the password, then?"

"Password? There is no password. You're a mirror. You must answer me."

"There *is too* a password, and you obviously don't know it, so I don't have to answer you at all." And the mirror turned black once more.

"I only wanted directions to the kitchen, for pity's sake," I said.

The mirror clouded up again. "You guessed the password!"

"I did? What was it?" I asked.

"To," came the answer.

"*To?* That's not a very good password, is it? Anyone might say it by accident."

"Yes, well, only those who are rude enough to insist on making inquiries at this hour of the morning."

"The kitchen, if you please, Mirror."

Some incoherent grumbling could be heard as the agitated clouds formed into a carnival mask, all black on one side, all white on the other. He was wearing a long, tasseled nightcap and yawning widely. "You must begin by opening your door. Then you must go down the long corridor to the right, like so." The mirror presented a picture of the corridor. "And you will come to the back staircase." The mirror presented a view of the staircase. "Turn left at the bottom of the stairs. From there your snout will lead you to the kitchen.

"Or else you should go out of your door and go to the left, then take another left after the portrait gallery." The mirror presented views of the route. "Go down another set of stairs, take a right, go to the end of that hallway, and open the door."

"Well, how do I begin? Go right or go left?"

The face raised one imperious black eyebrow. "I'm sure that's not for me to say. I'm merely presenting both sides."

"Both sides? Will both answers lead me to the kitchen?"

"No, only one will, but it's more fair this way."

"Fair to whom," I asked, "if one way is true and the other a lie?"

"Why, fair to the lie, of course. But there it is, a fair and evenhanded account. Equal time for opposite views. Now it's up to you. Good day."

5

A Trip to Paradise

❧

The savant's face clouded up again, and then shifted back into my own reflection. Clearly I would get no more information out of him. I went to my door and looked both ways, up and down the corridor. I decided to begin with the first set of directions, going to the right and looking for the back staircase. It did occur to me as I made my way down the corridor that the mirror might have been misleading me on both counts, but having no better choices, I persevered. At the bottom of the stairs, my snout detected the mouthwatering smell of fresh biscuits baking. My senses did indeed lead me directly to the kitchen, where the scene was one of pleasant hubbub.

The first person I encountered was Fairchild, who introduced me to the head housekeeper, Mrs. Gudge. She was an impressive older bear with an air of quiet authority. "Good morning, miss," she stated perfunctorily. "I hope you've found everything to your satisfaction?" Her tone brooked no objection, so I made no complaint about the mirror. She went on to introduce me to the kitchen staff and various servants who were bustling in and out, and I received curt nods from most of them. As I took in my surroundings, I became aware that Nurse was deep in a conference with several of the housemaids, who were bent over her, listening. There was a little burst of laughter, and then they all looked furtively around at me, quickly turned away, and laughed again. I could just imagine what stories she was making up at my expense, and I felt insulted and angry, but, seeing nothing I could do about it, I tried to ignore them.

Cook, a genial she-bear who kept up a running patter as she worked, pointed her spatula toward a small side table where a place was set for one, and said, "Right over there, miss. Biscuits will be up in a minute, if you'll be so patient, and well worth waiting for, if I say so myself."

"Won't the staff be eating too?" I asked.

"They'll eat when the morning chores are done."

"I see," I replied, and I sat down and surveyed a tall stack of pancakes covered with honey, and a large bowl of fruit, an ample start for the day by any measure. As I ate, I contemplated my solitary status at the little table. I had been warned of this lonely aspect of my vocation: that a governess, while too well educated to be considered one of the servants, could not be considered a part of the family either. Last night's inclusion at supper had been an act of kindness to welcome me here, but it seemed that, from now on, like any other governess, I must expect to take my meals alone.

I thanked Cook for the lovely breakfast, and asked the pretty little maid, whose name was Betsy, for directions to the schoolroom, which proved to be quite straightforward. My exploration seemed less daunting in daylight, and I found my way without too much difficulty.

Teddy and his mother were waiting for me in the school-room. Teddy greeted me warmly with a well-rehearsed "Good morning, Miss Brown," and a little paw full of flowers.

"Good morning," Mrs. Vaughn said. "I hope you've found everything to your liking."

"Oh yes," I responded. "My room is quite the loveliest I've ever had. And breakfast was very nice too."

Mrs. Vaughn smiled warmly and handed me a stack of books. "Here are some textbooks Mr. Vaughn ordered for you," she said. "And here are some of Teddy's favorite books as well. You may order more as you need them. There is a catalog included. Just give the list to Mr. Vaughn's clerk, Mr. Bentley. His office is adjacent to the library. Mr. Vaughn says you are to feel free to use the library during the day. There is a special section of cubs' books on the lower shelves beside the desk."

"Thank you. I'm sure that will be more than enough to get us started," I answered.

"At noon, luncheon will be served here in the schoolroom, if you like," she said. "Just ring for Betsy. Teddy is to have a short rest after the meal, then you may resume in the afternoon."

"Very good, madam. If it meets with your approval, I should like to take him out of doors, in the afternoons, weather permitting, for natural history and woodcraft?"

"Yes, that will suit perfectly, I'm sure. Just be certain to deliver him back to me by teatime. After that, your time is your own, though I understand Mr. Vaughn has set you to work learning Latin. Still, you should have ample free time. I hope you will feel at liberty to enjoy the grounds. There are miles of trails good for walking. You and Teddy might enjoy the walk to the waterfall this afternoon. It's very secluded and picturesque. You may go wading, if it's not too cold. Teddy knows the way."

She gave Teddy a little pat on the head, with an admonition to mind his governess, and make his mama and papa proud, and left us to our own devices. I sent my thanks Heavenward that my pupil's mother was so reasonable and generous.

I set out first to determine what levels Teddy had reached in his education, and discovered through some simple learning games that he was already proficient in reciting the alphabet, and could count to twenty. He also knew several of the stories from his storybooks by heart, and recited them as we turned the pages, making up little improvements here and there when the mood took him. I was charmed by these imaginative touches, and suggested that I could help him to write down stories of his own invention. This met with such enthusiasm that he wanted to begin right away, and I, capitalizing on the moment, sat with him and wrote while he spun me a fantastic yarn, peopled with brave and resourceful young bears, all manner of wizards and witches, and hideous fire-breathing dragons. When he had finished, I read it back to him word for word, and had the pleasure of seeing his soft brown eyes glow with delight. Suddenly he saw writing as a magical tool, something that could make his imaginings come to life, something he was eager to learn. I promised him that we would begin the very next day to make letters into words, looking forward to the day when he would be able to write his own stories.

In no time, it seemed, the lunch hour came, and I rang for Betsy and requested that we have a tray prepared to take outdoors. As this troubled no one, we found a comfortable spot under an enormous old oak, and ate our lunch of aged cheese, a dark, wholesome bread, and sweet mead. Then, while Teddy lay reluctantly down for his rest in the nursery, I spent my time getting ready for our nature hike. I found that the schoolroom was complete with nets, collecting jars, and an assortment of books on local flora and fauna. I was packing several collecting jars and a book on birds into a satchel when Mr. Vaughn entered the schoolroom with a most serious expression. "So, Miss Brown, I have just come from the nursery. Theodore tells me that he spent the morning making up stories. Is this true?"

"Yes, sir," I almost squeaked.

"And what is the reason for this? Surely you have better things to teach him than that!"

"It was a writing exercise, sir," I managed to respond. "I thought that writing his own story would excite his interest in learning to read and write."

"I suggest you excite his interest using something with a basis in fact, such as 'Jack and the Beanstalk,' or 'Snow White and the Seven Elves.'"

"*Elves,* sir?"

"Yes. Yes, *Dwarfs.* That's what I said. The important thing is to stick to the history books!"

"Yes, sir. I shall look into it. Just the facts," I responded as I secretly crossed my claws under the tabletop. The truth was, I abhorred the idea of stifling Teddy's splendid imagination. Though I was new to being a governess, I was still a cub at heart, and I remembered how a young cub's mind worked, and how to spark its interest. I thought I could find a way to pay lip service to Mr. Vaughn's directions while continuing with my own program.

That afternoon found Teddy and me meandering along the banks of Ambleworthy Stream, as delightful a body of water as one could wish for, bubbling gleefully as it slipped and plunged over black rocks, and resting here and there in transparent pools filled with frogs and minnows. Teddy and I were conversing on subjects from eating one's Brussels sprouts, of which he did not approve, to the saying of rhyming prayers, of which he did, and on to the finer points of making kite tails and spitwads. We had captured and identified four different insects, including a water bug and two butterflies, and hoped to catch several more.

Teddy was proud of his proficiency with the net, and prouder still to be my tour guide. I could tell by the soft, ever-present roar that we were near the waterfall. The path took a turn away from the stream, and into the deep woods, where the view was obscured for a space of time. Suddenly we stepped out of the woods and into a sunlit glade. There in front of us was a sheer rock face, perhaps sixty yards high, with a curtain of white water tumbling down, down, into a pillow of mist. Beneath the mist, a bed of jagged rocks tore the curtain into chaos and foam, and released it to the surrounding lagoon. I breathed a long sigh of pure pleasure, and strolled to the water's edge. In every direction lay such extravagant beauty that it seemed as if we had stumbled upon a small corner of paradise. I was still taking it in while Teddy took his shoes and socks off and gingerly tested the water with his toes.

"It's not too cold, Miss Brown, is it?" he asked, raising his voice to make himself heard over the rush of the waterfall. I bent down and plunged my paw into the clear pool, and, finding it acceptable, gave him a nod of approval.

"Stay near the shore!" I cried, sitting down to remove my own shoes and stockings, then tucking up my dress and petticoats so as not to get them wet. I set the collection jars out for him, and then waded into the water, wiggling my toes in the pebbly bottom as Teddy swooped his net after an elusive amphibian.

"I got one! I got one!" Teddy yelled. I fetched a jar for him and held it while he tenderly extracted the creature from the net, and placed him inside. I was oddly moved by Teddy's gentle touch with the tiny animal. It was a wonder to see such painstaking coordination and thoughtfulness in one so young. He looked up at me, straight into my eyes, and I thought, not for the last time, what an excellent little companion he made.

We set the captured frog aside to take back to the schoolroom. Together we made our roundabout way toward the waterfall, occasionally stopping here or there to capture another frog. These were just for sport; Teddy held each of them in turn between his two paws, and told them they were the best of frogs, and how pleased he was to make their acquaintance, then he released them with a splash back into the pool. We had come to the rocks at the edge of the falls, and paused there, staring out over the water, letting the fine spray dampen our faces. I found myself gazing, half hypnotized, at the patterns of light glancing off the wavelets, and for a time I basked in that feeling of rightness with the world that profligate beauty often confers.

I don't know what broke in upon my reverie, whether it was the violent motion I caught in the corner of my eye, or whether the apprehension of disaster seized me before I had turned my head, but I knew immediately that Teddy was in trouble, even before I heard his cry. I had not seen him leap to the wall of rock and begin to climb, but there he was, scrambling for a higher foothold, and wearing an expression of such panic that I cast about to see what was frightening him. Suddenly I saw it, the winding form of an adder at the foot of the cliff, coiling and ready to strike. I had been taught as a young cub to recognize the distinctive dark zigzag pattern on its back, and apparently so had Teddy. The creature, poisonous and agitated, crouched about five feet away at the base of the wall where Teddy had just been standing. I remained perfectly still, so as not to threaten the snake, and shouted up to Teddy to stop. I had no idea if he had been bitten, but I could do nothing for him until he came down. He seemed not to hear me, but looked down again at the adder, and then began climbing still higher.

6

Stranded

❧

"Teddy!" I shouted. "Don't go any further! Don't move!" Whether he heard me at last, or just couldn't find a foothold, he hesitated. "Don't move," I repeated, not knowing what to do next, trying to avoid the one idea I realized I had to face. I would have to move the snake. I had seen Papa do this once when I was small, but I recoiled at the thought of trying it myself. "Don't move," I repeated, knowing I could not go back for help and leave Teddy here. I must move that snake, even if it should bite me, and I must do it quickly, and get Teddy down before he fell. "Teddy," I called, "I'm running over to the edge of the woods to get a stick now. I'm coming right back!"

"Don't leave me, Miss Brown!" he yelled to me from above.

"I'm only going a little ways, to get something so I can move the snake. You can watch me. Just keep your eyes on me!" I turned and ran to the nearby undergrowth to find a long, forked stick. I was terrified, but determined. Though I could be paralyzed by a dread of unknown horrors in the dark, at least this was a fear I could see and name, and take action against, and, as there was no one else to do it, I must not fail.

I prepared myself inwardly, slowly approaching the snake from behind, and with a swift motion I pinned the creature's head to the ground between the branches of the fork. I knew I must touch it now, getting a good grip with my paw at the base of its head, and I was very loath to do it. Taking a deep breath, I accomplished this, a little surprised to find that its skin felt smooth and dry. I lifted the stick and picked the snake up at arm's length, still holding it fast behind his head and supporting its writhing body with the stick. Across the glade and into the underbrush at the edge of the woods I carried it, then I gingerly threw it a safe distance from me, and watched, shaking, while it shyly slithered away.

Running back to the waterfall, I looked up to see Teddy, who had now reached a ledge more than fifteen feet above my head. "Look, Teddy," I called up to him, "the snake is gone now. Are you all right? Did it bite you?" Eyes glazed with fear, he shook his head wordlessly, as if unable to speak. He still clung, frozen, to the rock face, perhaps just now realizing how far up he was. I felt a surge of relief that he had not been bitten, yet one glance at the jagged rocks below him told me he was still in terrible danger. I had thought to talk him down, but his obvious panic showed me that would be quite impossible. I reluctantly concluded that I must go up. I did not know what I would do when I reached him, but trusted to the moment to show me how to proceed. I had no confidence to marshal for the task. Nevertheless, I began to climb, sending up a desperate prayer for help. I was immediately dismayed to find the rocks slick with a film of moisture. Still, I pushed and pulled my way upward, concentrating so purely on my sense of touch that I might almost have had my eyes shut.

"What are you doing up there?" bellowed a voice below me, nearly jolting me from my place. I was far enough up to make for a nasty fall, if fall I should. Trembling, I looked down over my shoulder and observed a tall, powerfully built young bear, in the dress of a gentleman. His heavy brow was gathered in a scowl of outrage and disapproval. "What are you about?" he demanded.

"You nearly frightened me out of my life!" I shouted. "Can't you see I'm trying to climb? The cub is panicked. I can't talk him down."

"Come back down before you break your neck!" he commanded. "I'll go up after him!"

I must confess to a flash of anger at his peremptory manner. Though it seemed petty, I had managed the situation thus far, and I bristled at being ordered about like a child. "He's my charge," I shouted. "I should do it!"

"Don't be a fool!" came the response. "I can carry him down."

I didn't see how he could accomplish this, but I swallowed my pride and halted. "Teddy," I called, looking up. "I'm going down, but someone else is coming up for you. Someone big and strong. Just hold on!" I began my descent, thinking all the time how Teddy must be tiring, and what would happen if he lost his grip. The gentleman, meanwhile, had his jacket and shoes and stockings off, and was rolling up his sleeves. As soon as I reached the ground, he began to climb, expertly finding paw- and footholds where none seemed to exist, and using his claws to dig into cracks and crevices. He made his way up to Teddy's ledge, and began to talk to him. I saw him put his arm around Teddy's waist, and then he deftly maneuvered him onto his own chest. Teddy clung to him like a young monkey clings to its mother, with his arms around the gentleman's neck, and his legs wrapped around his middle. It seemed impossible to me that the bear could manage, burdened in this way, but slowly, precariously, paw by paw, he started downward. Halfway down, his grip failed as a shower of rocks came loose under one paw, but he quickly transferred his weight to his other paw and remained steady. One slow, deliberate movement at a time, he made the hazardous descent. When at last his feet reached the ground, I released a long-held breath. Teddy slid from the gentleman's arms and stood on his own two feet, a trifle unsteady, but unharmed and alert. I was overwhelmed with gratitude. "How can I—" I began. I was going to say "thank you" when he broke in on me.

"What the Devil possessed you?" the tall bear demanded before he had even caught his breath. "How could you permit him to climb in such a spot?"

"Permit him? I didn't permit him!"

"If it wasn't permissiveness, it was negligence, and that's no better," he declared. "Allowing a young cub to escape your supervision in a place like this is unconscionable. Inexcusable."

I was rendered speechless by this accusation, but I was unwilling to explain myself to this insufferable bear. His rush to judgment signaled to me a boorishness that placed him quite beneath my notice. No, if explanations were due, I would save them for Mr. Vaughn's ears.

Accordingly, I chose to ignore the obnoxious beast altogether, and focused my attention completely on Teddy. "Are you quite all right?" I asked him, checking his limbs for bumps or sprains. He nodded in the affirmative and gave a small sniff. He seemed none the worse for his adventure, though he was shaken and uncharacteristically quiet. Already I knew him well enough to surmise that this inhibition would not last for long. I thought it best to be as matter-of-fact as possible about the affair, so I took his paw and asked him if he was ready to go home.

"What, no thanks for the rescuer?" the tall bear asked sardonically. Determined not to behave as unreasonably as he had, I prompted Teddy to thank him.

"Thank you for fetching me, Mr. Bentley," said Teddy, a little unevenly.

Hearing this, I connected the name to my conversation that morning with Mrs. Vaughn. "Bentley?" I echoed.

"Yes," he replied, noting my recognition of the name. "I am Mr. Bentley, Mr. Vaughn's clerk. And you, I presume, are the new governess, Miss Brown."

"Yes," I answered briefly, and was silent. Had it been anyone else, I might have said "Pleased to meet you," but I wasn't, and I preferred to be silent rather than insincere. The moment stretched out, long and awkward, but I did not speak.

"You may ignore me if you like," said the gentleman, "but I assure you that I am on close terms with this cub's father, and you will have to answer to him for this day's misadventure."

"Then I will answer—to him!" I retorted, and I turned my back with great dignity to walk away. I had not gone many steps when something—a stray breeze, perhaps—made me conscious of my bare legs. With horror I realized that my skirts and petticoats were still tucked up from when I had been wading, leaving my pantaloons and bare legs exposed for anyone to see—for that arrogant cad to see. Appalled, I stopped and adjusted my clothing, only to hear a low chuckle behind me. I knew for certain no gentleman would have laughed at my predicament. Boiled with inner fury, I felt a scorching blush rise on my cheeks, and was thankful that it didn't show. Teddy and I picked up our things and returned to the path by which we had come.

Still fuming, I made a concerted effort to put the ill feelings behind me and concentrate on Teddy. With a little encouragement, he began to talk about what had just happened, and was soon chattering away. He quickly recovered his normal aplomb and began to appreciate the experience as one with great story-telling value. By the time we reached the Cottage, he was bursting to find an audience, and headed straight for Mr. Vaughn's den. I admonished him to knock first. Finding his father available for an interview, Teddy rushed to him, blurting disjointed exclamations like "I got way up higher than Miss Brown's head!" and "The snake almost bit me!"

Mr. Vaughn focused an intense gaze on me, saying, "Miss Brown? What is the explanation for this?"

Starting to tremble, I told the whole story from beginning to end while Mr. Vaughn sat in his chair, listening attentively, his expression tense and serious. Finally he nodded, and turned to Teddy. "Well, my boy," he said gravely, "you did nicely to recognize the viper. That's *Vipera berus,* you know, in the Latin. And you got yourself away from it. That's very important. Perhaps you needn't have climbed QUITE so high, but we won't quibble, eh? It was fortunate that Mr. Bentley often takes his lunch by the waterfall, fortunate indeed. I hope you thanked him?"

"Yes, Papa," came the reply.

"Very well, then. I'm glad to see you safe. Run along to the schoolroom now while I have a word with Miss Brown."

My stomach clenched. Would Mr. Vaughn blame me for what had happened? I braced myself to meet his condemnation as Teddy closed the door behind him.

Mr. Vaughn cleared his throat. He stood up and paced several times back and forth in front of his desk, holding his paws behind his back, and then he looked right at me. "I must ask you, Miss Brown, where your attention was while Teddy was encountering this snake."

"Well, to be honest, sir, I think I was looking at the water, but I believed Teddy to be standing safely nearby."

"And yet, had you been looking at him, he was not safe at all, was he?"

"No, sir. I heartily wish now that I had never taken my eyes off him."

He fixed his piercing gaze on me and knit his brow. "It is pointless, Miss Brown, to wish one had behaved differently in retrospect. It is rather more important to prevent such close calls from happening in the first place, is it not?"

"Yes, sir," I said, waiting for the ax to fall.

"Such incidents do not always end well enough to allow us the luxury of retrospection. Today, for example, there might have been a very different tale to tell—a tale of tragedy."

"Yes, sir."

"And surely you realize that in weighing the balance between your assets and your obvious shortcomings, this episode tips the balance heavily toward your shortcomings?"

"Yes, sir," I answered, my voice squeaking slightly.

"There is, however, the matter of the snake. I will say in fairness that it was very resourceful of you to handle the snake so well. Courageous too. I'm glad to see you are not one of those helpless females who faint at the first sign of danger."

"No, sir. At least not with snakes, sir."

"Well, then, let us say that on balance you have acquitted yourself adequately. I do expect that you will learn from this incident to be more attentive in the future. *Nolle prosequi*, Miss Brown, *nolle prosequi*. 'We shall not prosecute further.'"

I thanked him, allowing myself a moment's relief at my own narrow escape. Just as I was making my departure, Mr. Bentley came to the door. He bowed and held it open for me with exaggerated courtesy. "I regret that your employment here will be so brief," he said, under his breath. "A pity that there will be no opportunity for our further acquaintance." His eyes looked from my face to the frog in the jar I was still holding, and back again with obvious amusement, and I perceived, now that he was no longer in high dudgeon, that his face might have been considered by some to be handsome, though it was not so to me. I realized too that despite his height, he was younger than I had supposed: only a few years older than myself, I thought, probably just out of university. Still, old enough to know better!

"It is certainly true that there will be no opportunity for our further acquaintance," I said, just as softly. "I will see to that. As for the rest, you will have to consult Mr. Vaughn. Good day, sir." And with rather more dignity than the last time, I took my leave of him. Shrugging off my annoyance, I endeavored to put him out of my mind. Instead, I contemplated my encounter with Mr. Vaughn. Could he really expect me never to take my eyes off the cub for a second? Could I possibly live up to such a standard of vigilance? Could it really be good for Teddy to be so fussed over and protected? I could not help but wonder.

Back in the schoolroom, our immediate project was to fix up the new terrarium for occupation by the frog. This required the assistance of old George, the gardener, to supply us with a small patch of turf, and some mud and stones. After much arranging, Teddy and I created a snug little amphibian apartment, where the frog immediately made himself comfortable. All that remained was one last expedition to a damp corner of the garden to collect some of the insects, slugs, and worms that made up the typical frog diet. Teddy had no aversion to handling the slimier creatures, but he observed me carefully to see if I would shrink from them. Barely out of my tomboy days, I had no such inhibitions, and held up a juicy worm to demonstrate the fact. This earned me a satisfied smile from Teddy, as if I had passed some kind of test. Soon we had collected a whole frog feast. We returned to the schoolroom and stocked the terrarium with our catches.

I was pleased to think that all the activities surrounding the frog had put the afternoon's adventure right out of Teddy's mind. Or so I believed. How easy it is to make light of the minds of the very young, as if their spirits were no more complicated than the simple games we give them to play, while all the time it is their perceptions that are keener and brighter, their memories more indelible, beckoning to them forever after.

7

I Make a Friend and an Enemy

❧

Wishing only for a quiet space to set my jumbled thoughts in order, I took tea in my chamber. I found myself longing for someone to talk to, and so I wrote a long letter to Papa, detailing my first impressions of all my new acquaintances. Leaving out my dilemma over Nurse's flask and her nasty threat, so as not to worry him, I imparted a much-diluted story of the incident at the waterfall. As I came to describe Mr. Bentley's role, I wondered briefly whether I had been entirely fair to that bear. He had, after all, saved the day. Perhaps I shouldn't have minded so much that his manner had been peremptory and judgmental. My thoughts were drawn back to our last encounter at the doorway to the den, where he had been so impertinent: so smugly confident that I would lose my position. No. The bear was a cad. There was no room for compromise. I skipped his part in the story. Lastly, I assured Papa that Teddy and I were fine and getting on swimmingly.

The morning lessons went well, with Teddy peppering me

with all sorts of questions, like "What is the French word for *worm*?" and "Do frogs have ears?" Some of these I could not answer, but wrote them down to look up later. For the afternoon's natural history lesson, we stayed close to home, making a study of the trees surrounding the garden, their bark and leaves, and what color they were turning in the brisk fall air. We encountered nothing more dangerous than a wasps' nest, to which we gave a wide berth. By teatime Teddy seemed pleasantly tired, but I, being used to more exercise, was restless and fidgety, and so I resolved to take a walk into the village and mail Papa's letter.

I gulped down my tea, donned a shawl and bonnet, and made for the front drive. There the magnificent old trees had been left almost entirely in their natural state, a grove of somber giants abiding in their green tranquillity. A broad avenue had been cleared through their midst, with branches meeting overhead like the arches of a great cathedral. I set off down the drive, the very course I had taken only two days ago to come to the Cottage. I pressed on past the gatekeeper's lodge and through the big iron gates, and headed off in the direction of Bremen Town. About a mile further on, I came to a little country church, which I had passed by on the way to the Cottage. I had paid it little mind then, but in the late-afternoon sun the stone façade took on a golden glow, and I paused to admire it.

Stepping closer to examine the carvings on the big double doors, I was startled when they opened and a little white-haired man emerged. He was dressed all in black, and wore a clerical collar. "Oh! Good day!" he said, looking up at me. "I was just leaving. Were you coming to call? I'm in no hurry."

"Oh no, sir," I said. "I was just admiring the church—the workmanship in these carvings. They must be very old."

"Oh yes. They have been here longer than I have, and that is a very long time. You are new in these parts, I believe. Are you from the manor? I heard they were expecting a new governess. I am Reverend Dr. Snover, by the way. You'll find that everyone knows everybody hereabouts."

I answered that I was indeed the new governess, and introduced myself. He expressed great delight upon hearing my name, asking if I was the daughter of Ephraim Brown. It seemed that he too had known my father, having long ago been a professor of philosophy at the university where my father and Mr. Vaughn had studied. "I remember him vividly," he mused. "He was one of a small circle of students who came to my home on Saturday evenings to engage in all manner of intellectual conversations and arguments. He and Walter Vaughn were my shining stars. Your mother too. Dear Sarah. She joined the group a year after them. My three—they could think rings around the rest of them. Such a pity that you have suffered so great a loss. Please accept my condolences, my dear."

My mind was leaping to keep up. I felt as if I had stumbled across a great treasure trove of memories, and I didn't want to lose even one of them. "Reverend Snover," I said, "I'd love to hear stories of my parents in their youth. Perhaps when you have the time, you would share some of them with me?"

"Oh yes," he said. "That would be lovely. Lovely. I always wondered what Ephraim and Sarah's child would be like. My wife will be glad to know you too. You must come to the vicarage, let's say a week from Friday, and join us for supper—tell me how you've turned out, my dear."

I gave him a wry smile, and told him that perhaps I was not the best judge of that; he might get a different opinion from my employer.

"Ah. Having difficulties, are you? Do you find him a bit overprotective and demanding?"

I looked at him, somewhat startled that he should read my thoughts, but reluctant to speak any criticism of my employer out loud. "I'm afraid I've already upset Mr. Vaughn on several scores," I said vaguely.

"Perhaps there's something you should know, my dear. There is a reason why the Vaughns are so protective of their little Theodore. He was not their first cub, you see. There were two before him, neither of whom survived infancy, and another one after him—an infant girl cub who died just last year. There are three small gravestones over there under the oak tree. I'm afraid the Vaughns have had more than their share of tragedy. I'm sure you will find that the parents hold tightly to little Teddy and even perhaps overprotect him or spoil him. It's only natural, if you understand the history."

An image formed in my mind of the big, empty nursery, and my heart contracted painfully. I could imagine it filled with boisterous and delightful little cubs like Teddy. The story tugged at my heartstrings, and I felt moisture in the corners of my eyes. "How very sad," I said. "It all makes a kind of sense. I think the criticism will be easier to endure now that I know."

"I thought you would see it that way," he said, giving my shoulder a reassuring little squeeze. "You are a credit to your gentle parents."

"Thank you, sir. You could give me no higher praise than that. I should be glad to come for supper a week from Friday, if you're sure it's no trouble." The reverend assured me that he was looking forward to it already, and so I offered him my paw to shake and we parted. I thought him a most interesting person in spite of his advanced age, charming and not at all stuffy.

I continued my walk into the village. Bremen Town was a pleasant little place, lush with trees and hedges, and populated by the usual motley blend of characters to be found in the Enchanted Forest. The dwellings were as varied as the dwellers, ranging from several full-sized gingerbread houses—very much in vogue—to an inhabited pumpkin shell on the edge of town. Most of the occupants were friendly, nodding and offering a greeting to me as I passed, but of course there were always those who would cross the street rather than approach someone who was not of their own kind. This was more often than not a human person avoiding a creature like myself, as if by passing too near to me they might become infected with some exotic disease, or suddenly grow fur and lose all traces of civilization. I tried not to take it personally; after all, such people's existences must be so bland and narrow. And somehow it seemed that they always wore the same expression: their faces puckered up as tightly as if they had been sucking on lemons.

I suppose that it was because I had been contemplating these matters that after handing in my letter I noticed a certain bulletin put up at the Post Office. The announcement was for a meeting of the Anthropological Society. Its name seemed innocuous enough, but Papa had once informed me that the group was nothing more than a private club for humans only—humans who believed in the superiority of the human race, and its dominion over all other species. There were pockets of this hateful society here and there throughout the Enchanted Forest, and I had heard of other villages that had had trouble with them. The fact that this notice was posted openly in a public place implied that the society was tolerated or even supported here in this seemingly friendly little town. I examined the handbill more closely. It made the meeting sound like a village party, with a special guest speaker, a Mr. Morton Babcock, the new owner of the village newspaper, the *Town Crier*.

I looked around, half tempted to tear down the handbill and get rid of it, when a strapping young bear in work clothes walked into the Post Office and stood near me looking at the notices and reading some of them aloud. When he came to the announcement for the meeting of the Anthropological Society, he swore softly, reaching up and tearing the notice down in an angry motion. I looked into his face then, and was about to thank him for his act of courage when it became clear that he had been observed. Four juvenile humans focused their attention on the bear and swaggered over to him.

"What do you think you're doing? Huh? What you got there, animal?" snarled the tallest boy, crossing his arms over his chest. I froze, afraid for the bear who had grabbed the handbill, and afraid for myself. I had never encountered anyone so openly hostile and threatening. He was a great lummox of a boy, dirty and repulsive-looking, dressed in a bizarre assortment of clothing: checked trousers too large, a snuff-colored coat too small, and a threadbare velveteen waistcoat, all worn with a casual élan befitting a member of the gentry—or a highwayman. The truncheon dangling from his belt seemed to indicate the latter. "What you got there, animal?" he repeated.

"Just cleanin' the place up a little," responded the bear with studied casualness.

The boy snatched the handbill from the bear's paw and looked at it. "Why, you fool, this is about a private meetin'—a meetin' of the better folk in town. You got some objection to this meetin'?"

"I got some objection to bigots and bullies," said the bear evenly. "Most people around here do."

"So you're calling me and my friends names, are you?" the lummox demanded, seemingly enraged. "You'll take that back before we're through with you." He grabbed one of the bear's arms, and his friends grabbed the other, and they dragged him, struggling, out the door. Without thinking, I followed them out, yelling, "Stop! Stop it!"

I might as well have been talking to the wind for all the attention they paid me. I watched helplessly as they pulled the bear into a nearby alley and began beating him. I was hovering uncertainly at the alley's entrance, looking around desperately for someone to help, when a great brute of a woman came charging down the boardwalk wielding a sack of potatoes like a club. At least, I thought it was a woman, though the build was broad-shouldered and heavy. She wore a ragged dress and a drab scarf, and a cigar hung out of one side of her mouth. I flattened myself against the wall of the alley and looked on in amazement.

"Gabriel!" she roared. "Git yourself over here! Git away from there right this minute!"

Since none of the boys paid her the slightest attention, she stormed on into the alley and rained blows down on all four of them with the potato sack, until, finding themselves besieged, the three smaller boys jumped out of her way. But the biggest boy, the leader, had worked himself into such a frenzy of rage that he was impervious to her bashing, and he fought on like a whirlwind single-handed against the bear, pounding and kicking all out of control, while the bear seemed to hold himself in. I thought perhaps it was because it would go hard with him if he were accused of harming a human. The three other boys stood watching, slack-jawed, as the woman lit into the biggest boy with renewed vigor, finally knocking him to the ground and cursing him. At this, the poor battered bear saw his chance and took off at a run, brushing past me on his way down the street, bleeding from the snout.

"What in Hades do you think yer doin', fightin' in the alley like some wild animal?" she bellowed. "Do I have to keep tellin' you we can't afford no more trouble with the law? We're *poor people*," the woman said, emphasizing her point by kicking him. "We got to be *meek*," she said with another hard kick. Now he yelped with each blow, scrambling to get away from her. Gone was the swaggering bully I had seen in the Post Office. I'll admit to some satisfaction at seeing this treatment meted out to him. As he got to his feet, the woman grabbed him by the ear, and twisted it. Ignoring his cries of pain, she dragged him after her, though he was even bigger than she. They passed close by, and he caught sight of me, his eyes dilated with fury. "What are you looking at?" he snarled. "If you're smart, you'll look the other way and keep your *mouth shut*!" With that, he broke free and ran away while the woman swore and hurried after him.

The other boys scuttled past me and retreated in the opposite direction as I stood dumbly staring after them. I was rather shaken by the scene I had witnessed. What would those boys have done to the bear if no one had stopped them? He seemed not to put up a fight. What would they have done to me if I had tried to interfere? I had no experience in matters of violence, and did not know what to do. I stood there until my heart stopped pounding, and seeing no one about, I thought only to get myself home. It was not until I was well out of the village that I breathed more easily, and my steps finally slowed to a sedate walk.

Soon I was passing Reverend Snover's little church again,

and I was reminded of him telling me about the three little graves in the churchyard. What an unjust world, I thought, where the hateful people lived and thrived, and the innocents died young. I was unable to free myself from reflections on the episode in town, as well as the tragic story of the Vaughns' dear departed cubs, and a somber mood settled over me like a heavy yoke. The sun hung lower in the sky now, as if wearied by its own weight, and my shadow stretched ever longer, dogging my steps like some dark colossus. As I passed through the iron gates and down the long drive, the woods closed in around me and the world dimmed into half-light. It seemed a different place from the pleasant haven I had traversed earlier. What had felt tranquil and majestic before now seemed sepulchral and eerie. There was a hush too that I had not noticed formerly. No wind rustled in the leaves; no birds trilled overhead. I wondered if it was only my mood that tinged the surroundings with a subtle menace. I huddled under my shawl, shivering slightly, and hurried on my way.

I had not gone much further when I heard a branch snap. I whirled and looked behind me, but there was nothing out of the ordinary to be seen, only massive tree trunks towering in the gloom, overgrown ferns, and tangled clusters of underbrush. What had disturbed the utter stillness of the woods? I told myself that it was some wild creature, no doubt anxious to avoid me. I faced about and kept on walking, softly now, in order to listen. A little further on I heard it again, closer than it had been, and turned involuntarily to see. I caught a glimpse of something diving behind a tree. It had disappeared too quickly for me to make anything out, but I knew I had not imagined it. Had someone followed me, then? The hairs on the back of my neck bristled under my bonnet, but I kept walking. Only a short distance along the drive I heard another noise, almost on my heels, it seemed. The conviction came over me that this was no random noise either—that something, or someone, was in fact trailing after me. My immediate urge was to run, but a war for supremacy began in my conscience between Cowardice and Reason. Would I give in to a nameless fear, as I had that first night with the footsteps in the hallway, or would I be the self-possessed professional that I made myself out to be to my employer? Reason told me that my employer must not see me running away again. Cowardice quickly assured me that my employer could not see me now, and without further ado, I picked up my skirts and ran.

Once through the front doors, I nearly collided with Mr. Vaughn in the entryway. Struggling to slow my breathing, I removed my bonnet with trembling paws, apologizing profusely.

"Miss Brown, I observed you careening up the drive as if the Devil were on your tail. Is there some reason for this, or are you once again giving way to your imaginary fears?"

Thinking I had better defend myself, I decided to tell Mr. Vaughn what I had observed in town. "I'm very sorry, sir, but I thought I was being followed by one of the boys I saw fighting in the village."

"Indeed? Followed onto my estate? That seems most unlikely. You had better tell me all."

I described the scene that had taken place from beginning to end, including the boy's threatening words to me.

"You did right in telling me about this, Miss Brown. There has been the occasional trouble in town of late, and it's a shame you got caught up in it. In the future I trust you will try not to become embroiled in matters that don't concern you."

I burned inwardly at this, for it sounded like a rebuke, and

I thought I did not deserve one. I knew better, however, than to answer back, and so, swallowing my gall, I said only, "Of course, sir."

"Should the need arise, you may leave your mail with Mr. Bentley. He will see to it that it is delivered. Good night."

Perceiving that I had been dismissed, I said, "Yes, sir. Good night, sir." Then, struggling to keep to a sedate walk, I passed through the hallways and went up the stairs toward my room, wanting only to get to a place of peace and safety, and soothe my frayed nerves. Coming to the top of the stairs, I hurried down the gallery to the hall beyond, and around the corner where it turned toward the west wing. As I approached the nursery, the door banged open and Nurse's head thrust out. She saw me, and her expression turned to one of purest hatred. She reflexively opened her jaws and made a loud hissing sound deep in her throat. Feeling her malevolent glare almost as a physical blow, I staggered, suppressing a cry, and dropped my bonnet. For an awful moment I fought for my composure. Had she actually lain in wait just to scare me out of my wits, I wondered, or had I simply happened along at an inopportune moment? Either way I would not give her any further satisfaction. Determined to behave as if nothing untoward had happened, I picked up my bonnet, said, "Good evening, Nurse," and continued on my way.

8

A Presence

Safely in my own room, I realized I was trembling. Though I had put a good face on it, I was shocked by the ferocity of the badger's conduct. I wondered if poor Teddy had ever been treated to this spectacle, and how it was that Nurse kept this aspect of her character so well hidden from his parents. Twisting my handkerchief in my paws, I struggled to formulate some foolproof plan for avoiding her. There was no way to circumvent the nursery, as it was adjacent to my chamber on one side, and the schoolroom on the other, and I certainly had no way of controlling her comings and goings. It was out of the question to go to the master with my complaint. With a deep sense of melancholy, I came to the conclusion that I must simply resign myself to the specter of Nurse's hateful countenance popping out at me at any moment like some depraved jack-in-the-box.

Trying to calm myself, I still agonized over who or what had been hiding in the woods—and why? What honest business could anyone have lurking there? Had someone really followed me from town, or seen me leave by that route and waited on purpose for my return? It seemed a fantastic idea, but my mind was agitated and grasping at straws.

I spent the remainder of the evening at my desk, attempting to make sense of the Latin texts Mr. Vaughn had given to me to learn. Asking Betsy to bring my supper to my room, I applied myself to the most basic Latin lessons. *Amo, amas, amat.* "I love, you love, he loves." Though I scolded myself severely to concentrate on the texts, my thoughts were drawn once more to the little white-haired vicar who had known my parents. I carefully took off Mama's locket, my one cherished heirloom, and opened it to see the picture of her and Papa inside. They looked so young and happy! I had been a small cub when she was taken from us, so my memories of her were hazy and dim. This was the only picture I had of her and Papa, and I had always wondered what lay behind the hint of mischief in her smile. Wearing that smiling face next to my heart gave me the feeling that she was watching over me.

I set the locket carefully down, and tiredly struggled to refocus my attention on Latin, but my mind was still filled with the vicar and his account of the tragedy of the Vaughns' three lost cubs. Saddened, I laid my head down on my book and closed my eyes. For some time I hovered on the borderland of sleep, fantasizing images of the Vaughn family as it might have been. In my flight of fancy, I could see Teddy with his brothers and sister, somersaulting on the lawn; or the troupe of exuberant little bears filling the house with laughter; or the four of them tucked up snugly in the nursery. As I fell into a deep slumber, the dream cubs began to take on lives of their own, now scampering through the hallways in a game of hide-and-seek, the littlest one counting while the others fled to their hiding places. In my dream I joined the game, chasing after the fleeing cubs down hallways I had never seen, which stretched on and on and faded into nothingness. And then I heard it, the sound that was to haunt my dreams so often in times of distress or strain: the high, desolate wail of a human child. This was not like Teddy's gruff, solid cry. It had that poignant quality of the frail human, heartrending and insistent. I could not ignore it. In this dream I was overcome with a sense of urgency, a feeling that I *must* find the woeful child and save it. Yet even as I stumbled through a rising mist, down the next hall, up the next stairway, it remained always in the distance. Finally, overwhelmed, I knew I was lost, the weeping child forever beyond my reach. There I awoke, as I always would, feeling helpless and inconsolable.

Though my eyes were open, night had fallen. It took several minutes for me to orient myself, to realize that there was no crying child, and that I was sitting at the desk in my own room. Despite the faint moonlight filtering in through the windows, a tremor of fear went up my spine. Darkness, my old nemesis, had me surrounded. Groping my way to my candle, I desperately tried to spark a light from the flint and failed repeatedly. Finally giving it up as impossible, I faced the choice of changing into my nightgown in the dark or climbing into bed fully clothed. Not even pausing to remove my shoes, I dove under the covers and pulled them over my head.

For some time I lay there as still as death, with my ears attuned to pick up the slightest hint of sound. All I could hear was the wind howling around the corners of the house and rattling the windowpanes. But the windows were new, as was the rest of the house, and they fit the moldings as snugly as if the wood, stone, and glass were all of a piece. Yet something was undeniably rattling. Was it the windowpanes? No. It was my door. Abruptly, the rattling stopped. I froze, afraid to breathe, straining to hear I knew not what. A whisper? A soft shuffle of footsteps? A presence. My fur stood on end. I could not scent anything through the heavy coverlet, but instinctively I knew that I was not alone. My heart pounded a wild tattoo in my chest. I struggled to remain still, my muscles aching and trembling with the effort, and I gasped for air under the thick counterpane. My thoughts ran riot. Who could be in my room in the middle of the night? Who could wish me harm? Nurse's snarling visage came immediately to mind. Could she really hate me enough to attack me in my sleep? And who had been trailing me in the woods? Could they have gotten indoors? I lay contemplating all the possibilities until my lungs screamed for fresh air.

It seemed finally as if I must give away my hiding place or suffocate in it, and something deep inside of me refused to lie quietly any longer. I threw down the covers and sat up in one motion, bellowing "Ha!" as I did so, hoping to catch my nocturnal visitor off guard. My vision had adjusted to the dark sufficiently that I could tell in the moonlight that the room was empty—but my door was now open. Wide open. I was sure I had closed it when I had begun my studies earlier in the evening. Hadn't I? How could it have rattled if it had not been closed?

Suddenly I thought of Teddy asleep in the nursery next door. Was he safe? I had seen the little badger-sized bed near his and assumed that Nurse slept there, but I thought of her flask. What if she had imbibed, and slept too soundly to be awakened by an intruder? My heart shrinking in my breast, I realized that I would have to go and check on him. Without allowing myself to contemplate it too long, I got out of bed and tiptoed to the door, poking my head into the hallway. There were no windows here; in fact, there was no light at all. Could I feel my way to the nursery door? Sinking my face down onto my arm, I moaned and said a small prayer, then forced myself to step into the inky darkness and spread both paws on the cold wall. My breath came short and shallow while I tried to imagine what I would do if something came up and touched me. Thoroughly frightened, I began to count my steps as a way of blocking out the dreadful thoughts that threatened to overwhelm me.

"One . . . two . . . three . . . four . . . ," I whispered, sliding tentatively along the wall. Was that a noise behind me? After a short pause, I went on, "Five . . . six . . . seven . . ." At thirty-four I bumped into the doorknob on the nursery door. I tried to turn it with my trembling paw, but the knob wouldn't move. The door was locked. Without stopping to puzzle why this should be so, I felt a moment's relief that Teddy was safe behind it. Then the darkness seemed to close in on me again. My head swam with dizziness as I wondered who or what might lie waiting in this black void. Pausing only for a deep breath, I reversed my direction, counting my steps backward to my own door with all the speed I could muster. This having used up all of my thin store of fortitude, I found my bed at last, and dove in again, though this time I kept my snout out to breathe.

I don't know how long I lay there in the night with my dark imaginings. Someone had been in my room. I was sure of this even though I had not seen them. What could I do about it? I could imagine my employer's response if I went to him with such a tale. He would think me a hysterical fool. My mind continued to spin round in circles, with no helpful results. I could dimly hear the big grandfather clock in the great hall striking twelve, the quarter hour, the half hour. One o'clock. Two.

I must have slept a little, for I came uneasily awake with the first glow of dawn. I felt none of the benefits of having slept; my head ached and the inside of my eyelids felt dry and rough. It would be hours yet before I would meet Teddy in the schoolroom. I made a cursory inspection of my chamber in the faint light, to see if anything had been taken or disturbed, but I could see nothing amiss. Putting a wrap around my shoulders, I stepped out on my balcony to soak up the reassuring ambience of daybreak. I sat for some time in the comfortable wicker chair there, watching the morning star dwindle into the sunrise, struggling to achieve a more sanguine frame of mind.

Below my balcony lay the kitchen garden, nestled within its high stone walls. A motion in the mellow light drew my eye to a bent figure there collecting vegetables in a basket: Cook, I thought. Content in my solitude, I eased back in my chair so that I could not be seen from below, and allowed my thoughts to return to the events of the night before.

As daylight threw the solid objects of the landscape into stark relief, reality seemed a simple enough state to define. It could be seen, touched, smelled, heard. But what of that which could only be felt? Could I trust it? Now, in the light of day, I was forced to ask the question: Had anyone really been in my room at all? There had been a rattling that could have been the wind and a feeling—admittedly, a strong feeling—and a door that I might have left open. Had I really heard shuffling footsteps? Could I have heard anything clearly through the heavy coverlet? I gave myself a shake. It was nonsense, that was all. The overstimulation of the past days had whipped my imagination into full gallop, and there was only one cure for it. I must be ruthless and rein it in. I thought wryly that the only real danger I had to face was that, in allowing my fears to keep me awake most of the night, I had left myself too exhausted to do my job well. Now I must put all my fears aside and get on with my day as if nothing had happened—which, indeed, I realized, must be the case.

I tried to think of something to make me stronger. I thought then of Papa and the things he had taught me to appreciate: the priceless gift of a newborn day, the sweet essence of fall in the air, a wild madrigal of birdsong. As if on cue, a lone sparrow landed on the railing of my balcony, tilting its head in quick little movements as it eyed me up and down. It held its congenial pose for all of a minute, giving me the feeling that I had been smiled upon, then a noise in the far end of the garden startled it and off it flew.

The sun was fully up now, gilding even the most mundane objects with outlines of refulgent light, and I could see the door opening in the far end of the garden wall. My curiosity aroused, I watched as Fairchild stepped over the threshold. He was not in his butler's uniform, but ordinary town clothes, with plain trousers and a brown greatcoat draped loosely over his lanky human frame. Knowing that he had his own quarters near the kitchen, I wondered where he had been at this hour. Following his progress as he made his way between the garden rows, I perceived, as he drew nearer, an expression of black rage on his brow. Curious and concerned, I observed him carefully as he approached the kitchen door, confident that he, like most humans, would not look up.

"Good morning to ye," Cook called to him. Then, seeing

the intensity of his expression, the canny old bear lowered her voice and said, "What news? What's the mood in town?"

By now they were both outside my line of sight, directly below my balcony, but their voices drifted up to me, and, ignoring the good manners I had been raised with, I listened in.

"There's trouble brewing, and that's for sure," Fairchild's voice fairly growled. Then came a pause and his hushed inquiry. "Is anyone else about?"

"No one but us, and old Meg inside building the fire, and she's deaf as a post. What is it?"

"This is for the master's ears only, you understand, but you have a sister in Bremen Town, don't you?"

"Lord, yes. My sister Violet. Is this about the uproar there? Those musicians taking over the old Hawkins place? She says it's all anyone talks about."

"Well, there's some that will do more than talk, and she'd best be prepared."

"I told her there'd be trouble! It'll make no difference that those four musicians drove off a band of robbers, I said; they'll still say it's a bunch of animals that've run a gang of humans out of their own house. The society won't take that lying down!"

My ears pricked up at the mention of "the society." I recalled the handbill in the Post Office that had started so much trouble. Could she be talking about that? I leaned closer to the edge of the balcony and cocked my ears.

"Well, you didn't hear it from me," Fairchild's voice ground out, "but there's going to be the Devil to pay. By the time Babcock finishes whipping the townsfolk into a lather, those robbers the musicians chased out will be sounding like a pack of Sunday school teachers, and the sole support of their starving little grannies, and those poor old tired musicians will sound like a pack of wild savages. Nobody will blink an eye when— Well, never mind. You'd best get word to your sister, that's all. A week from Friday, you tell her to keep herself inside and lock the doors and shutters, and if she's smart, she'll see nothing, hear nothing— and above all, say nothing. Mind, you didn't hear it from me, or my neck's on the line."

"So you've been to their meeting, then? It's a dangerous game you're playing, Fairchild. Just let the constabulary deal with them."

"The constables? The constables are all in with them! There's even a judge that's one of the society! Slugby's his name, and he lives up to it! No, we can't rely on the law."

"But if ever they get onto you, I don't dare to think—"

"Don't worry about me, Bess. I'm not alone, you know. Just you stay out of it, and warn your sister to stay out of it too. You're no match for the likes of them."

"Well, I'll pray for the Almighty to watch over you, Fairchild. I can do that at least."

"That would be fine, Bess, and bless you for it. Now, where's the master? He'll be waiting to hear."

From my perch on the balcony, I heard the kitchen door shutting, and then silence.

9

A Theft, and a Mystery

I stayed rooted to the spot for another minute, trying to make sense of what I had overheard. What had the notice from the Anthropological Society said? I scanned my memory. I had read it in its entirety. It was to announce a meeting—a meeting that would have taken place last night. I felt sure this was "the society" Fairchild had spoken of—the one whose public notice had been the start of all the trouble in town—and it must be that Fairchild's dire prediction referred to some dastardly plan of theirs. I marveled at the realization that the stuffy old butler had risked his own neck to infiltrate the group and bring news of their doings to the master. What an unlikely hero he seemed—quiet, straitlaced Fairchild. And what would the master do with this information? Did I even want to know? My curiosity had already led me into matters far over my head. I had denied my fears of the night before, but this was all too real and could not be denied; there was trouble in this seemingly peaceful place.

I returned to my bedroom, washed, and dressed in fresh

clothes. My toilet completed, I reached to the desk for the locket I had placed there the night before.

It was gone. My mother's silver locket, my prized possession, vanished.

I searched frantically, anywhere it could have fallen, anywhere else I could conceivably have put it—even though I was certain I had left it on the desk—but it had truly disappeared. My sense of loss was bottomless and desolate. I thought of losing my mama all over again. This was my talisman to remind me that she was watching over me. Along with the loss went all the carefully constructed arguments with which I had convinced myself that no one had been in my room last night. Someone *must* have been in my room, right there, only a few steps from my bed, so close they might have almost reached out and touched me, and they had taken Mama's locket. My defenses shattered, I gave way to tears.

I could have cried the day away, but the hallway clock struck the quarter hour and I knew I had no time. I splashed my face with water and dried it, checking my appearance in the mirror, wondering what to do next. Could I go to the master about the locket? Surely the theft would prove that I had not just imagined the presence in the night, and yet I, still the newcomer, shrank from the prospect of telling him there was a thief in his household. The mistress, then? She seemed much more approachable, and it was she who managed the servants. Perhaps she would handle the matter with more understanding.

Only then did it occur to me that a solution might be looking me in the face. "Mirror," I said as I rapped smartly on the shiny surface. "Mirror. Do wake up. It's urgent."

My reflected image was obliterated by dark, churning

clouds. I knocked again. And again. Finally a dim outline of the carnival-mask face appeared, as if it were too much effort to create a full picture.

"What is the password?" came the surly response.

I cast about for the answer, but could remember only that it was something short and silly. "I don't have time for nonsense. Wake up and pay attention."

"Come on, give it a guess. This is the only fun in my humdrum life."

"Mirror," I said, "I must know who was in my room last night."

"Oh?" the supercilious voice drawled. "Do you mean you want me to SPY on someone?"

"I just want you to tell me who was in my room meddling with my things. That's not spying."

"I beg to differ. You want me to tell you someone else's whereabouts and what they were doing. That is unquestionably spying. If anyone else asked me where YOU were and what you were doing, you would certainly call that spying."

"Well, yes, of course, but I—"

"It's no use asking me. I simply cannot function in such a way. It's not in my household enchantment. The mistress wouldn't have it."

"But wait! It surely is not spying to tell me where an object is. Where is my locket? Just tell me that."

"Oh, lost objects. That's different. For that we have a special custom: the riddle."

"For Heaven's sake, can't you just give me the answer?"

"Quiet. I'm thinking. . . ."

I sank my head in my paws, clutching fistfuls of fur and counting to ten, then twenty.

"Let's see. . . . Floor . . . door . . . more," the mirror droned on. "No, too literal. I need a metaphor, or perhaps an allegory. Hmm. Something that collects shiny things . . . maybe a raven. Something, something a raven. But what rhymes with *raven*?"

"It doesn't have to rhyme!" I interjected. "Can't you hurry up?"

"These things can't be rushed. The hints must be subtle, yet tantalizing. You want a riddle of quality, don't you? This is a specialty of mine, and I'll tell you right now, it's going to take some time."

"How much time?"

"Oh, days! Five or six, I should think. I've had a few cases that took longer than that, but they involved the metaphysical."

"Oh!" I cried. "You are useless! Just useless!" I turned my back on the mirror and marched out into the corridor. After a moment's thought, I determined to find the mistress and enlist her aid. Down in the kitchen I asked Betsy where and when I might find Mrs. Vaughn, and she offered to take me to her as soon as she finished clearing the breakfast dishes. My stomach seemed tied in knots and I was sure I could not eat, so I waited, standing by the door, tapping my shoe impatiently on the tile floor until Betsy came to lead me away. She brought me to Mrs. Vaughn's morning room and left me there without inquiring what business I had with the mistress, but with the encouraging whisper, "Go on, then. She's not at all gruff like the master. She's a dear, she is. Just knock."

Mrs. Vaughn answered my knock with her soft, melodic voice, bidding me come in. She seemed surprised to see me, but welcomed me warmly. She sat at an exquisite little escritoire, made of some very dark wood with inlaid designs of mother-of-pearl. I thought how well the room suited her, from the vase of peach-colored mums to the framed photos of Teddy and of three other little cubs sitting on the mantel. I knew immediately who the three little cubs were. Suddenly I didn't know how to begin.

"How are you settling in, dear?" she asked. "Is your room satisfactory? I chose it because it's near the nursery and the schoolroom. This place is so big and sprawling; I know it takes some getting used to."

"I'm sure it's the nicest room I've ever had, madam. Thank you. And Teddy is a joy. He's been making me feel quite at home." We continued with such small talk for some minutes before she gently asked me if there was anything on my mind.

"I'm afraid there is, madam, though I hate to trouble you with it."

"You can come to me with anything, my dear," she said. "Now, tell me what's bothering you. Is it serious?"

"It is to me, madam. You see, someone was in my bedroom last night, and this morning I found that my locket was missing from where I had set it on my desk. I'm afraid someone's taken it," I said, tearing up. "It's not very valuable as such things go, but it's quite precious to me, as it was my mother's. It contains the only picture I have of her and my papa. . . . I don't want to accuse anyone, madam, but I think it must have been someone in the household."

I paused. Her expression was shocked, dismayed, even guilty, and I suddenly wondered if I had done the right thing in coming to her.

"Oh no!" she said. "Oh dear. This is entirely my fault. I should have said something, but I didn't want to frighten you off. I really had hoped there would be an end to it. Forgive me, dear. I should have told you to keep your door locked." She took an embroidered handkerchief out of her sleeve and pressed it to her forehead.

"Why? What is it?" I asked, concerned now that something was seriously wrong, and wondering what sort of danger I should have locked my door against.

After her initial outburst she seemed to suddenly regain possession of herself. She fell silent and turned slightly away from me, as if she did not want to meet my eyes.

Finally she answered, "Let me take care of this, my dear. Please don't ask me to explain. It's just that, well, there are things that have gone missing—just little things here and there—and I have an idea. . . ." She paused. "I think we may yet find your locket, but it may take time. Would you trust me to handle this in my own way? Just not mention this to anyone?"

I was somewhat taken aback. It was clear that she had a notion of who was responsible for the disappearance of my locket. It was equally clear that she was hiding something—and yet she was asking me to put all my faith in her. What did I really know of her? Her gentleness and sensitivity were obvious, but would she shrink from accusing anyone for fear of giving offense? All I really knew of her was that she had raised a fine young cub, and contemplating this, I decided that was reason enough to trust her.

"All right, madam, if you think it best," I said.

"Thank you, dear. Please believe that I won't rest until we've found it."

"Yes, madam. Thank you."

"Is there anything else I can be of help with?" she asked. "How is Nurse treating you? She can be terribly moody at times."

I was temporarily struck speechless while I quickly assessed how to answer the question. Was Nurse's frequent intoxication taken for moodiness, then? I could not tell Mrs. Vaughn what I knew, but I thought that if I inquired carefully into Nurse's behavior, I might gain some helpful insight into the badger's dreadful personality.

"I'm afraid I have gotten off to rather a bad start with Nurse," I said. "I believe she has taken a dislike to me."

"Ah, yes. I was afraid of something like that. You mustn't mind it, you know. It's just that she has always been so very possessive of Teddy. I do believe there are times when she even resents my relationship with him, and now she must relinquish him to your care for much of the day. Quite likely she sees you as a rival for Teddy's affections, or even as a threat to her position, though we have assured her that she will always have a place with us. I hope she has not been rude to you?"

10

A Wondrous Trip to the Library

❧

An awkward silence hung in the air. Finally, I choked out, "It's just a feeling I have when I'm around her, madam."

"Well, I hope she has not made you too uncomfortable."

I bit my tongue, hard enough to draw blood. "Oh no, madam. There's nothing that need concern you."

We concluded our interview, with her encouraging me to come and talk to her again, any morning at the breakfast hour. She had given me some small hope that she would be able to retrieve my locket, and I was grateful for that, slim as it was.

I made my way back down toward the kitchen, hoping for a late breakfast, but as I approached the door to Mr. Vaughn's den, I heard a lively spate of cursing that sounded like it came from the master himself. I had actually stopped to listen when Mr. Vaughn saw me and called me in. He stood with an open newspaper in his paws, and said, "Miss Brown, would you be so kind as to reiterate what you told me yesterday about the incident in town?"

Nervously, I repeated the story from beginning to end.

"Now let me read to you from today's *Town Crier.* 'Vandal Caught at Post Office. Yesterday our peaceful town was disturbed by an unidentified young bear who entered the Post Office just before closing time and became violent, vandalizing the announcements board and threatening other customers. Only the quick thinking and courage of a small group of boys kept the incident from spiraling out of control. The boys wrestled the suspect to the ground, but he was assisted by an outsider and got away. Anyone with information concerning the identity of the suspect, please contact Constable Murdley.' "

"Oh, sir!" I exclaimed, my temper thoroughly aroused. "How can they print such lies? It wasn't that way at all!"

"They can print them because old Mr. Babcock, the man who bought the *Town Crier,* is the Anthropological Society's grand high chief himself, and he controls the news. Since he's taken over, there have been more and more stories like this, inciting bad feeling against the Enchanted."

"But that's not right! No one is entitled to tell lies like that! Should I contact this Constable Murdley and tell him the truth? What will happen to that bear if he's caught?"

"I wouldn't be surprised if his family has already spirited him out of town. If you went to the constable, you would only be disbelieved, and perhaps become a target yourself. See to it that you don't go into town for any reason, and leave the rest to me."

"Yes, sir," I replied, and was excused.

Teddy was waiting for me in the schoolroom, as was Nurse. She glowered at me with red-rimmed eyes while Teddy greeted me with a spontaneous hug and a highly polished apple. The terrible thought occurred to me that Nurse might expect to stay with us through Teddy's lessons, and the idea depressed me unutterably. In a desperate attempt to dismiss her, I looked straight at Nurse and said, "Thank you for staying with Teddy while he waited for me. I was a little late today, but now that I am here . . ." I trailed off, not having the nerve to tell her to leave, but hoping she would take the obvious hint.

Nurse's expression went from hostile to inflamed. She seemed to swell up to twice her normal size, and then declared, "Now that you're finally here, I'll be leaving. But don't you go traipsing out of doors again without me, or there's no telling what trouble you'll get yourselves into. I'm keeping an eye on you, and that's certain!" She spun around and made her exit with as much gravity as her short, lumpy figure would allow.

My shoulders slumped. The prospect of Nurse's presence on what might have been pleasant rambles with Teddy completely disheartened me. I thought of going to Mr. Vaughn, or the mistress, and asking that they keep her from coming, but I knew this would fan the flames of Nurse's hatred. Her threat to implicate me as the owner of her flask hung over me like the Sword of Damocles. And with the incident at the waterfall still fresh in their minds, the Vaughns might very well decide in favor of having two sets of eyes watching their cub anyway. Ultimately, I turned to Teddy and asked for his opinion: Would he like to have Nurse join us on our nature walks?

"Oh yes!" Teddy answered immediately. "Nurse knows lots of good places to go."

My heart sank, but I told myself firmly that I would make a go of it for Teddy's sake. There must be some redeeming feature in the badger's personality for her to have earned Teddy's affection. And if Nurse's hostility toward me was really simple jealousy, perhaps it would help to include her in our outings. It might even be of some practical value to us to have a guide. But what a dark shadow she would cast! I gave an involuntary shudder.

Teddy and I started the day by checking on Rana, the frog, who seemed content enough in his watery lair. After that, the time passed quickly with lessons. I began teaching Teddy how to write the numbers and letters that he had already learned to re-cite, and how to write his own name. He caught on quickly and was excited almost beyond bearing, wanting to go immediately and show his parents his handiwork.

"I think we had better not interrupt your papa, Teddy, but perhaps we could show your mama."

Teddy's demonstrative face lit up—and then just as quickly sank in disappointment. "We can't," he said. "She's gone away."

"Gone away?" I asked, puzzled. "Where do you think she's gone?"

"I don't know," he murmured sadly. "She goes away in the daytime, and I don't know where."

I recalled then that she had said I could come and see her at the breakfast hour, but nothing about other times of the day. This struck me as an intriguing mystery, but I decided that to inquire any further would be prying. "Well, she is surely back at suppertime, isn't she?"

Teddy brightened, nodding.

I assured him it would be a great surprise to present his work to both his mama and his papa at supper, and the idea immedi-ately caught hold. We rolled up his papers, tied them with a bit of twine, and set them aside while Teddy chuckled to himself in anticipation.

Perceiving that only a complete change of scene would attract the cub's attention now, I proposed an exploratory foray down to the library. Teddy looked on this as a great treat, since he was not allowed in the library by himself. Our footsteps echoed as we entered the high-ceilinged room, and I imagined that we were waking the ambient spirits of the literary giants, captured here in the pages of hundreds and hundreds of glorious books. Teddy knew exactly where to find the books for cubs, and pulled out a large, well-worn volume with a rose on the cover, *Beauty and the Beast*. "This is my favorite!" Teddy said, his voice both contented and wistful. He clutched the book to his chest and asked, "Can we look at this one first? Could you read it to me? Please?"

I was touched by the earnestness of his request, and immediately acquiesced. We made ourselves comfortable on an overstuffed divan by the window. It was upholstered in shiny chintz with an exotic floral pattern, and though it looked as new as everything else in the house, it felt as snug and cozy as Papa's favorite chair at home by the fireplace.

"This is Sofie," Teddy announced, introducing me to the sofa. "We always sit on Sofie for book time," he said, bouncing a little. "Do you like her name? I named her."

"Yes," I said, surveying the colorful pattern. "It's a very fine name. Let's try her out, shall we?" We settled into a bright ray of sunshine coming through the tall window, bounced several times, and opened the book. I could see at once why it had captured Teddy's imagination. The illustrations lured us down, down, into the very pages, their enchanting alchemy of form, line, and color breathing life into the narrative. The Beast's palace seemed to grow up around us, steeped in splendor and mystery. And then there was the Beast—a hulking, bearlike character with sad eyes. I was half in love with him myself, and I could feel Teddy's empathy for the lonely creature as he asked Beauty again and again to marry him, and again and again she said no. Were they to remain separate forever because he was deemed an animal, and she was not? I thought how unfair such false distinctions were, and how easily they could result in tragedy. Teddy turned each page for me, reacting to every new development with undisguised emotion. As the poor Beast lay dying, a tear dropped on the page, though I couldn't tell if it was his or mine.

"But she really loved him, right?" came the hopeful little voice. I turned the page to find Beauty bent weeping over the dying Beast as she discovered that she truly did love him. It was a matter of history that they lived happily ever after, though many debated whether the Beast ever turned into a human prince. Anyone could see that the real magic of the story was that she came to love him exactly as he was.

Teddy sighed with satisfaction as he closed the book. My own eyes were drooping with the fatigue of having missed a night's sleep, but I shook myself awake. We paused awhile, sitting there in the sunbeam, easing ourselves back into the present.

"I have lots of other good books too!" Teddy informed me. He climbed down from Sofie and carefully returned the book to its spot on the shelf, then chose half a dozen others just as thick.

"These will certainly last us for a while," I said, and we headed back to the schoolroom, each carrying a pile of books.

Halfway down the hall a door opened, and Mr. Bentley appeared. I had not seen him since he had so sarcastically stated that the termination of my employment would prevent us from becoming acquainted. I still intended to prevent us from becoming acquainted. I put my snout up and tried to project an air of frozen dignity as I began to walk past him, but he stepped out in front of me, undeterred.

"Miss Brown," his deep voice rumbled, "I wonder if I might have a word with you?"

I looked at him as I might have looked at a particularly aggravating insect, but he stood his ground, blocking the way, and years of home training would not allow me to be so rude as to walk around him.

"I'm sure Teddy can spare you for a few minutes—can't you, Teddy? I'll bet he knows his own way to the schoolroom. Or perhaps you need him to show you the way?" He said this with a straight face, but I was sure I detected a wicked sparkle in his eye, and I knew immediately that he had heard tell of my getting lost on the way to supper on my first night. It was probably known to the entire household by now. I overcame my scruples and stepped to one side, intending to march past him, but he stepped aside too so that he was still blocking my way. "If I could just have a minute of your valuable time?" he asked again, smiling disarmingly.

Teddy cheerfully cried, "I can go to the schoolroom by myself, see?" and he trotted away down the hall, abandoning me.

"What is it that you want?" I snapped.

"I want to apologize, Miss Brown."

"Oh?" I replied suspiciously.

"Yes. I hope you will accept my apology for so badly misjudging you at the waterfall. Now that it has been explained to me, I see that I entirely mistook the situation, and your role in it. Had it been explained to me then, of course, the misunderstanding could have been avoided."

"Mr. Bentley," I answered after a cold silence, "do you consider that to be an apology? Because I have been apologized to before, and what you have just said bears very little resemblance to any actual expression of remorse. You have, in fact, blamed me for your misjudgment. Pray don't trouble yourself—or me—with any further declarations of spurious regret. Now, if you will excuse me . . ." I stepped around him once again, and continued on my way down the hall, not looking back, and he did not call after me.

Immediately, I questioned whether I had done the right thing. Tired as I was, I had spoken to him without restraint or forethought. Something about him rubbed my fur the wrong way, making me forget the formal manners that I had been taught at Miss Pinchkin's Academy as the only acceptable way of responding to a strange male.

Back at the schoolroom, Betsy arrived with lunch. Teddy's table manners, when not under the watchful eyes of his parents, tended to be overly enthusiastic; that is, food sometimes found its way directly to his mouth without the encumbrance of silverware. I was actually reassured to see that Teddy, who seemed such an angelic youngster, was not always on his best behavior. I saw no value in making cubs into miniature adults. Nevertheless, I prompted him, with gentle reminders and the promise of dessert, to slow down and use his silverware. Having thereby earned and consumed a dish of blueberries drizzled with honey, Teddy pushed away his plate, yawned widely, and announced that he was tired.

During Teddy's rest period, I wanted only to rest myself, but I was certain that once I laid my head down on a pillow, I would sleep the day away. Instead, I opened all the windows in the schoolroom so the bracing breeze would stimulate and refresh me, and set myself to writing out plans for tomorrow's lessons. I remember sitting at my desk, poring over my papers, one paw supporting my chin. I remember my pen seeming to slow down of its own accord. I remember the words on the pages before me swimming in a peculiar way, and then oblivion.

꒳

I awakened to hear someone calling my name, seemingly from a great distance away. My head was resting on my arm, and felt much too heavy to lift up, but the caller was insistent. "Miss Brown . . . Miss Brown . . . MISS BROWN!"

My head bobbed up, my eyes popping open, and I beheld Mr. Vaughn standing in the doorway with his arms folded, one shoe tapping irritably on the floor.

"Oh!" I breathed, getting to my feet. "Excuse me, Mr. Vaughn. I . . . I guess I must have nodded off. . . ."

"Yes, that much is obvious," he observed dryly. "And, if it's not too much to ask, where is your charge?"

I was wide awake now, and suddenly cognizant of how bad the situation looked from Mr. Vaughn's point of view. My throat constricted. "It's Teddy's rest period," I managed to say. "He's in the nursery."

"He WAS in the nursery, Miss Brown. Now he is outside on the drive, waiting with Nurse, who was good enough to report to me that Teddy's governess was ASLEEP in the schoolroom. Need I communicate to you my ire that your irresponsibility has once again required my attention?"

"Oh, I'm so sorry, sir. I was just working, and I don't recall— I don't know how it happened. I'm afraid I was overtired, and—"

"Overtired? Is your workload so heavy that you must sleep through the school day?"

"Oh no, sir. It's just . . ." I trailed off, not knowing how much to say. Should I tell him someone had been in my room and stolen my locket? When Mrs. Vaughn asked me to let her handle the matter, and not to mention it to anyone, did she mean to keep it from Mr. Vaughn as well? I responded with a half-truth. "I've not been sleeping well, sir. I'm afraid I'm not used to the house yet, and I was awake for the better part of the night."

"Perhaps I have erred, choosing a governess so young in years," he responded. "With this immaturity of yours, you have demonstrated that you are barely more than a child yourself, Miss Brown." I cringed inwardly at the criticism, but remained silent while Mr. Vaughn paced.

Finally, looking as if he had come to some decision, he turned to me and said, "From today, Nurse will oversee you and Teddy throughout the school day, and on your afternoon nature walks. All things considered, I see this as an opportunity for you to benefit from her greater experience and common sense while you do some growing up yourself. Until further notice, I will place you under her direction. You will teach. She will be responsible for Teddy's well-being. In that regard you will be guided by her wisdom and counsel. Do I have your agreement to this arrangement?"

"NO!" was on the tip of my tongue. My mouth had shaped the word and my vocal cords had begun the sound when I stopped myself. Papa. What of Papa and all his fond hopes and expectations? What of my own pride? And what of Teddy? If

I were sent away, I would be replaced by a new governess, of course, but would she appreciate his budding spirit as I did?

My throat constricted, and I felt tears welling up. Savagely I drove them back. I must not—MUST NOT—cry. Quickly, I weighed the obvious evil of having my every move overseen by Nurse against the alternative of accepting total failure. In those moments a resolve was born: Nurse would not get rid of me so easily. Whatever was set before me to do, I would somehow do.

"For how long, sir?" I managed to ask, hoping he would set some limit on my suffering and give me something to work toward.

"We shall review the situation in one month's time, but I make you no promises. If you demonstrate that you are willing to improve yourself, you will not find me unreasonable."

"As you wish, sir," I said, my heart sinking to my feet.

"Very good," he responded. "As Seneca, the great philosopher and Stoic, once said, 'True happiness is to understand our duties to God and Bear.' Remember, Miss Brown, *vincit qui se vincit.* Proceed with your plans for the afternoon, and remember your duties, and let there be no more reason for me to be disturbed."

I curtsied as he left the room. I quickly packed a bag with binoculars, a bird book, and a bag of seed for our outing. Throwing a shawl over my shoulders, I hurried to meet Teddy and the Horror.

11

I Am Supervised

Out on the drive, I approached Nurse with my head held high. It was my policy not to give her the satisfaction of seeing me upset, so I decided to act as if nothing had happened. "Good afternoon," I forced out. "We'll be studying birds today. Would you be good enough to choose a destination for our walk?"

"Huh!" she snorted. "You can quit your nicey-nice talk with *me,* chickie. *I'm* in charge now, right and square, and don't you forget it!"

With an effort that I thought might kill me, I mildly observed, "Yes, you're quite right, Nurse." My voice sounded unnatural to me, and I felt no connection to the words. "And I must continue to teach," I went on. "I'm sure you could take us to some likely spots for bird-watching?"

"Hmph," Nurse mumbled. Whatever reaction she had expected, I had apparently disappointed her, and I rejoiced at this small triumph. She countered by making an elaborate show of ignoring my existence. "Come, Teddy," she commanded, turning her back on me. She took him by the paw and waddled down one of the pathways branching off from the drive. "*We* know where the birds is." As I straggled along behind them, Teddy stole glances at me over his shoulder, and for his sake I tried to smile reassuringly. And so we progressed.

The path wound around hillocks and rock formations, and carried us deep into the old growth of the forest. Teddy looked up to me and said reverently, "This is the Giant's Walk. That's what we call the old trees."

I gazed about me. Venerable oak columns soared skyward, topped by a many-layered canopy that tinged the muted light a silvery green. There was a momentary hush as we entered the woods, and, on Nurse's signal, we went off the path and sat quietly down to wait. I marveled, briefly, that she should know of such a lovely place.

First one, then another, and then in chorus, the birds began chirping and trilling in the uppermost reaches of the foliage. I scattered some seed at a little distance from us to tempt them down where we could see them, and then we waited. Within a few minutes, we were observing delightedly as the little jewel-toned creatures fluttered down and took turns feasting and chasing one another away from the banquet.

Teddy and I were whispering to each other the names of birds we recognized. Each time we identified a bird, we would try to pick out its call. As we were absorbed in this activity, Nurse sat with her back against an enormous tree trunk, arms folded, radiating boredom, her worn red shawl wrapped about her like a blanket, and her ruffled dustcap slipping down over one eye. It was not long before I heard guttural snores emanating from her snout. Since I had just been demoted to a place under her supervision for the crime of napping, the irony was not lost on me.

For the next hour, we sat on the forest floor, very still, and waited and watched. Gradually birds came to investigate: a yellow wood warbler, a nuthatch with its long black beak, a little chiffchaff with its distinctive tail wagging, and many others. Teddy fairly glowed with pleasure. After a time, we returned to Nurse's tree and packed up our things, then contemplated what to do about Nurse.

"YOU wake her up, all right?" Teddy asked, standing behind me.

"Why, Teddy?" I asked.

"I don't like to wake her up," he said evasively.

"I'll do it, Teddy. Stand back."

I leaned in and tapped her shoulder. Getting no result, I pushed her shoulder gently, then shook it. She reacted as if stung, leaping to her feet, jaws wide open, with that same guttural hiss and hateful glare she had frightened me with the night before. I stepped back, nearly tripping over Teddy, who was hiding behind my skirts, and waited for her to come to her senses.

"Nurse?" came Teddy's tight little voice as he peered out from behind me. "Can we go home now? I want to go home."

Nurse's glare softened as she focused on Teddy, and as her ruffled fur settled, she seemed to make herself smaller and denser. "Home?" she repeated. Then, as if something had just occurred to her, she licked her chops and said, "Did you catch anything?"

With sudden clarity I understood why Nurse had come to know this place. Refusing to think about it, I answered in the negative and, taking Teddy's paw, headed back to the path.

Nurse quickly caught up and grabbed Teddy's other paw, pulling him away from me. Unwilling to put Teddy in the impossible position of being tugged in two directions, I relinquished his paw and took up my place behind them.

As a climax to our trip, a tiny house sparrow left the cover of the woods and darted directly ahead of us. Our eyes were naturally drawn to its motion. I told myself later that there was no way I could have prevented what happened next, or Teddy's seeing it. Almost instantaneously a sparrow hawk shot out of the upper canopy and plunged down on the little bird, snatching it from the sky and flying off with it clutched in its talons. As a few loose feathers drifted to the ground, my eyes went to Teddy. His mouth hung open in shock, and his eyes were tearing up. Nurse immediately turned and said, "Well, now you see what happens to BAD little birds, eh?" and laughed.

"I'm not bad, right? I'm good! Ain't I, Nurse? I'm good," quavered Teddy.

I was appalled. Uncaring of what Nurse might do to me, I knelt down to the cub, and, looking straight into his big, tear-filled eyes, said, "Yes, you're very good, Teddy, but if little ones are bad sometimes, we do not kill them. We teach them how to do better, and we give them another chance."

I was expecting a counterattack from Nurse—a verbal tirade, or a threat. She merely looked away, with what might have been embarrassment, and went, "Hmph!" Then her whole demeanor changed. She turned to Teddy and said, "There, there, duck. You didn't think I meant it, did you?" She stroked his paw as she continued. "Why, of course I didn't mean it. It was just a little joke between *you* and *me*—and now your nasty governess has gone and scared you!" She returned my glare here, as if I had been responsible for the whole thing. "Now just you come with Nursie, and we'll go home and have cake with our tea. Won't that be nice?" Without waiting for a reply, she gripped his paw firmly, and set off down the path again.

Teddy managed to recover some equanimity, and I was left to wonder, as I followed them along, how often scenes like this took place. Was Teddy so perfectly behaved because he had grown up terrorized by Nurse's thinly veiled threats? I could see that he loved her, but with his warm heart and innocence, it seemed that he loved her even when she mistreated him. Perhaps Nurse even loved him, in her way, and, like the sparrow hawk, simply couldn't help her own predatory impulses, but I found I couldn't exonerate her that easily. Everyone has their animal nature to overcome, after all.

Whatever the case, our school day was over, and since I had no choice but to entrust Teddy to Nurse's care, I took an affectionate leave of him, managed a stiff "Good day" to her, and returned to my chamber to freshen up before tea.

Back in my own room, I was once again reminded of my locket, and felt the pang of its loss anew. My paw went to my heart, where I was accustomed to feel it hanging, and I blinked back tears. Mrs. Vaughn had said it might take some time to find it, but I had allowed myself to hope that it would be found swiftly. I felt sorely in need of a sympathetic soul to pour out my troubles to, yet I could not bring myself to tell Papa about the stolen locket, or how I had been demoted, or Nurse's humiliating conduct toward me. There was no one else in whom I could confide—no one but my faithful journal.

Forgetting tea, I sat down at my desk to write. The supper hour came and went, but it was my wounded spirit more than

my body that needed ministering to. My pen traveled across
many a page before at last it rested, and my mind felt purged and
quiet. With a familiar melody floating through my head, I put
away my writing things and prepared early for bed. The dark
was coming again, but I told myself that this night I would be
exhausted enough to sleep through anything. I carefully locked
the door and set a lonely little candle in a shallow dish of water
for a night-light, as Papa used to do. Only after I had said my
prayers and climbed into bed did I recognize the tune that I had
been humming: "Abide with Me." It was Papa's favorite hymn,
and I knew it by heart. I closed my eyes and repeated the words
while I waited for sleep to come:

> *Abide with me; fast falls the eventide;*
> *The darkness deepens; Lord, with me abide!*
> *When other helpers fail, and comforts flee,*
> *Help of the helpless, O abide with me.*

Peace descended on me, and I slept a long and dreamless
sleep.

～

The days seemed to crawl slowly by. Nurse had become the bane
of my existence, but I had expected no less. She exercised her
grandiose authority at every opportunity, and seemingly with
the intention of driving me to the madhouse. If I opened a window for some fresh air, she said it must be closed again so that
Teddy wouldn't get caught in a draft. If I kept the windows
closed, she insisted they must be opened to provide Teddy with

healthy fresh air. She might say our afternoon walks were too strenuous for Teddy, and we must go home; or she'd assert that our walks were not strenuous enough, and we must continue. She even had the audacity to comment on my teaching methods, and correct the stories I read to Teddy. In these and a hundred other ways, she bullied and, yes, badgered me until my teeth ground against each other, but I held my tongue. Exercising control I didn't know I had, I continued with my teaching as if she had not spoken, feeling that I owed as much to Teddy. No less important, it was the surest way to deprive her of any satisfaction. All of her outrageous conduct I stored away for an imagined time when she and I would come to a day of reckoning.

Despite Nurse's tyrannical attentions, Teddy and I continued to forge a bond of trust and affection, and though he was frequently distracted by her interference, I was relieved to see that it did not affect his sunny nature. I concluded that her intolerable behavior was quite normal to him. Still, he seemed aware of the raging tensions that surrounded him, often looking from one to the other of us as if to check both authorities before acting.

Mercifully, it soon became obvious that Nurse was bored to distraction by Teddy's lessons. At such times she often sat apart from us, sullen and silent, attending to her knitting—or her flask, when she thought no one was looking—or pacing restlessly by the windows. Better yet, she sometimes napped for hours at a stretch, during which time the very air seemed transmuted—cleaner, lighter, and sweeter—and I sometimes succeeded in forgetting about her altogether. These were the times that sustained me through her insufferable campaign against me, and gave me hope that a brighter future was coming—a future that would be worth the pain and humiliation I endured every day.

୬

At last, Friday evening arrived, and I looked forward to accepting the vicar's supper invitation as a kind of reward for my suffering. I took some care with my appearance, more as a way of reviving my spirits than with any hope of impressing anyone with my great beauty. I had never seen myself as anything other than a plain, unremarkable she-bear. My snout was too short, and it was said that my eyes were too intense to be really pleasing, but I trusted the principle that no one who was healthy and well groomed could look too bad. And so I combed my fur, and dabbed my throat with rose water, and put on my good bonnet. The one shadow on my horizon was that I must travel again through the great woods along the front drive. I told myself how unlikely it was that whoever or whatever had followed me the week before would still be lying in wait, but I could not altogether erase my uneasiness.

I opened the front door and hesitated. As I looked down the drive, trying to magically divine any untoward presence, a deep voice from behind startled me. "Going out, Miss Brown?" I jumped, turning, only to find myself looking directly into Mr. Bentley's snout.

"Oh!" I said, nonplussed.

"Are you going out, Miss Brown?" he repeated. He was wearing his coat and top hat as if prepared for town himself.

"Yes," I said. "Alone."

"Wouldn't you prefer some accompaniment, Miss Brown? How far are you going?"

I wondered how I could answer him without speaking to him, but could think of no way to do so. "I'm going to the vicarage. Alone," I repeated.

"Imagine. I am going just that way. In fact, I was going to stop and say hello to the vicar myself. What a happy coincidence."

I made no response, but walked out the door and started down the drive. Mr. Bentley fell into step beside me. I walked faster, but Mr. Bentley easily kept up with me. I could go no faster without breaking into a run, and I was unwilling to make myself absurd, so I slowed down and took another tack. "Really, Mr. Bentley, meaning no disrespect to you, of course, but I prefer to be alone."

"Of course," he repeated, and tipped his hat to me. He halted as I walked ahead, and then fell into line a little way behind me and began whistling off-tune through his teeth. This state of affairs seemed no less absurd than trying to outrun him, but at least it spared me from further conversation with him. Despite this, I felt his presence keenly, and as he whistled the silly tune, it seemed as if he were practically breathing down my neck. At last, facing him, I said, "Really, Mr. Bentley, you are almost treading on my heels. Do you mind?"

Again he stopped and tipped his hat, and I went on. I had gone a little distance when I heard him call out to me. "Miss Brown? Excuse me, Miss Brown?"

Exasperated, I turned to him. He was a good thirty paces behind.

"Is this far enough, do you suppose? Or shall I make it a bit farther?"

He was too distant for me to see it well, but I was certain that there was a smirk on his face. I resumed walking, perfectly aware that he was laughing at me, and not knowing whether to be offended or to laugh at myself. A smile started at the corners of my mouth unbidden, but I took great care that he should not see it. This bear was too clever by half, and I refused to let him get the better of me.

I put my head down, concealing my face in the shadow of my bonnet, and continued without further comment.

And so things went, without another word, until I arrived at the vicarage, next door to the little church. It occurred to me then that at least I had not been troubled by the thought of anyone stalking me in the woods. Nevertheless, when I tapped the door knocker, I fervently hoped I would be admitted before Mr. Bentley caught up with me. I hoped in vain. Mr. Bentley reached the door just as it was opened by a harried young girl in a servant's uniform. She showed us into a cozy parlor full of knick-knacks and overstuffed furniture, with a cheerful fire blazing on the hearth. Though the flowered wallpaper was a bit faded, and the cushions a trifle worn, still the room seemed redolent of many companionable hours spent within its walls. Reverend Snover welcomed us effusively, and introduced his wife, a white-haired, apple-cheeked little woman. Her eyes shone bright and merry, and her wrinkles etched lines of both sorrow and laughter on her face. I was drawn to her immediately as she enfolded my paw in her hands and greeted me in her kindly way. Mr. Bentley seemed well acquainted with the two of them, and fell into conversation with them straightaway, so that I wondered how many evenings he had spent here.

"Jonathan, how fortunate that you have come by!" the vicar

enthused. "You must join us for supper. We'll have Maggie set another place directly."

For a moment I cringed inwardly, my heart sinking as I saw the evening ruined, but I was granted a reprieve.

"I do beg your pardon," Mr. Bentley responded, "but I just stopped to say hello. I'm afraid I must be on my way. I've a little party to attend on the other side of town."

Reverend Snover looked taken aback, but quickly regained his composure. Clapping Mr. Bentley on the shoulder, he answered, "Of course. Of course," then added under his breath, "Be careful! And if I can be of any help . . ." He let the sentence trail off as they shook hands and Mr. Bentley took his leave.

12

A Choir of Fugitives

❧

I did not immediately know what to make of this exchange. It was only later that I connected Mr. Bentley's "little party to attend on the other side of town" with the covert warning I had overheard Fairchild giving Cook that there would be "the Devil to pay" that Friday night in Bremen Town. Such was my ignorance at the time that I was merely relieved that he wouldn't be staying, and then forgot the matter altogether amid the pleasantries of the evening.

Reverend Snover made a grand host, with a memory as sharp as a pin, generously sharing a wealth of anecdotes from his teaching days at the university: stories of my father and mother, and Mr. Vaughn, as students, and of their exploits there. I marveled at his portrayals of my parents as young people, only a few years older than I was myself. He told tales of great academic achievement and lively intellectual exchange, of parties and pranks. I laughed aloud when he told me about a whole flock of sheep found shut up in the lecture hall, the culprits suspected but never identified. I could hardly imagine that my parents had ever been so young themselves.

The harried little maid served a simple but tasty supper: roly-poly pudding, boiled potatoes and carrots, and apple pie for dessert, all with that home-cooked flavor. The good reverend went on painting his retrospective with such broad strokes of warmth and humor that I laughed away the evening. Only after dessert was over and we sat gathered about the fire did the laughter mellow into quiet conversation, and Reverend Snover did his best to draw me out about my life with Papa and about how I was faring in my new position with the Vaughns. As tempted as I was to pour out my heart to him, something stayed me. I barely knew these people yet, and I still feared to be disbelieved if I cast aspersions on an old family servant like Nurse. I told him of Papa raising me after Mama died, and about his years as headmaster at his small school. I spoke a little of my education at Miss Pinchkin's Academy for Young Ladies. As for the Vaughns, I talked only of Teddy and how much I enjoyed him. I believe Reverend Snover may have known that some trouble afflicted me, but, if so, he left it to me to choose whether to share it in my own good time—for which I was most grateful.

The evening slowly drew to a close, and though we had only shared a short time together, they gave me the feeling that they would watch over me like the grandparents I had never had, and my heart warmed toward them. I had just had a flash of panic about going out into the darkness when Reverend Snover insisted upon walking me home. Too relieved to protest, I tied my bonnet under my chin and wrapped myself in my shawl, thanking Mrs. Snover for her kind hospitality as she saw us to the entryway. Even as we spoke, events were conspiring to drastically change the course of the evening. First, a frantic knock at the door. The maid moved as if to answer it, but the vicar waved her away and answered it himself. I was startled to see Fairchild standing there, hat in hand, asking quietly if Reverend Snover could speak to him.

"Excuse me, would you, my dear?" the reverend said to me. He stepped outside and closed the door. I could hear their low, urgent voices, but I could not discern anything that was said. The interview lasted but a minute, and then the reverend came back inside and turned to me. "I'm afraid there is a problem. Some gentlemen in rather desperate circumstances require my assistance. I wonder if you might lend a helping hand. I warn you, there could be trouble involved."

Trouble involved? I was mystified, and a little excited, by the urgency in his voice. Trusting to his judgment, I asked, "What can I do?"

"Do you play, my dear?" he asked.

"Play?" I repeated.

"The pianoforte, or the organ. Do you play? We have need of an accompanist. My wife is not musically inclined."

"Yes, I play a little," I answered. "I could accompany you."

"Good. Good. That will be splendid. We're having a rehearsal of the men's choir, you see. Just come into the sanctuary with us, and please!—whatever happens, don't say a word. Hurry. This way." He lit a lantern and stepped out into the night.

Following him to the little church, I wondered what could be transpiring that a choir rehearsal could require such urgency and secrecy, but I dared not ask. Inside, Fairchild awaited us with a tense gathering of Forest folk, a score of men, bears, badgers, and others, among whom I was astonished to see Mr.

Vaughn and Mr. Bentley. As the reverend led me to the organ, they all filed into the choir loft, lighting the tapers and quickly distributing hymnals. I observed that Mr. Bentley looked totally altered from the dapper, sanguine gentleman I had lately seen: his neckcloth was dirty and disarranged, his expression strained, and his movements clumsy. He was squeezed in closely on either side by Mr. Vaughn and Fairchild, as if they were holding him up. I wondered briefly if he could be drunk.

"Page 102," Reverend Snover announced. "'Blest Be the Tie That Binds.'" There was a flurry of page turning, and I began to play. One by one the assorted gentlemen chimed in uncertainly and sang. At least one could call it singing; it was vocal, and occasionally someone hit a random right note, but the effort was dissonant and distracted. It would not have surprised me then to learn the truth: that there had never been a men's choir before that night.

"Louder! Louder! With confidence!" the vicar called out. We were rounding in on verse three when the door banged open and several constables stepped in. "Keep playing," the vicar hissed to me as he conducted the motley choir. The discordant chorus continued as the constables looked the group over and the chief constable bellowed, "May I have a word with you, Reverend?"

I kept playing until the vicar signaled me to stop, then he called out, "What can I do for you fine gentlemen?"

The chief constable, whom I was to hear of later as Constable Murdley, swelled noticeably with self-importance and obvious malice. He was a burly human, looking for all the world like a bullmastiff in uniform. "We're looking for some troublemakers, Reverend. Traced them this way from the other side of Bremen Town. They've been disturbing the peace and assaulting good citizens in the streets. We think one of them was injured. Have you seen any criminal types hereabouts, or seen anything unusual at all?"

"Criminal types!" the vicar said. "Saints preserve us! No, I've seen no criminal types. Has anyone here seen anything unusual at all?" The assembled choir looked innocently at each other and solemnly shook their heads. No, they had seen nothing unusual.

Suddenly the mention of Bremen Town impacted me with its full meaning. I had heard Fairchild telling Cook that "the society" would be instigating some sort of trouble on the other side of town. I could only suppose that these hardy souls who made up the "men's choir" might be the "criminal types" the constable was looking for. Perhaps they had interfered with the society's plans in some way, and it seemed there had been a fight. It came to me too that Fairchild had said the whole constabulary, and even the judge, were hand in hand with the society. A chill unsettled me as I realized what was at stake with this little charade, and my paws began to tremble so that I was uncertain whether I would be able to play again if called upon. I clenched them tightly in my lap and waited.

Constable Murdley peered suspiciously at the choristers. "Awfully late in the evening to be holding a choir practice, ain't it?"

"Well, well, Constable, these are workingmen, you know. This was the only hour they could all get away. We just called this emergency rehearsal at the last minute. I'm sure you will understand why, having heard them sing."

The chief constable snorted—I could not tell whether in amusement or contempt—and he walked up the aisle to the choir loft, lifting his lantern and looking into the faces of the men's choir, one by one. He stopped when he came to Mr. Vaughn. "Oh, excuse me, Squire," he said with exaggerated deference. "I didn't know you were here! You singing with this bunch?"

"As you see," replied Mr. Vaughn, nodding condescendingly, lending his full dignity to the motley group. I noticed then with horror that Mr. Bentley was holding his hymnal upside down, but the constable passed him by, and, turning to Reverend Snover, said, "Do you vouch for these gentlemen, Reverend?"

"Oh yes, indeed," the vicar asserted manfully. "Yes, indeed. Fine citizens, one and all."

"Well, if you see anyone suspicious, report it right away! We'll have those troublemakers up before Judge Slugby. *He'll* teach them a thing or two!"

"We'll certainly keep our eyes open, won't we, gentlemen?"

The members of the men's choir all assented, wearing their most solemn expressions.

Constable Murdley seemed satisfied with this, and he and his fellows made a hasty departure. "Now, then, verse four," Reverend Snover called out loudly, and I shook myself to attention and forced myself to focus on the notes and play. Most of the choir joined in, and the reverend shouted, "Onward now! With spirit!" as he signaled a young man in the front row to go to the window.

We struggled valiantly on until the young man at the window said, "All clear. They've gone."

The singing stopped abruptly, and the atmosphere grew deadly serious. "Come now, get him to the house and into bed," the reverend urged Fairchild and Mr. Vaughn, and between them they half carried, half dragged Mr. Bentley to the door. I gasped as his open coat revealed a bloody shirtfront.

"You there, Wilson," the mild-mannered vicar barked to a young man. "Fetch the surgeon! The rest of you, to your homes! And for Heaven's sake, be here to sing for the service on Sunday. You can bet Constable Murdley will be checking up on us. Miss Brown, if you would be so good as to help my wife? Tell her we'll need hot water, bandages, and plenty of brandy. Mr. Bentley's been shot."

13

The Secret Patient

❧

I ran ahead to the vicarage, where Mrs. Snover accepted this information with equanimity. She asked no questions, but set a pot of water on to boil and gave me an old sheet to rip into bandages. As soon as Mr. Bentley had been put to bed, we set about cutting off his shirt, and some of his fur, and cleaning the injury: a bullet hole in his left shoulder. A small group remained at the patient's bedside; the vicar, Mr. Vaughn, and Fairchild were speaking in low tones, but not troubling to hide their conversation from me. It seemed that I had earned entrance into their little fellowship. My interest aroused, I pieced together from snatches of conversation that the Anthropological Society had attempted to burn down the house that the Bremen Town Musicians had moved into. Apparently, this band of villagers and Forest folk I had just met as the men's choir had fought to stop the arsonists. It looked like they might have prevailed and put out the fire until the constables, being conveniently near at hand, had begun shooting—not at the arsonists, but at the villagers and Forest folk who were trying to stop them. In the end the musicians' house had burned to the ground, but the little band of rebels had managed to spirit away the four Bremen Town Musicians unharmed. There had been only one casualty.

Mr. Bentley moaned, and I held his head and offered him a sip of brandy. He accepted this gratefully, then looked up at me and breathed, "Ah, a ministering angel!" I could feel myself blushing—a condition that, mercifully, was invisible to onlookers. Torn between sympathy and exasperation, I could have wished that he had expressed his gratitude in a less familiar way. "Don't fret yourself, Miss Brown," he muttered thickly. "It's the veriest scratch." Then he closed his eyes, and his head rolled heavily to one side. Concerned, I glanced at Mrs. Snover, who covered my paw with her hand, and said, "He's just unconscious, dear. He's better off this way," as if she thought I was in despair over him! Not knowing how to disabuse her of the notion, I kept silent.

The surgeon came at last, taking mastery of the situation. He asked me if I was queasy at the sight of blood, and, wanting to be helpful, I said no, whereupon he asked me to stay at my post to administer more brandy should the patient awaken. I swiftly found that not only did so much blood make me queasy, but it made me fairly faint as well, and it was only by counting backward from one hundred as I focused intently on Mr. Bentley's eyes that I managed to stay upright and keep from being sick. And so I tended to him while the surgeon worked, and Mrs. Snover assisted as his nurse. Little need be said here of the surgeon's skillful handling of the case, or of Mr. Bentley's quiet suffering, but at last the bullet was removed, the wound was cauterized, and Mr. Bentley lay resting. We could only wait now, and see if infection set in, but everything had been done that could be done, and it was time to go. I bid the reverend and his wife a fond goodbye.

Mr. Vaughn and Fairchild had waited for news of Mr. Bentley's condition, and so we returned home together, a circumstance I was most grateful for, making my way through the Stygian shadows of the night forest with one of them on either side of me. We traveled in silence until we entered the house, where some considerate soul had left rushlights burning, and then Mr. Vaughn stopped me with his paw on my arm, and said, "A moment, please, Miss Brown." Fairchild tipped his hat, said good night, and went on his way. In a hushed voice, Mr. Vaughn continued, "I'd like you to know, Miss Brown, how sorry I am that you have been drawn into events that are so ugly and potentially dangerous. You performed admirably, and your father would have been proud of you."

"Thank you, sir, but I barely understand what happened tonight. Who were you fighting when Mr. Bentley was shot, and why should they want to burn someone's house down?"

"You surely remember the Anthropological Society?"

"Yes. How could I forget? But what is happening? What do they want?"

"They are bigots and bullies. They masquerade as a harmless social club, but we have agents inside the group who tell us that their grand high chief, that same Mr. Babcock who took over the newspaper, wants nothing less than total separation between humans and the Enchanted animals of the Forest, and if that is accomplished, there's nothing to stop them from stealing away our voting rights and raising taxes on our property until we've nothing left. That is what we're up against. Right now they're waging a battle to sway the opinion of the populace, doing their best to inflame sentiments against the Enchanted, but tonight's violence is the worst we've seen. You understand why I don't want you getting mixed up with them? I owe it to your papa to keep you safe."

My heart was inflamed by his speech. How could I hear that my own kind were being plotted against and trodden on without wanting to help? "Please, sir," I said, "let me do something too. I believe Papa would want me to follow my conscience. Will the men's choir be meeting again? I could play the accompaniment for them like I did tonight. Please let me help."

"You can help by keeping this night's exploits a secret. *Una omnes posset condenabitis lapsu,* my dear. 'One slip could endanger us all.' I recognize that such secrets are a burden to carry, and I am sorry for that too. I must ask even more: that you will not breathe a word of this to Mrs. Vaughn. She tends to suffer from her nerves, and I have sheltered her thus far from knowing about the activities of our little band of rebels. She would worry all out of proportion."

I wondered if it was "all out of proportion" to worry when his little band of rebels were being shot at, but I dared not question him.

As if he had heard my thoughts, he said, "It's better this way. You must trust me, Miss Brown."

"Of course, sir," I answered. "I'll do as you say."

"Thank you, Miss Brown."

We went into the house, and parted. I lit a candle, and, facing the dark corridor, prepared myself to make the long trip to my chamber, alone. Holding my candle aloft, I straightened my spine and set forth. I traversed the seemingly endless passageways and the stairs with barely a quiver, refusing to allow my imagination to torment me. Only as I approached the door to my room did I stop and listen. Was that a shuffling footstep, or merely the soft murmur of the wind? Was there a wind? I had noticed none on the walk back from the vicarage. Whose footsteps could it be? Was the one I thought of as the Walker roaming the hallways tonight? What did he want of me? Quickly, I fumbled with my key and fit it in the lock of my door, opening it just as my nerves got the better of me and set me to trembling. I shut the door behind me and tried to lock it, dropping the key twice before I succeeded. Still apprehensive, I put my ear to the door and listened for any footstep, but heard nothing.

Finally, I leaned my head against the wall and allowed the tension to drain out of me. It had been an extraordinary night, and my mind was racing. I changed into my nightgown, climbed between the sheets, and tried to think of home and Papa, but I kept coming back to the image of Mr. Bentley smiling up at me despite his pain, and calling me his "ministering angel." Try as I might to banish it from my mind, this last obstinate impression persisted long after my eyes closed.

∾

I'm afraid that my mind strayed disgracefully during Reverend Snover's sermon on Sunday. The only thing that captured my attention was the heroic performance of the men's choir, and that was certainly more proof of their courage than of their musical talent. Noting that Mrs. Snover was absent, I could not help but wonder if she was attending Mr. Bentley, and how he was doing. Directly after the service, I called at the vicarage, and was shown to the sickroom. Mr. Bentley was sleeping fitfully, and Mrs. Snover was doing her best to comfort him with cool cloths against his brow. From her haggard look, I surmised that she had sat up with him all night. It seemed only right to relieve her and send her to get some rest, so I promised that I would tend to him in her place.

"His fever's quite high," she said. "We must try to keep him cool. He won't be out of danger until the fever breaks." She hesitated, then added, "I'm afraid it's rather improper for a young she-bear such as yourself to be sitting alone at a gentleman's bedside. Your papa might not approve."

"Oh no," I said. "I am convinced Papa would say that need takes precedence over propriety."

Mrs. Snover only smiled. "I will leave you to your nursing, then."

I changed the cloth on Mr. Bentley's head, and then settled down in the rocking chair that Mrs. Snover had lately occupied. Mr. Bentley tossed and turned, moaning softly in his sleep. From time to time he would call what might have been a name, but I could not make it out. Without thinking about it, I began humming a soothing little ballad Papa used to sing to me when I was ill and restless. I had been rocking and singing for some time before I realized that Mr. Bentley's eyes were open and watching me. Mortified, I stopped, and said, "Did I awaken you? I'm sorry."

"No," he rumbled. "It's nice. Go on." So I went on. He closed his eyes again, and seemed to relax into the pillows. I sang until I was sure he was asleep, then put a fresh log on the fire, and cast about for something to occupy myself with. Behind the rocking chair was a low shelf with a row of books on it. Expecting to see

Pilgrim's Progress, I was surprised to see *Faust, Gulliver's Travels,* a volume of Voltaire's essays, and similar fare. I picked up *Robinson Crusoe* and began to read.

As time passed, Mr. Bentley became restless again, and the fever showed no signs of abating. He muttered things under his breath, which I could make no sense of—except for two syllables that I finally made out to be "Amy." He repeated this several times: "Amy." I wondered who Amy might be that she held such a place in his dreams, though it was probably none of my business.

Eventually, the surgeon came and bled him, after which he seemed weak and debilitated. On through the afternoon I alternately tended him, or sang, or read to myself. The time crept by, but after several hours Reverend Snover came to relieve me. As I prepared to make my departure, he apprised me in low tones that the story they were giving about was that Mr. Bentley had been called home on some urgent family business, and would be gone for some time. No one was to know his true whereabouts, lest word of his injury should get out and arouse the suspicions of the constabulary.

I assured him that no one would hear a word of the truth from me—an odd vow, I thought, to be making to a vicar. Promising to return the following afternoon when I was done with my duties, I took my departure.

The sun was leaning low in the sky as I started out on my way home. It had not entirely escaped my notice that I would now have to make the walk unaccompanied through the woods. I tried to be philosophical about it and tell myself that no one, after all, had done me any harm yet, despite my fears. Even so, when I came to the gatekeeper's lodge, and through the gates to the long, wooded drive, my senses became attuned to the slightest irregularity, and I proceeded with such excessive caution that even the birds were scarcely aware of my passing. After painstakingly tiptoeing partway down the drive, I perceived a motion a little distance away, keeping pace with me, just out of sight, but too loud and clumsy to be any forest creature. I thought of the terrible boy from town who had threatened me, and wondered if he could somehow have followed me. It occurred to me that even a good, loud scream would not help me if I were confronted out here in the middle of the woods. With that chilling thought, I lost my nerve and broke into a headlong run. Halfway down the drive, I was struggling for air and cursing the fashionable dictates that kept women so tightly bound in their corsets that it was impossible to breathe normally. I paused and prayed that dizziness would not overtake me. What would I do so far from the house without a fainting couch? I staggered on to the Cottage in the Woods with what speed I could muster. Once safely home, I collapsed on the carved bench inside the door and waited for my heart to stop hammering in my chest. I had hoped that no one would see me there, but Mrs. Gudge, the head housekeeper, happened into the entryway and observed my distress.

"Why, look at you, miss!" she exclaimed, seeming slightly scandalized. "You're all done in! What'd you do? Run all the way from town?"

I was surprised by her question, as the servants seldom acknowledged my existence, let alone made inquiries into my well-being. "I did run a little way," I said, fanning myself with my bonnet. "I thought it would do me good."

Mrs. Gudge raised one eyebrow, seeing through my pathetic

attempt at dignity, and shook her head, chuckling to herself. She passed on down the corridor and out of sight, leaving me to wonder how the story would play in the servants' quarters that night. Thoroughly mortified, I vowed that I would not be frightened into running down the drive another time, come what may.

14

A Confrontation

꒱

That night I dreamed of the crying child; of searching and searching for it in labyrinthine passageways; of hearing its pitiful wail, but never coming closer; of losing myself in the same ominous mist. I awoke to darkness and silence, near tears at the loss of the dream child, and lay there in a welter of emotion for a long time before sleep came again.

It was a sleep that brought little refreshment. Morning found me droopy-eyed and gloomy in defiance of the bright new day. I arrived at the schoolroom hoping for something that would improve my mood, but it was not to be. Teddy and Nurse wandered in very late, Nurse offering no apology, and Teddy not speaking at all. I was compelled to wonder if he had been forbidden to do so. Not until we practiced some of the songs I had been teaching him did he open up and make any sound. By midmorning he seemed more himself, though he threw frequent glances at Nurse, measuring her reaction to his every word. It tore at my heart to see him, normally so full of life and enthusiasm, made so constrained and intimidated. Still, he tried to please her, making a present to her of his best drawing, delivered with a kiss. Much to my astonishment, she responded to this with an appreciative word and an affectionate squeeze. Observe them as I might, their relationship defied my understanding.

By the time my teaching day was done, there was a steady rain coming down, but having a good, sturdy umbrella, I was not deterred from my planned trip to the vicarage. If there was any movement in the brush, the noise was masked by the soft percussion of the falling rain, and so I was able to convince myself that there was no one lurking in the forest that day.

At the vicarage things were much as I had left them. Mr. Bentley still ran a high fever, sometimes sleeping fitfully, and sometimes delirious. For a long while I tended him in silence, and read to myself from *Robinson Crusoe,* but then he began to toss and turn, and seemed in some danger of opening his wound again. I sought to soothe him, saying, "Hush, now, everything's going to be all right."

"Amy?" he moaned. "Am . . . y?"

Taking his paw, I said, "Yes. It's Amy. Be calm now. You're going to be fine. Go to sleep."

With that, he quieted down, but he kept a grip on my paw for some time as he drifted off. I thought dispassionately, as I watched him lying there, that I had been wrong about his looks. He really was rather handsome, with a broad, even forehead, deep-set eyes, and glossy dark fur. Afraid that he might awaken and catch me staring at him, I returned to my book. Later, his eyes opened, and he saw me reading. "Read aloud," he whispered. To humor him, I turned back and started at the beginning.

"'I was born in the year 1632 in the city of York, of a good family,'" the story commenced. Now and then Mr. Bentley seemed to slip back into sleep, but if I stopped reading, he rallied and said, "Go on, go on," and so I ended up reading until my voice gave out. By then he was sleeping quietly, and I took my leave. Mrs. Snover coaxed me to join them for supper, but, being anxious to get home before the light faded, I made my excuses and set off for the manor.

The rain had long since ceased, but there was a steady dripping of water off the trees, and everything was still quite wet. Mud splashed the hem of my skirts until they were soaked through at the bottom and dragging heavily. Time seemed to slow to a crawl as my raw nerves reacted to every sound. I came to a place where the drive curved around a dense thicket, so that it was impossible to see ahead, and my feet seemed to stop of their own accord, as if they knew something that I did not. I tried to reason with them. I had no evidence of anyone's presence. The thicket lay downwind, so I could catch no scent, and even if there were someone there, I would certainly never get home unless I went forward.

Taking a deep breath, I managed to put one foot in front of the other until I was halfway around. Then I saw him, the leader of the gang who had beaten up the young bear in town. He was lounging against a tree trunk as bold-faced as if he owned the whole woods, casually slapping his long wooden truncheon into his open palm. He did not seem surprised to see me. His eyes looked me up and down with a gloating contempt, and he smiled in a sensual and disturbing way. I could not wait to get away from him. Indeed, my immediate instinct was to hurry past as if he were not there.

"Evenin', miss!" he called out, lifting his hat to reveal a greasy clump of hair. He stepped out in front of me as if sensing my intention to ignore him, and leered. "Lovely weather, ain't it, miss?"

I couldn't imagine why he was trying to be pleasant, but it seemed to me more threatening than if he had been openly hostile. "What do you want?" I snapped, backing up to a good four yards away from him.

"Why, I'm just tryin' to have a fren'ly little conversation now, miss. Ain't nothin' wrong with that, is there? A little parley between two of the squire's hemployees? Mebbe we got off on the wrong foot the other day, eh? Mebbe we got some common hinterests to talk about. Y'never can tell. What's a-goin' on in the manor house these days, eh? What's new?"

"I'm not in the habit of conversing with strangers. Please step aside."

"Why, I hain't no stranger, miss. Name's Gabriel. Like the hangel. Jus' call me Gabe. I works fer the gov'nor just like you. I'm the one what the master hired to keep a eye on the place—keep out trespassers and the like." Here he slammed the truncheon on the side of the tree trunk, as if to demonstrate just how he would deal with such offenders. "So you and me are hequals, like." He apparently expected some response to this, but I remained silent. "Well, if you don't like conversin', then just lissen," he continued. "There ain't no harm in that, is there, just lissenin'? See, I watches you an' I says to meself, Now, that teacher's a smart one. I can tell jus' by the look of 'er. That's one as knows how to turn things to 'er hadvantage. So I've got a little propisishun for ye, miss, an' I'll make it worth yer while too. I seen ye takin' this route back and forth, back and forth. Now suppose next time ye come this way, ye gives me a little report about who-all's in the house and what they're hup to. Such hinfermation would be very valuable to me, and me dear old mother. She's got a hankerin' to know how the rich folks live, see?" With this, he put his grimy hand into his waistcoat pocket and pulled out a large, expensive-looking watch on a dirty string. As I was wondering how this individual came by such a treasure, he dug deeper and pulled out a coin. "See this?" He held up a shilling, then bit down on it to demonstrate its authenticity. "Hit's fer you," he said, tossing it to me with an air of great magnanimity. I recoiled and let it fall to the ground. "G'wan, take it!" he urged. "Mother's been savin' up, like. She's got more where that come from!"

"Are you actually suggesting that I spy on the Vaughns for you—for money?"

"Oh, I see how it is," he answered, laying a finger beside his nose and winking. "We has scruples, eh? How much hextra are they a-goin' to cost, eh?" He laughed unpleasantly. "What's yer price?"

"I would certainly never do as you are suggesting at any price. Now let me pass!"

The boy's expression hardened, the little malicious eyes squinting narrowly. "So ye think our money ain't good enough for ye?" He seemed to tighten his grip on the truncheon.

The only answer I gave him was to hold my umbrella out in front of me like a lance and rush forward, thinking to drive him or push him out of my path. At the last moment he gave way and jumped aside, but just as I barreled past him, he grabbed my arm with a powerful grip and brought me up short. "Not so fast!" he growled. All pretense of pleasantness vanished in an instant, and indeed I recognized that same wild look of rage that I had seen in him before. "I'll lay it on the line fer you, Miss Priss. I want the rat, and I want 'er quick! You think about that; there's good money I offered you on the one hand, or sufferin' me mother's displeasure on the other. Let me tell you, miss, she hain't to be trifled with. And just you hunderstand that it's best not to mention this 'ere conversation to them at the 'ouse. If anyone was to come after me, I'd know fer certain who set 'em onto me, see? And I know how to settle a score, I do. Me dear old mum taught me well." He laughed hideously and his eyes dilated so that the whites showed all around his irises, then he shoved his pimply face closer to mine and I smelled his foul breath. "Ye'd have to come outside sooner or later, wouldn't ye, miss, and when you did, I'd be waitin'! I knows my way around every hinch of this place, and I'd be waitin'!"

With a desperate twist I wrenched my arm from his grasp, and ran. Not daring to turn and see if he followed, I held up my soggy skirts and pumped my legs as fast as they would go. Even so, it seemed to me as if time itself congealed, and I was caught in it, the seconds stickily slowing to minutes as my limbs fought in vain to move faster. Finally, with my legs threatening to buckle beneath me, I reached the manor and dove in the door, breathing like a winded horse.

And there was Mrs. Gudge again. She looked up at me from her dusting, taking in the picture from the muddy skirts to the open, panting mouth, and responded with her usual aplomb. "Been taking your exercise again?" Her mouth twitched at the corner.

I nodded, too out of breath to speak, but striving for a look of nonchalance.

"Do you a sight more good to take the shortcut," she said.

"Go out the door in the kitchen garden wall next time. The path takes you the back way through the pine grove. Comes out behind the churchyard. Save you ten minutes." With that she turned and withdrew down the hall, shaking her head and chuckling.

I could have kissed her—or throttled her. Why couldn't she have told me this yesterday? I was still trembling all over, trying to think what to do, trying to make sense of the ugly encounter with the horrid boy, but this piece of news offered me a way to evade him, at least temporarily. The brute had claimed to know every inch of the property, but he couldn't be everywhere at once. If I merely avoided him, what would he do? What was he up to? I could not guess the true motive of his clumsy attempt to buy information from me, or what his awful mother really wanted, and I could not fathom who or what "the rat" was, though I could be sure that his purpose was not honorable. Was it burglary he was planning? No sensible thief would have revealed himself so brazenly, and anyway, I knew of no way a thief could get into the house after it was locked up at night, unless he had help from a conspirator inside. But I reasoned that if he really had such a partner in crime, he would hardly have need of information from me. Whatever his designs, I had no doubt that he would make good on his threat if I gave him away. Everything in his appearance and manner indicated that he would be willing, if not eager, to engage in mayhem, and he hinted that his mother was even worse. Certainly what I had seen in town supported that claim. I came to the conclusion that it was not a risk I could take, and so I assumed the burden of keeping the whole story to myself. Surely that was nothing new. Nurse had blackmailed me to keep her drinking a secret.

Mrs. Vaughn asked me to keep the theft of my locket a secret. Teddy knew that his mother disappeared to some secret location every day. Mr. Vaughn wished me to keep his activities with the men's choir to myself. What was one more secret in this house of secrets, after all?

15

I Relent

✦

Safe at last in my own room, I tried to regulate my breathing. With my stays squeezing my middle, it was difficult to get one good, deep breath, and I longed to be free of the hated corset, but propriety won out over comfort as I wondered guiltily what my mama would have said.

As I did a dozen times each day, I unconsciously put my paw to the spot where my locket used to nestle against my fur. How I missed it! It had been like wearing a little essence of home, and keeping Mama's and Papa's love alive, and close to my heart. I longed to open its silver case and see their faces smiling out at me. A week ago I had entrusted Mrs. Vaughn with the task of finding the stolen locket, and though I had hoped daily for a reassuring word from her, there had been none at all. Wondering what else I could do, my gaze fell upon the magic mirror on the bureau. Could it possibly be worth another frustrating encounter with that eccentric apparition? He had said that he would take five or six days to come up with a riddle to tell me where my locket was; if he was ever going to help me, it would be now. I rapped on the glass surface and called out, "Mirror? Mirror, do wake up!"

No response. I tried coaxing. "Mirror, I need your expert advice. You know you promised me a riddle." Still no response.

I rapped smartly on the glass again and fairly shouted, "Wake up! Now! I need to talk to you!"

A disembodied voice cried, "All right! All right!" Then, after a slight pause, the carnival mask appeared, and added, "Say 'please.'"

I closed my eyes and counted to ten, then forced out a "Please."

"Well, that was a little insincere, but it will serve. I suppose you want something. They always do. The secret for turning straw into gold? A love charm? No doubt you expect me to tell you you're the fairest in the land—which would be too much, you know, because you're really not. Your snout is far too short, and there's something too direct about the eyes—"

"I don't care about any of that. I want to know where my locket is. You promised me a riddle."

"Oh yes. The locket. Well, I've read the signs, and some of the signs say it is in the *top* floor of the *east* wing."

"Well, that's not very specific! Go on."

"And some of the signs say it is in the *bottom* floor of the *west* wing. So the truth must be halfway in between! That would be on the *middle* floor of the *main hall*."

"Halfway in between? How did you decide it must be halfway in between?"

"Well, silly, that's what we call a *compromise*—and we must all learn to compromise."

"I don't care about that either," I said, growing hot with frustration. "I want to know exactly where my locket is!"

"Well, let's see . . . I know! We'll put it to a vote!"

"A vote? And who will do the voting?"

"Why, anyone. That's the beauty of it!"

"Anyone? But will they know anything about the matter?"

"No. But the vote will tell us where popular opinion believes it to be: upstairs in the east wing, or downstairs in the west. Whatever most people believe must be true."

"But what if most people are wrong?"

"Hmm. In that case I will give you an obscure riddle, based on my personal opinion, and you will just have to make the best of it."

"Well, I would rather have the truth, thank you all the same."

"Oh, but the riddle is all prepared. Just listen to this. Ahem . . ."

> *When the moon is full and rising, comes the raven,*
> *burglarizing,*
> *Stealing shiny goods and trinkets, pillaging from door*
> *to door,*
> *Silently and surreptitious, though it is not avaricious,*
> *Hiding stolen goods and riches, buried in a secret drawer.*
> *Will you find a shining locket buried in that secret*
> *drawer?*
> *Quoth the raven, "Nevermore."*

"That sounds familiar," I said, "and quite cryptic. But not very helpful. There are a million drawers in this house, and this 'raven' could have put it in any one of them. Can't you give me a clue who the raven is?"

"That is your problem. I make up the riddles; you solve them. Or just admire their cleverness and beauty. I must admit that was one of my better ones. Did you notice the rhyming of *surreptitious* and *avaricious*? A masterstroke, really."

"Yes, yes. You've made a marvelous little poem, and been no help whatsoever. Thank you all the same, Mirror. You may go back to whatever demon's dream you came from."

The carnival mask assumed a look of wounded dignity and vanished with a pop. I wondered if there had actually been any truth to his suppositions that the locket could be upstairs in the east wing, or downstairs in the west, but either possibility was so vague and vast that it was hardly worth contemplating. Was the Walker really the "raven," stealing shiny things and hiding them away? How could I tell where its lair was? I could not fathom it. My spirits sank as I came to the conclusion that all my hopes now lay with Mrs. Vaughn and her good intentions.

The accumulated strain of recent events, of Nurse's harass-ment, of not sleeping well, and sometimes forgetting to eat, had all taken a toll on me, and I hardly recognized the hollow-cheeked, dull-eyed creature in the mirror as myself the next morning. Somehow the school day was gotten through, and I was finally free to go to the vicarage. I easily found Mrs. Gudge's shortcut from the kitchen garden through the pine grove to the church-yard. Folk wisdom was that pine trees had their own spirits that lent an atmosphere of healing and serenity. Whether it was that, or simply my relief at avoiding another encounter with the boy Gabriel, I felt the accumulation of so many burdens ease away in the fragrant ambience of the softly swaying pines. Off in the distance I heard children's laughter, and thought I could make out their slight forms running about in the woods, and I smiled.

At the vicarage I found Mrs. Snover less exhausted than she had been of late. The patient was much improved, she said, though he was refusing the nutritious broth she had prepared for him, and he was asking for the next chapter of *Robinson Crusoe*. Upon entering the sickroom, I perceived that Mr. Bentley was very much awake, although still reclining weakly on the pillows, and that his attention was entirely focused on me. I suddenly felt unaccountably shy.

"Miss Brown!" he said hoarsely. "The very person I've been waiting for. I'm in terrible danger of my condition worsening on account of boredom. Have you come to rescue me?"

I suppressed a smile. "As it happens, Mr. Bentley, I have."

"Ah," he said. "Excellent girl. Do proceed with all possible speed. I fear I feel my fever returning."

"No wonder your fever is returning if you refused Mrs. Snover's broth. I could not even think about reading to you until you've taken some broth."

Mr. Bentley scowled. "Tyrant! Bring it on, then. I'll have it."

Ten minutes later he had swallowed the last of it, and I made myself comfortable in the rocking chair, opened the book, and began to read. Soon we were deep in the adventures of Robinson Crusoe dauntlessly overcoming immense obstacles to save his own life, not once but many times, before he was finally shipwrecked on the Island of Despair. I marveled at his great intrepidity and inventiveness as he set about creating his island home and providing for all his needs.

The clock struck the hour, and then another, before I stopped and lifted my head. Then I realized that Mr. Bentley was staring at me in a most peculiar manner. "What is it?" I asked. "Are you tired?"

He shook his head. "I was just thinking about that day at the waterfall when I first saw you and made you so angry—"

"Don't even think of it. It is my policy never to argue with invalids," I interrupted. "However, if you'd still care to debate about it after you are all well, I'll give you tit for tat. For the present, you must put it out of your mind. Now go to sleep, if you please. You need your rest, and I must be going."

"But when will you come again? You can't leave me here to languish—imagine having that on your conscience! I'm only thinking of you."

"Yes, I see that," I replied, putting on my bonnet and shawl. "I'll come tomorrow if I can. Now, good night." He bade me good night with a mock air of tragedy, and I took my leave.

I returned home by the shortcut, and settled in for a cozy evening in my chamber. Fall had come in earnest now, and I enjoyed a crackling fire in my fireplace. Cook had brewed up a hot toddy to warm me through, and I sat by the fireside thinking, too drowsy to work on Latin. As I stared at the yellow flames, my mind's eye kept tracing the outline of a certain face with a wide brow and a sculpted snout; the face looked suspiciously like Mr. Bentley's. But I disliked Mr. Bentley—didn't I? Examining myself candidly, I found that my grudge against him had lost its rancor. If I was honest, I'd have to admit that I wasn't just going to the vicarage to help Mrs. Snover, but that I took some satisfaction in nursing the patient for his own sake, and that I was happy to think of going back again on the morrow. And yet what did I know of him? I knew that he was a little older than I, probably just out of university. I knew his name was Jonathan, because I had heard Reverend Snover call him that. I knew that, along with the other members of the "men's choir," he had risked himself to oppose an evil deed. I knew that he was profoundly protective of young Teddy. I knew too that he could be irascible and judgmental, or quite charming when he chose. And I knew there was someone named Amy who was so important to him that he had called her name repeatedly while in his extremity. I pictured her as a round-faced beauty, laughing gaily with him, her arm linked with his as he quoted poetry to her. Realizing that I actually knew very little about Mr. Bentley, I concluded that I must be careful to guard my feelings. Long ago, listening to my classmates' endless accounts of love's vicissitudes, I had vowed that my own head would always rule my heart, and this could be the first test of that resolve. Forcing myself to sit down at my desk and open the Latin grammar book, I ruthlessly blotted out Mr. Bentley with Latin verbs.

16

A Wild Chase

❧

Several weeks passed, with little variation in my routine. Mr. Bentley was well on his way to recovery, so much so that he was bored and restless, and, now that he was able to take a little exercise about the room, it was proving difficult to keep him quietly hidden away at the vicarage. Though he was surely well enough to read on his own, he insisted to me that he felt too weak to do so, and that if I had any proper feeling of compassion, I would not deprive him of his sole entertainment. Telling myself that it was indeed an errand of mercy, and a temporary one at that, I went on with my trips to the vicarage despite my caution, and despite the continuing toll they took on my time and energy.

My walks through the shortcut remained undisturbed. I realized the grotesquely misnamed Gabriel might come looking for me there any day. I had had time to think over the encounter with the brute, and the more I thought, the more I came to doubt that he was employed in any capacity by Mr. Vaughn. Would Mr. Vaughn be likely to hire such a callow thug to patrol his property? Surely "Gabe" would have nothing to fear from exposure if he were, in fact, legitimately employed? The villain had made it all up in order to claim that he had the master's approbation, in a clumsy attempt to win me over. What was he really after? What information did he think I had? What was this "rat" he had demanded so angrily? The thoughts wore at me and worried me through my days and nights, try as I might to push them away.

My daily struggles with Nurse continued without abatement. It was now habitual for Nurse and Teddy to arrive to the schoolroom late. Since I had no hope of effecting any change in Nurse's habits, I used the time to come up with new activities for Teddy. And so the days went by as I seethed inwardly and tried to learn patience.

As might have been predicted, however, the day came when patience was not enough. I had applied myself to the morning's exercises for some time, inventing some simple counting games with colored buttons. The hour for lessons to begin came and went, and Teddy did not appear. The hallway clock struck the half hour, and still he did not appear. By the time the clock had struck ten, I made up my mind to go to the nursery myself and see what the matter was. There I found Teddy, with his sailor suit all awry, struggling to do up the buttons on his shoes. Seeing me in the doorway, he put his paw up to his lips and went "Shhh!" then pointed to the recumbent form of Nurse, dead asleep on her trundle bed. "Don't wake her up!" he whispered. "She's sick!"

Silently, I took his paw in mine and led him to the schoolroom. "Have you had breakfast, Teddy?" I inquired. His only response was to shake his head sadly and put out his lower lip a little. I washed his face and set his clothes and shoes to rights, and took him down to breakfast. Cook made much of him, chiding him for his lateness, but as it turned out, she had saved Teddy a plate of pancakes. He made short work of them, and we returned to the schoolroom to begin our day.

It was near noon before Nurse put in her appearance, and she looked puffy-eyed and disgruntled, the fur on one side of her face mashed flat where she had slept on it. I continued with the lesson without acknowledging her. She walked unevenly to the chair by the window that she routinely occupied, and after several tries she sat down squarely on the cushion, picked up a small book, and began trying to kill flies with it, cursing every time she missed.

Teddy and I resumed our counting exercises, sitting at the table using the piles of colored buttons, ignoring the occasional slam of Nurse's book. Nurse seemed to be paying no attention to us, until, lifting her head, she barked, "Shut that window over there! You'll have him sick!"

I ignored her.

She jumped off the chair, nearly apoplectic, and stamped her foot. "I said close that window! You do as I say!"

Teddy looked up, eyes dilated with alarm, obviously fearing a confrontation. Forcing my mouth to stay closed, lest I lose control and say something I shouldn't, I crossed the room and closed the window. Nurse's hideous smile of victory made my stomach wrench, but Teddy visibly relaxed. It suddenly became clear to me that the day would come when Teddy himself must throw off her tyranny, and that there was nothing but my example to teach him how to do it. What could I say? The time had come to be audacious.

"I would have closed it at once, Nurse, if you had asked me nicely," I said for Teddy's benefit, and I returned to the table, not looking to see what reaction this might have elicited.

Behind me, a high, mocking voice mimicked, "'I would have closed it at once, Nursie, if you had asked me nicely.' You make me sick."

"Perhaps we should send for the apothecary," I suggested innocently. "He will be able to tell what is making you sick." This comment got the better of her, though she stewed in fury for the next two hours. I should have known then that she would have her revenge.

Soon it was time for our afternoon outing. We had gathered by the fern beds bordering the west lawn, beyond which lay a wilderness, and I remember telling Nurse that I had no special destination in mind, and that she might take us wherever she would.

I watched her expression go through a series of swift changes, as if she were calculating a list of possible outcomes, each more pleasing than the last. Suddenly she grabbed Teddy by the arm and cried, "Ha! All right, then!" and dove into the trackless woods at an all-out run. Never would I have suspected from the badger's squat build and surly temperament that she was capable of such speed. Teddy was dragged along as she went, his little feet fairly flying to keep up with her. She had nearly disappeared into the dense underbrush before I realized what was happening. Belatedly, I picked up my skirts and ran after them. A frenzied chase followed in ever-changing directions, over puddles and fallen branches, and into virtually impenetrable thickets where my clothing kept getting caught on branches and brambles. My greater size and voluminous skirts and petticoats were a handicap in the thick of the woods with no path to follow, and despite my longer legs, the runaways widened their lead on me.

Glimpsing Nurse's red shawl up ahead, I called out to Teddy. He giggled and ran on. I was sure he thought the headlong flight was some kind of game, and I knew I must not blame him for it, but my composure was about to snap. Finally I lost sight of them beyond a copse of juniper. For several minutes I followed the sounds of their movement, but my foot slipped and lodged firmly between two fallen logs, bruising my ankle, and by the time I extricated it—tearing the upper from the sole of my shoe—the only sound I could hear was of the wind rustling in the leaves. They had gone. I stood there thinking very indecorous thoughts of Nurse. Still, I knew that I could always find my way back alone. Of course, this would have to involve some accounting for where I had left Teddy and Nurse, and how we had become separated. I feared I would be blamed regardless of the explanation. There was no help for it. I must play Nurse's outrageous little game: follow them by their scent and their tracks and catch them up.

With my ankle still throbbing, I set off. After a bit of investigation, I picked up their trail, leading east toward a cluster of low hills. It led me in tortuous circles and turns, but I managed to stay with it for some time, angrily planning what I would say to Nurse when I caught up with her, and thinking too what I should say of this matter to Mr. Vaughn, for I was determined now that he should hear of it, even if I were disbelieved.

I came upon Teddy sitting at the foot of a large tree, building bug-sized dwellings out of twigs. "Miss Brown!" he cried, jumping up, obviously both surprised and pleased to see me. "You found us! Nurse said you would never find us! She said it was a holiday." His expression when he said this was just guilty enough that I could tell he knew better.

"Teddy, this is not a holiday. It is a school day, and it was wicked and rude for Nurse to run away with you the way she did."

Teddy looked down at his toes. "I'm sorry, Miss Brown," he whispered.

"You needn't apologize, Teddy. I know it was not your fault," I said, patting his head gently. "Where is Nurse?"

Teddy pointed to the opposite side of the tree. Stepping around it, I found her sleeping form propped against the tree trunk, and I nudged her shoulder until she burst into her habitual hissing, growling, and panting wake-up ceremony.

"You!" she spluttered. "What do YOU want?"

At that moment it seemed that some dam within me broke, and the words poured out. "What do I want? I want you to stop this war you are waging against me. I have borne every indignity you have inflicted upon me, but this time you have gone too far!"

She showed all her teeth in a slow, dangerous smile. "And what will you do about it, eh, chickie? What's the smart, edji-cated teacher going to do about it?"

"I will go to Mr. Vaughn, and tell him the whole story."

"The story of how you dawdled so that you couldn't keep track of an old badger and a cub? That ain't too complimentary to you, chickie, now is it?"

"No, I'll tell the truth, the whole truth: of the way you bully and frighten Teddy; of the way you imbibe; of the way you sleep through entire mornings and afternoons, and still can't get up and get Teddy to the schoolroom on time; and of the way you stole Teddy away on this wild-goose chase today—all of it. Whether he believes it or not, I will tell him!"

The badger glared at me, nearly choking on her own bile, her eyes flaming with rabid intensity as she seemed to search for sufficiently lethal insults. Then something seemed to give way, a fissure in the brash countenance, a trembling of the lower lip, and Nurse whipped out her handkerchief and burst noisily into tears.

17

Night Terror

ↄ

The effect on Teddy was immediate: his expression turned to one of sorrow and dismay, and he rushed to her and threw his arms around her. Nurse looked over her shoulder at me to see if I was appreciating the full scope of her power over him, then she leaned her head against him and sobbed pathetically. "To think it should come to this," she gulped, "after all these years of loving care and sacrifice. And me with no other home but this one, and no other family but this to love like they was my own . . ." She trailed off, alternately crying and moaning.

I folded my arms and tapped my damaged shoe in agitation. Teddy looked up at me with his big, liquid eyes, and said, "We don't have to tell, do we? She didn't mean to do anything bad!"

How could I explain to a mere babe in arms that the creature he had looked to his whole life with trust and affection was cynically using him even as we spoke? In all his innocence, he was simply incapable of understanding or believing it. Even worse, Nurse would see to it that Teddy would blame *me* now for her tears, and for any ill consequences to her that might follow my report to his father.

"Teddy," I said, taking his paw in mine, "you trust your papa, don't you? Doesn't he always know what to do? And your mama too? Do you know that she told me Nurse would always have a home with you?"

Teddy looked at me hopefully, but the look was erased by a fresh round of blubbering from Nurse. Finally, seeing that the performance was not likely to come to an end while there was strength left in her body, I informed Teddy that we must get her home.

Thus began the long, lachrymose journey back to the Cottage, with Nurse stumbling blindly through her supernatural supply of tears, and Teddy pulling her gently onward by one paw. Progress was slow, partly due to my sore ankle and ruined shoe, but mostly because of Nurse's amateur theatrics, which she seemed to be honing and augmenting as the expedition advanced. In one inspired bit of display, she hit on the stratagem of hurling herself to the ground, and lying there wailing convulsively until Teddy and I each took an arm and lifted her up again. This had the effect of drawing sympathetic tears from Teddy's eyes, so of course she made it a regular feature of her repertoire from that point on.

We arrived at the Cottage exhausted and bedraggled, but I repaired straightaway to Mr. Vaughn's den, undeterred by Nurse's histrionics. Nurse managed, despite being incapacitated by grief, to edge her way in front of me in order to be the first to Mr. Vaughn's door, and so when Mr. Vaughn responded to my knock, she collapsed against his leg, weeping profusely.

"What's this?" Mr. Vaughn demanded, in a tone that brooked no nonsense.

All eyes turned to me, so I spoke up. "I'm very sorry to interrupt you, sir, but I urgently need to talk to you."

Teddy sniffled. Nurse released a torrent of incoherent verbiage, ending with "Lor' knows I've done the best I can!" then resumed her wailing. Mr. Vaughn's strained expression seemed to indicate that he would rather be anywhere than in the middle of this scene. He reached down and patted her awkwardly, saying, "There, there, Nurse. Pray calm yourself." To me he said, "I will hear you out as soon as I have dealt with Nurse." Then he ushered her into his den and shut the door.

My spirits sank. I couldn't even guess what half-truths and outright lies she would spin for him behind that closed door, but all I could do at this point was tell him the truth and hope for the best. Teddy sobbed openly now, and I held him close and comforted him.

"Remember what I said, Teddy. Trust your papa." Even as I spoke, I thought privately that I was not at all sure that Mr. Vaughn could remain objective in the face of Nurse's emotional onslaught. I knew that this incident could result in either Nurse's dismissal or my own, depending on whom he believed, but I dared to hope for Teddy's sake that it would be neither. Though I longed to eliminate Nurse from Teddy's life—and mine—I knew that his attachment to her was very strong, and that he would suffer if she were suddenly torn away from him.

As I was lost in these thoughts, Mr. Vaughn opened the door and summoned me in. I sent Teddy on ahead to the schoolroom, and entered Mr. Vaughn's den, mentally rehearsing how I would begin. Nurse was seated in an upholstered chair, many sizes too big for her, looking so devastated and forlorn that I nearly wanted to comfort her myself. Far from calling her performance amateur, I was now convinced that in her earlier life she had had professional training for the theater.

Mr. Vaughn sat down in his chair and left me to stand on the opposite side of his desk. "Before you begin, Miss Brown, let me say that it has come to my attention that I have perhaps been insensitive in assigning Nurse to supervise you."

I was stunned. I had imagined several different outcomes, but never this. Was he seriously apologizing to me for imposing Nurse upon me?

"I utterly failed to take into consideration that Nurse is getting on in years, and that the position might be too much for her. It seems that I have—unconsciously—produced much strain and difficulty for her. Perhaps you were not aware of this—though it seems her distress must have been obvious. In the future I hope you will come to me with any problems immediately and not allow them to go on until things have reached such a pass."

Only then did it dawn on me that Mr. Vaughn was apologizing not to me, but to Nurse, for inflicting the added responsibilities on her. None of this should have surprised me, either that Nurse had come up with a perfect story that would make any criticism I made of her seem cruel and insensitive, or that Mr. Vaughn was actually chiding me for failing to bring Nurse's fictional problem to his attention. Still, it took me a few moments to adjust to the new reality. I quickly realized that I could hardly have hoped for better: Nurse was being effectively retired from her supervision of me, and yet not discharged from her position. If I let Nurse's story stand, I would have my freedom back, and also avoid upsetting Teddy with her dismissal.

I became aware of Nurse's gaze focused on me with burning

intensity, and it seemed to me that her mask had slipped. She wore an expression of naked fear, as if pleading with me to play along with her. Though I later understood this was as feigned as the rest of her act, it served its purpose. I made a split-second decision, and, trying to keep the irony out of my voice, I said, "I'm so sorry, Nurse, that you have been under such a strain. I didn't realize." Then, turning to Mr. Vaughn: "Sir, maybe I can be of some help to Nurse by taking over her morning duties and getting Teddy ready for his school day? It would be no trouble to me, and it would make it possible for her to get a little more sleep."

Nurse looked as if she would object, but covered it quickly. What could she say when I had taken care of Teddy that very morning due to her being "sick"?

"That sounds like an excellent idea," pronounced Mr. Vaughn. "I will personally be looking in on you from time to time, Miss Brown, a task which I perhaps should have undertaken to begin with."

If I suffered a little dismay at this pronouncement, it was still minor in comparison with my relief at being liberated from Nurse, who allowed herself a malicious smirk in my direction.

"Is there anything else we need to discuss, then?"

Nurse and I both looked guilelessly at him and said, "No."

"Very good. *Fiat tantum pax.* 'Let there be peace.'" Mr. Vaughn saw us to the door. It had barely shut behind us when Nurse turned on me with teeth bared.

"Don't you be thinkin' you've got the best of me, chickie," she spit. "I'll get my chance. Sooner or later I'll get my chance to do you dirt, and when I get it—I'll take it!" She was gone before I could think how to respond, and I was left with the chilling knowledge that she meant it. I could only marvel that she had the strength left in her to make threats after the exhausting melodrama she had enacted all afternoon. I myself felt drained and enervated.

Nevertheless, it was with a light step that I walked to the schoolroom to talk to Teddy about the conversation with his father. He didn't question the story that Nurse was simply too old and tired to keep up with us all day, though I thought it must seem a patent falsehood to anyone who'd had to run to keep up with her as he had that afternoon, and he seemed to have no qualms about the proposed solution.

That afternoon, for the first time since Mr. Bentley's injury, I did not make the trip to the vicarage to read to him. Indeed, I was so tired by teatime that I could barely make the journey to my own chamber. There I found that an envelope had been slipped under my door. It was a letter from Papa. I rang for Betsy to make a fire in the fireplace, and serve tea in my room, then settled down in my chair to savor the tidings from home. It was like being at our old place again, sitting companionably with him at the close of day while he smoked his pipe and talked of great things and small, and listened to all my childish joys and sorrows. How I wished I could be there by his side! I could only hope that Lucy, our housemaid, was taking good care of him. Intending to answer his letter, I added a log to the fire and sat down at my desk to write, but I did not get much past the salutation before the accumulated fatigue of the day and the soporific warmth of the fire combined to make my eyelids heavy and my thoughts blurred. I set my pen aside, and, after preparing myself for bed, I climbed into my big four-poster, and fell into a dreamless sleep.

৵৩

I could not say what awoke me. My nighttime candle had burned out, and it was dark, except for the glowing embers in the fireplace. Afterward I could recall no sound, only an unfamiliar scent—and yet I sensed a presence: something in the darkness that did not belong. The Walker. A stinging bolt of fear shot through me as I tried to remember whether I had locked my door. I had. I knew I had. So how could there be anyone here? Yet once before, I had disbelieved my own senses only to find that there actually had been an intruder—an intruder who had stolen my locket. I would not be so quick to disbelieve again. Someone *was* here.

Light. I must have light! For a long time I debated whether I had the courage to take the burned-out candle at my bedside and light it from the embers in the fireplace. What would the Walker do if I moved? Would he attack me? Would he flee? After what seemed an age of helpless agonizing in the dark, I came to the conclusion that the light of a candle would be worth almost any risk.

With painstaking slowness, I sat up on the bed and reached out a trembling paw to grasp the candle. Had I heard something? A rustling? Some furtive movement? My ears nearly quivered, attuned to the slightest sound, but it was gone. I listened intently for a full minute more, then I slowly stood up. Was the Walker watching? Was it too dark for him to see me? I tried to guess how many steps to the fireplace. Ten? Twelve? I began what seemed like the longest journey of my life, putting one foot in front of the other like a tightrope walker, aware that my next step could precipitate some disaster. There—that rustling again, from somewhere in the corner. Casting away all caution, I ran to the fireplace and frantically blew on the glowing coals as I held my candle to them. Interminable seconds passed. I imagined that the Walker would see what I was up to—see that he was about to be exposed. Would desperation make him violent? I couldn't think about that. I stirred the embers with the fire iron and blew some more, and saw my efforts rewarded with a little spurt of flame. Keeping the iron in one paw, I lit the candle with the other and slowly stood up, bracing myself for whatever I might encounter.

No one was there. Only dim shapes and looming shadows surrounded me in the flickering light. No sound gave away the Walker's presence, but I smelled the acrid odor of fear—whether my own fear or the intruder's, I could not tell. I raised the candle and began to search, my nerves stretched as taut as a violin string, my fur bristling. I forced myself to go about the room, checking under the bed, behind each curtain, illuminating each shadow, until I had checked everywhere but the corner beyond the wardrobe. All that was necessary now was for me to step to the side of the wardrobe and throw light into the shadow, but I could not do it. I stood like a statue a little distance away. I stood until my muscles ached while an argument raged in my head whether to go forward or not.

And then I heard a small sneeze.

18

I Receive a Shock

At once I stepped to the side of the wardrobe and raised the candle. There I saw what looked like a little bear, until, in the flickering light, a pair of human eyes looked up at me. For a moment I could not make sense of what I was seeing. The small figure had the furry body and ears of a bear, but the delicate face and hands of a human child—a child in a bear costume. Seeing the fear in its eyes, I stepped back and put down the fire iron. Here was an uninvited guest that I could manage. My mind raced, wondering where the child had come from, and a dozen other questions. Choosing the one most obvious, I said, in soothing tones, "What brings you to my room so late at night, little one?"

There was no response, almost as if it hadn't heard me, but the eyes seemed a fraction less frightened, the posture a bit less stiff. I took a slow step forward and bent down to the child's level, in order to be less intimidating. "Where do you come from, dear? Are you lost?"

The child took several steps backward—soft, shuffling steps made by two furry slippers. I had heard those shuffling steps before: in the hallway, in my room, in my darkest imaginings. And yet, this was just a frightened child.

"Are you lost?" I repeated.

Still no answer.

"It's all right," I said. "You're quite safe here. I am Miss Brown, the governess." Slowly I reached out a paw to stroke its head—or rather stroke the furry hood with the bear ears sewn on. The child flinched. Close-up, its features seemed feminine, almost fragile. Impulsively, I pushed back the hood and beheld a cluster of long golden curls. While I marveled, she darted under my arm and ran for the door, leaving me alone with all my questions and an empty feeling in my middle.

This, then, was the Walker, the menacing creature who roamed the halls between dusk and dawn, the thief who had taken my locket? But had she? Having looked into those limpid, innocent eyes, I found it hard to believe. Surely this frightened child was not the danger Mrs. Vaughn had warned me to lock my door against at night! How on earth did she get through that locked door? And what about the Vaughns? They must know of this youngster. Whose child was she? What was she doing traipsing about their hallways in the dark?

Distractedly, I climbed back into bed, not bothering to close my door again. In the morning I would go to Mrs. Vaughn and ask for an explanation.

❧

Daybreak came with a spate of doubts. A child in a bear suit roaming the halls of the manor at night? It seemed too improbable to be true. I could almost believe that I had dreamed it, except for my open door, and the fire iron lying where I had left it on the floor.

I went early to Mrs. Vaughn's morning room hoping for an interview, and found it empty. Not to be deterred, I sat in a chair just outside her door and waited. The distant chiming of a clock told me an hour had passed. At last, I heard light footsteps approaching, and turned to find her looking at me quizzically.

"Miss Brown? Was there something you wanted?"

"Yes, madam, I wished very much to speak with you. It's rather important."

"Well, then, my dear, you must come into my room and make yourself comfortable. I am free all morning, so take as much time as you please."

Accepting her invitation, I chose an overstuffed pink chair and sank into it as she settled into another.

"What can I do for you, dear?"

She waited calmly for me to begin, but I did not know quite how to do it. Finally, I blurted out, "Mrs. Vaughn, there was a child in my room last night! A little human girl in a bear costume! I'm convinced it's not the first time either. Who is she? Why does she wander the hallways at night?"

Mrs. Vaughn gulped, as if she were swallowing a lot of air all at once. "Oh dear," she said, looking anywhere but at me. "Well . . . I guess you've found our little secret. We were going to tell you soon anyway, my dear. Really we were. We were just waiting for the right time, you see."

"Please, madam, I want to know all about her. Tell me how she got in my room last night with the door locked."

"Oh dear, did she? She *will* pick the locks. I just cannot find one she's unable to open. The most they do is slow her down.

I imagine she mistook your room for the nursery. I found her there once, at night, watching Teddy sleep."

"But where does she come from? What is her history?"

"Well, as you've seen her, I suppose I should tell you the whole story, at least the part that I know. It would be a relief, actually, to get it off my chest. I daresay you will tire of it before I'm through."

"No, really, madam. I'm fascinated. I'll gladly listen."

"All right, then," she said. Picking up a bundle of knitting, she started to work with the regular rhythmic motions of an experienced knitter. She relaxed and cleared her throat.

"This all happened in a morning," she said, "but it really began earlier, with the weather. It was just four months ago now, the hottest, driest June that anyone could remember. The birds and crickets had stopped chirping. The wild creatures had become bolder and bolder, coming onto the grounds, even up to the house, seeking water. Old George, the gardener, reported he'd seen wolves drinking at the koi pond. After that, Mr. Vaughn declared that Teddy and I must not go out alone for our walks. Everyone's nerves were on edge, just waiting for a good, cooling rain.

"And then came that morning. We were all looking forward to some nice, refreshing berries for breakfast. Well, wouldn't you know Cook would choose that morning to serve us piping hot porridge. Mr. Vaughn was scowling, and even Teddy threatened rebellion. I wanted to send the stuff back to the kitchen, but was afraid of inciting open warfare with Cook. 'Look,' I said, 'it's not so bad,' and I took a big spoonful, burning my tongue badly.

"'Enough!' declared Mr. Vaughn. 'We are going out. We shall leave this mush to cool off while we go berry picking.' He stalked into his den and came back a minute later with his musket, shoving several minié balls into his vest pocket.

" 'Is that really necessary, dear?' I remember asking.

" 'Better safe than sorry,' he said. He locked the front door, and we set off for the glade where the strawberries grow. The berries were small and scarce because of the drought, but we proceeded to make a snack of them. Not until the first thunderbolt split the air above us did we pause and look up. The treetops were dancing in the wind with a mad rushing and roaring. Suddenly we heard a loud crack, and a branch plummeted down within a few feet of us. I was startled, but more than that, I was filled with the conviction that we must go back. I turned to Mr. Vaughn and said, 'Something's wrong. I feel it. I want to go home.'

"I expected that he might laugh it off. He generally has no patience with presentiments and portents, but this time he looked into my eyes, and quoted—I remember it so clearly—'For my mind misgives some consequence yet hanging in the stars.'

"We grabbed Teddy and hurried back up the path. The wind howled at our backs; thunder and lightning raged overhead. We clambered into the house just as the skies opened and unleashed the deluge. We had made it safely home, but my mind was still unquiet. Mr. Vaughn was tense too. 'I'll just check the drawing room doors,' he said. 'They never do shut right.' He set off down the hall. Teddy and I followed at a distance. We stopped at the entrance and watched as Mr. Vaughn went to close the French doors, which were wide open.

"Well, we were barely seated at the breakfast table when we realized that someone had gotten into the porridge. Why,

Teddy's was all gone! Mr. Vaughn and I looked at one another. Then he rose from the table and picked up his musket and loaded it. 'Stay here,' he said. 'I'm going to look around.'

" 'I won't stay here,' I said. 'We're coming with you.' And we all trooped through the downstairs, inspecting each room for anything moved or missing, until we came to the back parlor. At the far end near the fireplace, we found Teddy's little chair in several pieces.

" 'Vandalism!' said Mr. Vaughn.

" 'Oh dear. The silver candlesticks are missing,' I said. 'But perhaps the servants have taken them for polishing.'

" 'And will you look at this!' said Mr. Vaughn, going to his own favorite chair. 'Someone has moved my newspaper, and my pipe and glasses are on the floor! By Heaven, someone has been sitting in my chair!'

" I looked closely at my own favorite chair and saw similar signs. My knitting had been disturbed, and my favorite afghan was missing! 'Whatever shall we do?' I cried.

" 'Do?' Mr. Vaughn said, cocking his gun. 'I know what I shall do! Stay back!' He marched out of the room, down the hall, and up the grand staircase. Teddy and I hurried after him. Into each of the rooms on the second floor we went, and on to the master bedroom. Here I knew immediately that something was wrong. I had made the beds carefully myself that morning, as it was the maid's day off, but now they were all rumpled and unmade, and a pillowcase was missing from Mr. Vaughn's bed. And wasn't he furious!

" Suddenly I noticed that Teddy had gone on ahead, and it worried me to have him separated from us. I called out his name, but there was no answer.

" 'Try the nursery,' Mr. Vaughn said.

" 'Teddy? Teddy?' I called as we went. Still no answer, and I felt a little chill of fear, wondering where he could have gone, or what could be preventing him from answering. We opened the nursery door, and there stood Teddy, at the foot of his bed, staring, entranced, at what was on it. He turned to us, his eyes glowing as if he had just witnessed a miracle, and put his claw to his mouth, going 'Shhhhh.' He pointed to the little figure lying there, and whispered, 'You'll wake her up!'

"Well, there we stood, we three, looking at the child. She was very dirty, dressed in rags, with a tangle of mud-colored hair and no shoes on her grimy little feet. I remember that her thumb was in her mouth. In the other hand she clutched my missing afghan, and next to her lay the missing pillowcase, out of the corner of which stuck the end of a silver candlestick. But the little face was what drew one to her, and grabbed at one's heartstrings. It was a cherub's face, utterly serene and innocent, only where there should have been round, rosy cheeks, there were pale hollows, and a trail of dried tears. I think I fell a bit in love with her at once.

" 'The little angel,' I whispered.

" 'The little thief!' said Mr. Vaughn.

" 'Can I keep it?' Teddy asked.

"Mr. Vaughn rang for young James, the footman, then motioned me out of the room. We had a hurried conference in the hallway.

" 'Don't go getting attached to it,' he said quietly. 'I'm sending for the constable. It's a human child; let them determine what to do with it.'

" 'Yes,' I said indignantly. 'Just see how well the humans have taken care of her so far! She's only a wee little thing, and half starved! She needs love and nurturing. What's the constable supposed to do with her? Put her in jail?'

" 'What would you suggest? Give her the run of the place? Should we lock up every valuable we own, or simply let her rob us blind? Besides, she must belong to someone. You can't just KEEP a child, you know. That could cause a world of trouble.'

" 'Maybe we should put an advertisement in the papers,' I suggested. 'We could take care of her here until someone answers, and if no one answers, then why shouldn't we keep her? I'm sure that would be all right. Please, Walter. She looks so thin and pathetic. I doubt if she can survive much longer without being cared for, and you must know she'd catch her death out in this storm.'

"Mr. Vaughn shook his head. 'So it would seem I'd be guilty of murder, Mrs. Vaughn, if we don't keep her? Well, all right, then. I've come this far in life without murdering any innocent children. I suppose I can wait a little longer. We'll keep her here, and care for her, but I'm putting an ad in the paper. Someone must know something about a missing child—or a burglar at large.'

"Teddy came out of the nursery and took me by the paw. 'Come on. I think she's waking up,' he said. A little moan escaped the girl's lips, and her eyes began to open. 'For Heaven's sake, Mr. Vaughn,' I said, 'put the gun down. You'll frighten her!' He laid the gun on the mantel, and we all continued to stare at her as she watched the three of us.

"I've asked myself time and time again what we could have done differently, but of course we had no idea what was to come. She lay there so peacefully. Then the child's expression changed.

She sprang from the bed like a scalded cat and bolted for the door. Mr. Vaughn reached it first, and shut it. The girl gave a strangled little cry, but she never slowed. She simply swerved to the side and ran the whole perimeter of the nursery, and then did it again, dodging each of us, and running straight up and across Teddy's bed as if it weren't there. She finally halted at one of the windows, climbed up on the sill, and wrenched it open. The rain drove down, soaking her, but she seemed oblivious to it, looking frantically at the ground as if she might actually jump from the second story. My heart was in my mouth. I started talking to her, quietly introducing each of us, and asking her name. She seemed not to hear me. I took a step closer to the window, and with another wild cry the child jumped back into the room and resumed her frantic running. Little Teddy stood mesmerized by her, then he began to run too, as if he were being pulled into her frenzy. I tried to call him to a halt, but it was useless. 'Just let them wear themselves out,' Mr. Vaughn said, but that didn't look likely to happen.

"In the next instant the child made a leap for Nurse's chair, and from there grabbed Mr. Vaughn's musket off the mantel. She held the heavy gun awkwardly, but knew enough to place the stock against her shoulder and take aim for the door. Teddy stopped his charge, and we all stood still for an awful moment, mouths hanging open, paws in the air, held hostage by a child with a cherub's face, and eyes of flint. 'You don't want to do this,' Mr. Vaughn said, calmly backing away from the door. 'That gun is loaded and cocked, and unless you're very careful, it will go off.'

"Then three things happened so quickly that we could barely react. James arrived and, knowing nothing of the drama within, opened the nursery door. Then instantly, the child dropped the musket and ran toward the door, whereupon the gun went off, narrowly missing Mr. Vaughn.

"He and the child both dove for the door, but Mr. Vaughn got there first. He grabbed her up in a bear hug that completely immobilized her. 'Whoa, little hellion!' he said, and he held her, rocking his body back and forth like he used to do with Teddy. Whether she was actually comforted, or simply found herself unable to struggle anymore, the child seemed to relax into his chest, and she was still.

"Mr. Vaughn asked James to stay with Teddy in the nursery while we took care of her, but Teddy objected loudly, saying, 'Where are you going? I want to come too!'

"'She has to go home to her own house now,' Mr. Vaughn said. 'It's time to say goodbye. You must stay here with James.' At this, the child started squirming again, and James had to restrain Teddy from following us.

"As soon as the nursery door was shut, I started to speak to Mr. Vaughn about this change of plans, but he interrupted me. 'You've seen how fascinated Theodore is with her. I think you'll agree that we cannot expose him to the behavior of this little wildcat? I'm simply making sure he won't come looking for her. I hate to lie to him, but it can't be helped. Now, where, my dear, do you suggest we keep her?'

"'Of course. You're right,' I said. 'She must be kept away from Teddy. She must be some place safe, where she can't jump from a window—and spacious. And out of the way of the rest of the household, I think.'

"'Yes, out of the way, by all means. You do realize, my dear, that there are those who would make a great deal of trouble over us harboring a human child. I don't doubt she'll be a great deal of trouble in any case. How do you propose to go about civilizing her? Have you thought of that? A child that doesn't even speak? She may be deaf, or dull in her wits.'

" 'Walter,' I said, with all the seriousness I could, 'I only know she needs me.'

"Mr. Vaughn let out a big sigh, and said, 'Lead the way.'

"I chose a suite of rooms up under the eaves in the east wing, much too high to jump from, where nobody goes unless we have company. They had been done up as a lady's chamber, and never used, but I thought they could be made into a comfortable home for a little girl.

"I gave Mr. Vaughn a short list of instructions for James, chief among them being to bring a rocking chair, and some food. Mr. Vaughn transferred the girl to my arms, with only a brief struggle from her, and I said to her, 'This place is for you now, dear. You're safe here,' and I cautioned Mr. Vaughn to lock the door on his way out. The child remained calm until she saw the door close, then she fought to get down. She ran to one of the dormer windows. I thought she was checking the distance to the ground, but she gave a strange, hoarse cry and bolted away as if something had terrified her. She ran to a big, overstuffed chair and squeezed in behind it. I went to the window to see what had frightened her so, but all that was visible was the torrent of rain and the empty drive. I wondered what she had seen. Was an accomplice waiting out there somewhere? If so, he must have abused her terribly to inspire such fear in her. If I could help it, he would not get the chance to do so again.

"All through that afternoon she stayed in her little hideout, ignoring me. Finally, it occurred to me to try singing. She peered out from behind the chair as if she were paying some attention to me. It seemed that she was not deaf, after all. When the food arrived, she wouldn't come near the tray until I had backed away from it, and then she ate as if it were her last meal—and with such appalling manners! But what could you expect from the poor little mite?

"That evening Betsy and I gave her a bath. The girl fought like a tiger at first, but then the warm water seemed to relax her. It wasn't until we had washed her hair that we discovered that startling color—as gold as a gold sovereign. That's when Betsy started calling her Goldilocks, and so we have called her ever since, for the child has not spoken as much as her name from that day to this.

"So that's the story of little Goldilocks," Mrs. Vaughn finished. "It's been four months now, but she still behaves like a wild thing. It wasn't long before I realized that she was picking the locks and roaming about the house taking valuables. You see, she could have opened any door and run away long since, but she seems to have decided she is less afraid of us than of whatever she saw outside. To this day she won't go near a window." Mrs. Vaughn sat back and put down her knitting, apparently tired by the long narrative.

I thought of Gabriel lurking around the drive, his unhealthy interest in the comings and goings in the house, and his ugly threats. Could he be the one the child feared? If so, I shared her fear of him. I wondered, not for the last time, whether I should tell all to Mr. Vaughn and hope that he could find a way to protect me from the brute. Turning my thoughts back to the girl in her lofty rooms, I asked, "Who looks after the child now? You can't be with her all the time."

"I've been spending several hours a day with her, and she's become accustomed to my presence. Young James suggested his mother, dear old Mrs. Van Winkle, for her nanny. What a treasure she is! She raised ten children all on her own after her husband disappeared, and she has a way with little ones. She's actually gotten the girl to sit on her lap and be rocked. Of course she's getting on in years and does sleep rather too soundly herself."

Now I knew where Mrs. Vaughn disappeared to in the daytime.

"And what of the advertisement?" I asked.

"Mr. Vaughn insisted on putting the ad in the papers. I was most unhappy waiting to see if some dreadful criminal type would try to claim her, but the weeks went by and no one answered. I feel certain now that she was raised by some band of thieves, and taught her pilfering ways. Poor innocent! All she knows is picking locks and stealing valuables. I tried to keep her nighttime activities from Mr. Vaughn. I was afraid he wouldn't be so understanding about her wanderings and her bad habits. Most things I was able to retrieve before he noticed them missing, but he is too acute to be kept in the dark for long. Just last night his pipe went missing, and he announced to me that he was perfectly cognizant of the thievery and who was behind it, and that if I would be so good as to restore his pipe to its rightful place, I needn't trouble myself to hide the fact anymore. It is unfortunate that I still haven't found the pipe. I'm afraid she has some hiding places that I have not yet discovered. I believe your locket must be in one of them, but it's possible that I will someday find it."

I thought of Mama's locket: a shiny trinket to the child, a

treasure beyond price to me. Would I ever see it again? Tears threatened to appear as I contemplated that I might never get it back.

"And you do have some hope," I asked, "that she'll be able to change her ways?"

"Yes, I do have hope. She's such a little thing, I think she can hardly help but respond to love and kindness, and when she's been 'civilized,' as Mr. Vaughn says, perhaps we can let her join in the family activities. I made the little bear suit so she would feel more at home—just like one of us—but even though I spend a part of every day with her, I do so long for the time when she can be with the family. For now, though, we've only told Mr. Bentley and a few very trustworthy servants: James knows, and we had to tell Cook and Betsy. And Nurse, of course."

I thought of my first night in the manor, of Teddy and me hearing shuffling footsteps and running all the way to the nursery, then being reprimanded by Mr. Vaughn. I reasoned that Mr. Vaughn must have been in the dark about the child's wanderings then.

"If you don't mind me asking, madam, do you think that someday she will live with you openly?" I asked.

"Oh, I do hope so, when she's ready. Mr. Vaughn says we shall see what to do when the time comes. No doubt there will be some trouble about it, but in the end I'm sure he'll not allow himself to be influenced by hateful human prejudices. After all, we're only taking care of an abandoned and misused child, and that can't be wrong. What do we have to fear?"

19

A Confession

I contemplated Mrs. Vaughn's question for a while in silence. It seemed to me they had a great deal to fear. Maybe everyone would be against them. Maybe the little wild thing they had taken into their home and hearts could never be "civilized," or return the affection lavished on her; could never stop her nighttime wandering and pilfering. I thought of all this, and then I thought of how colossally generous and warmhearted the Vaughns had been to her, and my opinion of them underwent a change. I had always respected my employers, but I hadn't really seen this side of them; Mrs. Vaughn had been a figure of mystery, and Mr. Vaughn had his gruff exterior. I perceived them now in a different light. Now I could see beyond Mrs. Vaughn's lovely surface. At last I could see Mr. Vaughn as the kind of bear who would once have been a kindred spirit to my own dear papa.

Looking into Mrs. Vaughn's eyes, I said, "I think that you are doing a very fine thing, madam. May I help? May I visit her?"

"I was hoping that you would," she replied. "In fact, I don't know whether she is teachable. I'm sure it would be quite a challenge, but if you could perhaps work with her in your spare hours? I do think she's intelligent."

Though I felt some apprehension, I set it aside, and said, "Of course I'll do whatever I can, madam. How old do you think she is?"

"I think perhaps Teddy's age, or a bit younger. Six or seven. You may see her now, if you like. She's just rising about this time. She sleeps quite late, you know, after all her nighttime exertions."

I immediately agreed, and we set forth to the east wing. On an impulse, I asked if we might make a detour to the library and take some books along. I quickly picked out several I thought likely to capture the imagination of a little girl. As we walked on to Goldilocks's chamber, Mrs. Vaughn warned me not to expect too much. We arrived just as Betsy was coming out with the breakfast tray. It looked like a wild animal had been after it. "Did she do that?" I asked.

"I'm afraid so," Mrs. Vaughn replied. "Such a blessing that dear Mrs. Van Winkle is so patient with her."

We entered an attractive sitting room with a pale green sofa and striped chairs, and a large dormer window with a window seat. A comfortably corpulent, elderly woman sat in a rocker doing needlework, fairly exuding a sanguine calm. Mrs. Vaughn introduced her as Mrs. Van Winkle. The child was sitting on the floor in the center of a plush carpet, in her bear suit, surrounded by toys. I thought they must be Teddy's castoffs—a stuffed bear, a boat, a pile of blocks—but she seemed not to know what to do with them. When she saw me enter the room, she jumped up, ran to the furthermost corner, and crouched behind a chair, peeking out just enough to keep an eye on me. I could see that this was her habitual refuge by the afghan and pillows and assorted objects she had apparently stashed there.

Undaunted by the girl's retreat, Mrs. Vaughn introduced us, calling her "our little friend Goldilocks," and coaxed the youngster to come out, assuring her that I liked children very much, and had come especially to see her. The child stared intently at me, and I thought I saw a flicker of recognition on her face, though she didn't stir from her lair.

"It's quite all right if you don't want to come out yet," I said. "I've brought some books to read. You can listen from where you are." I placed the books on a low table, and smiled at her.

Mrs. Vaughn excused herself, saying, "I'll just leave you to get acquainted, then."

I settled into a comfortable chair across from Goldilocks, and, exaggerating my gestures, I opened one of the books. The girl didn't move, but she watched me closely. I picked up a lovingly worn volume, and said, "This book tells the story of a little girl. The smallest little girl you can imagine—a girl no bigger than your thumb! Would you like to hear it?" I thought I detected a spark of curiosity. I began to read the story of Thumbelina, of her birth from a flower, and the long saga of her adventures that followed: how she was kidnapped by a toad to be a wife for her toad son, the way the beetles rejected her as too ugly, and her long employment as a housekeeper for a mouse— and there I stopped, hopefully leaving little Goldilocks wanting to hear more.

"That's all I have time for today," I said, "but if you like, I'll come and read the rest of the story tomorrow." I watched her carefully as I said this, and if ever a child looked bursting to say something, this was the child. I smiled to myself, and, picking up the books, I lightheartedly said goodbye.

As I walked back from the east wing, I thought of the plight of this silent child. I could not deny my growing conviction that there was some connection between the little girl we called Goldilocks and the volatile brute who had confronted me on the drive. What else could she have seen out the window that would have frightened her so? And Gabriel's skulking about, hunting for information, might have been an attempt to locate the girl. Why the urgency? I wondered. Surely not out of any concern for her welfare. It occurred to me that she probably knew too much that would incriminate him and his dreadful mother, but what difference would that make if she couldn't speak? All the rest of that day and on into the night, I wrestled with my quandary over Gabriel, and his threat to "settle a score" if I told anyone about him. Now that I knew some of Goldilocks's story, his lurking on the grounds seemed far more sinister. What if his villainous machinations did involve this innocent child? It no longer seemed sufficient or right to simply try to avoid the problem. As my last thought before sleep, I admitted to myself that it was time to confess the secret I had been keeping, and tell Mr. Vaughn all about my experience with Gabriel.

❧

Sunday, after church, I was standing at the door to the parlor, reluctant to interrupt the family's time together, when Mr. Vaughn noticed me there and asked whether I needed something. My request to speak with him alone was answered forthwith, and he ushered me down the hall and into the den.

"Has this to do with the little girl?" he asked. "I understand that you've met her. You can appreciate, I hope, why you weren't informed of her presence sooner."

"Yes, sir. As to whether it has to do with her, I don't know, but I'm afraid it might."

"Suppose you explain from the beginning, then," he said. So I started from the first time I had encountered Gabriel in town, which Mr. Vaughn already knew of, to the time he had accosted me on the front drive, and his attempt to bribe me to inform him of activities in the house. When I told of his threat to come after me if I gave him away, Mr. Vaughn exploded with majestic wrath.

"By Heaven, this is not to be borne! This *cur*, this *knave*, dares to trespass, dares to attempt to spy on my household, dares to threaten a member of my household on my own property! Of all the infernal—" Here he made a visible effort to calm himself, though his paws were balled into fists.

"Then he is not in your employ?"

"He is most certainly not in my employ."

"I suspected that he was lying about that, but I believe he meant his threat, sir. I hope that you can help me somehow."

His voice tightly controlled, he said, "There will be no opportunity for him to harass you further, Miss Brown. I will instigate a manhunt—today! Furthermore, I am putting one of the gardener's bears, Harry, at your disposal. He has not much to say for himself, but he's intensely loyal, and a crack shot. Whenever you are outdoors for any reason, he will escort you. He must accompany you on your daily walks with Teddy as well, of course."

Though this seemed almost too much protection, relief flooded through me like a warm tide. For the first time I actually felt grateful for Mr. Vaughn's indomitable will. "Thank you, sir. I'm sure I shall feel quite safe."

"I take no chances where my son's safety is concerned, Miss Brown, and your father would not forgive me if I took chances with yours. *Ne accipias periculis non necessarium.* 'Take no unnecessary chances!' I thank you for having the courage to bring the matter to my attention."

"If I might inquire, sir, Mrs. Vaughn has asked me to try to teach Goldilocks in my off-hours. Does this meet with your approval?"

"Yes, you may assume so, though I'm afraid you'll find all your efforts to be in vain. As long as it doesn't interfere with your regular duties, you may try your hand with her. You'll be compensated accordingly, of course, for your extra efforts. Just keep in mind, as I have already apprised you, Miss Brown, that I will be monitoring your progress in the schoolroom closely."

Our interview ended with Mr. Vaughn's warning to stay indoors for the remainder of the day while he and the male staff searched the grounds. I had planned to go to the vicarage, but being compelled to change my arrangements, I went instead to the library, then on to the east wing for my second session with Goldilocks. There I found things much as before, with Mrs. Van Winkle rocking and humming, and Goldilocks sitting cross-legged on the floor, idling in the midst of Teddy's cast-off toys. Upon my appearance, she jumped like a startled fawn, and ran to hide again behind her fortress chair.

"Never you mind about that," Mrs. Van Winkle reassured me. "She'll warm up to ye in a while. Jest move slow and quiet-like. She'll come to ye after she's looked ye over good. Poor young 'un has been about scared out of her own skin by someone, if I'm any judge. More skittish than a cat."

Signaling my thanks with a smile, I walked slowly to the same striped chair I had occupied last time, and said "Hello" to Goldilocks. She retreated further behind her fortress. "Hmm," I said. "I wonder what to read today. What was I reading yesterday? It had something to do with a toad, and a beetle, and a mouse—and what else?" I watched her as an expression of avid interest animated her face. "Oh yes! A little girl. A *very* little girl called Thumbelina. I wonder what happened to her. Shall we find out?" I asked, looking directly at the child. She quickly looked away. "Let me see," I went on. I returned to the place where I had left off, and resumed reading the story. Goldilocks kept her eyes on the book as I read of tiny Thumbelina taking pity on a sick bird, and nursing him all through the winter; of the mouse trying to make her marry a mole; and of how she flew off on her bird friend to a faraway land, and found her handsome fairy prince.

"And that's the end of the story," I said. "Of course, I have many more books full of stories. I have one here called *Beauty and the Beast*. It's Teddy's favorite. You know who Teddy is, don't you? He is the little bear cub who lives downstairs." I paused, curious to observe any change in her expression, and was gratified to see that her attention was all on me.

"Shall I read this one?"

She nodded ever so slightly, which seemed promising.

"All right, then," I said with some delight. "This book has the most beautiful pictures imaginable. You might want to come closer to see them."

I opened *Beauty and the Beast* on my lap, and began to read, holding each illustration up to tantalize her. It was a long story, and I had read about halfway through when I noticed the girl slowly coming out from behind her chair and sidling along the wall to a spot behind my chair, so that she could view the pictures over my shoulder. When I came to a lush illustration of Beauty exploring in the Beast's palace, I held it up in front of her and waited for a reaction. At first she cringed backward against the wall, but staring hard at the picture, she leaned in closer and reached out to touch it, running her hand all over its surface like a blind person, as if she expected to find it three-dimensional. After a moment she withdrew her hand and I went on with the story, showing her each illustration in the same way, but she didn't try to touch them again, apparently having learned that they were only flat.

I smiled inwardly. It seemed that books could work their magic on this tormented child. Throughout the whole long story, she hovered behind me, listening and watching until I reached the last page and slowly closed the book, then she slid away as silently as she had come.

20

Teddy Misbehaves

❧

That evening, Mr. Vaughn sent word to me through James that they had found no one on the property that afternoon. James related that more help would be coming from town, and that the grounds would be patrolled regularly in the days to come. I sent my thanks back to Mr. Vaughn, and settled down to write a response to Papa's letter of a few days ago. So much had happened, and I was eager to share it with him, and so I wrote a long letter before retiring, telling him the story of the child, and how I was trying to befriend her.

I was nudged awake by Betsy the next morning, drawing me out of a deep slumber. Reluctantly, I climbed out from under the warm bedclothes into the chilly room.

"Good morning to you, miss. Cook's serving breakfast downstairs. I thought I ought to wake you, you was sleeping so late." I thanked Betsy and hurried through my waking routine, then went to the nursery and roused Teddy while Nurse snored away, unconscious of us both. Seeing to it that he washed his face and paws, I set out Teddy's clothes and encouraged him to dress himself as best he could. Though it would have been much faster for me to finish dressing him myself, I believed it would be better for him to do it on his own, and so we arrived a bit late in the kitchen for breakfast.

There, things went badly from the first. Cook served up big helpings of porridge, a sure sign, as I had learned, that she was out of temper. Whatever her motive, Teddy steadfastly refused to eat the stuff. He further offended Cook by sculpting half of it into little mountains and valleys and slopping the other half liberally on the tablecloth. Considering how uncommonly good Teddy usually was, I sometimes let some minor misbehavior pass, but this drew a scolding from me. Finally, Cook removed the mess with a huff and substituted a glass of milk and a piece of toast, with the warning that it would have to last him until lunchtime. Since no better fare was going to be served, Teddy nibbled at this with maddening slowness, taking little bites out of the toast to make designs in it, and gargling with his milk. Seeing that he was more recalcitrant than hungry, I declared that the meal was over and we adjourned to the schoolroom, but not, as it turned out, soon enough. Mr. Vaughn stood in the doorway, holding his watch and waiting for us.

"You're late," he announced, tapping his claw against the watch face. "This is not an auspicious beginning to your first day without Nurse's supervision. Have you so quickly forgotten the primary requirement of professionalism? One must begin, Miss Brown, by being on time. *Tempus fugit,* Miss Brown. *Tempus fugit.*"

I had to remind myself at this point that Mr. Vaughn had a softer side. Fearing that my explanations would sound defensive and inadequate, I simply replied, "I'm sorry, sir. It won't happen again."

"Very well, Miss Brown. See that it doesn't," he countered. "I'm afraid that you have already put me behind schedule, but now that I am here, I would like a full report on Theodore's progress in each of his courses of study."

"That would be an easy matter, sir. His progress is excellent in all subjects."

"Good. Good. And the Latin? What progress in that?"

"I'm afraid I haven't mastered the Latin sufficiently to begin teaching it to Teddy as yet, sir. It will require a little more time."

"More time. Hmm. More time. May I suggest, Miss Brown, that though your assistance at the vicarage has been invaluable these past weeks, your presence there is no longer necessary? I think you'll agree that with your new duties, and your Latin studies, your days will be too full to allow you to continue volunteering your time there?"

I hadn't expected this, though I should have guessed Mr. Vaughn would be aware of my activities. More than that, I knew that though he had framed it as a question, it was really a command, and that I had better obey it. I had a fleeting thought, all unbidden, of Mr. Bentley waiting impatiently to hear the next chapter of *Robinson Crusoe;* of what he would say about my desertion, and of his tone of voice, and of how his face would look when he said it. Then, with a start, I reminded myself of my resolve to put him out of my mind. My employer's directive made a perfect rationale for ending my association with Mr. Bentley altogether. Surprised and mortified by the tremor in my voice, I gave the only response I could: "Yes, sir. I'll see to it."

"Very good. In a week's time I shall measure your progress

in the Latin, and again at regular intervals. I'm sure that for a young bear of your talents, serious application to the subject will yield results. *Labor omnia vincit,* Miss Brown. 'Labor conquers all things.'" Patting Teddy on the head, he said, "Carry on, carry on," and departed.

I stood unmoving for a time after Mr. Vaughn's exit. I felt as if he had left some residual specter of himself in the room observing my every word and action. I reflected then that Mr. Vaughn's manner of supervision could be every bit as much of a trial to endure as Nurse's, though in a very different way. At least his criticisms would be genuinely meant to improve the quality of Teddy's education, rather than interfere with it, but I wondered faintheartedly if I could possibly live up to his lofty expectations. I reminded myself that I *had* been late today, though not by much. Still, if I wanted Mr. Vaughn's respect, I must do better.

Teddy, however, had ideas of his own. His dawdling over breakfast had apparently been only the beginning of a determined campaign of minor naughtiness. He fidgeted at his desk, tapped the floor continuously with his feet, and scraped his claws across his slate. At my reprimands, he would merely change tactics. When I asked him to count to one hundred, he had the impudence to begin with one hundred and count backward. As this was no minor accomplishment in itself, I allowed him to keep on all the way to zero.

"That was very good," I said. "Why didn't you count forward to one hundred?"

"I dunno how," he said, staring at his shoes, which he had begun tapping on the floor again.

"Perhaps you will remember in a little while," I said, putting off a confrontation.

From that point on he responded to all my questions with a vapid "I dunno."

After about an hour of this maddening behavior, I snapped, "Teddy! What is the matter with you today? I have never seen you misbehave so! What am I to do with you?"

Instantly, his expression changed from one of dull inattention to one of real alarm. His feet fell still; he sat rigidly erect with his paws clasped tightly on the desk in front of him. His frightened brown eyes searched my face, as if to read his own fate there. "Are you going to tell Uncle Ruprecht to come and get me?" he asked, his voice barely audible.

All at once the morning's misbehavior made a kind of sense. Apparently, Teddy had been testing me for a reason: to see if I would use the same draconian style of discipline as Nurse. What would the rules be now that Nurse was absent, and what would happen if he broke them?

"Teddy," I said, reaching out to pat his head affectionately, "even if Uncle Ruprecht were real—and he's not; he's just a picture—but even if he were real, I would never, ever, no matter what you did, tell him to come and get you, because that is no way to treat little bear cubs, even naughty ones."

"Oh," he said, thinking about it. "Then would you pinch me? Hard?"

"No, Teddy, I wouldn't pinch you either. I suppose if you were very bad, you would have to sit in the corner and think about things—about what you had done wrong, and how you might improve."

"Do I have to sit in the corner now?"

"I don't know. I think perhaps you are done being naughty. What do you think?"

Relief spread over his face like the sun coming out from be-hind a cloud. "I guess I'm done now," he said, and picked up his slate and chalk as if to signal his readiness to work. I patted his head again and resumed the lesson, keeping a careful watch over his behavior, but the naughtiness had faded away, except for the occasional foot tapping, and I reflected that I might see a more natural side of Teddy once he truly realized that I would not try to bully him into perfect submission. Little did I think then how dangerous such a course could be.

Our afternoon walk took on a different flavor that day, as Nurse was no longer there casting her pall over the proceedings, but we were joined instead by Harry, as Mr. Vaughn had de-creed, for our safety. Harry was a seemingly gentle giant, though no doubt capable of doing great damage when roused. Shaggy-browed and powerfully built, he was an uncomplicated bear, stolid and faithful. He wore drab trousers and a coarse tunic over his shirt, belted at the waist, all very clean, the wholesome effect of which was offset somewhat by the incessant dripping of his snout, and the trite expedient of wiping it on his sleeve. This subtracted nothing from his imposing presence, however, and I felt we were quite safe in his care.

Though Teddy's immediate interest was in Harry's musket, Harry put him off with a solemn explanation that it was for Teddy's father to say when he was old enough to learn about guns, and until that day he had better content himself with watching. This Teddy did assiduously, picking up a heavy stick and holding it just as Harry held his gun, even down to imitat-ing his gestures and gait. When our little excursion was done, and we returned to the manor, I had no doubt but what he had learned more of Harry's mannerisms than he had of the day's botany lessons, but I hoped that this fascination would diminish as Harry's presence became commonplace to us.

At the appointed hour, having turned Teddy over to his mother, and taken tea alone in my room, I climbed to the little bower in the east wing where Goldilocks was sequestered, trying to prepare myself mentally for the task of building a connection with the child. Though I surmised that she had had a hard life, I dared to hope that she was not too different from young cubs I had known, and I thought I would trust my own intuition as events unfolded. I greeted her with a sunny demeanor, paying no attention when she scrambled to her hiding place behind the furthest chair. With a companionable "Hello" to Mrs. Van Winkle, I took my place in the same large chair where I had sat before.

"My, my," I said. "Here I am with new books, and no little girl to read them to. Perhaps I should come back another day."

A little face appeared, peeking from behind the chair, as if to give proof of her presence, and then retreated.

"Well! So there *is* a little girl here, after all! Then I shall be happy to read to her, if she would only help me choose a book. Let's see. We have a yellow one, which is about fairies, and a green one, which is about Jack and the beanstalk, and we have a blue one, which I chose especially for her." I waited for several minutes to see whether this would have any effect.

Just as I thought I would have to try some other strategy, Goldilocks emerged from behind her chair as cautiously as a wild forest animal, keeping her eyes locked on mine, ready to leap away at the smallest alarm, and crept over to the table where the books lay. Like a flash, she grabbed the one on top and absconded with it back to her little den.

21

A Look, and a Question

❧

I almost laughed aloud, but immediately stifled it, not wanting to encourage an act of thievery. Instead, I thought to bargain with the child, interested to see whether she heard and understood me, and whether she could reason.

"Now you have got the book, Goldilocks, and that book has another wonderful story in it, but without reading, books are silent. Would you like me to read that book to you and tell you its story?"

She looked at me with suspicion, and gripped the blue book tightly to her chest.

"If you bring the book to me, I will read it to you. You can sit right here beside me if you like, and turn the pages." I moved to one side of the spacious chair and patted the empty spot beside me in the universal signal for "Come sit here," then I settled down to wait. Soon Mrs. Van Winkle struck up a conversation with me, telling me all about how she had raised her large family, and so I ignored the child for some time, letting her think this over. I did notice out of the corner of my eye that she had opened the book, and was—rather roughly—turning the pages as if looking for something. Mrs. Van Winkle had just delivered a homily on the special problems of raising twins when Goldilocks appeared at my side, thumped the book down in my lap, and swiftly tucked herself behind my chair to watch.

"Oh, what a lovely book!" I said. "Now, where has this come from?" I made a great show of looking all around the room, but not at her. I thought I heard a suppressed giggle behind me. "Well, I suppose since someone has put it in my lap, I should read it," and so I began. It was "The Seven Swans": the story of seven brothers who were turned into swans by a spell that could only be broken if their loving sister wove them seven shirts out of stinging nettles. I had chosen it because the sister in the story had to remain mute for the many years that it took her to weave all the shirts. I thought it might capture the child's interest, or evoke some sign of empathetic feeling that would tell me whether she understood what I was reading. As I read of the maiden's plight, Goldilocks moved slowly, almost imperceptibly, out from behind my chair until she was standing next to me, her tear-filled eyes locked on the book as if it were telling her own story. Again, I patted the space beside me, then continued casually reading. This went on for some time as I told of the king falling in love with the mute maiden and carrying her back to his kingdom to make her his queen—and suddenly there was Goldilocks, climbing into the chair and settling down next to me. Without pausing in my narration, I slid the book over so that it was spread across our two laps.

Reaching the end of the page, I said, "Now I'll turn the page," demonstrating the act with exaggerated care. At the next page I said, "Now *you* turn the page," and waited to see what would happen. To my great satisfaction, she copied my motion and turned the page with careful precision. I was moved to pat her on the head as a sign of approval, but this was a mistake. With a little cry, she shoved my paw away and leaped down from the chair, retreating to her hiding place on the other side of the room. My heart sinking, I made a brief but sincere apology, looking her in the eye, and then went on with the story. Slowly, she crept back to her viewing spot behind my chair. I read on to the close of the story, which seemed to keep the child spellbound. Then I pronounced, "The end," and gently closed the book. In an instant Goldilocks maneuvered from behind the chair, grabbing for the book as if she would carry it off again, but I was faster. While I was greatly pleased that she had formed such an attachment to the book, and though I wanted her to have it, it seemed a poor choice to simply allow her to snatch it.

"Nice people have a custom when they want something. They say 'please.' Suppose we make a way for you to say 'please.'" Thinking quickly, I wedged the book between my leg and the side of the chair for safekeeping, and showed her my paws put together palm to palm, as if in supplication. "Can you do this?" I asked. By this time she had grown surly. Her lower lip stuck out in a pout, and she crossed her arms over her chest in a clear gesture of refusal. "If you say 'please' like this, I will let you keep the book until tomorrow, and then I will read it again." Her eyes glittered with mischief, and she made another grab for the book. I was faster this time as well. She stamped her foot and then threw herself on the floor, kicking and beating her little fists, and making an incoherent noise. I ignored this and, setting the book in plain view on my lap, I resumed my earlier conversation with Mrs. Van Winkle, who, after ten children of her own, was an old hand at ignoring tantrums.

In the course of our conversation, I asked her whether any of her children had a special talent. A quarter of an hour later, I knew the full names and special talents of all ten of her offspring, as well as their first words and what childhood diseases each of them had had. Trying to bring the discussion around to Goldilocks, I asked Mrs. Van Winkle if she would like me to leave some books for her to read to the little girl.

"Oh, Lor' no!" was her response. "I ain't never larnt to read, miss! Me dear ol' pa didn't believe in eddicatin' girls. Me and me sisters was all he had, an' he didn't eddicate none of us."

I asked if she had ever tried to teach Goldilocks anything.

"Oh, ye'll get nowheres with her," the old lady assured me with a nod to the child, who was now lying exhausted and quiescent on the floor. "You can't hexpect to suddenly civilize a wild liddle savage like that. No good raisin' yer hopes. Don't go breakin' yer heart over her like the missus."

At that moment I was aware of some motion. There came a little tug on my sleeve. I turned to find Goldilocks with her two palms together, signing "please," with a guarded expression that told me she half expected some trick from me.

"Yes, dear," I said to her. "You may have the book until tomorrow. Take great care of it, won't you?" I watched as her hands closed around it and her cherub's face flushed with surprise and delight, and for a moment I saw what she could be, perhaps, with time and effort and affection: a happy, well-mannered child.

To Mrs. Van Winkle's warning, I replied, "Break my heart over her? Yes, perhaps I will."

∼

After several days of working with Goldilocks, I felt I could report to the Vaughns that the child could learn. So far I was satisfied that she understood what was being read to her, that she was capable of empathy, that she was able to pay attention for long periods of time, that she could understand a bargain and its consequences, and that she could follow simple directions—at least when she chose to. It seemed a promising start.

Upon my next meeting with Mrs. Vaughn, I asked if some physician might be consulted to evaluate whether the child was physically capable of speech. This being immediately approved, I screwed up my nerve and consulted her about the child's costume.

"If I may say so, madam, I'm afraid she's not comfortable in her bear suit. It seems heavy, and too hot for her."

"Oh dear. I only thought to make her feel like she was my own cub."

"That was very kind of you, madam. Very kind. But I wonder if she might be more at ease if she were allowed to simply be a child. Couldn't we get her some little things in town?"

"Oh. Oh dear, I suppose you're right. We should accept her as she is. I never thought of it that way before." There was a quiet pause as she gazed unfocused into the distance and put her handkerchief to her snout. Finally, as if she had come to some decision, she said, "I believe I have the very thing. Come with me."

I followed her through various passageways and up several flights of stairs to the attic. Since the house was still quite new, there was very little stored away there: a few boxes and trunks, and a child's velocipede sitting in an enormous empty space under the rafters. Mrs. Vaughn began moving boxes, and uncovered a beautifully carved chest with a cleverly worked brass hasp. She opened this as if it contained precious jewels. I could only see something flat wrapped in tissue paper, but she unfolded it to reveal a little dress, just about Goldilocks's size: a creation in white lawn and crocheted lace, with a wide pink ribbon about the waist. "It was my little Jane's," she said. "That was Teddy's sister, though he barely knew her. She was with us such a short time. She lies in the old churchyard now, with two of her brothers, William and Thomas. I thought I could never part with her things, but they're just moldering away up here. I would much rather Goldilocks wear them. They'd only need to be taken in a little on the sides, don't you think?" She held up the frock for me to see.

I was so touched by her generous heart that I could barely find words. "Dear madam," I said, "you are so kind and good, but I think that these are much too precious to you to be dirtied and torn by an active child. She has no manners at all as yet. I'm afraid this dainty outfit would be ruined in just one meal."

"Yes, yes, I see your point. Well, there are some things here more suitable for play. Suppose we start with those." She gently sorted through the little garments and made a small stack of them in my arms: rompers and cotton frocks, assorted undergarments, and a dimity sailor suit. Then she carefully rewrapped the remaining clothes, closed the chest with a sigh, and led the way back downstairs.

Before the day was out, Dr. Robinson, the local physician, had been consulted, and on his recommendation a letter had been posted to the eminent Dr. Bernhard Ehrlichmann, requesting his presence at the Cottage in the Woods for an examination of the child, since it was thought that Goldilocks was too mercurial and fearful as yet to travel. Also an order was sent to town for a small pair of button-up shoes, and a certain toy I had suggested, suitable for a little human girl.

That was the day I discovered that Mr. Bentley had returned unexpectedly from his convalescence at the vicarage, and had resumed his duties, as well as his habitual professional deportment. I had succeeded, the day before, in sending him a note explaining the impossibility of any more visits at the vicarage, and had begged his pardon, but when I consulted with him over sending out the orders, he gave no indication that he had received my note, and I could not bring myself to ask. In my surprise and confusion, I barely knew how to speak to him at all, so I imitated his impersonal formality while we took care of the business at hand. Not until he followed me into the hall and asked to have a word with me did I recognize the more relaxed and charming Mr. Bentley I had come to know while he was recuperating.

"Miss Brown!" he announced with solemnity. "I must take you to task."

"For what, pray, Mr. Bentley?"

"For your heartlessness in abandoning me to my lonely sickbed. I was forced to cut short my recovery for want of company. Surely you don't intend to leave Robinson Crusoe alone with all those cannibals, do you? A very unwholesome state of affairs, to my way of thinking."

I had to suppress a little smile, trying not to be swayed by his charm. "I do apologize for leaving off my visits so abruptly. I sent a note. Didn't you receive it?"

"A note!" he remonstrated. "A fine substitute that makes for the spoken word!"

"I must say you seem to be in adequte good health and spirits to read the rest of *Robinson Crusoe* on your own. I'm afraid I've no time for reading. I have a new pupil in the afternoons, and in the evenings I must devote myself to learning Latin. I'm to begin teaching Teddy soon, or suffer Mr. Vaughn's displeasure." I made this pronouncement with the satisfied feeling that with these explanations I had barricaded myself quite effectively from any further association with this bear, but this was not to be.

"Learning Latin?" he repeated. "As it happens, I am a great proficient at Latin. Please allow me to offer my services as your tutor. You won't find a better one in all the county."

"I could not possibly pay you what your services are worth, Mr. Bentley. Please don't trouble yourself about it. I'm managing on my own."

"Miss Brown," he replied, suddenly serious, "I wouldn't think of taking tuppence from you. I am so greatly in your debt for your many hours of nursing and attention; surely you couldn't be so cruel as to deprive me of a way to repay you. What possible reason could you have to spurn my offer?"

Nervously, I cast about for some excuse sufficiently urgent to refuse him. The truth was I did need the help, and had no better reason to turn him down than that his nearness was making my insides flutter. How could I tell him the danger he posed to my peace of mind?

"It's a very kind offer, Mr. Bentley, but you owe no debt to me. I only did what any decent bear would do."

"Then you will kindly allow *me* to do what any decent bear

would do, and repay you by sharing my rather remarkable expertise in Latin. Think of Teddy. I will be helping both of you."

Exasperated, I couldn't suppress a little laugh at how he had gotten around me. Perhaps I didn't try hard enough to find more excuses for turning down his offer, but my mind did not seem to be functioning properly. "Indeed, if you are in earnest, Mr. Bentley, I can think of no reason not to accept you. Thank you," I said, and abruptly fell silent, kicking myself.

"Good, then shall we begin this evening? Perhaps we could make ourselves comfortable in the kitchen, at that small table by the fireplace? There is always someone bustling about in the kitchen. That would be quite proper, would it not?"

"Yes, quite," I said, and so it was arranged. Every evening after the dinner hour, Mr. Bentley and I met at the table in the kitchen and worked by candlelight, our heads bent together over the books, until the hall clock struck eight. At first I could barely overcome my self-consciousness at his close proximity and attention, but as time went on, his nearness became quite comfortable; more than that—though I could not admit it to myself—I looked forward to it. For days I told myself that my regard for him was simple friendship and respect as a fellow teacher, and indeed, under his guidance, Latin became a living language, and its mysteries of grammar and syntax opened up to me. I began to appreciate it as the mother of many languages, and it became our game to connect common English and French words to their Latin roots. It started when he pointed out that the words *veracity* and *verify,* and the French word *vérité,* come from the Latin word *veritas,* meaning "truth." He said this looking directly at me, which disconcerted me.

"Oh?" I choked. "Do they?" I stared down at my lap to avoid his gaze. "Are there others?"

"Oh yes. Many others. *Liber,* the Latin for 'book,' can be traced to the Italian word for book, *libro,* the Portuguese *livro,* and the French *livre.* We find it in the English word *library* and, interestingly, in the word *liberty.* In Latin the word for 'book' is the same as the word for 'freedom.' And of course we have the words *amity* and *amorous,* and the French *amour,* all coming from the Latin word *amor,* meaning 'love.'" He said this as casually as he would say any other word, but he looked directly into my eyes, until I felt the heat rising in my face.

I wondered what he meant by staring at me so; or was it only my own excruciating sensitivity warping my perceptions? I had more sense than to believe that he was captivated by my beauty, but I thought his looks seemed to speak of longing, and I had to cover my confusion with a cough.

For the rest of that lesson, I smiled and nodded and managed to be attentive, but my concentration was faulty, and to compensate, I endeavored to study for another hour alone in my room after the tutorial was finished. Even then I found myself distracted and troubled by the memory of his eyes staring into mine. What did it mean? In retrospect I could not say that he had given any indication of a special tenderness for me. Certainly, there had been no declaration, only the light banter that we sometimes exchanged, no more than any two friends might engage in, and yet in my heart of hearts I knew there was something: a quiet thrill, a charged atmosphere between us, like the air before a lightning strike. For the first time in my life, I allowed myself to wonder whether I might be in love, without chastising myself for a fool, but only telling myself to wait and see.

22

Rebellion

～

Several weeks went by. Out of doors, Nature ran riot, splashing leaves with extravagant reds, oranges, and yellows, then driving them to the ground with blustering winds and rains in the ancient cycle. Now the naked branches stood exposed and forlorn, awaiting the onslaught of winter, and we in the Cottage drew closer to our fires and counted our blessings.

Up in the east wing, I was seeing good progress with Goldilocks. She no longer hid when I entered her room, but ran instead to the chair where I habitually sat to read to her, and imitated my gesture of patting the place beside her. Her appetite for stories of all kinds seemed endless. Her flashes of temper and of taking fright continued, but I expected very little of her as yet, thinking it important to first establish a bond with her. To aid in this effort, Mrs. Vaughn insisted that I be the one to present to Goldilocks the new toy we had sent for from town, a golden-haired doll, very like the child herself, and dressed in a miniature sailor suit and Lilliputian shoes. I watched Goldilocks's face light up as she opened the box, and beheld the little figure within. As a measure of the progress she had made, she looked up at me and signed "please."

"Yes, dear," I said. "You may have her to keep. She is just for you." The little girl's eyes spoke her wonder and gratitude. Her first instinct was to run with it behind her hiding chair, as if fearful that I might change my mind and take it away. There she alternately examined every inch of the doll and its clothing, and hugged it to her chest with both arms, smiling incandescently. How often that happy image comes to me now, in the quiet hours. Would that I could always have kept that shining smile on her innocent face, but I had no such magic.

My work with Teddy continued to be a source of satisfaction and even amusement, his sweet nature and quick perception rewarding my efforts many times over. The difficult task was to avoid laughing at his occasional mischief, for in truth I was delighted to see such evidence of spirit.

But then there was Nurse. For weeks I had seen no sign of her other than her sleeping form when I went into the nursery to wake Teddy. I let myself believe that my problems with her were in the past. It didn't seem to have penetrated her sensibility, however, that her presence was no longer needed in the schoolroom. By the end of a fortnight, she began wandering into the schooloom at odd times, planting herself immovably on her old chair and watching my every move with an aspect as malignant as the plague.

At first I cordially voiced my objection, reminding Nurse that Mr. Vaughn had decreed that it was not necessary for her to tire herself further by spending time in the schoolroom. When I suggested this, however, the furry face screwed up into an expression of such tragedy that Teddy immediately ran to her side and smothered her in a small bear hug.

"I ain't causing no trouble! I never done nothing!" she sobbed, gulping and sniffling to great effect. "I just wanted to be with my little Teddy. An' all I hear is I ain't wanted and I must go away, when there ain't no other place for me, an' no one else who loves me on this here earth!"

It struck me that, though the performance was clearly manufactured, the old badger might be telling the truth: in all likelihood, her sullen visage was not welcomed anywhere else, and I had no trouble believing that there really *was* no one else to love her but Teddy. Her impact on him was exactly as she had calculated: he looked up at me with tear-filled eyes and said, "Please can't she stay, Miss Brown?"

"The lessons must not be interrupted," I insisted, trying to hold my ground.

Teddy immediately agreed, and Nurse sniffled loudly while writhing around uncomfortably in what might have been a nod of assent. In the end, Teddy's love for the cantankerous old badger was stronger than my polite objections, and so it came about that Nurse was with us again. She typically arrived midmorning, in varying states of sobriety, and was sure to make her presence felt with a loud belch, or a noxious passing of wind, before settling down in her poisonous little corner. There she lurked, exuding malice, making messes with little wads of paper and dead flies. The remarkable exceptions were when I praised Teddy for performing particularly well at his tasks, or when he took some work of his to show to her. Then a transformation took place: her evil old face cracked into a smile, and she'd say, "That's my duck! What a clever one he is!" and the little bear's eyes shone.

It seemed that she was now content just to be in the school-room with Teddy, where she could sit quietly and kill me with her looks. And yet, for all her hostility, I thought I observed her in unguarded moments to betray a hint of interest in my lessons. On several occasions when I was verbally examining Teddy on some short words, I noticed that she started to call out the answer, then cut herself short, and camouflaged it with an exaggerated sneeze. Could it be that Nurse could not read? Pondering this, I realized that I had never seen books in the nursery. It occurred to me that Nurse was learning to read along with Teddy. This thought gave me pause. I wondered if my teaching her to read could possibly change her behavior toward me: whether opening the world of books to her might actually improve her character, or whether she would just use the ability for composing poison-pen letters and ransom notes.

One day, after the lessons were done, and I was having tea in my room, I received a note from Mr. Vaughn asking whether I might play the accompaniment for the men's choir that night. If so, I would be escorted by himself, Mr. Bentley, and Fairchild to the church at the appointed hour. My heart skipped a beat upon reading this epistle. I dearly wanted to be of some practical use in the cause for which they were fighting, and I was excited by the spark of danger present.

An hour before sunset, I met the others at the door and we departed silently. Mr. Bentley fell in next to me, and I smiled up at him, hoping he was walking beside me on purpose, but Mr. Vaughn soon consulted him about something, and Mr. Bentley moved to his side to speak with him. I confess, I listened in on their conversation. In truth, I longed to know more of what the men's choir was trying to do. Though I was full of questions, I was loath to make a pest of myself, so I thought it better to keep quiet and see what transpired.

When we arrived at the church, the others were waiting for us, having taken their places in the choir loft and passed around the hymnals for good show. I was asked to play the pianoforte while the gentlemen spoke among themselves, so that anyone approaching the church would hear the music. I started with the first hymn in the hymnal, "O for a Thousand Tongues to Sing," and began to play. Mr. Vaughn called the meeting to order, and gave a quick summary of their recent activities before opening up discussion on conditions in town, and suggestions for their future exploits. A short black bear stood up and reported that many of his longtime human customers, friends and neighbors, were forsaking his grocery store, taking their business to a human greengrocer clear across town. Several raccoons then complained that they had been denied credit at the general store, and that their favorite fresh fish restaurant, where they had been regulars for years, had last night seated them next to the kitchen, and that nobody had waited on them until all the other diners were finished. Finally, an elderly man, introducing himself as Mr. Weatherby, began to talk about the village newspaper, the *Town Crier,* and the way it was twisting and revising the news. I soon deduced that he was the editor of that paper. He objected to Mr. Babcock, the new owner of the paper, and grand high chief of the Anthropological Society, ordering him to run articles that maligned the town's Enchanted citizens, firing up old resentments, pitting neighbor against neighbor—articles that had little or nothing to do with the truth. Mr. Vaughn then introduced a case in point, the article calling that young bear I had seen in the Post Office a vandal, and praising the boys who beat him up. He asked me to stop playing briefly and tell the true story, which I managed to do, though I was so nervous to be the center of so much attention that my voice quavered.

"They've no shame at all!" I heard one bear say as I went back to playing the hymns.

"How can we stop it?" others began to ask.

"We can't, but maybe we can beat Babcock at his own game. Mr. Weatherby," inquired Mr. Vaughn, "what if I asked you to work for me? With you as our editor, we can set up our own printing press, have our own newspaper, tell people what's really going on. We can work out of my basement if we've nowhere else. I'll be the backer."

"I would be pleased and honored to become your editor, sir," said Mr. Weatherby. "If we can publish our own paper, we can shed some light on the ugly facts!"

There were cheers and cries of approbation. "And we'll deliver them!" cried one, and the others quickly joined in. "We'll all deliver them!"

It was an exhilarating moment, and I happened to be playing "Take Up Thy Cross" when the weasel watching at the door gave us the signal that someone was coming. My heart seemed to do a somersault, and I lost my place as I realized that this was where the intrigue really began. Reverend Snover gave me a reassuring smile, and I tried to focus on the page in front of me, knowing that these men were counting on me to play my part, and I must not let them down. "Page 160!" I called out, and everyone started humming along, frantically flipping pages, joining in with the words when they found the place. By the time the door opened and Chief Constable Murdley walked in, there was some semblance of a choir singing, with Reverend

Snover conducting, and me silently thanking Papa for all those years of piano lessons. Constable Murdley made himself comfortable in a back pew and settled down to listen, leaving us to wonder why. Did he still harbor suspicions about the men's choir, after all, or did he just like music? If it was the latter, he was doomed to disappointment. I played all four verses with the choir limping along in something like three-part harmony, and then Reverend Snover shouted out the next hymn number and we went through the whole process again with "He Leadeth Me, O Blessed Thought" and "Rise Up, O Men of God." Still, Constable Murdley sat and listened, and Reverend Snover stopped the proceedings a few times to correct some minor points, or to encourage the tenors or baritones to sing out, apparently for a touch of realism. I admired his panache, a little surprised to find such a talent for subterfuge in an elderly man of God. I myself was making enough nervous mistakes to cast doubt on the whole endeavor, but no one seemed to notice. I could feel the perspiration dampening my brow as the charade went on for another half hour. At last Constable Murdley stood up and ambled out the door appearing satisfied with himself. Breathing a sigh of relief, I played on until the watch weasel signaled that the constable was well out of range.

"Now, then," Reverend Snover commenced. "Where were we?"

"The new printing press," put in Mr. Vaughn. "I'll order the machinery delivered with all possible speed. It may be a month or more before we're set up and ready to print. In the meantime, if Mr. Weatherby would look into hiring or training whatever staff he will need, the rest of us can be on the lookout for likely stories, stories that the *Town Crier* would never print. We will give our citizens the plain truth."

"The *Plain Truth*! A great name for our paper!" called out an enthusiastic badger, amid cries of agreement.

Mr. Vaughn smiled and nodded. "So it is. So it is." And so it was decided.

The meeting was soon over, and it seemed to me that, despite Constable Murdley's interference, the men's choir had gone from a discouraged group of martyrs to a hopeful band of mutineers in the course of the evening.

"Until next time, friends," said the reverend. "Keep your eyes and ears open and your lips closed. And look out for one another. God go with you."

23

An Evening Out

～

Though I found myself in this period of my life greatly occupied by work and study, I did have one amusement left to me, and I looked forward to it all the week long. It had become the regular custom for me to dine on Saturday evenings at the vicar's, along with Mr. Bentley and whatever interesting company the Snovers had assembled. Reverend and Mrs. Snover seemed to know all the most colorful characters in the town and countryside, and none of them were nearly so dull and straitlaced as I had at first feared they might be. I had met a charming old lady there, Lavinia Hubbard, following the opening of the first gallery show of her paintings. Hers was a fascinating story of having been discovered at the age of seventy-eight by a great art connoisseur. Her cupboard, which had once been bare, was now full to overflowing. She often came to these soirees with the Little Crooked Man, a fearsome literary critic by the name of Snark, whose twisted perspective of the world he had adapted into a flourishing career. We were often joined by some of the local Enchanted creatures, and Mr. Bentley and I were always included in the mix as the young people. I had become accustomed to similar gatherings when Papa had occasionally invited his circle of scholarly friends in for an evening at our home. Though much of their conversations had gone over my head, I enjoyed grasping at their meanings, and I felt it a special treat to be included.

On the night of the first snowfall, Mr. Bentley and I, accompanied by Cook, and Harry with his musket, were heading to the vicarage. Cook was coming to help out the Snovers' maid, Maggie, for the evening, and Harry was our faithful guardian. We had come to the vicar's front door when a strange bear in a black greatcoat entered ahead of us. In the friendly confusion that results when everyone is arriving at once and taking off their outer accoutrements, the young stranger seemed to hold himself apart, but the vicar immediately pulled him into the chattering circle and introduced him as Reverend Abraham Wright, his new curate. "Fresh out of seminary! Here to assist an old man in his ministerial duties. He'll increase the spiritual quality of the parish by one with his presence, and by many with his salutary influence."

Reverend Wright looked awkward and embarrassed, but smiled stoically and nodded to the company at large. Despite his obvious youth, he wore an air of considerable gravity. It was as if the social occasion were not a thing to take lightly, but a challenge requiring unyielding strength of character to survive. He was tall and spare, with his fur brushed back severely, and his classical features were overwhelmed by a thick pair of spectacles, so that he looked ecclesiastical and bookish. I was just imagining what sort of literature he might generally like to read when we heard a loud knock—more of a kick, really—and cheerful voices calling out. When the maid opened the door, I beheld a donkey, a dog, a cat, and a rooster, each of them a little bony and gray with age. Our hostess introduced them as Wallace, Zeke, Tallulah, and Ernest, respectively, the Bremen Town Musicians. Intrigued, I quickly observed that their motions were all in unison, as if keeping time with some inaudible metronome. I selfishly hoped that they would favor us with a musical performance later in the evening, but even more I was curious about the turns their lives had taken since that fateful night when their house had been burned to the ground.

As we all went in to dinner, Reverend Wright shyly offered me his arm, and I could not refuse without being rude. I took my seat next to him, expecting very little of him by way of conversation. Indeed, he was rather quiet, but I noticed he took an intense interest in each speaker as the conversation traveled about the table. He seemed to be divining their deepest characters, so that I felt reluctant to draw attention to myself by contributing to the discourse. Nevertheless, his attention did focus on me, and there it remained, until I began to wonder whether something was actually amiss with my apparel or grooming. Mr. Bentley, who sat across from me, broke the spell by inquiring whether Reverend Wright planned on joining the men's choir. It was an innocent enough question on the surface, but one with an important meaning for those brave souls resisting the injustices of the Anthropological Society. A hush fell over the table. All eyes turned to the curate. I could not help but wonder if he had any inkling of the troubles in this seemingly peaceful little parish. He looked around, taking in the whole gathering, cleared his throat, and stated that his singing voice was possibly the worst in three counties, but that he would consider it his duty to assist the men's choir in such ways as he could. Mr. Bentley and Reverend Snover exchanged quick glances, the reverend almost imperceptibly nodding in the affirmative. From this I inferred that the curate did indeed understand the true nature of the men's choir, and was committed to their cause. After that, I was inclined to be sympathetic to him.

Mrs. Snover, in her grandmotherly way, made an effort to draw him out, asking questions about his background and family. It was then that he artlessly confessed that the bishop had suggested to him that he take a wife. I was suddenly stricken with the thought that his attention to me had some deeper purpose, and I felt myself blushing furiously. Thankfully, no one could see it. Though some of the girls at Miss Pinchkin's Academy had thought of nothing but love and marriage, I had always held myself separate from such ambitions. I thought I must take care now to keep my conduct to him cordial, but not encouraging.

As the evening progressed, the conversation turned from the usual lively topics of religion and politics to more eclectic subjects. There was some debate about the validity of the research techniques of those controversial historians the Brothers Grimm. When that subject was exhausted, there was hearsay and gossip about the habits and eccentricities of the aristocracy. I enjoyed listening to the give-and-take, though I did not contribute much myself. One might have expected some inhibition in consideration of the clergymen in our midst. In reality Reverend Snover and his good wife seemed to possess such largeness of spirit that all foibles were seen as endearing, and all subjects food for thought. In such a welcoming environment, ideas flowed freely about the company. Only Reverend Wright was reserved. His face remained impassive, but his eyes took everything in with manifest interest, always seeming to return to me when he thought I wasn't looking.

Mrs. Snover noticed my discomfort and, turning to Reverend Wright, claimed his attention by asking him whether he had much association with the sons of the nobility while at seminary.

Blinking several times, as if making an effort to switch his focus to her, he answered, "Well, yes, I suppose you could say that. My roommate in my last year was the second son of a baron, but of course younger sons in this land inherit nothing; they are simply commoners."

Here Reverend Snover, who had been listening to the exchange, broke in, saying, "Ah, yes, but commoners with a difference. Ask our own Mr. Bentley here. He is the younger son of a viscount, and has grown up among lords and ladies. What do you say, Mr. Bentley, has your background given you an advantage?"

I was so stunned by this revelation that I very nearly choked on my sweetmeats as every eye turned to Mr. Bentley.

Mr. Bentley did not seem at all pleased by this attention, and he thought for a moment before he spoke. "For myself, I have had many advantages, not least of which was a rigorous education. Of course, I have also had the example before me of my elder brother, so petted and indulged as the heir that he really had no chance to learn self-discipline or self-reliance. I now consider myself much the more fortunate of the two, as a simple commoner." He said this with a searching look in my direction, as if to elicit my response, and I returned it with a reassuring smile. Though I had been momentarily put off by the disclosure of his noble ancestry, his pronouncement served to dispel any fear that he was not still the same, congenial Mr. Bentley that I had perceived him to be. I only hoped he would volunteer more about his history, as I did not like to question him, despite my curiosity.

"Remarkable that you have not suffered any of the weakness of character generally displayed by those of the upper classes . . . ," Reverend Wright proposed, trailing off into silence as he apparently realized that he had just insulted Mr. Bentley's entire family and perhaps many of his acquaintances as well.

"Yes. Isn't it, though," Mr. Bentley replied evenly.

"Oh, do excuse me if I've offended. I've such a talent for saying the wrong thing," said the flustered curate. He closed his mouth abruptly and looked at his plate. I felt sorry for him, as I believed that he had meant no harm.

"I suppose that people and creatures come in all stripes, whatever their station in life," said Mrs. Snover, in an attempt to smooth things over. "And what a dull world it would be if they did not! Of course, here in the Enchanted Forest, the popular tendency is to blame everything on magic."

"Yes, and whose magic?" Mother Hubbard joined in. "Why, the way people tell it, the whole land is just teeming with witches, wicked fairies, and evil old crones, all of them casting spells and curses, poisoning apples, eating small children. You'd think little old ladies were the most dangerous characters in creation!"

"You mean they're not?" quipped Reverend Snover, winking at Mrs. Snover. She gave him an enigmatic smile and handed him an apple, which he cheerfully bit into. "Am I a frog yet?" he asked, looking about the table. "No? How disappointing."

Wallace cleared his throat. He stood at the table's edge, his companions the dog and the cat sitting in chairs on either side of him, and the rooster perched on his back. "It's not just old ladies who are maligned, you know. My comrades and I were each about to be destroyed by our former masters, whom we had served so well! And for what? The great crime of growing old!" Zeke, Tallulah, and Ernest all cried out in assent, making a perfect chord of alto, tenor, and baritone. Wallace chimed in with a resounding bass, and the rest of us listened, entranced.

"There is music in us yet!" Zeke intoned, then Wallace drew them to a close with a dramatic swish of his right ear. I had expected some cacophony of howling and braying, crowing and caterwauling, but it was obvious that the musicians were capable of making their own, eerily sweet style of music.

"Oh, I do hope you will sing for us this evening," Mrs. Snover effused. "Tell us, how are you faring, all of you? We've been terribly concerned about you since the night your house was burned. Are you quite safe in Farmer O'Dell's barn? Are you still getting threats?"

"Oh, dear lady," said Wallace, "if you only knew the half of it. You'd think folks would thank us for driving that gang of thieves out of the house, but it seems some preferred the thieves living in their midst to a troupe of Enchanted musicians. The abuse has tapered off now that we're living in a barn—like good animals. It's a nice barn, as barns go, but not as good as our little house was. Still there are those who hurl insults, or sometimes stones, when we go through town. Even children can be cruel to us. There's a disreputable-looking gang of them that all seem to use us for target practice!"

I was appalled at this disclosure, not realizing that things were so bad in town.

"It's only a minority that are stirring up trouble," Zeke interjected, "but they're a loud minority indeed! Too much in love with the sounds of their own voices to listen to what the good reverend tries to teach on Sunday mornings. 'Humans only!' is their slogan. I know, because we've heard them chanting it, and it was written on the bricks they used to throw through our windows. I don't believe the malcontents will rest until they have silenced us all."

"Silenced us all!" Ernest repeated, rustling his feathers and bobbing his head up and down for emphasis.

I felt great sympathy for the musicians, and wanted to apologize to them for the way they had been treated, though it was not really my place to do so.

"Ah, yes, of course," sighed Reverend Snover. "Silence, like blindness, allows evil to flourish. A certain miserable faction of our citizenry thinks that they can make themselves less miserable by being cruel to others. They seek to silence the Enchanted while they deprive them of their rights and jobs and property, and reduce them to living in the wild, or as unpaid laborers—or as targets for their sport."

"Sport!" squawked Ernest. "Sport! Ha!"

"Things are getting ugly," Tallulah fretted. "One gang of rogues asked me why I wasn't wearing a collar—and offered to put one on me! People can be so rude! I'm almost afraid to speak out loud in public these days. Safer just to act like an old stray cat."

"That is precisely what they want," the reverend responded.

"They are no gentlemen!" Mother Hubbard exclaimed.

I had the thought that our own newspaper could not come soon enough. More people needed to hear the stories of those like the four musicians, but since the new printing press and its location were to be a secret for now, I refrained from bringing it up.

"Why do they call themselves the Anthropological Society?" I asked.

Unable to resist playing Devil's advocate, Mr. Snark spoke up, quavering in his little crooked voice. "Anthropology, after all, is merely the study of man and his culture. The society is simply a fraternal organization for humans who wish to preserve their human heritage. What's wrong with that? Why, they've been known to make donations to widows and orphans, and hand out Bibles to Sunday schools. You're all being alarmists!" Mr. Snark sat back to watch the effect of his declaration, as if he had just poked a stick in a beehive and stirred it around. There was only a troubled hush.

"Even if all you've said is true," Reverend Wright spoke up, "it is easy to mask evil with a few good works."

"They take care to keep their surface appearance respectable," Zeke added. "Babcock and all his followers! Perhaps it cannot be proved that they sully their own hands with the dirty work, but at the very least they incite a lot of weak-minded ruffians to do it for them."

"Weak-minded ruffians!" Ernest interjected.

"Not only the weak-minded ruffians," Reverend Snover put in. "Many of them are educated men who should know better. In fact, I am ashamed to say that some of them are clergy. They've tried to recruit me more than once."

"Surely not!" I cried.

"Pray, how can that be? Men of conscience?" Mother Hubbard demanded, giving voice to my own question. How *could* a clergyman be such a hypocrite?

"A conscience can be twisted to suit just about any deed or dogma, my dear. Many of the constabulary have joined as well. I've found that even the lowest criminal may justify his crimes with a skillful contortion of his morals, so that he counts himself as a righteous and misunderstood man."

This revelation sobered us, and we all fell silent. Perhaps the others pondered, as I did, just how elastic their own principles might be if challenged.

"Well, enough of darkness and disillusionment," Mrs. Snover interjected at last. "We can buoy one another up through anything the future might bring; for the present, let us do as the Good Book instructs us: we shall think on that which is lovely, and that which is admirable. I do believe the time has come for some music, my friends, if you would be so kind." Wallace, Zeke, Tallulah, and Ernest, seemingly happy enough to change the subject, graciously acceded to this request, regrouping themselves about the fireplace in the cozy parlor and treating us to a medley of sentimental ballads.

I had not heard them perform before, so I could not tell how this night's artistry compared to their usual fare, but it seemed to me, as I listened to their poignant refrains, to be singularly stirring. Indeed, when they sang the haunting melody of "The Blue Hills of Home," it struck me forcefully that this band of weary old pilgrims, betrayed by their masters, could never go home again. As I felt a lump growing in my throat, I glanced about and saw many a glistening eye.

That night stood out in my memory long after it was over.

Though I had become accustomed to older people failing to take me seriously because of my youth, that night I felt befriended by them. That night, the mantle of fellowship that had enveloped us all through the evening seemed to cling to each of us as we bade one another farewell and went our separate ways. How thankful we would be in times to come for such good and faithful company.

24

A Fledgling in the Schoolroom

~

The last cold weeks of fall were upon us. Up in the schoolroom, Teddy—and Nurse—and I kept busy as the world outside turned white, and frost etched diamond-bright patterns on the windowpanes. The days grew shorter, the nights grew colder, and even we Enchanted ones were not totally removed from our animal instincts. Though we did not hibernate, the household retired by eight, and slept past sunrise.

My duties, already stretched to include afternoon lessons for Goldilocks, and my evening Latin instruction from Mr. Bentley, were now condensed into even less time, so that I went from one task to the next with scarcely a breath in between. My letters home to Papa became hastily scribbled notes assuring him I was well, but Papa, generous as he was, responded with long, colorful missives, filled with love and encouragement, which inspired me to persevere through many a demanding day.

In truth, I was grateful to be busy. Latin lessons with Mr. Bentley were, as I had feared, proving to be a hazard to my peace of mind. My moods were unquiet, alternating between confused melancholy and a tenuous euphoria, depending upon whether I felt that he was indifferent to me, or was developing a fondness for me, or was merely trifling with me.

The hours I spent with the fractious Goldilocks strained my abilities to the fullest. She was completely untutored, capable of communicating only through spontaneous hand signals and facial expressions. I found that she could count, for example, but only up to three. Three fingers held up seemed to stand for every number larger than two, whether it was five or one hundred—a common enough limitation among many here in the Enchanted Forest, where things are so often counted in threes. We practiced counting fingers, chairs, stockings, and anything else at hand. I also tried the button games that had worked with Teddy, but Goldilocks had a habit of absconding with as many buttons as she could hold in her little fist and refusing to give them back.

Communication being the most urgent issue, I impatiently awaited the arrival of the specialist the Vaughns had called in to evaluate the child's mute condition. This was the distinguished Dr. Bernhard Ehrlichmann, who, intrigued by Dr. Robinson's description of the patient, had agreed not only to come out of retirement and take the case, but to travel to the Cottage in the Woods to examine her. Mrs. Vaughn informed me that they had decided that a human doctor would be most suitable for this little human patient, and that Dr. Robinson had vouched for Dr. Ehrlichmann's trustworthiness and his disdain for all forms of interspecies prejudice.

The doctor arrived one cold, clear day in December, a wizened little man with an air of courtly authority and great intellect. What hair he had was white, and his monocle gave him the aspect of a one-eyed owl. I was assigned the task of introducing him to Goldilocks. However, the child's reaction upon his entering her chamber was to produce one of her little incoherent cries and retreat behind her hiding chair. This was fortuitous, in that he was able to hear for himself the only sound that she seemed capable of producing, but it was clear that his first task must be to win the little girl's trust.

"You spend a great deal of time vith the child?" he asked me.

"Several hours a day, sir—as much as I can manage."

"Und vat are her faforite toys, her faforite occupations?"

"Oh, by far her favorite thing is to be read to. She listens attentively and seems quite thrilled by the illustrations. Her favorite toy is that doll you see her with just now."

"Very goot. I think it best if I am left qvite alone vith her for a time so that she might depend on me for her entertainment, und become accustomed to me. Iff you vill excuse us, please? Und perhaps iff you vill haff sent up some small portion uff her faforite dessert from the kitchen?"

Mrs. Vaughn looked a little doubtful, but the doctor treated her to his wrinkled smile, rich with the warmth of a lifetime of gentle good humor, and reassured her that he would only try to win the child's trust with kindness. Mrs. Vaughn's concern melted away; she rang for Betsy, then she and Mrs. Van Winkle and I retired to the little sitting room next door in case we should be wanted, and Dr. Ehrlichmann spent the afternoon sequestered with Goldilocks. We could only speculate whether his befriending of her might take days, or whether she might accept him more quickly because he was human.

He emerged from her chamber several hours later, and reported that while she did finally come close and look over his shoulder, he did not want to alarm her by trying to examine her as yet. Plans were made for him to spend the night and continue on the morrow. This proved to be propitious, as he related the next day that Goldilocks's initial gesture to him upon his entering her apartment was to hand him her favorite book to read, and that after a little coaxing, she had seated herself by his side. He felt that she was ready now to accept his touch, and enlisted our help for the examination itself. In the beginning, I thought he intended for us to hold her still for him, and worried that this might damage the trust she had built up in us, but I soon realized he had something else in mind. His stratagem was to first examine Mrs. Vaughn, Mrs. Van Winkle, and me in front of Goldilocks, all of us making it seem like a great deal of fun. And so he proceeded, first to check on our general health, then to test our hearing with a series of tuning forks, followed by a contest to see who could open our mouths the widest while he looked in our throats. In a bit of inspiration, the doctor asked Goldilocks if he might inspect her doll. The request was at first met with reluctance, but with a little entreaty success was achieved, and the much-loved toy was handed over to his care. The distinguished doctor solemnly proceeded to give the doll a thorough going-over, and, pronouncing her fit, returned her to her owner. Finally, Goldilocks all but insisted on her turn, plunking herself down in front of the doctor and opening her mouth wide. He scrutinized her with gentle efficiency, talking softly to himself as he went along—"Mmm . . . aha . . . yes"—but we dared not question him.

At last he finished, patting Goldilocks on the head and telling her she was a good girl, and, putting away his instruments, he directed us into the sitting room, where he questioned us at length about the child's brief known history and behavior.

Finally, he gave his diagnosis, which was both hopeful and disheartening: he had found nothing, he explained, no physical reason why the child could not talk. Her little strangled cries proved that in unguarded moments her vocal cords were capable of producing sound, and the examination showed no physical impediment to speech. Some great shock, perhaps, or pathological fear had silenced her, but her disability lay only in the inner reaches of her own mind. He offered no more than slim hope that with time and care she might recover.

"If anything vill induce the child to speak, it vill be the company uff other youngsters," he said. "That is my prescription. Und a vord to the vise: do not try to compel her. Iff she ever does begin to attempt speech, it vill be ven she feels safe und free to do so. I vish you the best uff luck." With that, he took his departure, and I waited with budding optimism to see whether the Vaughns would take the doctor's advice and allow Goldilocks to associate with another youngster—namely, Teddy. My own belief was that both young ones would benefit from the contact: he could act as a good example to her, and she could help alleviate the loneliness of his being an only cub. I knew the decision was not so simple, that once Goldilocks was introduced to the schoolroom, there would be no keeping her presence in the household a secret. Still, they surely weren't planning on keeping the child shut up in the east wing forever, and I had faith they would do what they could for her.

Later that day, the Vaughns proceeded to question me about both Goldilocks's progress and Teddy's, and then, seemingly satisfied with the answers, Mrs. Vaughn asked me if I thought I could manage the two of them together, still meeting the specific needs of each.

"Before you answer," Mr. Vaughn interjected, "I must

remind you of how tumultuous their encounter was on the day we found the child here, and how mesmerized Teddy was by her. Far from being a calming influence on her, he was drawn into her frenzy and ran after her. Should you agree to this new arrangement, you will be responsible for maintaining order, as well as holding them to high academic standards."

"I understand, sir," I said, "but I'd like to try. Goldilocks has learned to trust me, and she adores hearing about anything that Teddy says or does, so I think there is no reason for her to fly into a frenzy again."

"If they are so taken with one another," Mrs. Vaughn put in, "then perhaps their companionship should be made contingent on their good behavior, so that misbehavior would result in separation. That is probably the best motivation we could give them to do well."

"May we attempt it, sir?" I asked.

The Vaughns concurred, and so it was decided. The next morning as Teddy and I sat working over his primer, Mrs. Vaughn opened the schoolroom door and leaned in, informing Teddy that he was to have a visitor—that she was here to do her schoolwork, and if they were both very good, and got their work done, the visitor would come again tomorrow. Teddy, whose eyes had grown wide, stood up and said, "I'll be good, Mama! I can be *very good*, can't I, Miss Brown?" He turned and looked at me.

"Yes, Master Teddy," I responded. "You can be very good, and you can help your visitor remember to be good too, can't you?"

At that moment, Mrs. Vaughn stepped through the doorway, holding Goldilocks's hand, and the two youngsters saw each other. Goldilocks's eyes sparked with instant recognition. Teddy's realization came a moment later, perhaps because her appearance was changed so from the first time he had seen her. "It's her!" he cried, and the two flew into each other's arms like long-lost friends.

My eyes met Mrs. Vaughn's and observed them glistening with restrained emotion. "I'll leave you to it, then," she said, smiling, and withdrew from the room.

Only then did I glance to Nurse's corner by the windows and notice Nurse, standing at attention, an expression of shock and consternation writ large on her countenance. Though I knew she had been one of the few servants informed of the girl's presence in the house, she had clearly not expected this, just as I had neglected to take Nurse's presence into account when we were making our plans for Goldilocks to join us in the schoolroom. A chill of apprehension shot through me as I contemplated the possibilities for mayhem. The situation would require vigilance. Perhaps it would be sufficient that out of consideration for Goldilocks's dread of windows, I had placed the youngsters' desks on the opposite side of the room from Nurse's accustomed spot.

Despite this shadow on the horizon, the morning got off to a fine start, with Teddy eagerly showing Goldilocks to her somewhat oversized desk, then taking his own seat, head erect, paws folded formally on his desktop, the very model of an attentive student. A meaningful glance to his smaller schoolmate was all it took for her to straighten her spine, and fold her hands carefully in imitation of him. This augured well, I thought, for the new arrangement. As we progressed through the morning lessons, I encountered my first dilemma, which was that every time I turned my back on my students, I would wheel around only to find the two of them squeezed into Teddy's seat, hands and paws folded decorously on the desk, silently signaling their intentions to be ever so good if allowed to remain together.

"Teddy," I finally inquired, "do you like this arrangement, then? Can you do your work with Goldilocks next to you?"

"I don't mind it," he answered shyly.

I quickly evaluated the possibilities for benefit or for trouble. In the end, guided by the conviction that they might learn as much from each other as they would from me, I simply went on with the lessons.

From that point on, things improved, though I soon found that Goldilocks's attention was all for Teddy and Teddy's lessons, and that her desire was to imitate him in everything. Thinking it better to take advantage of this impulse than to quell it, I encouraged Teddy to try to teach Goldilocks the simple counting games I had played with him. Though she continued to hold up three fingers in answer to every problem, I could almost see the little brain working, grasping at the concepts that Teddy revealed like glimpses of so many stars flashing tantalizingly in the night sky. Teddy never seemed to rush her or lose patience with her. The child watched his face, harkening to his every word—comprehending him or not, we could not tell—until from time to time her own impatience and frustration would erupt in a brief show of temper, characterized by her banging the desktop with her diminutive fist, and covering her face with her hands. Then Teddy, captivated by her mercurial moods, would curl his arm about her shoulders and coax her into trying again. And so, their education proceeded, and the preternatural bond that was to grow between them took root. Nurse looked on from her corner lair, brooding and inscrutable.

It had been arranged that the child would stay until lunch-time. Beyond that I could not foresee. I hardly dared hope that even Teddy could induce Goldilocks to come outdoors with us for the afternoon's natural history lessons, which we observed in all but the most extreme weather. She still would not go near a window, let alone outdoors. Was it that devious lout Gabriel who had terrified her? Could he have some hold over her even now? We could tell Goldilocks that the grounds were patrolled now, that the faithful Harry had been assigned to protect us in our wanderings, but it would take a great deal of trust indeed for the child to believe that we could protect her from one such as Gabriel.

25

Papa

❧

The winter holidays were soon upon us. I had a fortnight free to spend at home with Papa, and though I looked forward to it with longing, I had some anxiety about leaving Goldilocks at this stage of her development. Her progress in the schoolroom was quite encouraging, and it seemed an unfortunate time for the schooling to stop. Mrs. Vaughn proposed that Goldilocks might continue to spend her days with Teddy in the nursery, but I could foresee all manner of trouble under Nurse's tender ministrations, and so I suggested that Teddy instead be allowed to visit Goldilocks's chamber under the supervision of Mrs. Van Winkle. It was a simple matter to convince Mrs. Vaughn that it would be too much to ask of Nurse to handle the two youngsters all day on her own. And so it was decided.

Having done what I could for Goldilocks and Teddy, and said my goodbyes, I packed my valise and bid my cantankerous mirror goodbye as well.

"Just cover me up, then, if you please," it replied. No sooner had I done so than a mellow snore reverberated through my chamber. I calmed myself, and giving a last look to my cozy little room, I picked up my bag and closed the door, thinking of the inexperienced young bear I had been when I first set foot there, and how much I had changed since that day. Then, on an impulse, I proceeded to the east wing, where I leaned in at Mr. Bentley's office doorway to bid him farewell. I was greeted only by an empty seat. Having no time to search for him, I swallowed my disappointment and went on my way.

The ever-faithful Harry escorted me to town, patiently standing by while I went into the bookstore looking for a gift for Papa. At last I found a beautifully bound volume of his favorite book, *Don Quixote,* to replace the old, worn-out copy he kept by his chair. I set off on the afternoon train with a light heart, my valise in one paw, my carefully wrapped package in the other.

Papa's old housemaid, Lucy, was there at the station to greet me at journey's end. Normally a sturdy, cheerful person, she seemed uncharacteristically depressed. "I'm so glad you're here, miss," she said fervently. "Your papa's been poorly and couldn't come himself."

"What is wrong?" I asked as she helped me with my bag and we began the walk home.

"He's quite ill, miss, though he won't admit it. You know how good-natured he is, even in times of trouble. It started with a little cough, but now it affects his breathing. It's keeping him up at night, and sapping his energy so that he's stopped doing most everything that he used to do," she continued. "He insists it's just a touch of the grippe, and won't give me leave to call in the doctor."

We walked down the street in a worried silence as I told

myself that it couldn't be that bad. Papa had always been so strong and vital! Surely all he needed was some tender, loving care, I thought when we turned up the hill toward home. As we approached, I paused and stared at the old homestead with fond eyes, noting that it seemed a little smaller and a little shabbier since I had seen it last. I saw that Papa's rose garden, usually so carefully cut back and wrapped in burlap against the winter freeze, stood withered and frozen, the last wrinkled brown blossom teetering in the wind. A cold foreboding seized my heart. I hurried through the door and made my way to the familiar old parlor, where we had spent so many contented hours sitting by the fire when I was but a cub, Papa watching over me in steady benevolence, the Gibraltar of my little world. At first I did not espy him, so shrunken did he seem, propped up in his overstuffed chair, draped with a heavy shawl. I went to him, kneeling at his feet and looking up into the dear, tired face, thinner now than I remembered. His eyes seemed to focus on something very far away as he puffed on his old pipe.

"Papa? Papa, I'm home."

The brown eyes fluttered, and turned to me, a little dim but still twinkling, and a slow smile spread over his furry face.

"Ah, if it isn't my own wee Ursula, the apple of my eye and the beat of my heart," he croaked, lifting his paw to pat the top of my head. His speech was a hoarse echo of the rich, deep voice I knew so well. "Home at last, are you? I've been waiting for so long." He dropped his paw heavily, and an icy knot formed in my chest. How frail he was! I kissed him on the snout, noticing now that it was streaked with silver, and found that it was hot and dry.

"Papa," I announced, hiding my fear. "Papa, I must be stern

with you. You're ill, and you belong in bed. Let Lucy and me help you up to your room, then I'll send her for the doctor. Be good now."

"No, no," Papa objected. "Don't fuss at me. I'm perfectly all—" He broke off in a fit of coughing that seemed to shake his whole body as I watched helplessly.

"That's it," I declared, more cheerily than I felt. "It's off to bed with you this minute. Let's get you settled before the doctor arrives."

He treated me to an expression of pained martyrdom. "Termagant!" was the choked rejoinder.

"Here, Mr. Brown," Lucy cajoled. "You heard Ursula. Just lean on me. I'm strong as an ox!"

With a mix of patience and determination that I had learned from Papa himself, I soon had him bundled into bed, sitting against the pillows and sipping some good hot chamomile tea. I sat by his bedside, telling him stories, all the while, of my life with the Vaughns, and about young Goldilocks.

When Lucy finally returned with Dr. Deeb, he greeted Papa with, "Well, my friend, what are you up to?" and swiftly banished me from the room. Obediently, I went downstairs to the parlor to await the doctor's verdict, while Lucy retired to the kitchen to busy herself with supper. For a time I paced back and forth, listening to the floorboards creak. Then I sat in Papa's chair by the fireside, staring at nothing while anxious thoughts crowded in. Daylight was fading. Lucy brought a tray from the kitchen, but I wasn't hungry. To keep my spirits up, I lit the candelabra and began to hum a familiar melody, then recognized that it was Papa's favorite hymn. As the words went through my mind, they both alarmed and sustained me:

Abide with me; fast falls the eventide;
The darkness deepens; Lord, with me abide!

From the top of the stairs, Dr. Deeb called me. "Your papa needs to speak with you."

I climbed the stairs, hope and dread mingling in my heart, and searched Dr. Deeb's face for hints of either, but I could read nothing in his features beyond his characteristic calm and compassion. I moved past him, into the room, where Papa lay resting on the big bed.

Then his eyes met mine, and I knew.

"Papa! Oh, Papa!" I cried, all my mature reserve abandoning me as I flew to him and lay my head against his chest. His steady paw stroked my head as he waited for the wave of despair to subside.

"There, there. Have your cry, then. Let it go," he murmured. How like him to be comforting me in his own darkest hour! Indeed, I could no more have stanched the flow of hot tears than have held in the tides, or stopped the sun from setting. I gave myself up to the pain of losing the one I held most dear in all the world while I accepted the bracing comfort of his arms.

Crying out my shock and sorrow, I came to the realization that Papa must count on me now to be the strong one, to do whatever could and must be done. Perhaps this was the only gift I could give him. I pulled out my handkerchief and dried my eyes. Looking up at the doctor, I asked, "How long?"

"His lungs are filling up, I'm afraid. He has a little time. Enough to settle his affairs."

I nodded, and took Papa's paw in mine, promising to stay by

his side, lending him my youth and strength, and carrying out his wishes as best I could.

That evening I composed a letter to the Vaughns to apprise them of my plight, then I sent my fervent prayers Heavenward that Teddy and Goldilocks might continue to thrive in one another's company while I was absent, and that Teddy would not suffer too much under Nurse's volatile governance.

From that point, my life became a concatenation of duties, caring for Papa's needs as he rapidly failed. Lucy and I took turns sitting with him, day and night. Sometimes, during his wakeful periods, I read aloud to him from his old favorite classics, or we talked quietly together when he was able. Papa explained to me in fits and starts what he wished done with his few possessions. He regretted that he had nothing of value to leave me except his books, which he looked upon as old friends. Though I did not even want to think about such things, he directed me to sell them, and set the proceeds aside for myself, for a rainy day, and this I promised I would do.

Christmas was fast approaching. At Papa's bidding, we decorated the house, arranging evergreen boughs on all the mantels and candles in the windows. We decked out the sickroom with bright poinsettia plants. Though my heart was breaking, for his sake I would do my utmost to imbue this last Christmas together with all the holiday spirit I could summon, though it be the most difficult task of my life.

Then, late one night as he lay awake, he took my paw in his. He told me his fondest hope for me was that I would someday find someone who would be to me what he and Mama had been to one another: a soul mate and beloved companion to share my life with. At this, Mr. Bentley's likeness came unbidden into my mind: the deep-set eyes alive with wit and intelligence, the rogu-ish grin, the handsome dark fur. I quickly blocked the image out, afraid to ask myself if he could ever mean so much to me, but Papa caught my fleeting change of expression and smiled.

"Is there . . . ?" he asked hoarsely.

"I don't know, Papa," I replied. "There's someone who . . . I don't know. He hasn't declared himself to me. I'm afraid of get-ting my heart broken."

"Is he worthy? Does he make you happy?"

"Oh yes, Papa. I think you would like him very much."

He paused, breathing heavily, obviously tired. "Don't worry too much about your heart getting broken, pet," he wheezed. "Love is not for the fainthearted . . . and even broken hearts can heal."

"You always know just what I need to hear, Papa."

He signaled me to come closer, and whispered, "When you know it's the right one, remember, my dear, that you have my blessing."

He lay back, exhausted but smiling, and I sat with him, holding his paw until he fell asleep, grateful for our short time together.

He slept fitfully, more and more as the days passed. Christ-mas morning arrived, a reminder of all that is beautiful and good. Lucy and I had made preparations for a small Christmas dinner, and she had brought home a fat goose, and a little of everything to go with it. She and I set to peeling, chopping, baking, and roasting, until the old house was redolent with holi-day smells. First I took a plate up to Papa, and tried to tempt his appetite. He swallowed some potatoes and gravy, and tasted some of the plum pudding and port jelly, then he urged me to go down to my own supper while he napped. Despite the pervasive cloud of melancholy, I sat next to Papa's empty place and said grace, then Lucy and I attempted to do justice to the fine meal. Though I was hardly hungry, the nourishment lifted my spirits, and we ended the repast with a bit of mulled wine. Thinking it might be good for Papa, I stood by his bed, wondering if I should wake him. He opened his eyes and, smiling wanly, croaked out, "Happy Christmas, my angel."

I smiled too, wanting to keep things cheerful, and said, "I'm no angel, Papa! You should have heard what I almost said this morning when I burned my paw on the cookstove! And on Christmas too!"

This brought on a weak chuckle.

"*Almost* doesn't signify, does it, Papa? It's not like the time you hollered 'Blast!' in the middle of church. Remember? The minister stopped the service."

"That couldn't be helped, you know," he whispered. "Something *bit* me!"

We laughed companionably, and I, not wanting the moment to end, summoned more happy memories to share. We talked on quietly till the fire burned low, and our hearts were mellow and content. For a time, all the old jokes and mishaps were infused with fresh life. For a time, laughter and tears flowed together in unbearable sweetness, and love banished fear from the Valley of the Shadow.

That was the last day I had with Papa. By nightfall, he had sunk into a kind of insensibility, drawing each breath more painfully than the last. I listened helplessly, holding his paw and unconsciously holding my own breath, waiting for him to inhale once more.

Here I draw a curtain over our travail, saying only that Papa, like his Don Quixote, fought a valiant fight against an unbeatable foe. He found his blessed release in the early morning of New Year's Day, and died with Mama's name on his lips.

✧

Numbly, I proceeded to follow the forms and rituals of death, dressing myself all in black, shunning any ornament. Through those dark days I leaned heavily on dear Lucy, who treated me as fondly as any parent, taking over all the funeral arrangements and leaving me to my grief. The Vaughns traveled down on the next train, and Mr. Vaughn came to me as a godsend, asking whether he, as Papa's oldest friend, might be allowed to defray the funeral expenses and help with the settling of Papa's affairs. I accepted this gratefully, as a gift for Papa, and raised Mr. Vaughn up several levels in my estimation.

He also delivered to me a letter from Mr. Bentley, a very proper message of condolence, which left me strangely unsatisfied. I found myself wishing they had brought Mr. Bentley himself instead of this polite note. I had thought of him so much throughout my time away, but especially since my talk with Papa, that I frequently allowed myself to imagine how different things would be if he were by my side. I smiled when I thought of him meeting my papa, and how they would have gotten on. I imagined how much easier the grief would be to endure with his broad shoulder there for me to lean on.

Nevertheless, I put on a brave face for the many visitors who came to pay Papa their last respects. These were friends, colleagues, and students of his from all walks of life, from Mr. Vaughn, to the greengrocer, to the mayor, for Papa was on the best of terms with all manner of people, from the wealthy and preeminent to the humblest talking creature.

When Papa had been laid to rest, and the last of his many well-wishers had said farewell, Mr. Vaughn took me aside and informed me that things had gone sadly awry with the children in the short time I had been away. My stomach lurched when he said this, and I asked him to elucidate.

"We can talk about that later. The sooner you come back to continue your work with Master Theodore and Goldilocks, the better," he urged. He inquired whether I needed help in finishing up Papa's affairs. I replied that I had only a few belongings to pack up and some of Papa's books left to sell, and then I would follow them back on the train. I packed up Mama's wedding dress, the only thing I had of hers now, and I saved only one book, Papa's worn and tattered copy of *Don Quixote*.

Finally it was time to say goodbye to the old house. I stood at the front gate, realizing that I would never cross that doorstep again, and I let the tears flow.

26

Nurse Is Punished

With a heavy heart, I boarded the train, and, having no task to occupy me, I beguiled the time by turning my thoughts to the life that awaited me at the Vaughns'. I was most worried about Goldilocks and Teddy. Whatever the trouble was, I knew that they needed my help, and now, with no other home to go to, it was more important than ever that I earn my keep. I must do better than my best, try to go on in a way that would win Mr. Vaughn's approval, and more importantly, a way that would have made Papa proud. My paw went to my heart seeking the comfort of the locket with Mama and Papa's picture—the locket that was not there. Now that Papa had passed on, it would be all the more precious to me if ever it were returned. I sighed heavily and tried to think of something else.

My thoughts wandered to the men's choir. Had I missed any new developments? I thought how grateful I was to be allowed to be of some help to them and their cause. I remembered the last night when I had played the accompaniment for them, and Mr. Vaughn had proposed the new newspaper. Perhaps the printing press would be delivered soon, I mused. Surely it would not be long now until the first edition would be printed, and the *Plain Truth* would be spread far and wide. Would it make a difference? I wondered.

But mostly my mind kept harking back to Mr. Bentley. Did he think about me as much as I thought of him? Did his heart feel the same thing, soul-stirring and sweet, that grew in mine? Had he ever given me any indication? No, he hadn't, I chastised myself, and tried to push the thoughts from my mind, but the rhythm of the wheels seemed to chug out his name, and I hastened along in the inexorable train, lost in a deep reverie.

On my arrival, Mrs. Vaughn informed me only that Mrs. Van Winkle had been called home for a week because of a family emergency, so that instead of playing together in Goldilocks's chamber as had been planned, Goldilocks and Teddy had been allowed to play in the nursery under Nurse's supervision, the very thing I had sought to avoid. Now Nurse claimed that Goldilocks had bitten her—that she had run in a perfect frenzy of rage and defiance about the room, knocking into furniture and throwing things. It had so far been impossible to determine exactly what had incited Goldilocks to violence, but having laid down the rule at the outset that any misbehavior would be punished by separating the two youngsters, the Vaughns had no choice but to confine Goldilocks to her chamber. There Betsy and Mrs. Vaughn herself had attended to her until Mrs. Van Winkle returned.

Teddy was brokenhearted, moping about, refusing to be comforted, refusing to talk, and scarcely eating. Nurse, meanwhile, went about with an ostentatious swath of bandages around her paw, her arm in a sling, and limping on alternate feet, as the mood took her. The Vaughns were distraught, with Teddy in a decline and their confidence in Goldilocks badly shaken. Having neither an explanation for nor a resolution to the dilemma, they looked to me for a remedy.

It was with great trepidation that I made my way to the east wing to see how Goldilocks fared. I had come prepared with some of her favorite books, and finding her firmly entrenched behind her hiding chair, I tried to coax her out with the stories and illustrations she loved, but to no effect. She either would not or could not respond, and I began to be afraid that some lasting harm had been done. Mrs. Van Winkle, who had warned me so specifically not to break my heart over the child, refrained from saying "I told you so." She merely explained in a sorrowful tone that she bitterly regretted having to leave the child.

"Please, Goldilocks," I said, trying the direct approach, "do come out. I miss you. Teddy misses you. He's very sad without you." It had been a full day since my return, and the child had not budged from her old hiding place behind the chair, or even given any indication that she saw or heard me.

"Please, Goldilocks," I tried again. "I'm so sorry I had to go away, but won't you give me a chance to try to make things right?" I watched her closely for any response. Perceiving no change, I decided to forsake my schoolteacher dignity and sit down on the floor beside her hiding place to wait, hoping my nearness would communicate my compassion for her. This at least elicited a reaction: she stiffened her shoulders and turned her face away from me. Ignoring this, I sat very still by her side while the afternoon waned, sometimes talking softly about why I had been away for so long, about my papa's illness and death, and about how much I had missed her. Sometimes I hummed or sang; sometimes I was silent. I sat with her while my poor body rebelled at the hard floor, and my uncomfortable position on it. She remained unmoved. Finally, I dared to ease my paw gradually closer to her, and I touched her hand. To my astonishment and gratification, the little hand grasped my paw tightly. The slight body leaned near to me; she dropped her head down on my shoulder, and began to sob. I too was overcome with emotion. Until that moment, I had not even known for a certainty that she *could* cry. I had never seen her do so, though I had witnessed occasional bouts of silent grief. I held her in my arms and let her cry it out.

And so began her journey back to us. The Vaughns were pleased to hear of her progress, but they were now of the opinion that she was in need of moral instruction. This they would shortly arrange with Reverend Snover, stipulating also that Goldilocks must find some way of apologizing to Nurse. They had granted that I might reunite Teddy and Goldilocks in the schoolroom at my own discretion. But being unsure as to how I could arrange the requisite apology, I thought it best to give the child a few more days in which she might recover her sangfroid.

At the same time, I hoped to somehow discover the origins of the fateful tantrum in which Goldilocks had actually bitten Nurse. Since Teddy was the only one who could speak, I looked for some time to be with him when Nurse was not present in order to sound him out. This proved to be no great challenge, but getting him to talk to me was another matter.

"Master Teddy," I inquired over breakfast one morning. "I've been thinking of what I can do to make Goldilocks feel better so she can come back to the schoolroom with us. It would help if I knew what happened to upset her so. Can you tell me?"

Teddy stopped eating, with his fork halfway to his mouth, and paused a minute before answering, "I dunno. I didn't see."

"Really?" I asked. "I think it must have been something quite momentous for her to behave in such an awful manner. I'd hate to think Goldilocks would suddenly turn wild for no reason at all. We couldn't trust her then, could we?"

Teddy dropped his fork and looked down at his lap, considering. After a long silence he asked in a small, tight voice, "Miss Brown?"

"Yes, Teddy."

"What are Gypsies?"

Perplexed, I responded, "They are travelers. They move from place to place, carrying their homes with them."

"But do they buy children?"

I nearly gasped as I realized the likely source of such a cruel threat, and felt a rush of anger at Nurse's perfidy. "No, Teddy, they do not buy children. That's a terrible fib."

"What about bear cubs? Do they buy those? Do they make them do tricks for money?"

I answered carefully: "I don't know about wild bears, Teddy. Perhaps they do. But not with Enchanted bears, like ourselves. There are laws about such things."

He seemed to contemplate this for some time, though he spoke no more of the matter. I tried to go about the school day as usual, but Teddy was so listless and preoccupied that I might as well have been talking to myself. Only when Nurse put in an appearance did he show any reaction, and that was to fold his arms on his desk and bury his face in them. Nurse could hardly have missed the gesture, and I found it a fascinating study to observe her demeanor as she met with this and other blatant forms of Teddy's rejection throughout the day. Each time she tried to approach him, he turned his back on her, folded his arms, and brooded, precisely as I had seen his father do on occasions when he was displeased. This was unprecedented. Nurse's expression flickered between pain, anger, and melancholy. Whatever her role in fomenting this trouble, she had obviously not counted on Teddy's complete alienation from her, or his brokenhearted pining after Goldilocks. As the days passed, and his rebuffs continued, I saw a humbled Nurse, a deflated and repentant Nurse. Dared I hope this represented a turning point in her checkered career? Could she reform, for the love of Teddy?

Meanwhile, I prepared Goldilocks to make her apology to Nurse. I told her, first, that I was convinced Nurse had done something to provoke her, though I did not know what, but the fact remained that she had bitten Nurse, and thrown a tantrum, and for that she must apologize, just as any good little girl would do. She could accomplish this by offering her hand to Nurse in friendship.

"This may seem unfair," I told her, "but manners are what separate us from the wild beasts. Besides, the Vaughns want to be proud of you, as I do."

At first Goldilocks shook her head vigorously and stamped her foot, but I spoke to her at some length during the following days, assuring the child that I would be watching over her; that if Nurse mistreated her in any way, she had only to bring it to my attention; and most of all that Teddy was waiting for her, and was distraught without her. At this she finally nodded her acquiescence and threw her arms about my skirts.

Thinking it best to prepare Nurse for the encounter as well, I privately apprised her of my plan, and requested that she accept the child's hand when offered. What her true response might have been I could not be sure, for she opened her mouth to speak, but, seemingly thinking better of it, closed it with a little pop. Then her expression changed into a sickeningly sweet smile, and she answered, "Oh, of course, of course, the little darlin'," while rubbing the big bandage she still wore. "Won't that be charmin'?"

Finally the morning came when Goldilocks was returned to the schoolroom, whereby a joyous reunion occurred with Teddy. At first I thought Nurse would not put in an appearance, but she wandered in shortly before noon, red-eyed and weaving slightly. I quickly prompted Goldilocks to make her gesture, and held my breath as the child walked purposefully over to Nurse, made a commendable curtsy, and bending down, extended a hand to her. An awkward moment passed while Nurse reached out and took Goldilocks's hand, raising her other paw as if to strike her. I quickly moved to place myself between them, when Nurse, smiling sweetly, carefully stroked Goldilocks's golden hair, and murmured, "Pretty-pretty. Teddy's play-pretty." Goldilocks froze, suffering Nurse's touch with palpable reluctance, but Teddy called the child's name out just as she began to tremble, and she retained her self-control. The critical juncture had passed. Nurse unsteadily retreated to her polluted little corner and soon began to snore, Goldilocks resumed her place next to Teddy, and my schoolroom was at last restored to its former felicity.

Though I did not relax my vigilance in the days that followed, I saw no sign in Nurse of hostility toward Goldilocks; rather, she seemed to regard the child now as Teddy's pet, or toy, to be looked after because it made Teddy happy. Teddy responded by returning to his previous sunny disposition. His manner toward Nurse was once again unfailingly affectionate, with an important difference: Nurse now understood that Teddy, having once withdrawn his affection, might do so again if goaded. The lock had cracked, and the chains were slipping. Her unwholesome hold over him had developed a fatal weakness in the form of a diminutive golden-haired girl, and I privately rejoiced at it.

The Vaughns, upon hearing of Goldilocks's gesture of contrition, appreciated that the girl's apology marked a new step in her "civilization," and from that day began to include her in their nightly family time, a decision that increased exponentially the frequency of Goldilocks's pink-lipped smiles. I was also invited to join them whenever I was free, as I had such a good rapport with the child and could manage her and read some of her gestures. Though this was another demand on my time, I found it very satisfying to be of such use to the family and the child. I did find it worrying that this new arrangement also increased the odds that someone among the household would spread the news of a human child living with the family of bears. What ripples that news would make in the Enchanted Forest, only time would tell.

27

Heartache

❧

By day, my little world had returned to peace and order. The children were doing well, and the Vaughns were pleased with my handling of the crisis. By day, my time was regimented, my thoughts were occupied. By day, I was too busy for grief. But by night, my self-possession deserted me. Now once again I was alone in the darkness, easy prey for all my fears and sorrows. Even now, it seemed impossible that Papa was gone, and many a night I soaked my pillow with missing him.

At the same time, Mr. Bentley was constantly in my thoughts. I had seen him only once since my return, a glimpse down a hallway, and a quick disappearance—enough to send my pulse racing, but no welcoming greeting to warm my heart. I even thought he might be avoiding me, no difficult task as we worked and resided in different wings of the manor. Alone in the dark, I asked myself if I could possibly have imagined the depth of feeling between us, or had he merely thought better of it once I was away? Had he perhaps had time to consider the difference in our stations? Wouldn't the son of a viscount expect to marry a female of some fortune? And I, a dower-less nobody, what did I have to offer him, except myself? And yet, I envisioned again and again the way he lit up with happiness at the sight of me, the way his eyes melted into mine when he spoke to me, and I asked myself whether that could be merely kindness.

Perhaps it was this aggregate of grief, loneliness, and uncertainty that finally dismantled all my carefully erected defenses. I had confessed to Papa that I was afraid of getting my heart broken. I admitted to myself now that it was already too late, for in the long separation from Mr. Bentley I had more than missed him; I finally accepted what I had avoided for so long: that I admired and loved him. In the lonely hours of the night, I dreamed of belonging to him, and he to me. I even dared to dream of a lifetime by his side; of a family of cubs around our feet; of growing old together, and tottering off into the sunset. If he was going to break my heart, I thought, then let it be broken thoroughly. "Love is not for the fainthearted," Papa had said, and so I dared to be bold. I resolved to seek Mr. Bentley out about resuming our Latin lessons, and see what developed. If he rejoiced to see me, his expressive face would tell me so, and if he was polite and distant, that too would give me an answer. All through the next day, my intended visit to Mr. Bentley was constantly on my mind. My confidence failed me several times as my inner voice whispered that I should wait for him to act, that if he wanted to see me, *he* would seek *me* out, but I felt that I must know his heart or perish.

At teatime, I made my way to Mr. Bentley's office with a mixture of hope and dread. Seeing that his door was open, I hesitated, then stepped in. Mr. Bentley was seated at his desk.

He looked up at me, and joy lit his face—and was just as quickly pulled back, to be replaced by an amicable but businesslike demeanor, with unmistakable sadness in his eyes.

"Ah, Miss Brown," he said politely. "How nice to see you back. Please allow me to express my condolences on your loss."

"Thank you," I responded. "I wanted to tell you how much I appreciated your note."

"How can I be of service to you?" he asked, a little briskly, still with the sadness in his eyes.

"W-well," I stammered, "I've come to consult with you about the Latin lessons."

"Ah, yes, about the Latin lessons," he said, looking like a bear in torment. "Your progress has been so admirable, Miss Brown, I was going to suggest that your proficiency is probably adequate by now to begin teaching—"

"Just what I was going to mention," I lied, trying to make it easier for Mr. Bentley, and save my own pride. I launched into a well-rehearsed speech that I had prepared against this eventuality. "I'm teaching the basics to Teddy now, and I feel confident that I have sufficient expertise to continue learning on my own. You've been an enormous help to me. I can't thank you enough."

"My pleasure to assist you, ma'am," he responded formally, after which an awkward silence ensued. This was nothing like the warm, companionable silences we had often shared in the course of my lessons. I felt suddenly chilled, almost frozen. I cleared my throat and said, "Well, then, that's settled. I won't take up any more of your time. Thank you again, Mr. Bentley. *Au revoir.*" I held my paw out for him to shake in an equally formal manner. His eyes turned suddenly brilliant and gentle as his paw grasped mine, but instead of shaking it, he slowly bent his head and kissed it. My breath stopped, as if that could keep the moment from passing, then he straightened, resumed the businesslike demeanor, and roughly bade me goodbye. I backed out of the room, then turned and ran, my thoughts a jumble of confusion and grief.

Alone in my own room, I had no tears. I sat staring at the cold, empty grate, dreams shattering silently in my soul. As daylight faded into darkness, I tried to make sense of the encounter. I had seen the momentary joy in his expression, I still felt his kiss on my paw, yet it was certain that our old association was at an end. Something had changed. Something else was stronger, more important, and it had come between us with a deadly efficiency. I might never know what, or who, or why. I had no right to demand such explanations, but how could I fight an enigma? Papa had not schooled me, after all, in the feminine arts of flirtation and romantic intrigue. I had only my simple heart to offer, and it had not been asked for.

Whatever moved him, I clung selfishly to the hope that the feelings he had for me would not be so easily set aside, for I knew that he returned my sentiments, as surely as I knew my own heart. Not until I could look into his eyes and see neither joy nor torment there would I believe that he had stopped caring for me, and that conviction that he cared would have to be enough for me; perhaps it was all I would ever have.

"Papa," I said aloud, "I need you now!" There seemed to be only an empty echo where Papa's encouraging voice should have been, and this thought at last released a flood of hot tears, which racked my body as the darkness gathered around me. Finally, I lit a candle, and then sat up most of the night watching its feeble light flicker on the walls, rejecting the tray of food that Betsy brought me, all corporeal matters seeming crass and unendurable now.

I thought it odd, as I forced myself to go about my tasks the next day, that the sun still rose; that the sky was still a heart-stopping blue; that people still looked at me, greeted me, as they always had; that no one seemed to notice that my world had stopped turning. Only Teddy and Goldilocks approached me, as my attention wandered for the dozenth time, gently patting me on the face or arm to draw me back to them. I observed them as if from a great distance. Sometimes I thought that I must leave the Cottage forever or lose my mind, but there was Goldilocks. What would become of her if I abandoned her again now? What would become of Teddy, left at Nurse's mercy? I was trapped by my responsibilities, compelled to go through the motions of my normal life whether I would or no.

Weeks came and went in this manner while I waited like a dumb beast for the pain to pass. I took refuge in books. Books made it easier to get through a day. In lieu of lessons, I read countless fairy tales aloud to my charges, sometimes in the re-vised human versions to please Goldilocks, and sometimes in the original bear accounts. I lost myself in other people's stories, for I could not endure thinking of my own. This was not with-out its effect on me: the tales of courage, wisdom, compassion, and self-sacrifice inspired me to look further than my own trou-bles. Through it all, I was learning that my life would still go on, day by painful day, with or without my consent. Though no force on earth could erase Mr. Bentley from my heart, I began to understand that I must keep him in a safe, secret corner of it, where only I would know he resided, and take up the reins of my life once again.

First I assessed Teddy and Goldilocks to see how much they had regressed while I had been so remiss in my teaching efforts. I was pleased to see that there had been little backsliding. In fact, Goldilocks's good progress made me hopeful of assisting her to try something new. Now that she had come to trust us, her biggest fear was of the windows. I couldn't help but wonder if she had been frightened by the sight of that skulking brute, Gabriel, who had accosted me on the drive, but with the guards Mr. Vaughn had patrolling the grounds, I believed Gabriel's trespassing must have ceased. The only disturbance they had reported was a gang of village children roaming the property. I was optimistic that with the patrols, and our faithful Harry guarding us, I might eventually succeed in tempting Goldilocks to accompany us on our walks, which would surely be of great benefit to her health and vivacity.

Each day, after checking to be doubly sure there was no one outside to be seen, I enlisted Teddy's help to coax her a little closer to the windows, reassuring her that no one was about but those who were employed to keep trespassers away. Teddy pointed out to her that if anyone were nearby, we'd see their footsteps in the snow, and that there were none. One day, Goldilocks came all the way to the corner of a window and, with Teddy by her side, took her first quick peek outdoors. I actually smiled that day, making much of her, and was rewarded by her own tremulous smile, and another peek, slightly longer than the first. I was greatly encouraged by this, and even requested Mrs. Vaughn to send into town for some warm outdoor clothing and boots sized for a small human girl, in case we should succeed in persuading Goldilocks to join us in the snow.

Some days later I hit upon a strategy for convincing the

child to come outdoors. Goldilocks, who had done so well with looking out of the schoolroom windows, had been instructed to wait in her chamber with Mrs. Van Winkle until the clock struck two, then to look out her window. By that time, Teddy and I were dressed for the outdoors, and stomping our way to a place on the snow-covered lawn just below Goldilocks's window, where her little face duly appeared. We waved wildly and threw snowballs. Teddy had the idea of making snow angels, so, once again abandoning my schoolteacher's dignity, I sank backward into the snow and flapped my arms and legs until a respectable representation of an angel was made, next to Teddy's smaller one. Goldilocks was seen to clap at our efforts. She smiled down on us, nose flat to the glass, as we rolled up three big balls to make a snowman, but we had nothing at hand to make a face with. We decided that Goldilocks should have the honor of placing the features the next day if she would come out. This offer melted away the last of her reserve.

The following day, Goldilocks was bundled into her new outdoor clothes, and we three stepped out into the mantle of white. We made our way to the unfinished snowman, armed with coals for the eyes, a carrot for the nose, a corncob pipe, and an old scarf and hat. The child's cheeks were flushed and rosy, and her eyes sparkled as I lifted her to place the hat on the snowman's head. Already the fresh air had done her good, and I was inordinately pleased at the trust she had placed in me in taking such a step. I resolved to use all my influence with the child to encourage her to come on our jaunts and enjoy the benefits of Nature. And as innocently as that, the die was cast.

28

Intimidation

❧

It was at about this time that the Vaughns, having come to the decision that Goldilocks was not ready to attend a large social gathering like church, requested that Reverend Snover come to the manor for the child's private religious instruction. I had no qualms about this, knowing that Reverend Snover, always a great favorite with youngsters, would charm the child. Teddy was to be included, on the supposition that it would make the lessons more palatable for Goldilocks, and would do Teddy no harm. And so it happened that Teddy and Goldilocks and I waited in the schoolroom one morning for Reverend Snover's arrival.

He was due at half past nine, but the half hour chimed and he had not put in an appearance. We entertained ourselves by watching out the window as Mr. Vaughn's new printing press was being delivered in crates amid much hubbub on the ground below. Strong bears in work clothes ferried each wooden box to the cellar doors and vanished within. I wondered how long it would take before the press was up and functioning, impatient for the time when our own paper, the *Plain Truth,* would begin to circulate in the community. Mr. Babcock might say what he liked in his slanted newspaper. We would soon have the means to refute it!

As I was lost in these thoughts, the clock chimed ten, and still Reverend Snover had not come. I wondered what could have detained him. I was beginning to be concerned by half past ten, when Fairchild came to the schoolroom door and beckoned me out into the corridor. There stood not Reverend Snover, but his new curate, Reverend Abraham Wright, his eyes staring at me from behind his thick glasses.

"Miss Brown, Reverend Wright is here to instruct the children."

"Oh," I said, struggling to keep the disappointment out of my voice. "You are most welcome, Reverend Wright. Is Reverend Snover well?"

"Reverend Snover is well. He is much occupied these days, but I shall do my utmost to fill his shoes," Reverend Wright pledged, with excruciating sincerity.

"I hope you like children?" I ventured.

"To be perfectly frank, I've had very little experience with children. I hope that won't be an impediment. They are persons, are they not?"

"Oh yes, most assuredly. But Goldilocks may need some time to get used to you. You might try storytelling. That is how I first befriended her. I must tell you that she is also easily frightened."

"Perhaps we can concentrate on cultivating the virtues, then, and leave sin and eternal condemnation for later."

I stared at him openmouthed, trying to determine whether

he was joking. Nothing in his physiognomy or deportment betrayed any hint of a sense of humor. Then the smallest of grins crossed his face. "A little joke," he said, so softly that I barely heard him. "Do excuse me. I'm a bit nervous." It occurred to me that he had also had very little experience with females, since his magnified eyes continued to stare at me so admiringly, as if he had never before seen one.

"Perhaps I might remain in the room, as a calming influence on Goldilocks?"

"Yes, thank you. That would be greatly appreciated."

With my most bracing smile, I welcomed him into the schoolroom, and introduced my students. Goldilocks, who had been hiding behind me, promptly forsook the shelter of my skirts and squeezed onto Teddy's seat with him, clutching his paw with her little white hand. Reverend Wright was wise enough not to insist that she sit at her own desk and merely acknowledged her presence with a nod. Without preamble, the somber clergyman launched into a homily on the nature of the Almighty.

Goldilocks seemed both fascinated and mystified, making me wonder if she had ever even heard tell of such matters before, and what questions she would ask if only she were able. As the good reverend continued on at some length, however, her attention wandered and was lost. Even Teddy, sitting politely upright, began to look a little out of focus, so that I watched for an opportune moment to request that the curate read the youngsters a story.

"Oh yes," he acknowledged. "I almost forgot." He immediately took the suggestion to heart and launched into the first story of them all, the biblical account of the six days of Creation, describing each new day in vivid detail. Once again

Goldilocks's eyes grew wide with interest, until the curate began to expound on the theme with a scholarly analysis. I loudly cleared my throat, and the reverend, looking my way, took my hint, and moved on to an elementary instruction in how to pray. Goldilocks put her palms together in imitation of Teddy, but her expression was troubled. Indeed, she seemed on the verge of tears, until Reverend Wright, intuiting her difficulty, explained to her that her prayers would be heard even though she could not speak them aloud. She rewarded him with a glowing smile.

Finally, the lesson over, the good reverend and I adjourned to the corridor, where I thanked him sincerely for his efforts, a gesture that he accepted in a vastly inflated proportion. "Oh, I thank *you*, Miss Brown," he effused. "I couldn't have done it without you and your consummate direction. I do hope you will make a habit of attending our lessons."

"I would be happy to attend the children's lessons if you wish," I responded, "but you give me far too much credit. I have done nothing to merit such praise."

"Really, I'm sure your helpful hints to me made all the difference."

I smiled and steered the conversation toward "goodbye," while Reverend Wright proffered his hope that he would see me at Reverend Snover's regular Saturday-night soiree. I had not attended one of the Snovers' gatherings since my return from home, in light of the fact that Mr. Bentley had always accompanied me to and from the vicarage each Saturday night, and that, even if I knew that he were willing, I felt unequal to spending an evening in his company. I brushed off Reverend Wright with an excuse, and offered to see him to the door. As we walked, we conversed in a desultory way about each of the youngsters, while I privately thought what an unusual bear he was: undeniably handsome except for the thick glasses magnifying his eyes to twice their normal size; good-hearted, but awkward and pedantic; and though conspicuously versed in knowledge gleaned from books, quite out to sea in ordinary relationships. I wondered how he might be improved by Reverend Snover's care and guidance.

It was later that same day, just as Teddy, Goldilocks, and I were coming in from outdoors, that the summons came from belowstairs for the three of us to join Mr. and Mrs. Vaughn in the front parlor. Mystified, I gave a cursory wash to the youngsters' faces, a brushing to Goldilocks's hair, and and a straightening to their clothes. As we approached the room, a stranger's raised voice could be heard within, which quieted suddenly as the little ones entered behind me, hand in paw. Mr. and Mrs. Vaughn were seated together on the divan, and standing directly in front of them was Chief Constable Murdley, with his mastiff-like jowls.

"Children," Mr. Vaughn said, "this gentleman is Chief Constable Murdley, from the police." Goldilocks immediately hid behind my skirts, but at my urging, managed an abbreviated curtsy and then ran to Mrs. Vaughn and climbed up on her lap. Teddy gave a little bow, then took his place next to his father. I stood off to one side, sensing the strained atmosphere, and wondered what Constable Murdley could possibly want with the children. He was stiff and imposing, and I hoped that he would not frighten them as much as he did me.

Mr. Vaughn calmly turned to Goldilocks and posed a question. "Constable Murdley wishes to ascertain whether you,

Goldilocks, are being well taken care of here. What is your opinion, young lady? Can you tell us yes or no?"

Goldilocks nodded vigorously and put her arms around Mrs. Vaughn's neck.

"As you can see, Officer, she has come a long way since we found her here, ragged, half starved, wild as a Tasmanian devil. Now she is well fed, well clothed, civilized, and happy. Furthermore, she is being educated in all appropriate subjects, including religious instruction. Most importantly, she has formed bonds with the family; obviously, she is much attached to my wife, and she and Teddy are playmates, schoolmates, and fast friends."

"But no *human* playmates? None of her own kind?" the constable interjected.

Mr. Vaughn's brow lowered ominously, and for a moment I thought he would not answer. "No," he finally said. "Mrs. Van Winkle, the woman who minds her, is human. Until recently the child has been too easily frightened to introduce new people to her." Turning to me, he inquired, "Have you anything to add, Miss Brown?"

I wanted to shrink from the constable's attention, but I sensed how important it was to speak up on the child's behalf. "She is applying herself in school. She has nearly caught up with Teddy in a very short time. They work well together, and spur each other on."

"Well?" the constable snorted. "How can you tell that when she doesn't even speak? What about that? The girl doesn't even speak!"

Mrs. Vaughn responded with elaborate courtesy. "Sir, we have had a specialist in to examine her. It was his opinion that the child suffered some trauma before she came here, which caused her to lose her voice. No one can tell if it will return."

"As for the schoolwork," I added, trying to keep the resentment out of my voice, "it only takes a little ingenuity to test her comprehension. For example, I might write 'Stand up' or other instructions on the blackboard. If she follows the instructions, then I know she reads and comprehends."

"If you please," added Mrs. Vaughn, "now that you've seen the child, I'd prefer to send the little ones from the room rather than speak in front of them. You can see, can you not, that she is in good health and spirits and well cared for?"

Constable Murdley emitted a deep "Harrumph!" then added, "She needs to be with her own kind! *That's* the truth of the matter."

I felt as if I'd been slapped. With a few callous words he had dismissed all we'd done for Goldilocks! The Vaughns too looked affronted and appalled as the tension mounted.

Mrs. Vaughn ushered Teddy and Goldilocks to the door, requesting that Teddy lead her back up to the schoolroom, then she turned on the constable. "Her own kind left her starving and ragged, stealing for a living. I see no special virtue in that."

"She belongs to someone, begad!" he expostulated. "You can't deny it!"

Mr. Vaughn stood, his wrath like a force of nature. Pulling himself up to his full height, he looked down into the constable's face and said tightly, "I know my rights, sir. We advertised in all the local papers, and no one's claimed her. She's had great care here, and I have the receipts to show for it, so unless you have a candidate with actual proof of parentage, she belongs to *us*!"

The constable harrumphed again, but he stepped back a

pace and slid a finger inside his collar as if it were suddenly too tight. His jowls trembled as he sought for words. "Well, ahem," he spluttered. "Ahem, we may not have the parent, I grant you, but you can bet there's one out there somewhere. I wouldn't get too used to this unnatural arrangement if I were you, that's all. No sense in getting attached to what don't belong to you."

"Thank you, Officer," Mrs. Vaughn interrupted, playing the role of peacemaker. "We'll take your words into consideration. Now, will you have some tea?"

"No, thank you, ma'am. I've said my piece, and I'll just be on my way. But this isn't over, I can tell you!"

Mrs. Vaughn called for Fairchild to see the constable to the door while Mr. Vaughn visibly restrained himself from saying more. Fairchild answered the call with such alacrity that he must have been standing directly behind the door, and I caught a glimpse of Betsy, too, so that I wondered if they had been listening at the keyhole. I speculated on how long it would take for the details of today's interview to make the rounds of the staff.

No sooner had the constable departed than Mr. Vaughn erupted. "The officious, impertinent blackguard! The cur! If he's so concerned about children, why isn't he out rounding up those village brats who insist on trespassing on my land? Why isn't he talking to *their* parents about *their* welfare? I'll tell you why! He simply dismisses our household as an 'unnatural arrangement'! 'Unnatural arrangement,' is it? As if kindness were unnatural! As if benevolence and affection were unnatural! If that isn't the Anthropological Society for you! He's one of their grand high chiefs, and so is Judge Slugby! And Babcock is the grand high chief of them all! Ever since he took over the *Town Crier,* he's been spreading his poison, and now it's come to my own doorstep! They've somehow gotten word that the girl's here, and they're going to make as much trouble as they can, mark my words. Of all the venomous, detestable snakes!"

Mrs. Vaughn cleared her throat and, catching his glance, nodded over to me. Mr. Vaughn stopped short and turned to me.

"Oh. Pardon me, Miss Brown. I'm afraid my temper has gotten the better of me." Then he turned back to Mrs. Vaughn, and continued: "The black-hearted swine! If he thinks we're going to be intimidated by him throwing his official weight around, he's sadly mistaken! I'm sending for my solicitor—I'll hire a whole team of solicitors if necessary! As if what I do in my own home is any business of the likes of him!"

"Mr. Vaughn, dear," interrupted Mrs. Vaughn, "couldn't we make Goldilocks our ward? Would that put everything right?"

He looked at her as if a fairy had just materialized in front of him. "Why, Mrs. Vaughn," he exclaimed, "that might just settle the matter! She *is* our ward, is she not? If we're not her guardians, I don't know who is! Won't *that* set the society on end! Why, I'll get Mr. Bentley moving on this right away!" He hurried toward the door, then stopped and turned to us, saying, "Oh. Please excuse me, ladies," and made his exit. Fairchild, apparently having heard him coming, opened the parlor door and stood well aside, as if making room for a passing whirlwind.

Mrs. Vaughn gripped my arm for support and put her paw on her heart. "Oh, they mustn't take her away!" she breathed. "Suppose she is claimed by some terrible people? People who will neglect and abuse her the way she was before?" She pulled out a lace handkerchief and dabbed at her eyes. "Poor little thing! Such an appealing child she's become. And Teddy. Just think of Teddy if she is taken away. Oh, calamity! Whatever would we do without her?"

29

The Plain Truth

꒰

I returned to the schoolroom, only to find it empty. On a hunch, I went down the hall, looked into the nursery, and discovered Teddy, Nurse, and Goldilocks kneeling next to the open trapdoor to the laundry chute, heads cocked to one side. Curiosity drawing me closer, I soon realized that they were listening to voices from down below, perhaps from the kitchen. I recognized Betsy's voice, clear as a bell, resounding up the chute, giving a somewhat exaggerated account of the confrontation with Constable Murdley in the parlor.

"And then the constable, 'e says, 'She belongs to *someone*, begad!' An' the master, 'e lit right into 'im. 'I know my rights,' 'e roars—"

"Teddy! Goldilocks! Come away from there," I called, at the same time marveling that it had taken less than five minutes for the story to spread to the kitchen, and now to the nursery. Teddy and Goldilocks looked up, startled, while Nurse hissed, "Shush!" and listened on. Though I abhorred her eavesdropping, I could think of nothing to do about it. I merely took the children into the schoolroom and tried to explain what had happened in terms they could understand. Teddy asked me, wide-eyed, "Did Papa fight the constable? Did he beat him up?"

"No, Teddy, that is not how civilized people solve their problems."

"But is the constable going to take Goldilocks away?"

"Not if your mother and father can help it," I answered. Since Teddy had implicit belief in the omnipotence of his mama and papa, this answer satisfied him.

Meanwhile, Goldilocks, her pale face taut with worry, fastened herself to Teddy's paw. I knelt down to the child's level and looked her in the eye, saying, "Mr. Vaughn is already making plans for how to keep you safely here, dear, and he'll have many others helping him. You must try not to worry."

"My papa will fix it!" Teddy added. "He can fix anything!" Somewhat reassured, Goldilocks still kept her grip on Teddy's paw.

I suffered a sudden pang as I was reminded of my own papa, and the faith I once had in his ability to "fix anything." Longing to feel that he was still watching over me, I would reflexively move my paw to the spot over my heart where my locket used to lie. Such a little thing it was, but so precious to me! I had even tried questioning Goldilocks about it, but my inquiry was met with only a blank stare. There was no use in getting angry at the child, but I wondered for the hundredth time if I would ever see my locket again. Putting away the thought, I turned my attention back to the children, and spent the rest of the afternoon with them out of doors in the snow, happily forgetting about the scene with Constable Murdley.

At teatime, I returned to my room determined to try one more time to elicit from the magic mirror some clue to the whereabouts of my locket, for I was sure that he knew more than his obscure riddle had revealed to me. Though all my dealings with him before had ended in frustration, I had now worked myself up into an angry heat, and was bent on having my own way. Accordingly, I rapped on the surface and urgently called to him. "Mirror! Mirror! Wake up!"

The mirror's carnival mask appeared dimly, and groaned, "Please. I have a headache."

"Then answer me quickly, and I'll leave you alone. Where is my locket? No hints this time. I want the facts."

"Oh, very well. You've caught me. The locket is inside the jade vase in the drawing room."

"Really? Really, Mirror, are you telling me the truth? Don't toy with me now!"

"The locket is inside the jade vase in the drawing room. Say it with me: The locket is inside the jade vase in the drawing room."

"You really mean it? All this time, the locket has been inside the jade vase in the drawing room?"

"Yes, the locket is inside the jade vase in the drawing room. Come on, say it! The locket is inside the jade vase in the drawing room. The locket is inside the jade vase in the drawing room. Doesn't that sound true?"

"What do you mean, 'sound true'? Is it true or not?"

"Just repeat it a few more times: The locket is in the jade vase in the drawing room. The locket is in the jade vase in the drawing room. Doesn't that seem true to you now? You can do the same thing with numbers. Try: Two plus two equals five.

Two plus two equals five. Two plus two equals five. Two plus two equals five. When you say it again and again and again, it seems true, don't you think? Just try it."

"Mirror, you are driving me to distraction. I don't believe for one minute that my locket is inside the jade vase in the drawing room!"

"You really must keep saying it, you know. Get all your friends to say it too. Get *everyone* to say it! Before you know it, it will seem really true, and that's just as good as truth. The locket is inside the—"

"Stop that!"

"Or you could try writing it! Anything written must be true."

"Stop!" I cried, banging my fist down on the top of the bureau.

"Two plus two equals f—"

"Stop it right now!"

"All right, but your locket is in—"

"I'm leaving now! Go back to sleep!" Instantly, the mirror went black, and once again I turned away in frustration. I knew the mirror was lying, but I couldn't stop myself from going down to the drawing room and discerning for myself whether the locket could be there inside a jade vase. Just in case. It took only a minute to determine that there was no jade vase in the drawing room. I buried my face in my paws, and gave in to despair. I felt it was time I accepted it: I would never see my locket again.

❧

It was two weeks later, as I was resting in my chamber after a tiring day, that Mr. Vaughn sent a message by way of Fairchild that the men's choir would be gathering in the basement at sunset, and that I was welcome to attend. I was thankful they had included me as part of their organization, but such a welter of angst and indecision was precipitated by this friendly invitation! With my whole heart I desired to go, but I had managed to avoid Mr. Bentley altogether for the past six weeks. Was I ready to face him again? I wondered if it were possible for us to have a simple friendship when it would always mean so much more than that to me. I imagined spending the evening hiding out in my room instead, while the meeting went on without me, and quickly rejected the idea. Refusing to think about it anymore, I decided to go. Momentarily forgetting I was in mourning, I tried to decide what to wear, then admonished myself for my vanity.

At the appointed time, dressed in my plain black mourning frock, I followed Fairchild to the lower cellar, only to find Mr. Vaughn and many other familiar faces gathered around the new printing press, which was now assembled and functional. The editor, Mr. Weatherby, was explaining that this was a Stanhope press, made entirely of iron—small and squat, but capable of producing 250 copies per hour. He was giving a demonstration, cranking out copies of the last page of our new newspaper, the *Plain Truth,* as others collated and folded them. Spotting Mrs. Snover among some of the other wives there, I went to stand with her. I couldn't help looking around furtively for Mr. Bentley. At first I could not see him. Our numbers had grown so that there was quite a crowd in the lamp-lit cellar, but when Mr. Weatherby began passing out printed pages, Mr. Bentley stepped forward and began to speak. My tears welled up involuntarily at the sight of him, with his deep, bright eyes and his noble demeanor, and I stepped behind the large gentleman standing next to me so that my distress would not be seen while I mastered my emotions.

"I've just learned that the society is pressing the town fathers to enact a curfew," he informed us. "No Enchanted animals on the streets after sundown. It's said to be for our own protection. Of course, all the town meetings are after sundown; this is just another tactic to silence us. With the Enchanted out of the way, they can pass any law that they like."

"They think they can stifle our voices while they legislate away our rights," said an outspoken pig in a dapper suit. "Most of you know me. I'm Edgar Pig. I'm the sole survivor of three brothers, and the head of my own masonry company. I've been around a long time, and it ain't hard to see where this thing is heading. If they pass this curfew, it would be just a matter of time before they make it illegal for humans and the Enchanted to mix at all."

"Surely most humans wouldn't go along with the society if they understood their agenda," Mrs. Snover objected. I thought of what such a law would mean to the Vaughns and Goldilocks, let alone the whole parish. Such a thing mustn't be allowed to happen!

"We can fight back!" cried Edgar. "Let the whole country-side know what's going on! And you can bet I'll be at the next town meeting, curfew or no! Babcock and the Anthropological Society won't have it all their own way!"

Exclamations of hearty agreement erupted among the assorted creatures and menfolk. "Here we have it," Reverend Snover announced. "'A few honest men'!"

"Ah, yes," Reverend Wright spoke up. "'A few honest men are better than numbers.' Lord Cromwell, I believe. Is it a war, then?"

"It is a challenge," answered Reverend Snover gravely. "We could, of course, contest the legality of such a curfew; we might even win. The greater battle is for the sympathy and good opinion of our ordinary citizens. Perhaps we can change some minds at the next town meeting. Let's make sure there's a good turnout!"

"I've got the notice right on the front page," pointed out Mr. Weatherby, "here in bold print: 'Big Doings at the Next Town Meeting!' I haven't said what the doings are; everyone will have to come and find out for themselves."

"That will suit our purposes quite well, thank you," said Reverend Snover while the members of the men's choir and the wives admired the notice on the front page. Much discussion followed as to possible stories for their next edition, and Mr. Vaughn asked me if I minded telling their reporter the story of the fight I had witnessed in town, saying that they would like to run a rebuttal of the version told in the *Town Crier*.

He assured me that they would not use my name, but only describe me as a bystander, and so I agreed. I was taken off to a desk in a corner and interviewed by a fast-talking raccoon with a piercing gaze, who asked for the "who, what, when, where, and why" of the story and recorded it with great dexterity. I was fascinated by his proficiency with words, and even thought I should like to try my hand at writing for the paper someday.

The gathering continued for some time after that. Many beasts and men had their say, but whether I would or no, my eyes followed Mr. Bentley. His observations seemed always full of discernment, courage, and reason, and I allowed myself to revel in being able to look at him and hear him without being noticed. As the meeting drew to a close, I was most sorry to tear myself away from this pursuit. At last we were all sworn to secrecy as to the location of the printing press, and each stout-hearted member of the group went carrying his bag of news-papers into the night to be delivered. As I turned to leave, I was detained by Mrs. Snover's hand on my arm.

"We haven't seen you at our Saturday-night gatherings since before Christmas," she said. "Won't you come tomorrow? Mother Hubbard will be there, and I'll be making your favorite roly-poly pudding." How could I explain to her how loath I was to encounter Mr. Bentley face to face? He had always walked with me to the Snovers' on Saturday nights. Would he even come if he knew I would be there? Was he avoiding me as well? I had given up my only entertainment in order to evade all such questions, but now I rebelled at the thought that I must hide from him. In the end I resolved to take the risk—to go to the Snovers' and let things unfold as they may.

30

A Skirmish

❧

On Saturday evening I lingered by the door with the ever-faithful Harry and his musket, trying to concentrate on breathing in and out as I waited to see if Mr. Bentley would appear. A footstep sounded on the stairs promptly at six o'clock, sending my pulse into wild glissandos of elation. I looked up to see him, to determine what his manner was, whether formal or friendly, so that I could quickly match it with my own. He was polite as ever, if a little subdued, and neither of us quite met the other's eyes as we said our brief hellos. Falling into step with a careful distance between us, we set off for the Snovers'. Before long Mr. Bentley began a light conversation about the weather, remarking on how lovely the snow looked on the evergreen trees, and pointing out signs that it would soon be spring. It required very little response from me, but it comforted me to hear his deep voice, and served to smooth over the awkwardness between us. By the time we reached the vicarage, the strain had dissipated, regardless of the river of emotion streaming just below the surface.

Reverend Snover greeted us with open arms. Though the white-haired little man only came up to my chin, he gave prodigious hugs, which warmed the heart and welcomed the soul. The assembled guests gathered about us while he made the introductions. Peter Pumpkin-Eater and his wife were there, as nice a pair of hedgehogs as you could ever hope to meet. Mother Hubbard, who helped me with my coat, informed me in an undertone that it was the first time Mr. Pumpkin-Eater had let his wife out of the house in years—that it was all due to the patient counseling and influence of Reverend Snover.

I was pleased to meet the Snovers' other guests: Edgar Pig, who had spoken up at the meeting of the men's choir the night before; Reverend Wright, treating me to his usual admiring stare; and a Mr. Drood, a mysterious man, new to the area.

Once we had gotten acquainted, and had our pleasant conversations over dinner, we adjourned to the parlor, where Mother Hubbard was the first to say, "You'll never guess what I found on my doorstep this morning! A newspaper! Not the *Town Crier,* but a new one. It's called— What was it? Oh yes—the *Plain Truth*! Imagine! Someone's gotten up a new newspaper, and it seems to be a whole different viewpoint, speaking out about some of the outrageous goings-on in town. It's certainly time somebody did!"

"Yes, it was delivered to me as well," stated Mr. Drood. "It seems to me like stirring up a lot of trouble. There will be some dire consequences when the Anthropological Society finds out who's publishing this paper."

"Maybe things need stirring up!" squeaked Mrs. Pumpkin-Eater, surprising everyone with the vehemence of her opinion. "Maybe if females had the vote, things wouldn't have come to such a pass!"

At this her husband appeared mortified and irate, and Reverend Snover, who was sitting next to him, placed a calming hand on his prickly back, and said, "We're all entitled to our own point of view, now, aren't we?" Mr. Pumpkin-Eater looked up at Reverend Snover's reassuring smile and took a deep breath as if he were trying to relax. Mr. Bentley, Edgar Pig, and Reverend Wright kept silent, as it had been agreed upon at the meeting the night before that everything about the paper was to be kept secret, with mail to be held at the Post Office until called for.

The talk quickly turned to the Anthropological Society, and its manipulation of local politics. The gossip about Constable Murdley's attempt to intimidate the Vaughns had spread over half the countryside by this time, with several melodramatic touches added in. When Mrs. Snover asked me if I could corroborate the story, I replied that contrary to what they had heard, neither Constable Murdley nor Mr. Vaughn had actually thrown any punches, and that the children and Mrs. Vaughn had not been reduced to tears.

"Let me commend you, my dear," said Reverend Snover. "I could use a great many more like you, dousing inflammatory rumors and innuendos. I've found that no situation is so bad that gossiping tongues can't make it worse."

"But it's not all idle gossip, Reverend, is it?" Mother Hubbard asked.

"No. The threat is quite real, but we must meet it with logic and justice, not hysteria and vengeance." Just then there was a knock at the door. A moment later Maggie entered the room, telling Reverend Snover that he was wanted urgently—that Constable Murdley's young daughter was ill and had taken a turn for the worse.

"Do excuse me, all of you," the vicar said. "I am so sorry to leave, but duty calls. Please continue without me—the evening is young yet."

Some among us reacted with muted outrage. "Duty? Begging your pardon, Reverend, but is it your duty to minister to that snake Murdley?" cried Edgar. "Him what is stirring up all the hatrid ag'inst us?"

"Exactly so," replied the reverend quietly. "His innocent child is in need, and he too is one of my flock." He smiled benignly and added, "Perhaps a lesson in kindness will do him good."

The grumbling quieted at this gentle rebuke. Mrs. Snover exhorted everyone to please stay and keep her company. The reverend bade us good night, and the group was soon deep in discussion again. It seemed that the mysterious Mr. Drood had escaped some trouble, back in the city he had once called home, and had come to this quiet village expecting to find a safe haven. Now he wanted only a peaceful life, and, like so many, did not wish to involve himself in the strife. I wondered what it would take to move him, and others like him.

Outside the unshuttered windows, the wintery evening light was fading, and the mood turned somber. Mrs. Snover, ever the sensitive hostess, suggested that we join in some singing, asking me if I might accompany the group on the pianoforte. At this, Reverend Wright stationed himself by my side and assiduously turned the pages of the music for me. We struggled through some country ballads, and were finishing up with a few favorite hymns when there came a pounding at the door. Mrs. Snover answered it herself, and brought the caller directly into the parlor. It was Fairchild, looking harried and grim, and breathing heavily, as if he had run a long way.

"They've done it!" he rasped. "They've gone and done it! The dirty scoundrels! Mr. Vaughn sent me to warn you."

"Who? Who has done what?" we all cried.

"Slowly, now," Mrs. Snover urged him. "Is anyone hurt? Tell us from the beginning."

Fairchild took several deep breaths, then continued. "Mr. Vaughn just got word. Certain handpicked members of the City Council have just had themselves a secret meeting, and they've passed the curfew! They've got the constables and a gang of newly sworn-in deputies out tracking down the Enchanted, and they're looking to make an example of someone. Mr. Vaughn says that his people especially will be targeted to make him look bad. I'm sorry to cut your evening short, but the curfew started at sundown, and it's already dark. Some of you had best hurry on your way before the deputies catch up with you."

This was met with cries of "Villains!" and "Blackguards!" Reverend Wright stood up to his full height, quite tall for a bear, and said, "They can make an example of *me.* I'll go toward town till I find them, and lead them away from the rest of you. Let them arrest a member of the clergy and see how that plays out with the public." Without waiting for a response, he strode to the door, grabbed his coat, and was gone, leaving us all marveling at his unsuspected temerity.

"I have to pass through town to get home," Edgar observed anxiously. "I'd better go quickly."

"Perhaps you should stay the night," Mrs. Snover suggested. "All of you can stay the night."

"That is most gracious of you, dear lady," replied Edgar, "but I wouldn't give them the satisfaction. I'll take the long way around by the railroad tracks. Pigs can be stealthy enough when they want to be."

"We'll go through the forest," Peter Pumpkin-Eater said. "They'll never even see us."

"What about you?" Mr. Bentley asked me, rising. "Shall we stay safely here, or give them a run for their money?" There was a glint in his eye as if he rather relished the thought of outsmarting the law. With a rush of exhilaration, I leaped at the chance of sharing an adventure with him. If this were folly, I would deal with the consequences later.

"I believe we should go," I said, throwing caution to the winds. I gave a quick embrace to Mrs. Snover, thanking her for the delightful dinner and good company, and said goodbye to all. In a matter of minutes, Mr. Bentley and I were gathered at the door with Harry and Fairchild, taking our leave.

"Any sign of them?" asked Mr. Bentley.

"None yet," answered Fairchild, "though Mr. Vaughn's man said they were headed this way, coming by the Old Jones Road."

"Then we'll stay away from the roads, and take the back way through the cemetery and the woods. It's an overcast night, with no moonlight, so they'll have a hard time finding us." This plan being agreed upon, Fairchild, Harry, Mr. Bentley, and I set out through the churchyard, splitting up as we quickly wove our way back and forth around the gravestones in order to make our tracks more confusing.

Suddenly a dark figure lurched from behind a large tombstone, grabbing me by one arm, and I gave a little scream of surprise. From the corner of my eye, I could see more figures coming out of hiding—men, from the size of them—and our group being set upon. Aiming a hard slam at my attacker, I managed to loosen his grip enough that I was able to wrench my arm free, and, not pausing to look back, I made for the shortcut through the woods on the other side of the churchyard as fast as I could go. Listening for signs of pursuit, I dodged around tombstones, bushes, and trees, intent on putting some distance between myself and the band of men. I had almost reached the path through the woods when I heard footsteps gaining on me. Realizing I could not outrun my pursuer, I turned to meet him, and collided with the fast-moving form of Mr. Bentley coming up behind me. Before I knew what was happening, we were stumbling to the ground with his arms around me to break the fall. I found myself flat on my back in the snow, with the wind knocked out of me, and Mr. Bentley by my side whispering to me to breathe. I had several terrible moments where I was afraid my breath might never come again, or that the men would find us there, but my breath did finally return, bit by agonizing bit, and we were apparently hidden from the view of our pursuers, so we remained still and silent as the men roamed through the cemetery in the darkness with ever-louder threats and growing frustration.

"It's a crime to resist arrest!" one shouted. "Just wait till we catch you. The constable will throw the book at you!"

While the deputies searched in vain through the cemetery, Mr. Bentley and I quietly rose and sneaked toward the path and into the woods, where we found Harry already waiting for us. Fairchild, the only human among us, hung back on the path to see if anyone followed. Soon several of the men ran up, all out of breath, and Fairchild, pretending to be one of them in the darkness, shouted, "They didn't come this way! Try over there!" and pointed in another direction. The men hurried off after the false lead. We bears crept further into the dense woods, with Fairchild following behind.

We traveled silently toward home, straining our ears to hear sounds of pursuit. After a time we perceived raised voices behind us yelling, "This way! The tracks lead into the woods!" and I felt a rush of trepidation as I tried to place each foot quickly and quietly in front of the other, all too aware of the tracks we were leaving in the snow. I could only hope that the night woods were dark enough to conceal them. We went deeper into the wildest part of the forest, where dense thickets of underbrush were nearly impenetrable, and there we made several false trails, doubling back to hide in the thick brush. We crouched there silently as the men's voices became louder, and then they were nearly upon us. We held our breath as a group of armed and angry men approached, muttering imprecations. One of them stopped, not ten feet from where we hid, saying, "Look sharp, men. They must have come this way!" For a few dreadful moments the men milled about, unseeing, then passed on. Still, we hid, for perhaps a quarter of an hour, not making a sound.

At last Mr. Bentley stood up. "I think they've gone," he said in a hushed voice, and we each stretched our cramped limbs and climbed out of the thicket. "Are you all right?" Mr. Bentley asked solicitously as we made our way through the dense woods. I assured him that I was only shaken.

"We were caught right in their trap!" he exclaimed. "It's no secret that Reverend Snover entertains all kinds of mixed company on Saturday evenings. What better place to lie in wait and catch the Enchanted at night?"

"Really? Do they know who we are, then? Do you think they could recognize us if they saw us again?"

"I doubt that very much. It was quite dark, and they can barely tell us apart in daylight. They might guess who we were, but they can't prove anything."

As we traveled carefully along, we agreed that we were fortunate that no shots had been fired, probably because the gang of men were worried about shooting each other in the darkness. It had been a narrow escape, and we wondered if those who had departed before us had gotten safely away.

By the time we were halfway home, the clouds had broken up somewhat and a sliver of moon was trying to illuminate the snowy landscape. Harry was forging ahead, and Fairchild, having a harder time slogging through the deep snow, was lagging behind us. Mr. Bentley and I went on together, with him frequently helping me over some fallen log or other obstacle by holding my paw. How can I express what his simple touch did to my still-raw emotions? After weeks of despair and numbness, this unforeseen adventure had brought us together again. I found myself transported from that old, sad time, smiling to myself over nothing.

31

An Ending, and an Offer

❧

It seemed to me afterward like a particularly happy dream, traipsing along by Mr. Bentley's side, through the ethereal landscape, with our easy rapport restored. We came upon the back of the Cottage, traveling across the kitchen garden and up to the kitchen door. Reveling in Mr. Bentley's company, I found myself unwilling to go inside. Once I went in the door, the night was over.

I looked at Mr. Bentley, and he at me, and a moment passed. Suddenly he gripped my shoulders, holding me at arm's length. "Forgive me," he said. "I've done it again, despite all my vows."

"Done what again? What vows have you broken?"

"I've allowed my feelings to override propriety, and I've been totally unfair to you."

"Please, explain. How have you been unfair to me? It was just an exciting interlude."

"Much more than that to me, but I have no right to say so."

The happy warmth that had suffused me shrank into a cold,

hard little ball as I felt us getting to the heart of the matter, but still I asked, "No right? Why not?"

"I'm not free, Miss Brown. I am betrothed to my cousin, Amy Wallingsford. I have been since childhood. I can only beg your forgiveness for my conduct. In the beginning I told myself I meant only to befriend you, but my feelings—I have no right to mention them."

Suddenly everything fell into place with irrevocable force. The name he had called out in his illness: Amy. "No," I said, flinching as if from a blow. "No. No, you don't have any right to speak of your feelings, and I've no right to mention mine. But you've nothing to apologize for. You've behaved every inch the gentleman."

"Please understand, it was my father's and my uncle's idea, before I was even old enough to object. Amy and I were practically raised together, and we're so close, it would be unforgivable of me to break it off. She's already planning the wedding."

"Then say no more," I urged, shrugging out of his grasp. "It will be an easy matter for me to stay out of your way. You needn't fear that I'll make things difficult for you. I'll give up going to Reverend Snover's on Saturday nights."

"That won't be necessary," he said, the look of torment back in his eyes. "You see, I leave on the morrow. I've been called home—I don't know for how long. My brother, the viscount, is very ill, and I'm required to manage the estate's affairs until he is well."

I was temporarily struck dumb while I took this in. He was going away. Tomorrow he would be gone.

Finally, I recovered my voice. "I am so sorry to hear of it. I hope your brother recovers swiftly. I suppose I shan't see you again for some time, then. It will be easier that way. I'll take my leave now, Mr. Bentley, and wish you all the best," I said, forcing the polite words out of my mouth even though I could feel my heart splintering.

I opened the door and entered the kitchen, only to find it in almost complete darkness, with just the dimmest glow from the fire banked down in the hearth. A rush of cold dread sent shivers down my spine.

"Mr. Bentley, could I ask you for one last act of chivalry?"

"Name it."

"Could you walk me to my quarters? You see," I confessed, "I'm afraid of the dark." Never had I confided this to another soul, and I waited, stiff-shouldered, for the scoffing rejoinder. It never came.

"Of course," he replied, as naturally as if I had said, "May I borrow your umbrella? It's raining." He felt around on the mantel until he found a candle, and managed to uncover some embers with which to light it. "Lead the way," he said, handing me the candle, and we wended silently through the halls and stairways to my room. His solid presence calmed my fears, even as I struggled with the realization that this was the last time he would walk by my side. All too soon, we arrived at my door. A quick glance within reassured me that Betsy had left a fire burning for my return.

I set the candle down on a side table, searching for the right words. "Thank you, and Godspeed, Mr. Bentley."

At that he moved toward me, and kissed me on the cheek, but that was not enough. He reached for me, and I for him. We held each other in a tight embrace, as if the whole world were ending. With that bear hug, I told him everything I felt for him, everything I had dreamed of and hoped for with him, and all of my grief, and I felt his love and sorrow flow back to me in his strong arms. It seemed to last forever—or was it only a few moments?—until I wanted so much more, and I could no longer ignore the voice of warning within. I separated myself from him and stepped back, tears in my eyes.

"Let us not have anything to regret," I gently chided. "I would rather leave you with your conscience clear than full of tormenting memories."

He laughed softly to himself, his eyes shimmering with unshed tears. "How like you to worry about *me* when I was intent on toying with your affections. Very well. Goodbye, Miss Brown. No doubt when you see me again, I will be an old, married man, but you will always have my heart." He stepped back, only touching my cheek with his paw in a last caress before he picked up the candle and walked away.

I nodded speechlessly, and watched the candle's glow as he retreated down the hallway.

ᘐ

Morning found me bleary-eyed and numb, searching for a way to go forward with my life. I would lock away the broken pieces of my heart, and live with what was left. I thought it could be done; people lost limbs, or eyes, and somehow managed to get along with what remained. A heart was not so necessary, after all. I still could go through the motions of my life. I was grateful that Mr. Bentley had been honest with me. At least now I understood, and I knew it wasn't because he didn't love me. I thought that perhaps I should be trying to accept the truth gracefully—to be content to wish him and his bride every happiness. I knew that something more was required of me: that I should pray, for his sake, that he would eventually forget me. But despite the fact that he belonged to another, I clung to the knowledge that his heart was *mine*! This sat uncomfortably on the jagged edges of my conscience, but I could manage no better.

I wondered if Mr. Bentley had departed as yet. The thought of being left behind here while he took his leave was unbearable, and so I forced myself to go to church, despite the state I was in, it being somehow less terrible if I was not here when he left. I walked to the little church alone, unwilling to share my thoughts with anyone, and unwilling to have them interrupted. I sat in the back and forced myself to take an interest in what was going on around me. The service was packed with all sorts of villagers who were very interested to hear what their beloved minister would have to say about last night's developments. Entering the sanctuary, as if by some unspoken understanding, the humans and the Enchanted split off from one another and took up positions on opposite sides of the aisle, giving tangible proof of the growing divisions in what had always been a friendly congregation.

Reverend Snover was inspired that morning. Betsy had quietly pointed out to me that some very important members of the Anthropological Society were there. Mr. Babcock sat ostentatiously in the front row, decked out in a checked waistcoat and matching trousers and a large bow tie, and wearing an expression of the most profound disapproval. And yet, spurred on by the injustice of the outrageous curfew, the humble clergyman fired a cannonade of denunciation that echoed in the rafters of that little church, and rattled the consciences of those within.

In a speech born of outrage and love, his rhetoric soared like thunderheads streaming on a wild wind, so that afterward many swore that their hymnals had been blown shut, and their hats had tumbled away. Then, holding their attention in the palm of his hand, he quieted to dulcet tones, enticing his flock back to sanity and kindliness, and exhorting them to love their neighbors. This last was delivered with such eloquence that sniffles could be heard on both sides of the aisle. Still, some prominent citizens, Mr. Babcock chief among them, remained unmoved. Indeed, they sat so stiffly that it appeared their spines might snap with the strain. I wondered what trick of logic or rationalization allowed them to remain so impervious.

Reverend Snover closed the service with the announcement that Constable Murdley's young daughter had succumbed to illness during the night, and asked for the congregation's goodwill and prayers for the Murdley family. Everyone murmured in sympathy and assent, even among the Enchanted, who had presumably suffered many an injustice at the hands of Constable Murdley over the years. Despite this moment of unity, when the congregation lined up at the door to greet the minister and shake his hand, there remained an awkward distance between the human and Enchanted members of the congregation, and some left by a side door rather than face one another. Mr. Babcock, however, made a point of walking past Reverend Snover as if he had not seen him.

When my turn came to greet the reverend, I thanked him for his sermon, and asked him about the fate of Reverend Wright, who had run off to get himself arrested the night before, and was now nowhere to be seen.

"Ah, he'll be fine," Reverend Snover declared. "Only his

pride was hurt that no one would arrest him. He wandered around half the night looking for law enforcement. Three times he found them, only to be sent on his way with a warning. They didn't want him, you see, him being a clergyman. All he got for his trouble was a nasty cold. Mrs. Snover's tending to him over at the vicarage."

I felt a flash of sympathy for the unlucky curate. I had the thought that it might distract me from my own wretchedness to do a good deed and go cheer him up. Choosing between that and an afternoon alone with my own suffering, I made my way past the churchyard to the vicarage, knocking at the kitchen door. Mrs. Snover and Maggie were busy preparing Sunday dinner, but Mrs. Snover led me into the parlor, where Reverend Wright sat bundled in blankets by the fire, with his handkerchief at hand, soaking his hind paws in a pan of hot water.

"Oh, Biss Brown, how kind of you to cobe," he enthused, his eyes shining feverishly. "Do sit down."

"I'm so sorry to see that you are sick, Reverend Wright. Can I bring you anything? Some tea, perhaps?"

"Oh no. Bissus Snover keeps be well supplied. I was only needig a little copany. And here you are."

"I'm afraid you've had a difficult night of it. How are you feeling?"

"Oh, that is hardly ibportant. Feelings pass. What is ibportant is to do what is right and needful, don't you think?"

"Is that why you went rushing out to face the deputies last night?"

"I suppose it was righteous indignation. And, well, vanity."

"Vanity?"

"Yes, I bust confess. I was hoping to . . . to, well, hoping to ibpress you."

"Impress *me*? Whatever for?"

"Well, you see, Biss Brown, I'b very glad you're here. I have subthing to ask you," he said, blowing his snout into his handkerchief. "I believe there is a proper forb to follow. Please forgive be if I ab not doing this correctly, but, well . . ."

Dragging his blankets around him, he stepped out of the pan of water and went down on one knee before me, creating puddles on the parlor floor. "Biss Brown, will you barry be?"

I nearly recoiled with astonishment. At a loss for words, I was suddenly reminded of Papa's injunction to be kind to gentlemen offering marriage, whatever your answer might be. "Reverend Wright," I began, thinking fast, "you take me by surprise. It's a very great compliment, but how did you settle on me? You barely know me!"

"Yes, well, you see, Biss Brown, since first we bet, I have been observing your conspicuous virtue and ladylike debeanor, not to bention certain talents that would be bost helpful and attractive in a clergyban's wife: a certain social ease, for exabple, which I'b afraid I lack. It is clear to be that your influence would bake be a better and bore effective pastor. I ab convinced that you are precisely the sort of febale I should like to have as a help-bate in by vocation."

"Help you in your vocation? That sounds very businesslike, Reverend Wright. Am I the first female you have made such an offer to?"

"Well, there was another, shortly after by graduation frob sebinary. A very ebotional febale, as it turned out. It ended rather badly."

I marveled inwardly at his impenetrability, though it seemed more like naiveté than callousness, and I thought I might try to be of help to him.

"Perhaps you neglected to mention anything like romance to her?" I hinted.

"Oh, but I don't believe in baking such a decision based on subthing as changeable as robance. Far better to deterbine suitability with the intellect and good sense. By own parents had such a batch, and they got on rather well together. Of course, by buther has barely spoken for the last thirty years."

Seeing that it was hopeless to guide him to any other way of thinking, I considered it best to give him my answer quickly: a standard speech Miss Pinchkin had counseled her charges to have always at the ready. "Reverend Wright, I am sensible of the great honor you have bestowed on me, and I believe you will make some fortunate female an excellent husband one day, but I must tell you that what you ask is impossible."

"Did I do it wrong?" he asked, despair written on his face. "Perhaps you are overcub by by ibpetuosity? Perhaps in tibe you bight look on the batch bore favorably?"

"No, Reverend Wright. It is only fair to tell you, my heart belongs to another."

"Oh? But I don't bind. That needn't be an obstacle—unless subone has already bade you an offer. Are you hitherto engaged?"

The question pierced my heart like an arrow. How I wished I could tell him I was. I cleared my throat and said, "That does not signify."

"Oh? Then you're not engaged?" said the bear, sneezing vehemently. "Perhaps I bay hope?"

"Reverend Wright, do get up. This can't be good for your cold. I've given you my answer. Please accept it. Here, now put your feet back in the pan. Shall I add some more hot water?"

The dejected bear raised himself unsteadily, slumped back

into his chair, and sighed. "I suppose," he said. I fetched the tea-kettle from the kitchen, asking Maggie to mop up the puddles, and I returned to the parlor and poured steaming water into the pan.

"Now, would you like me to read to you? Something amusing, perhaps? *Gulliver's Travels*?"

"You would read to be?"

"Of course. Can we not be friends?" I asked, moved by my own aching heart to treat him with sensitivity.

He smiled broadly as I adjusted the blankets about his shoulders, settled into the chair opposite him, opened the book, and began to read. "'My father had a small estate in Notting-hamshire; I was the third of five sons.'" I read on for some time, until Reverend Wright seemed relaxed and sleepy, and the awkwardness of the sudden proposal was forgotten. We parted amicably, and despite the absurdly businesslike nature of his offer, I reflected that it was, after all, my first proposal. I should feel complimented, but I was overwhelmed by the thought that it was from the wrong bear. I felt myself tearing up at the cruel irony, and though Mrs. Snover put her head in the door and invited me to stay for Sunday dinner, I politely turned her down and took my leave.

32

Nurse's Kindest Sympathy

❧

The first day of spring announced its presence with a wail of wind and a slashing torrent of sleet. By noon a glittering glaze of ice encrusted every surface, accumulating drop by deadly drop until even mighty branches cracked with the weight of it and fell to earth. We remained cooped up in the schoolroom, dreaming of warm breezes and fragrant blossoms, watching dejectedly at the windows as the elements colluded against us. The children especially became fractious without their regular exercise.

Then, within days, a sudden thaw gusted in, turning the forest into a dripping morass of melting snow and mud. Harry and I ventured out to survey the surrounding woods and see if they were safe for the children. We slogged through the cheerless landscape, picking our way carefully around puddles and fallen branches. No gentle zephyrs wafted by, portending winter's end; no birdsong called awake the nascent buds; no small green shoots hinted at better things to come. All of Nature seemed to be conspiring to withhold the blessings of spring, waiting. Harry, being of a superstitious bent, said it was an evil sign, and kept crossing himself when he thought I wasn't looking. Ambleworthy Stream, usually so placid and contained, had transformed overnight into a roiling river, subsuming its banks and everything in reach, leaving treacherous black pools in the hollows. Only the path we called the Giant's Walk, named for its population of huge old trees, was well above water, though slick with mud.

"What is your opinion?" I asked Harry. "Is it safe to bring the children out here?"

"Safe enough, if we keep to the path, and away from the stream. A bit of mud never hurt, and they'll have the two of us watching over 'em. Not like that band of dirty ragamuffins what runs loose all over these parts with nobody lookin' after 'em at all. One of these days one of 'em will come to a bad end. See if they don't!"

"Where are the parents? I wonder."

"Eh, miss. From what I hear, these wild 'uns all come from one mother, and she's enough to make yer blood run cold. Maybe they're here in the woods hidin' out from 'er."

∼✺∽

Back at the Cottage, Harry repeated his assessment of conditions to Mr. Vaughn, who encouraged us to resume the youngsters' healthy outings, and instructed Harry to keep the unsupervised village children off the property for their own good. After that, Teddy, Goldilocks, Harry, and I continued our daily walks, doggedly venturing out in the dismal weather. Day after day, we trod carefully down the Giant's Walk, determinedly searching for hidden proofs of spring, as an incessant drizzle fell from the slate-gray sky above, and the brown mud beneath us sucked at our boots. The only colors to be seen were in the soft rose tint of Goldilocks's cheeks, and the golden halo of her hair.

At about this time, I was invited to a family celebration held in Goldilocks's honor. Sweetmeats and punch were being served in the back parlor, for Mr. Vaughn had chosen the moment to announce that Goldilocks was officially his legal ward. The child was given to understand that she was now part of the family. To demonstrate the fact, Mrs. Van Winkle had been retired with a handsome pension, and Goldilocks had been moved from her apartment up in the east wing to reside with Teddy in the nursery, a special treat for both the children. I had immediate misgivings about this, knowing what Nurse was, and what she was capable of, but the decision was not mine to make. I could only hope that Nurse would continue to regard Goldilocks as Teddy's beloved plaything, and look after her accordingly. After recent developments with Teddy, I was all but convinced that Nurse's better nature was on the ascendant, but alas, it was not to be.

The next afternoon, I lingered in the schoolroom after the children had gone to tea. I was putting things to rights and making notes for the next day's instruction, as was my habit. I sometimes took my tea there if I had a lot to do. I had been sitting for some time in the empty room, reading, when I sensed a presence behind me. Startled, I turned about to behold Nurse lurking there, rubbing her paws together and looking unbearably smug.

"You," I said, a little testily. "You startled me."

"Oh, I just poked my head in and seen you sittin' here all

alone," she answered, suddenly bursting into inappropriate laughter, which faded off into periodic snickering.

"So you thought you'd keep me company? That's very considerate of you."

"Yes, company," she agreed, "seein' as how you're all alone."

"Well," I said, wondering what she was up to, and struggling to maintain a light tone, "was there something you wished to talk to me about?"

She began tittering again. "Oh, I just been havin' a little conversation down in the kitchen with Betsy and Cook."

"Yes?" I said, with exaggerated patience. I had no interest in the kitchen gossip, if it was even offered to me, which was rare. However, it was clear Nurse was full of some news she wanted to tell me, and I only wanted to get it over with.

"Oh, I thought you might like to hear. It's about a *friend* o' yours."

"Yes? Which friend?"

"Why, none other than your old *friend* Mr. Bentley!"

I should not have been surprised to hear her call Mr. Bentley my friend in such a suggestive way. From the time that we had begun my Latin lessons, the household gossips had linked us romantically. It would make the perfect excuse to torment me with news of him. Suddenly apprehensive, I asked, "Is he well?"

"Oh, he's *more* than well, I'd say. It's his brother, the viscount, that ain't so fortunate. He's the one what's died, leaving the title and all to Mr. Bentley. That's *Lord* Bentley now to the likes of you, eh, chickie?"

I paused for a moment, taking this in. "How very sad about his brother. I hope Mr. Bentley—"

"*Lord* Bentley!"

"Lord Bentley," I echoed. I looked straight into her eyes and said, "I hope that he'll be happy in his new life."

She covered her mouth with her paw and snickered convulsively.

"Surely you don't find his brother's death so comical?"

"Oh no, chickie. You ain't heard it all."

"Yes?"

"Oh, I hate to say, miss, you bein' such good *friends* with him an' all. I'd hate to think I might *upset* you."

"You positively concern me. Pray give me the news and be done with it."

"We-e-ell," she drawled. "It seems Lord Bentley is engaged! To his cousin! Has been since he was a cub!"

"Yes, I know," I responded without emotion, wondering if Mr. Bentley's engagement was now household gossip.

Far from discouraging her, this seemed to propel her onward. She leered evilly for a moment, literally hugging herself with delight. "Well, it seems they're plannin' a big bust-up of a weddin'. The invitations are goin' out to all the gentry. Imagine! All the finest people will be there to see them married, includin' the Vaughns. And then his cousin, Miss Wallingsford, will be *Lady* Bentley."

I struggled to keep my expression impassive as her beady little eyes nearly scorched my face, searching for a reaction, some telltale sign of anguish she could savor ever afterward, and report gleefully to the others. I stared dispassionately back, pretending to myself that she was speaking of someone else, refusing to think about it until I should be alone and able to allow myself to feel.

"'Course I don't expect they'll be sending an invitation to

the *governess,* but p'raps it would be just too awful for you any-ways, eh, chickie?" Here she patted my back with one paw, in mock sympathy, while she sniggered into the other.

As the full effect of Nurse's cruelty hit home, I pushed her away from me and rose from my seat, needing to be rid of her, but she clutched my paw in her own and stroked it, her manner fawning, intimate, and insufferable as she continued her cruel parody of concern.

"Oh, now don't tell me I've upset you!" she lamented. "Oh, the poor dear! And here I thought you'd rather hear it from a *friend.*"

"That's quite enough," I asserted, withdrawing my paw from her grasp.

She pulled at my skirts instead. "Does chickie want to be left alone? Oh yes, we'll leave her alone. All alone." She treated me to a particularly poisonous glare, and ground out, "Better get used to it, poor thing!"

I stood there, riveted by her eyes, those eyes that held no ember of warmth, no glimmer of pity toward me. Blinking, I pulled myself loose of her grasp and walked out of the room, her malicious cackle echoing after me.

It seemed an eternity before I reached my own chamber door, and still I could hear her unholy laughter, though I refused to look round and see if she was actually following me. Closing the heavy door, I was finally blessed with silence.

I sank into a chair as the news hit home. Shaken as I was, I told myself that nothing had changed. Mr. Bentley was now Lord Bentley, making an impossible barrier between us. But it had already been impossible. Nurse had only made it a little more real. Alone, she had said, I would be all alone, and she was right. All I could see ahead of me was a spinster's life, caring for other people's cubs, and eventually outliving my usefulness. And yet I could not let go of the thought of Mr. Bentley's last words to me: that I would always have his heart. I could still hear his deep voice saying it. I could still feel his powerful arms around me. I knew that I should try to wipe it all from my memory, but I clung to it more selfishly than ever, loathing my own weakness.

33

Ambushed

A week ground slowly by. When I thought of Mr. Bentley, I took refuge in a kind of unreality, avoiding the painful facts until such a time as they might actually stare me in the face. Meanwhile, Nurse had pared her mockery down to its distilled essence—that is, her intolerable meaningful looks, and a chronic snickering at the sight of me.

Since Goldilocks had been moved to the nursery, I had been keenly alert for signs of trouble from Nurse. Now I redoubled my vigilance, afraid that the crueler side of Nurse's nature, having been quiescent for so long, was once again on the rise. Yet it seemed from questioning Teddy that the worst she was guilty of in the nursery was frequently leaving the children to mind themselves while she napped. Under the circumstances, I could only be grateful that her malice was reserved for me.

The unnaturally cold and wet weather continued unabated, chilling the body and depressing the mind. In spite of this, another meeting of the men's choir was to be held. Though they would all meet afterward in Mr. Vaughn's cellar to gather the week's newspapers for delivery, Reverend Snover had pointed out that now that we had started the ruse of the men's choir, we had better keep up with it for appearances' sake. I heard Mrs. Snover say laughingly that many of the members had not set foot in the church for years before the invention of the men's choir, and that Reverend Snover was taking advantage of a good thing while he had the chance. Whatever the rationale, I was called on once again to play through the hymnbook while the gentlemen talked and kept a lookout.

I listened to the menfolk with half an ear while I played. It seemed that last town meeting had nearly erupted into violence. The Enchanted had arrived at the town hall in great numbers before sunset in order to beat the curfew, and then, after a very contentious meeting, they had simply stayed the night in the town hall, frustrating the intentions of the City Council.

The first issues of the *Plain Truth* had also provoked much excitement. Subscriptions were already streaming into the Post Office from enthusiastic customers, but there had also been incidents where ruffians—Babcock's men, no doubt—had chased away or beaten up those who tried to deliver the papers. Fairchild and others reported that the Anthropological Society was hopping mad about the new paper. They called it sedition, and fomentation, and vowed not to rest until they had found out who published it. I was alarmed to hear that there had even been talk of smashing the printing press.

Mr. Vaughn snorted at this. "They will have to find it first! This is precisely why we've kept the location a secret, but even if some of you are followed, and they find out where it is, they cannot get to it. There are still laws about private property."

"Yes," said Reverend Snover, "but they can make life very difficult for you, and for all of those who've volunteered to deliver the papers." I couldn't help but wonder just how the Anthropological Society would go about making life difficult for Mr. Vaughn. Though I admired his intrepidity, I was filled with a vague unease.

Mr. Vaughn suggested that our people go out in groups. He said to make sure there were some good fighters in each group, and to stick to the woods and the back ways as much as possible. His suggestion was accepted favorably. Reverend Snover led the gentlemen in a couple of hymns to sing for the following Sunday, and when the rehearsal was finished, they formed up in parties of three or four, a sturdy bear or scrappy badger with each, and made off into the night. I heard no more of the fate of the brave adventurers through that long weekend, and so hoped there was no more serious trouble.

$\sim$

Life in the schoolroom went on as usual, though we were growing as dull as the gray weather. It had snowed several times in recent days, in defiance of the spring season, and the wind was biting cold, but we were marching stalwartly along the Giant's Walk one afternoon, breathing deeply, when some distance away a human child appeared, bobbing his head out from behind an enormous tree, and pausing as if deliberately waiting to be seen. Goldilocks gave a strangled cry and immediately hid behind me.

"Look at that! Bold as brass!" bellowed Harry. "It's one o' that gang o' vagabonds what's always playing about on the master's property as if they owned it!"

"Are they village children? Who looks after them?"

"No one tends to them at all. The master says to send them on home for their own sakes before one o' them gets hurt, but they're a canny lot, and I've yet to catch one." It was clear from his tone how deeply this rankled him, as if it were a reflection on his own abilities.

At that moment two other children, behind two other trees, a bit further away than the first, briefly revealed their grimacing faces and laughed in a provoking way, as if daring us to do something about it. The effect on Harry was just as desired. "Here!" he spluttered, handing me his gun. "Keep it pointed up. If you need me, fire into the air." Then he took off at a run while the offending children scattered from behind one tree trunk to the next, appearing and disappearing, taunting him and throwing stones until they had lured him some distance away, and I could no longer see him in the woods. I wondered briefly what he would do if he did manage to catch one, or if he even had a plan, the chase having become an object in itself.

So engrossed was I in this development that I had barely noticed Goldilocks, struggling to wrap herself inside my voluminous coat, and making a soft keening noise that I had heard from her on occasions when she was very frightened. Teddy stood by helplessly. "Goldilocks," I pleaded, "come out, dear. There's nothing to be afraid of. It was just some children, and now they're gone."

The girl shook her head vigorously, still keening, and, separating herself from my coat, grabbed one arm free of the gun, which I had been holding with both paws, and tried to pull me back toward home.

It was at that moment that I saw the child, then two, then

perhaps ten, come out of hiding. Turning, I saw that there were more than I could quickly count, approaching us on every side, as grimy and sullen a lot of human young ones as I could ever imagine: an assortment of big and little, boys and girls, wearing a haphazard variety of flimsy clothes inadequate for the weather, surrounding us all in a ring. These were like no children I had ever seen. Faces too cynical to be childlike, eyes dull as lead, they pushed and jostled and kicked one another like savages, so that I barely knew whether to feel compassion or dread.

"Hey, Rat!" one of the big boys barked. "Where do you think you're going?"

Cries of "Hey, Rat!" and "Yeah, Rat!" rang out around the circle.

Goldilocks clung to me now, tears rolling silently down her cheeks, looking very small and defeated. And then it struck me that *she*, apparently, was "the rat" they were jeering at.

"Goldilocks," I said softly to her, "do you know these children?"

She wouldn't look at me, but hid her face in my coat. Teddy, bewildered but steadfast, stood next to her, holding her arm and shielding her with his body.

"Where you been, hey, Rat? Looks like you been living it up," a girl sneered, looking Goldilocks up and down. "I like that coat. I think it would just about fit me."

Another shouted, "Somebody go get Gabe! Won't *he* be tickled!"

My heart began to race as two of the children ran off. Gabe. That would be Gabriel, no doubt, the same overgrown, unwholesome brute of a boy who had accosted me on the driveway. I was suddenly reminded of his enigmatic insistence that he wanted "the rat." Now at last it was clear that he wanted Goldilocks! But why? My throat went suddenly dry. Where was our faithful guardian now? At least I still had the gun. "Fire into the air," Harry had said. This was not as simple as he must have assumed, since I had never fired a gun before, but perhaps the thing would be useful for intimidation if the need arose.

"Who are you? What do you want?" I asked with a feigned calm. I thought quickly that I might have an opportunity here to shed light on the tantalizing mystery of Goldilocks's previous life, and so I must tread carefully.

"Why, we're Rat's *family*," brayed one boy, "ain't we, Rat? Did you miss us?"

Taken aback, I scanned the dirty faces for any resemblance to Goldilocks's features—the wide forehead, the turned-up nose, the little pointed chin—but, at a quick evaluation, none seemed like hers. I bent over and whispered to Goldilocks, "Is that true? Are they relations?"

She stared soulfully into my eyes and shook her head. I wanted to believe her, but I had to wonder whether she would deny their relationship out of fear of them taking her away from us. A healthy fear, one for which I could hardly blame her.

I turned back to the boy who seemed to be their unofficial spokesman, and said, "If you really were her family, surely you would have claimed her long before now! There were advertisements in the newspapers."

"In the papers? So what? Ain't none of us can read." There was considerable mirth over this, not like children's laughter, but hard and mean, as if they had never really been children at all.

"Then how did you think to look for her here?" I asked, suspecting that Gabriel had known where to look for her from the beginning, but wanting to see what they might reveal.

"Gabe told us," piped up one of the younger girls, only to be met with a chorus of reprimands, and a vicious kick from the boy next to her.

"Hush up!" exclaimed the first boy. "Don't you say nuthin' 'bout Gabe! He'll be here any second." This resulted in a communal silence as they exchanged alarmed glances with one another.

"Is Gabriel your leader, then?"

"He's our *brother*!"

Another revelation. I wondered if there was any chance that the vile creature was actually Goldilocks's brother as well. My fears for her multiplied with each passing minute.

"And where are your parents?" I asked, trying another tack. This was evidently a splendid joke. They reacted as if they had just been asked to deliver up the man in the moon. "Wouldn't you like to know!" hooted the older boy. Then the group's hilarity ended in an instant as heavy footsteps behind me signaled the arrival of their big brother. I turned, and confronted him. I held Goldilocks close with one paw while Teddy stayed glued to her opposite side. In my other paw I tightened my grip on Harry's musket, deciding in a moment whether I would really shoot Gabriel if he threatened us. With some surprise at myself, I realized that yes, I would. I did not immediately take aim at him, hoping to avoid the necessity.

"Well, ain't this just prime!" the snide voice resounded as Gabriel approached us. "Look what we 'ave 'ere! If it ain't the teacher lady 'erself, and—what's this?—my own little sister what's been livin' it up, havin' tea and crumpets while 'er own family starves. Praise be! Won't it warm *dear old Mother's heart*?" He followed this with a laugh so ironic and insolent that had I been closer to him, I might have slapped him. The gang of children laughed when he laughed, and stopped when he stopped. "You make me sick!" he growled suddenly. "Livin' with a bunch of filthy animals! Puttin' on airs! And look at this little whelp, born with a silver spoon in 'is mouth!" He glared at Teddy. "Think yer sumthin' special, I bet. Nothin' but a worthless *animal*, I say! Somebody oughta taught ya yer *place*!"

He continued his approach until I put my paw up and said, "That's far enough." Eyeing the weapon I held, he stopped. "What do you want with us?" I asked, with as much civility as I could summon. Goldilocks burrowed deeper in my coat, still hiding her face, and Teddy, wide-eyed and frightened now, stayed staunchly by her side.

"Why, we're just lookin' out fer our dear lit'le sister what we 'ave missed lo these many months." He took off his battered felt hat and clutched it to his heart in mock sincerity, and I noticed a fresh-looking scar on his forehead.

"You've suspected where she was all along," I countered, refusing to refer to her as his sister until that had been proved.

"Why, what's she been sayin' to you? You can't believe a thing she says! The truff of the matter is, miss, she's a terrible liar and a thief, though we've tried to change 'er ways. She's such a 'ardened criminal that when I saw 'er 'eaded toward the manor one day, I suspected she'd be up to 'er thievin' tricks, and I followed 'er. I lost sight of the whelp, going in, and when she didn't come out, we thought for sure she'd been caught red-handed and sent hoff to jail. Y'see, we knew she'd end up behind bars sooner or later. She's a bad 'un, she is."

Goldilocks showed her face then, as outraged and indignant as one small face could be.

"So you had no idea whether she was here today? You just happened to run into us by chance?"

A cunning look came over his detestable face, and his voice lowered as his hand crept toward his belt. "Oh, I've got my reasons, miss. See, I've got a coupla scores to settle with you. First is this," he hissed, pointing to the red puckered scar on his forehead. "This is what I got from my dear old mother that day when you wouldn't accept my little commission. Just a little cooperation from you is all it woulda took. Wouldn't 'ave cost you nuthin, but it cost me somethin', see? A stick of firewood upside the 'ead is what. Me dear old mum don't like bein' thwarted, not 'er. And then you went an' ratted on me, miss, and after I was so careful to hexplain to you that you mustn't cross me."

His voice lowered to a dangerous growl. "Don't think I don't know why all these guards have been set about the place, or who set 'em after me, but they won't do you no good." He slipped his hand under his coat, and brought out a lethal-looking dagger, glinting like his steely little eyes.

"No, Gabe, no!" a tiny voice squeaked beside me as I raised the gun to my shoulder, and inexpertly pointed it in his direction.

34

Evil in the World

❧

I dared not withdraw my attention from Gabriel to look down at Goldilocks, or to register my astonishment that she had spoken. Gabriel now turned all his malice on her.

"What did you say, Rat?" he snarled, his malevolent eyes boring in on her, either not seeing the pointed gun or not caring.

"D-don't hurt her, Gabe. She didn't do nothing. It was me. I saw you out the window and I told!" Goldilocks's rusty little voice was stronger now as she lied to protect me.

"So you've been shootin' off yer mouth, eh? What'd I tell you? Eh? What'd I tell you?"

"It's not true!" I interjected desperately. "These are the first words I've ever heard her speak! She's been mute, from the day she came here."

"Mute, eh? Then she better go *back* to bein' mute if she knows what's good fer 'er! You hear me, Rat? You hush your mouth, or you know what I'll do! I *told* you, didn't I? I'll cut your *gizzard* out, I will!" He accompanied his threat with an illustrative thrusting and twisting motion of the knife, and Goldilocks clutched her throat as if she literally felt it being ripped open. With a choke, she fell silent again, and Teddy, who had remained by her side, stepped forward and with astonishing courage interposed himself between Gabriel and the terrified child.

Meanwhile, I lowered my eye to look down the length of the gun barrel at Gabriel. Aiming as best I could for the broad target of his middle, I said, "This child is the legal ward of the Vaughns, who own this property. If you threaten her, you'll face the full force of the law. Also, you are trespassing. Drop that knife and remove yourself at once, or I *will* shoot."

Gabriel looked considerably less cocky, staring down the barrel of my gun, but he kept a firm grip on the knife. The children on either side of him backed swiftly away from him, as if they did not trust my aim, while I prayed that it would not be obvious that I was trembling, and tried to recall having seen a musket fired, and how it was done.

With a quick look around his audience, Gabriel seemed suddenly aware that his dignity was at stake. He puffed out his chest, and blustered, "Ha! You don't have the nerve!"

"I assure you," I responded, "I do have the nerve." My right paw fumbled for the small metal switch on the back of the gun, pushing and pulling at it until something clicked, then I slipped my claw around the trigger. "Drop the knife," I repeated. Perhaps it was that little click, cocking the gun, or perhaps it was the decision I had already made to shoot him that showed in my eyes. The color left his face. He dropped the knife, and put his hands in the air. The gang of children scattered and melted back into the woods.

"Now get off this property," I demanded, hoping he would not hear the quiver in my voice, "and stay off!"

He backed up slowly until he reached the safety of a large tree trunk, then, darting behind it, he stuck his head out and growled, "I'll settle with you another time!" Pointing a finger directly at Goldilocks, he ground out, "This is yer fault, Rat! You went and opened yer big mouth after what I told you! You think you've got yerself a real sweet deal with all yer new friends! A regular princess, ain't you! But just you wait until Mother hears about this! *She'll be comin' for you!* You can betcher life on it!" With that, he wheeled around and bolted away into the woods.

I pointed the musket into the air and fired, the recoil of the gun knocking me off my feet. Realizing that that was my only shot, and that I had no idea how to reload the weapon, I prayed that Harry would be swift in coming. The musket had fallen to the ground, and I left it there as I struggled to my feet again and turned to Goldilocks and Teddy. I found them in tears and clinging to each other for comfort. Kneeling down, I held the two of them close, and felt them trembling as much as I was. Though I tried to keep my voice calm and soothing, its pitch went up an octave as I told them how brave they had been, and that the danger seemed to be past.

"I want to go home," cried Teddy, his courage dissipating now that the crisis was over, and Goldilocks nodded her assent. I wondered with a pang whether we would ever hear her voice again, or whether Gabriel's threats had once more frightened her out of the power of speech. I paused to collect the gun, and Gabriel's knife, so that it would not be there if he came back for it. Keeping the children close to me, I set off with them in the direction of the manor, traveling along the Giant's Walk, where Harry could find us.

At first Teddy peppered me with questions—the questions of an innocent having first discovered evil in the world. Who was that bad man? Why was he so cruel to Goldilocks? Why did all those nasty children tease her so? I had no answers, except to point out how terrible it must be to carry all that meanness within oneself all the time, that perhaps they were jealous that she had found a home among gentle and loving bears. He accepted this idea with a thoughtful expression beyond his years.

The two little ones soldiered bravely on, though Goldilocks sometimes staggered, her nerves having suffered a terrible blow. Teddy kept one arm about her, looking over his shoulder uneasily from time to time as if checking to be sure we were not being followed. When we heard something large crashing through the forest, I halted, placing myself in front of the children and raising the musket, but it turned out to be Harry.

"I heard your shot!" he cried. "Are you all right?"

I assured him that we were all unharmed as I gratefully turned the gun and the knife over to his care, and took the drooping Goldilocks's hand. As briefly as possible, I related to him all that had happened in his absence, in response to which he hit himself repeatedly on the forehead with self-reproach, until I bade him stop. Again and again he lamented that he had allowed himself to be played for a fool, and endangered those he was dedicated to protect.

On the long walk home, I found myself going over the encounter in my mind, trying to make sense of it. Surely Gabriel hadn't devised that whole plan just to avenge himself on me? He had wanted something badly enough to put quite a bit of thought and effort into organizing the trap, for certainly this meeting had been no accident. I could not help but see the cleverness of sending a gang of children to find us. Though I did not understand it all, the scheme implied more intelligence than I would have attributed to the flat-browed Gabriel. Where adult trespassers could be kept off the property with gamekeepers and guns, no gamekeeper would shoot at children, let alone suspect them of anything sinister, and there were too many of them to catch. I thought they must have been watching our movements for some time; they waited for us on what had been our regular route of late, along the Giant's Walk, and chose an area with enough massive tree trunks to hide an army, then lured Harry away, all evidently in order to settle a score with me, and to find a child they didn't seem to actually care about or want. Gabriel's only concern with the child was to see to it that she wouldn't talk. What did she know, what might she say, that was so dangerous?

At least now I recognized the source of the fear behind Goldilocks's muteness. Perhaps it would be possible, with time and care, to help her overcome it. So much made sense now. If that herd of barbarians really was Goldilocks's family, it would explain the savage tendencies she displayed when she first came to the Cottage in the Woods. Gabriel had called her a liar and a thief, and I could see perfectly plainly how she might have learned such habits, or even been trained in them by such a tutor as himself, for there was no doubt in my mind that it was he who had sent her into the Vaughns' house to steal. It was his own culpability that had kept him from simply coming to the front door and claiming her, had he really wanted to do so. How utterly sanguine was he in his supposition that she'd been arrested and sent to jail! And if she had been, how content he'd seemed to leave her there to rot. Clearly, his only concern was to terrify her into keeping silent about it all, or to convince me that anything she might say would be a lie.

And what of the terrible "Mother" Gabriel threatened Goldilocks with as his parting shot? Was that violent shrew who had come after him in town the one who had spawned him and this whole gang of miscreants? Could she be the brains behind today's ambuscade? And the most horrifying question of all: Would she really come for Goldilocks? I held tightly to the exhausted child at my side, and prayed.

When we reached the Cottage, I called for the mistress and explained to her that the children, especially Goldilocks, had had a terrible shock. She hugged them both closely, saying, "Oh, my dears!" then sent me to report matters to Mr. Vaughn while she took care of the little ones.

Harry had already given Mr. Vaughn his own account up to the point where he had handed me the gun and chased after the children, so I went on to describe the details of what followed. Mr. Vaughn listened with a cool self-control that seemed more dangerous than rage. Yet, as I came to the end of my story, he shook his head in wonder. "To think that she spoke," he marveled, his voice heavy with emotion, "that she spoke up in order to save you." I was astonished to observe that he was struggling to retain his composure. He turned away for a minute, collecting himself. Harry and I watched silently as he paced about the room, thinking, for several minutes, then he began to speak.

"We must give thought to reporting this thug to the police. We could press charges against this 'Gabriel' for trespassing and menacing. And yet whom do we report him to? Not Constable Murdley! That toad! The minute he hears there is a human family claiming young Goldilocks as their own, he and the whole Anthropological Society will be tripping over themselves to offer *them* the best legal counsel. No, I will summon my own team of lawyers. I think we must find out everything we can about this entire clan, and the mother, then determine how to proceed." He rang for Fairchild, who was, as usual, waiting just outside the door. The master did not bother with the polite fiction that he needed to repeat the story to the butler, but simply assumed that he had been listening.

"Fairchild, I have a task for you. I wish you to go among the servants, each and every one of them, and find out if any of them have knowledge of this brute Gabriel, or the band of wild children he claims as siblings, or their mother. These people must have a name. They must go somewhere to sleep at night. Tell the servants to ask everyone they know. Ask everyone *you* know, even the members of the men's choir. Consider this your sole duty until further notice."

"Yes, sir," Fairchild said grimly. "Immediately, sir."

"Miss Brown, you have done well today, acquitted yourself very bravely. Now, do you think you can coax the child into speaking again? She must have much information that would condemn this so-called mother, or they wouldn't be so intent on keeping her silent."

"I doubt that Goldilocks will put much faith in anything I say, sir. I'm the one who convinced her that it was safe to go outdoors, and yet Gabriel got to her in spite of all my reassurances. I wonder if she will ever trust me again. I will talk to her, sir. All I can do is try."

"Very good. You may retire. Now I wish to speak to Harry privately."

I retraced my steps to the nursery and found Mrs. Vaughn with the weeping Goldilocks on her lap. Teddy sat beside her on the bed, with Nurse standing behind him, patting his back solicitously. I marveled, not for the first time, that the merciless harridan seemed capable of genuine tenderness toward Teddy. I quickly assessed that Goldilocks was too overwrought as yet to even try to speak, and, feeling the strain of the day's adventure on my own nerves, I begged Mrs. Vaughn to be excused and retreated to the solace of my own room.

That night I was visited again by my old nightmare. Once more I found myself wandering dark passageways, following a child's heartrending cry. Nearly beside myself to find the suffering child, I rushed headlong to look for it around the next corner, and the next, deeper and deeper into the darkness and obscuring mist, until I was overcome. I awoke, as I had so many times before, inconsolable. But this time calling out a name: *"Goldilocks!"*

My nighttime candle had gone out. Only the smallest glow remained in the fireplace from the banked coals of last night's fire, and I lay in the darkness remembering the night I discovered the child in my room, bundled up in that ridiculous bear suit. How far she had come since then! How I treasured the girl's trust, for which I had worked so hard and so long. And yet how much the worse for her now, if she should be forced back into the clutches of this family of savages, to have been denuded of the hard veneer of insensitivity and distrust that her former life engendered. What would be the value, in such a life, of a few golden moments? Would their light survive the ugliness? Would it live to flower, on some future date, in her own acts of kindness? Or would it only serve to illuminate her misery?

35

A Mother's Love

Morning brought its own sense of dread, reinforced by a somber, oppressive sky. A heavy pall seemed to hang over the manor, drifting down the chimneys and seeping over doorsills like a pestilential fog. Afraid of what the day might bring, I neverthe-less put on a cheerful face for Teddy and Goldilocks, who were out of sorts and preoccupied after yesterday's encounter. Since Goldilocks had moved into the nursery, I had assumed the re-sponsibility for rousing both children each morning and prepar-ing them for school while Nurse snored blithely on. Taking the opportunity to try to coax Goldilocks into speaking, I gathered her onto my lap and praised her for her courage the day before, in speaking up to Gabriel in order to protect me. I told her in all earnestness that I would never forget what she had done, and that I was in her debt.

She seemed not to want to be reminded of the confrontation. She shook her head and covered her face with her hands. I rocked her gently for a while. Teddy, who had been listening carefully all this time, leaned in close and whispered a long, secret message in her ear. Whatever it was, it brought the barest hint of a smile. By the time we left for breakfast, her self-possession was restored, and we continued on to the schoolroom, though both youngsters remained moody and distracted, and I was not much better.

While I was struggling to focus the children's attention on counting exercises, a message was delivered from Mr. Vaughn requesting my presence. I considered rousing Nurse to mind the children while I was downstairs, but quickly reasoned that they spent quite a bit of time in the nursery minding themselves while Nurse slept or was otherwise incapacitated, and that they were probably better off that way. I assigned them some simple tasks to do in my absence, and left them busily working together.

Entering Mr. Vaughn's den, I was met with a small gathering of individuals, some unknown to me, some familiar—among them, Reverend Snover, and some other humans; a handful of the Enchanted; and a group of bears, badgers, and weasels in fine suits whom I took to be the Vaughns' lawyers. It was soon made clear to me that each of these persons, besides the lawyers, had come here in response to Fairchild's quest for information about Gabriel and the gang of children, all having some knowledge of them to report to Mr. Vaughn.

Mr. Vaughn called for silence, explained the situation briefly, and said that Goldilocks's alleged mother might actually show up at any moment to claim her. He then called on each of the group to say their piece, and asked me to tell whether their descriptions fit the characters I had encountered. Several had tales to tell very similar to the Vaughns' story, of having caught some hungry-looking, ragged child in the act of burgling their

96   THE COTTAGE IN THE WOODS

homes, and having had no heart to prosecute. Mr. Wiggins, the greengrocer, told of having his store nearly picked clean by a gang of dirty children operating in concert while two of them created a diversion with a fistfight. One woman with a kindly face said she had often noticed such a gang of children lurking about in her neighborhood, where many of her neighbors had fallen prey to the little thieves in one way or another. Owning a large dog, she had escaped their pilferage, but out of pity she left occasional bundles of food and her own children's old outgrown clothing sitting on a tree stump, beyond the reach of the dog's leash, and these disappeared quickly. Even she did not know their name, or where they lived. Reverend Snover only knew of the children through stories he had been told. He had come in the hope of finding information so that he might offer some charity to the family, though we all begged him not to venture after them alone.

Finally, a quiet gentleman came forward, introducing himself and the crow on his shoulder, who was Enchanted. The crow cleared his throat and started to speak.

"When Mr. Fairchild came looking for information about this band of wild children," he croaked, "I volunteered to take to the air and seek them out. I began my search high above the forest, looking for chimney smoke, or for clearings in the deep woods, where I might spot an isolated dwelling. I scouted out locations that would be nearly impossible for a person to find from the ground. Spying one such place, I glided lower and observed a number of children cavorting about a structure that looked like an enormous shoe—which might in fact have been a giant's shoe, with a roof attached on top and a chimney spouting smoke. I came in for a closer look, and did indeed observe a great many children of various ages, dirtier than any forest animals, and dressed in rags. No sooner had the children spotted me than they began to make a sport of firing pebbles at me with slingshots. No parents were evident to curb their behavior, and I quickly ascended out of range, taking careful bearings so that I could find the place again."

"So they hide out in this great shoe," Mr. Vaughn mused, "and they make their living by robbing their neighbors blind. Can we assume that the mother this Gabriel spoke of is behind it all? Can we even assume that all those children are hers?"

"They could be," said one of the badger lawyers, who had introduced himself as Mr. Caswell. "There could be enchantment involved—fertility beyond the normal number of years, an abnormal number of twins or even triplets."

"Did you notice anything like that, Miss Brown?"

"Honestly, sir, they were so dirty I couldn't tell. It's clear that no one takes any care of them at all."

"Excuse me," put in Reverend Snover, "but perhaps the woman just has so many children she doesn't know what to do? We must withhold judgment until the facts of the case are known. What we must ask ourselves is, now that we know of this needy family, how can we help them?"

"There's one question I'm asking first," Mr. Vaughn responded. "How do I keep my ward safely away from them?"

Mr. Caswell turned his attention to me. "You say they only wanted to secure her silence?"

"Yes, that's true."

He turned back to Mr. Vaughn. "My advice to you is to wait. Let the mother come to you, if she dares, and see if she can be convinced to do what's best for the child."

At that moment, Fairchild entered the room, his legendary composure somewhat rattled, and, with what clearly cost him some effort, announced to Mr. Vaughn that he had a visitor: a certain woman whom he had been expecting.

"You mean," Mr. Vaughn responded, "the mother?"

"I'm afraid so, sir."

"Show her in."

There was a murmuring among the assembled townsfolk as Fairchild went to call for her. He returned a minute later, announced, "Mother Shoe, sir," and withdrew. The gathering parted like the Red Sea as a tall, burly figure stepped into the doorway. At first glance I thought she was a rather ugly man, an impression aided by the large brown cigar she held between her teeth, but the dress and the scrawny baby dangling at her hip argued for femininity.

She halted, looking over the spectators, and, arranging her face in a gruesome imitation of loving concern, said, "Where's me dear little girl?"

It must have been my mind playing tricks on me, or something about the way the light angled in through the window, but suddenly, instead of a human, I saw a great predator, such as those ancient fossils found on the seaside cliffs: a bony monster with gaping jaws and pointed teeth. My heart missed a beat, and I had to quell the urge to grab the baby out of her arms.

Mr. Vaughn, apparently not about to make things easy for her, drew himself up to his full height and said gruffly, "Who are you? State your business."

Mother Shoe rearranged her face, taking the cigar out of her mouth, and assuming an exaggerated deference. "Oh, now, you must be the master of the house. 'Ow delighted and honored

I am to make your acquaintance, kind sir," she effused, dripping honey, but her falsity was tangible; the great predator's eyes glinted behind her gaze.

"As to my business, sir," she continued coyly, "I was 'opin' I could speak with you private-like, about my dear little girl what's been missin' lo these many months, and what's been found by my boy Gabe, livin' in the grand style 'ere with you good people."

Mr. Vaughn held a short conference, sotto voce, with his lawyers. "Very well," he agreed. "Ladies and gentlemen, if you'll please excuse us, I thank you all for your help." The group trickled out the door, giving Mother Shoe a wide berth, and yet unable to look away from the spectacle she presented. Mr. Vaughn turned to me and said softly, "Would you be so good as to bring Miss Goldilocks here? Say no word to her. We must see her spontaneous reaction."

"Yes, sir," I responded, knowing it had to be done, but afraid of what the effect would be on the child's already shaken equilibrium. Finding the schoolroom empty, I hurried next door to the nursery and beheld both children and Nurse crouched around the laundry chute once again, listening to the servants' voices filtering up from the kitchen below.

I cleared my throat loudly, and the youngsters' heads popped up. They had the grace to appear embarrassed, while Nurse did not move an inch. Knowing full well that the minute I left the room she would be listening again, I decided to bring both children with me. Informing Goldilocks gently that Mr. Vaughn desired to talk to her, I was gratified to see that this elicited no negative reaction, and concluded, with some relief, that the kitchen gossips had not yet received word of Mother Shoe's arrival.

Leaving Teddy to sit outside his father's door, I entered the den once more, holding Goldilocks by the hand. Mother Shoe turned to face us, showing all her teeth in a grotesque leer, with her fat cigar hanging from the corner of her mouth. "Well, if it ain't my little Rat— Um, um, I mean, um, M-Mary!" she stuttered. I couldn't help but wonder if she had made the name up on the spur of the moment.

Goldilocks recoiled as if she had been struck—as if she too had seen the great predator's gaping jaws and pointed teeth. She gave a little scream and darted behind me, clutching me with both arms.

Mr. Vaughn sat coolly observing this from behind his desk. "It would seem she is not happy to see you," he commented to the woman. To Goldilocks he said, "Is that your true name? Mary?"

The child shook her head, eyes wide with fear.

Mother Shoe shrieked. Striking a pose with the back of her hand dramatically pressed to her forehead, the woman moaned, "You've turned 'er against me! Oh Lor', you've ali'nated 'er affections! Oh, my dear, my darlin' deary chile! She don't want to know 'er own lowly mother what lives in a shoe! She's 'ad 'er 'ead turned by livin' in the lap o' luxury. Oh, woe is me, woe is me—" The scrawny baby let out a mewling cry as the mother hauled him from one hip to the other like a sack of meal, her cigar dropping ashes perilously close to his head. My arms fairly ached with the urge to take the baby from her arms.

Mr. Vaughn looked on, appalled. Then, perhaps realizing he could do nothing for the baby, he turned his attention to Goldilocks. "Come to me, child," he said. "Don't be afraid. I won't allow her to hurt you."

With a swift glance at the woman, Goldilocks ran to Mr. Vaughn's side. He put a protective arm around her and said, "Now, I'm going to ask you some questions, yes or no, and it's very, very important that you answer them truthfully. Do you understand?"

She nodded.

"First, do you know this woman? Don't be afraid, just tell the truth."

Goldilocks stared down at her shoes and stuck her lower lip out, but she nodded slightly in the affirmative.

"Good. Now, tell me, is she your mother?"

She shook her head vigorously and put both arms around Mr. Vaughn.

"Perhaps you can't do it here today, child, but is there anything you can tell me, with your own voice, about who you really are and where you came from? That would help me very much."

Goldilocks's gaze seemed to be pulled inexorably to the woman who claimed to be her mother. The great predatory eyes focused on the child with deadly intensity. I watched in horror as she took the cigar from between her teeth, and used it to make a stabbing and twisting motion aimed at Goldilocks, exactly as Gabriel had done with his knife the day before to illustrate his threat to "cut her gizzard out" if ever she spoke again.

"Stop that!" I cried in outrage as Goldilocks turned white and grabbed her throat protectively. Mr. Vaughn observed with some puzzlement, but did not interfere as I continued. "Stop it, I tell you!"

The predator was suddenly the meekest and most innocent

of women. "What? Why, that's just a little private sign language between me and me own dear little girl to tell her how much I love her!"

"Madam," Mr. Vaughn replied, "nothing can make me believe that you have the smallest regard for this child. Suppose you tell me what you came here for."

"I come for me precious daughter, of course! She's the light of my life, that one is. Me and her brothers and sisters are plumb brokenhearted without her." At this point she began to blubber unconvincingly, and squeezed out a few tears. "And I'm just a poor woman," she gulped, "what lives in a shoe and tries to do 'er duty by all 'er darling childrin, but me 'usband's off at sea, an' 'e don't send no money 'ome, an' 'ow are we to live? I'd like to know. T'isn't right this 'ere child has everythin', an' the rest of us have nuthin'! Now maybe you could make it worth my while . . ."

"Ah, so we get nearer to the point. So you *might* be able to give her up for the proper price."

The predator whipped to attention, smelling blood. "Oh, sir, how could you even think of me givin' up me favorite child, me treasure, but . . ."

"Yes?"

"But p'raps," she said, wiping her eyes and nose with her dirty hand, "I could bring meself to make the sacrifice, if it would 'elp to provide the necessities for me other precious babes. What a terrible, in'uman choice to 'ave to make, but I shall 'ave to bear it!"

"So you're willing to sell her to me."

"Oh, now, sir, don't you be saying that! It would just be me, a brokenhearted mother, leavin' 'er precious young 'un to the care of a fam'ly what could provide 'er with the foiner things in life, and you, sir, expressin' yer friendly gratitude and p'raps wantin' to 'elp out a fam'ly of poor needy childrin. No need to talk of sellin'!"

"I assume there's a record of her birth, perhaps in one of the local churches?"

Mother Shoe snorted. "I don't need no record! I know me own child! I have all her brothers and sisters to witness her growin' up from a golden-haired babe! She's mine and I want what's comin' to me!"

"How much?" Mr. Vaughn asked pointedly.

Without hesitation, she named a sum that would have set her up quite nicely for life, twenty-some children and all, one thousand pounds. The figure seemed to echo in the resulting silence.

"You can't be serious," Mr. Vaughn finally replied.

Abruptly, Mother Shoe's insinuating manner changed. All social graces vanished. "Not serious, am I?" she snarled. "Not serious? A big, important bear like you might think you can just go round the countryside snatchin' up poor people's children, but I've got somethin' to say about that, an' I'll say it at the top of my lungs until everybody 'ears me, I will! You'll pay it and be glad to afore I'm done!"

"Get out," he replied, needlessly ringing for Fairchild, who almost fell into the room, with Teddy stumbling in after him. "Escort Mother Shoe to the door," he ordered. "To the front gate if need be."

"Don't think I'm done with you!" she snapped, glaring at the child with pure malevolence as she repeated the threatening motion with her cigar.

Mr. Vaughn rose, placing Goldilocks behind him, and, as if in response to the woman's unspoken intention, said, "This child is my ward, and she is under my protection."

Mother Shoe grew quiet. In a voice dripping with acid, she hissed, "But you can't watch 'er *every* minute, now, can you?" Spreading her mouth into the hideous leer once again, she cackled to herself, stuck the cigar in one side of her mouth, and threw the wailing baby over her shoulder. "Goodbye for now, dear little Mary. You be a *good* girl, won't you?"

And with that, she brushed past the awestruck Teddy, and was gone. Goldilocks reached her arms up toward Mr. Vaughn in an obvious request to be picked up, which he immediately granted, then she wept on his shoulder with discernible relief and gratitude. Teddy ran to his father and hugged him about the legs, while out from behind some heavy drapes stepped one of the lawyers, the diminutive Mr. Caswell, who had apparently witnessed the entire encounter.

"We have not heard the last of the woman, sir," he warned. "It is my belief that she's known where the child was all along, and left her here to give you plenty of time to become attached to her before making her demands."

"I'm afraid you're right. If that's what she's about, her plan has worked. The child is like one of the family now, but I won't give in to that woman's extortion. If she's cynical enough to use the child this way, it's a safe bet she'd never stop coming back for more."

"That's almost certainly the case, sir. But she can indeed foment trouble for you, if she makes enough noise. If the Anthropological Society hears of her complaint, you'll have the very Devil to pay. They're trying to push through a law to keep humans and the Enchanted separate. This would make a perfect case for stirring up public opinion in favor of their cause."

"Then let us hope that the Anthropological Society and this evil woman never connect. They travel in rather different circles, after all. I should think even members of the society would not want to dirty their hands dealing with the likes of her."

36

A Party

❧

Back in the schoolroom with Goldilocks and Teddy, I caught a motion out the window, and a flash of red. Curious, I leaned closer to the window for a better look, and recognized Nurse's small figure, wrapped in the red shawl she habitually wore out of doors, moving at a furious pace in the direction of the front drive. I watched her until she was out of sight, wondering what could motivate her to exert herself so uncharacteristically. It seemed likely that she must have heard the whole story about Mother Shoe's visit by now through her listening post at the laundry chute, and the chilling thought occurred to me that she might be running to catch up with the woman. I asked myself whether Nurse would really collude with that harpy. All that would be required was a word from Nurse to direct Mother Shoe to Constable Murdley, and he and the rest of the Anthropological Society would line up their considerable weight on Mother Shoe's side. Though it was fruitless to speculate, and there was nothing I could do to stop her in any case, the thought that Nurse would betray us all preyed on my mind.

Goldilocks was badly shaken by the confrontation with Mother Shoe, and Teddy, having witnessed the woman's tempestuous departure, was full of questions, so academic studies were temporarily set aside. I had so many questions myself that there was little I could say to them. Was Mother Shoe really Goldilocks's mother? What kind of mother would try to terrify her own child? What kind of mother would leave her child with strangers until they had become attached to her, and then try to sell her to them? I had no answers. What was wanted was a diverting outing, but Mr. Vaughn had quite rightly put a stop to our going outdoors. Instead, we marched through the hallways on a pretend safari to the library, where we looked up wild animals from the African continent, and copied engravings of them from books. Having thus conquered the beasts, we climbed onto Sofie, the overstuffed sofa, and lost ourselves in our favorite storybooks for a time, before retracing our route to the schoolroom. Between this "outing" and Teddy's occasional whispered messages to her, we had managed to distract Goldilocks from her distress, and restore the smallest of smiles to her face. Though the whispering was a behavior I'd normally discourage, I dared to hope that it might lead Goldilocks to whisper back to him, and so I pretended to ignore it.

At the end of the school day, Betsy knocked on the door and handed me a note from Mrs. Vaughn, a request to come and see her in the solarium when my duties were done. At dismissal time, I accompanied the children into the nursery to see if Nurse was back from her mysterious errand. There she sat, demurely stitching away in her place by the fire. When she looked up at me and smiled sweetly, it was painfully obvious that she had been up to some mischief. I stood watching her, wanting to question her, though I thought it would be futile. Finally,

Nurse, uncomfortable under my gaze, looked straight at me, and snapped, "What?!"

"I saw you running toward the front drive after that woman left," I said accusingly.

"I was just minding my own business, chickie. You should try it!"

Our eyes locked in a contest of wills, but, realizing that opposition would just make her more stubborn, I looked away in frustration. Bidding the children goodbye, I hurried on to see what Mrs. Vaughn wanted.

As I entered the French doors to the solarium, I was met with the garden scents of fresh foliage and moist earth. Making my way between the potted palms and philodendrons, I found that dear lady seated on a wicker love seat, surrounded by a plethora of decorative pillows. She greeted me with a sad smile, and invited me to sit by her side.

"I needed someone to talk to, my dear, and you are such a sweet child, almost like a daughter to me, and you understand about Goldilocks and how we love her, and how she is one of us now." She took out a handkerchief and dabbed at her eyes.

I had come to know Mrs. Vaughn better in the months since Goldilocks and I had been part of the Vaughns' family gathering each evening, but this was the first time she had specifically invited me to talk. "I'm honored, madam, that you thought of me. What troubles you?"

"Well, I really believe I haven't a friend left in the world," she announced.

"How can that be, madam? Surely you are mistaken."

"Yes, how can it be? I ask myself the same question. It started with all this ill will and prejudice the Anthropological Society has been stirring up against the Enchanted, and then word got out that we had Goldilocks living with us. In the past few weeks, my friends have dropped away from me one by one."

I struggled for words, mindful of the difference in our stations, and not wishing to insult these females who had been her friends, but I was unsure how to comfort her. I wanted to put my arms around the dear soul, as if she were my own mama, but I dared not take the liberty.

"Perhaps it is not the end, madam. I think that if they really knew the whole story, they might understand. Wouldn't it be worth a try to explain matters to those who have been your particular friends?"

"Explain? After the way they have humiliated me? They have removed themselves forever from my sphere!"

I was silent, and she shook her head and said, "Listen to me. I sound like one of them. I believe you could be right, dear. I think I will try to explain to them. Perhaps if they met the dear child, they'd see. Maybe all is not lost, after all." She dried her eyes and bade me stay awhile and keep her company.

She seemed to have talked out her distress over her friends, so I considered whether to apprise her of the morning's visit from Mother Shoe. Though my urge was to shelter her, I believed that she would want to know the worst. I proceeded to fill her in, describing the horrible woman and all that had transpired as objectively as I could. Mrs. Vaughn was terribly alarmed. Her first thought was for Goldilocks, and the shock it must have been to her.

"The poor child," she bemoaned. "How much more can she stand? It is just unthinkable for her to fall into the hands of those people! Mr. Vaughn should have paid the woman, paid her anything!"

"I'm afraid, madam, that if he had once given in to her

demands, she would have come back again and again to demand more. You would never have been free of her."

"Yes, I suppose that's true, but are we free of her now? We can't even allow the child outside to walk about on our own property! And I'm afraid Mr. Caswell is correct in assuming that we haven't heard the last of her."

❧

Three days later Mr. Vaughn received the summons, a legal demand for him to appear in court in the matter of *Shoe v. Vaughn,* to decide the custody of one Mary Shoe, aka Goldilocks. I was visiting again with Mrs. Vaughn in the parlor, her invitations to come and talk having quickly become a daily habit, when Mr. Vaughn entered the room, jaw clenched and eyes blazing, to show her the awful document. Though he was making an effort to be calm and stoic, I could see that Mrs. Vaughn was deeply dismayed, near to panic.

"Oh, how could this happen?" Mrs. Vaughn gasped, clutching my paw for solace.

"Someone's gotten to that Shoe woman," Mr. Vaughn growled, "and I'll wager she's wasted no time getting herself hooked up with the Anthropological Society. It has to be some group with very deep pockets to have retained this law firm. Someone like Murdley and Babcock, and their bunch of fearmongers."

I believed I knew in that moment just who had "gotten to" Mother Shoe, and directed her straight to Constable Murdley, but I had no proof and could not accuse her. To think I had ever allowed myself to believe that Nurse's better nature was winning out! She had only been biding her time to find some other way to work her devilish will. My stomach tightened into a knot.

"What are we going to do?" Mrs. Vaughn asked, trying to match Mr. Vaughn's attempt at calm. She and I both hung on his words.

He said, "Our solicitors are already working on it, building a case against Mother Shoe and her son Gabriel, charging them with using that gang of children as thieves and pickpockets. If only Goldilocks could speak, I'm convinced she could tell us all about it. As it is, I'm sure we'll have no problem finding a dozen villagers who will be willing to testify against them. Strictly speaking, the woman should be dragged off to jail. No magistrate in his right mind will award our Goldilocks to her by the time we are through." He said this, but he wouldn't meet Mrs. Vaughn's eyes.

"There's something you're not telling me," Mrs. Vaughn insisted.

He sighed heavily. "The case will be heard by Judge Slugby, charter member of the Anthropological Society, in a week's time."

Her grip on my paw tightened until I almost cried out, and I felt my eyes watering, while Mrs. Vaughn seemed to deflate, and shrink into herself like a little old woman.

Mr. Vaughn put a bracing paw on her shoulder. "Mrs. Vaughn," he said, "remember yourself. We must be strong and resolved. If Slugby rules against us, we will appeal to the high court!"

Mrs. Vaughn raised her chin and straightened her spine, as if preparing herself to meet bad news. Looking him in the eye, she said, "But if the decision goes against us, they'll take her.

She'll fall into the hands of that loathsome woman and her mis-begotten son. Even if we win the appeal and get Goldilocks back after that, how will we ever heal her, or rebuild her trust? And Teddy! He loves her so, and he has total faith in us. What would it do to him?"

"We will face whatever we must when the time comes," he replied. "And meanwhile, let us not give up hope! Come, Mrs. Vaughn, you will only make yourself ill imagining the worst. *Labium superius dura!*"

"This is no time for your Latin phrases!" she responded.

I smiled, and translated for her. "It means 'stiff upper lip.'"

"Very good, Miss Brown," Mr. Vaughn acknowledged. "I hope that I may call upon you to testify on the child's behalf?"

"Yes, sir. I'll do anything I can."

"Excellent. Then I'll leave you two to each other's care. I must confer with my solicitors with all due speed."

When he had gone, Mrs. Vaughn shakily asked me to stay and take tea with her, and I of course accepted, but I reminded myself that she was lonely now, and though her motherly affection was genuine, such invitations would probably cease once her old friendships had been repaired. We sat side by side on the divan and she spoke to me of her worries for a long time, until she had calmed herself. "We must do something to keep our spirits up," she said, and immediately hit on the idea of a party.

"A party every night!" she cried. "Since all my friends have deserted me, it will be just for us, and we shall decorate the drawing room, and you shall play for us, and we shall have music, and fine things to eat, and all manner of games, and it will be splendid!"

". . . I'm sure it will, madam," I concurred, admiring her determination, but having private doubts about how cheerful we could be.

Noticing my hesitation, she turned her full charm on me. "I've heard how talented you are, my dear. Really, I am counting on you! Surely you can do it for Goldilocks's and Teddy's sakes!"

She went on in this vein until she had won me over, and I was able to set my doubts aside.

❧

I approached the drawing room that evening with a smile fixed on my face, determined to do my part. Mrs. Vaughn greeted me warmly, taking me by the paw and bringing me to the fireside. She was garbed in a lovely blue silk dress, with ruffles and matching ribbons, and even Goldilocks was attired in a party dress of white lawn and lace. Impulsively, I looked down at my own stodgy dress. Still in mourning for Papa, I wore my black bombazine, and no ornament. I comforted myself with the thought that I had dressed for Papa, and that they must take me as I was.

As the evening progressed, I got into the spirit of celebration. Mrs. Vaughn's good cheer was indeed so irresistible that my smile soon turned genuine. True to her word, there were delicious desserts and punch to drink. She soon had us all laughing with a game of blindman's buff. Teddy was blindfolded and groped about the room until Mr. Vaughn allowed himself to be caught. After a few more rounds, Mrs. Vaughn called upon me to accompany her in a solo. I found that she had a fine contralto voice, perfectly suited to the sentimental old song she chose.

Just a song at twilight, when the lights are low,
And the flick'ring shadows softly come and go.
Tho' the heart be weary, sad the day and long,
Still to us at twilight comes love's old sweet song.

Listening to her sing these words brought a lump to my throat, but I played on. Several verses later, we drew the performance to a close, amid enthusiastic applause. The merrymaking continued, though I thought I noticed a rather desperate edge to Mrs. Vaughn's laughter. I knew very well that behind the bright smiles she was not forgetting about the upcoming court case, which could take away the little girl we all cherished. Watching Goldilocks, subdued and somber since the confrontation with Mother Shoe, I almost could imagine the child on her way to the gallows, so crushing would it be to her budding spirit to be given back to Mother Shoe and Gabriel, but the Vaughns had not told her of the situation as yet, and she sat by Teddy's side, contentedly holding his paw, all unaware. When it was time for the children to retire, I volunteered to escort them up to bed. Upon reaching the nursery, I discovered Nurse, inebriated and reeking of strong spirits, muttering confusedly that *she* knew how to behave in fine company, *she* had been with the family since Teddy was born, and *she* should have been invited to the family party instead of me. I found that I actually had some sympathy for her, miserable and lonely as she was, and I ended by putting all three of them to bed.

Back in my own cozy chamber at last, I thought of Nurse, doomed to outgrow her usefulness. But then, so was I. Teddy and Goldilocks would not need a governess forever. When they were grown, I might, with luck, obtain a position with another family, but eventually I would find myself alone, just as Nurse had taunted me. I had better get used to it, she said, and perhaps she was right. But I would always have my thoughts of Mr. Bentley. I could imagine seeing him again, watching the changes on his noble features, the quick intelligence and warmth of his eyes, the gentle strength of his bearing. It was like acid on my soul to tell myself that he belonged not to me, but to another. My mind began to work feverishly, asking questions I had asked so many times before. He had said that it would have been "unforgivable" to break off the betrothal. I knew that he had grown up with Amy, that both families had expected them to marry from the time they were small. Indeed, I began to see how breaking off an engagement with a lifelong playmate might seem unforgivable to an honorable and noble-hearted bear like Mr. Bentley. Against all logic, the possibility made me love him all the more, a thought that contained as much guilt as joy. Caught between my heart and my conscience, I prayed on my knees that night for some manner of relief, for a way out, for an answer.

37

Trouble and Foreboding

❧

Determined not to give in to despair, Mrs. Vaughn continued with her evening parties, though the festive mood seemed to vacillate and falter. The approaching trial hung over the household like a shroud, and we, the inmates, crept around silently as if afraid to disturb it. Only the children remained unaware of the gathering darkness. Even so, it was clear from her grave little face that Goldilocks sensed something. I felt strongly that the child must be told about the trial and what it might mean for her, and that Teddy must also be prepared, but the Vaughns wanted to maintain the children's happy innocence for as long as possible. I was instructed to keep their lives as normal as could be, and this I endeavored to do, for such time as might be left to us.

A week had passed since our confrontation with Gabe in the woods, and we had not been outdoors since the encounter, though Mr. Vaughn had doubled the patrol of the grounds. Deprived of exercise and fresh air, I found myself staring longingly out the window in unoccupied moments, despite the gray and wet weather. I was engaging in this activity when suddenly my eyes beheld the disturbing visage of someone standing, hands on hips, on the lawn below, daring and defiant, looking up at the second-story windows as if trying to work something out. It was Gabriel himself. In an instant he spotted me, and had the audacity to respond with an evil grimace before he vanished into the shrubbery. I was shocked, and frightened. How could he get past all of Mr. Vaughn's patrols? Was no place safe? With an unreasoning fear of leaving the children in the schoolroom alone, I hurried them down the stairways and passages with me to the kitchen, leaving them there with Cook while I went to Mr. Vaughn's den. Barely stopping to knock, I reported the incident to him in detail, though I acknowledged that in the time it had taken me to get to his office, the villain could have gotten well away. Mr. Vaughn, cursing in outrage, rang for Harry and Fairchild and began giving orders. He assured me that all doors and windows would be locked, even during the day, which allowed me to breathe more easily.

I quickly returned the children to the schoolroom, convincing them it was all a game, but I was badly shaken, and contemplated just what Gabriel was hoping to accomplish by showing himself. Was it simply a desire to terrorize us, to prove that he could penetrate all our defenses at will? I wondered how far he would go to wreak his vengeance on me, or on Goldilocks, who had so bravely and foolishly told him that she had been the one to betray him. Would he do murder? Remembering his berserk fury that day when he beat up on the bear, I even wondered whether he was altogether sane.

With the trial date only days away, we all gathered once

again in the drawing room and made the best of things. I played the pianoforte, while Mrs. Vaughn tried to teach Goldilocks some dance steps, and Mr. Vaughn was showing Teddy card tricks. We heard a distant noise, very soft at first, like the buzzing of angry bees, then gradually becoming louder. Mr. Vaughn raised his paw to silence us so that he could listen. He had just gotten up to go to the window when a brick came flying through it, scattering glass over half the room and landing in the center of the floor. After being momentarily too stunned to move, Mrs. Vaughn and I quickly leaped up and thrust the children away from the windows.

"Get them upstairs!" Mr. Vaughn commanded, but before we took another step, a second volley came through the broken window, this time a ball of fire, landing virtually at our feet. I heard screaming then, and some of it was my own, as we backed away from the fiery mass. Mrs. Vaughn grabbed Teddy, and I held on to Goldilocks, as Mr. Vaughn swiftly dumped the water from a vase of flowers on top of the fireball, stamping out the flames that remained.

"Cowards!" he bellowed out the window. "I'm coming out there, and if any of you have the nerve, you can stand and fight me like a bear!"

In through the window came shouts of "Shut down the printing press!" and "Shut it down if you know what's good for you!" and "Next time we'll burn the whole place to the ground!" There seemed to be a dozen voices or more, and I feared what might happen if Mr. Vaughn went out among them, as he seemed intent on doing. Mrs. Vaughn held firmly on to his arm, trying to calm him and talk him out of leaving the house, but when Mr. Vaughn refused to be deterred, she said, "All right, but keep your temper, Walter, or you'll only make it worse." This finally seemed to sober him, though it did not alter his determination.

"I'll take care of the children and the servants," said Mrs. Vaughn.

"Don't go upstairs!" Mr. Vaughn was now contradicting his earlier directive. "There may be a fire. Get everyone to the kitchen and stay near the door, ready to leave." I directed my attention to the children, who were terribly frightened and bewildered by what had happened. Teddy was in tears, and Goldilocks looked to be in shock. Mrs. Vaughn and I half dragged them to the kitchen, and she quickly explained to the group of servants there what was happening. James and some others filled buckets of water, in case they should be needed, and the call was sent round for everyone to be ready to exit in case of fire. I saw Nurse arrive, fairly sober, and hover protectively around Teddy and Mrs. Vaughn, and I was relieved to see that she kept her head. Mrs. Vaughn called Nurse and me to her and said desperately, "Take care of the children! I must go and see what is happening with my husband!"

But upon hearing this, Teddy clutched her skirts in a death grip and cried, "No, Mama, no! Don't leave! Don't leave us!" and began to weep so piteously that Mrs. Vaughn, with a torn expression, bent over to comfort him. Goldilocks, who had begun crying as well, joined Teddy with a poignant appeal of her own, grasping Mrs. Vaughn's paws and pulling her away from the door.

Mrs. Vaughn turned to me over her shoulder and said, "I can't leave them. Go and see what's happening and report back to me! I must know what transpires!"

"Yes, of course, madam," I answered, and slipped away

without the children noticing that I was leaving. As I made my way with a lonely candle toward the main entrance of the house, I was surprised by the quiet. I had expected to hear angry raised voices, but there were none. Approaching the foyer, I could see clearly the open front door, and Mr. Vaughn's towering form standing on the outside steps, and beyond him the glowing torches of a small crowd of men. Staying out of sight, I set my candle down and took up a station in the darkness a little way back from the door to watch and listen.

Mr. Vaughn was speaking quite calmly, addressing himself to the men. I speculated that he must know some of them, had perhaps even done business with some. As I listened, he called several by name.

"Mr. Harkness, Mr. Judd, Mr. Greeley," he said with gravity. "There were women and children in that room where you threw your missiles. Is that the size of your courage?"

The men looked a little embarrassed, but one of them cried out, "What about this paper of yours? All you're doing is stirring up trouble!"

"Have we printed any lies?" demanded Mr. Vaughn.

"That's a matter of opinion!" growled one old-timer.

"Some of what we offer is opinion, and is labeled as such. The rest of it is fact, backed up by trustworthy witnesses or valid documents. If you think we're wrong, then present your evidence and prove it! No one has taken away your right to speak your own minds. Write a letter to the editor! If it's civil, I'll print it."

There was an uncomfortable pause, and then I saw Mr. Vaughn move closer to them, saying, "You all have a right to your opinions. You have a right to make yourselves heard! What you don't have is a right to commit mayhem in order to silence the opposition! Don't you see that if *one* person's voice can be silenced by those who disagree with him, then *none of us are safe*. When mobs rule, your own voice could be the next one silenced. Let us rather devote ourselves to protecting each other's right to speak freely, as we have always done here in the Enchanted Forest."

I was moved by his speech, and his deft effort to turn aggression into comradeship. There was a tense silence while the mood of the crowd teetered in the balance.

"You going to write about this, then?" piped up one voice.

"Gentlemen," said Mr. Vaughn, "you have been my good neighbors for many a year, and I hope shall be again. If you go in peace now, that will be the end of the matter."

At this they conferred among themselves, and there was a low muttering. In the dim light I thought they looked rightly ashamed of themselves, peering at one another guiltily out of the corners of their eyes, and then, apparently having nothing more to say, the group started to break up and fade back into the night.

$$\sim$$

"They're all gone now, and I don't expect they'll return," I assured Mrs. Vaughn as I reported back to her and the anxious staff members gathered in the kitchen. I had described the scene at the front door as accurately as I could, trying to convey the eloquence of Mr. Vaughn's speech, and he arrived soon after me to assure us all that the crisis was over. There was a long communal sigh of relief from the staff, and Mrs. Vaughn, after treating Mr. Vaughn to a rare public kiss on the cheek, turned her attention to the children, and asked my help to get them to the nursery. There she tucked Teddy in and sat by his side, holding his paw and talking reassuringly to him, while I rocked Goldilocks until her head grew heavy on my shoulder. Long after the children were asleep, I lay awake, staring at my ceiling and thinking how close we had come to having the place burned down around us. Where would it all end? I felt that I was bound to a chain of events that I was powerless to sever. Excruciating as it was, the constant ache caused by my hopeless love was nearly over-shadowed by the still-stronger sense of some inescapable threat that time suspended over our heads.

꿍

We tried to carry on with some semblance of normalcy. The window was quickly replaced, and the scorched carpet was rolled up and taken away. But nothing could take away the wounded look in Teddy's eyes. It seemed that his innocence had been dealt another blow, and I feared that his faith in the world of adults had been sadly shaken. For Goldilocks, who had lost hers long ago, it was but one more reason to be mistrustful. What made it worse was the knowledge that we were running out of time, and the Vaughns must now explain to them about the trial.

On the eve of the trial date, as I joined the Vaughns in the parlor for our last "party," all pretense of gaiety was dropped. The sweetmeats and pastries went untasted, the cards and other games untouched. Even Mrs. Vaughn seemed caught up in the whirlpool of her own sadness. When Goldilocks, sensing her melancholy, climbed onto her lap and put her arms around her neck, Mrs. Vaughn looked as if she might cry. Mr. Vaughn moved to her side on the divan, and, pulling Teddy onto his own lap and putting a bracing arm about his wife's shoulder, said to her, "It's time. We mustn't leave them unprepared. Do you want me to tell them?"

She nodded, holding Goldilocks tightly as Mr. Vaughn began. "You see, children, we've received something called a summons. A summons means that someone has a problem with us, and a person called a judge must use the laws to help us solve it."

"But who?" Teddy asked innocently. "Who could have a problem with us?"

The children watched Mr. Vaughn's face intently, as if sensing from his serious demeanor that some blow was about to fall.

"It's Mother Shoe. She says Goldilocks belongs to her, not to us, and she says she wants her back."

Goldilocks emitted a desperate wail and hid her face against Mrs. Vaughn's shoulder.

"This means there has to be a trial. A trial is where Mother Shoe and your mother and I each tell our sides of the story. We have people called lawyers to help us, and they will ask all sorts of questions, trying to find out the truth. We hope to prove that Mother Shoe is a terrible mother, and that she shouldn't have Goldilocks back, and that we can give her a better home. The judge will listen to everybody and decide where Goldilocks must live. If the judge decides against us, she may have to go back to Mother Shoe—"

Goldilocks caught the full import first. Hearing the words, she collapsed in a full swoon, sagging against Mrs. Vaughn. Teddy gave a little scream and, jumping down from his father's lap and bending over Goldilocks's prostrate form, called her name repeatedly. Receiving no response, he whispered a long message in her ear, as he so often did to cheer her up, but there was no answering smile. The rest of us gathered around the desperate little scene, our tears flowing freely, and Mrs. Vaughn called for her smelling salts. The administration of these brought the child's eyes open, then the pallid little face crumpled and she began to sob. Mrs. Vaughn clutched the golden head to her bosom, rocking back and forth as if in agony.

"Listen, dear, listen! That won't be the end of it!" she said, in a desperate effort to reassure her. "If this judge takes you away from us, we'll go to a higher judge! We'll try and try until we get you back!"

"Oh, Mama, Papa, don't let them take her," cried Teddy, and then he too dissolved into tears. Mr. Vaughn picked him up and held him close while Mrs. Vaughn attempted to comfort the weeping Goldilocks. We stayed in our protective circle for some time, until the little ones had cried themselves out, and our own handkerchiefs were thoroughly damp. At last the Vaughns carried the exhausted children off to bed and the evening was over.

That night, I felt submerged in a witches' brew of trouble and foreboding. Though I had agreed without reservation to testify on the Vaughns' behalf, now that the time had come, I was filled with dread. What if I failed to make clear how much Goldilocks loved and needed them? How would I live with myself if my failure resulted in the child being taken away from them? Papa had always told me that my best was all anyone could expect of me, but never before in my life had there been so much at stake. I must do better than my best tomorrow. Throughout that whole long night, my mind continued to spin, rehearsing over and over everything I wanted to say.

When the first morning light appeared over the horizon, I gave up on sleep and made myself presentable, anxious to see how the children were faring. As I entered the nursery, I passed Mrs. Vaughn, who was just leaving, barely containing her emotions. The children sat solemnly together on the floor, hand in paw, enervated by grief. Goldilocks's little face was red and swollen from crying. Nurse sat up dizzily and groaned, holding her head with both paws, suffering no doubt from the ill effects of her indulgences the night before.

Sitting down on the floor next to them, I pulled Goldilocks onto my lap, but she was unresponsive. I asked Teddy then to try to whisper to her, as he often did to cheer her up.

He leaned over to her ear, and this time I could hear his whispered message. "I won't let them take you, no matter what!" Brave little Teddy! I thought of the way he had shielded Goldilocks with his own body that day in the forest, and I did not doubt that he would do anything he could to save her. But he was just a cub, I thought, and as helpless as the rest of us in this matter.

As the Vaughns and I met at the front door for the trip to town, I felt uneasy about leaving the children, and so I pointed out to Mrs. Vaughn that Nurse was indisposed. She called for Betsy and gave her instructions to look in on the nursery from time to time and see if she could be of any help. The other household servants were gathering round tearfully to wish the master and mistress success.

Our little company set off for the courthouse, picking up additions along the way, some who had agreed to testify for the Vaughns, and others who tagged along out of loyalty or simple curiosity, so that as we approached our destination, we became quite a crowd. A much larger crowd awaited us when we neared the courthouse; from as far away as the hotel halfway down the street we could see them, some humans, some Enchanted, many of both descriptions carrying signs with slogans like "Blood is thicker than water!" or "Stick to your own kind!" or, conversely, "Home is where the heart is!" I also saw a number of placards with insulting epithets aimed either at the Vaughns or at Mother Shoe. A surly murmuring emanated from the mob, and our little group formed a protective circle around me and Mrs. Vaughn while we moved in toward the door. I experienced a thrill of fear as we pressed our way through.

Inside, things were chaotic, with characters of every kind milling around, jockeying for the few available seats. Mrs. Vaughn had warned me the courtroom was a small, shabby space that received very little use, since, in days past, the populace prided itself on working out its own disagreements amicably. Our solicitors led us to a roped-off area with our own uncomfortable benches. As we settled ourselves, Mr. Vaughn assumed his most impressive attitude of respectability and authority, and Mrs. Vaughn maintained flawless deportment. I sat next to her, craning my neck and looking nervously around.

Reverend Wright appeared directly, and shyly offered me his best wishes, which I accepted with good grace. I had tried to be sensitive to the bear's mood and manner since the day I turned down his proposal, but I was pleased to note no stiffness between us, only a slight diffidence on his part. He and Reverend Snover were moving about among the assembly, speaking earnestly to both humans and the Enchanted, trying, I was sure, to promote peace even now. I recognized some of my acquaintances there—among them, Lavinia Hubbard, on the arm of the Little Crooked Man; Wallace, Zeke, Tallulah, and Ernest of the

Bremen Town Musicians; the Pumpkin-Eaters; Edgar Pig; and
many other familiar faces from the men's choir. There were also
a great many humans with angry, self-important looks; most of
them were gathered about the table of solicitors for the opposing
side. I recognized Mr. Babcock, the one who published all the
incendiary articles in the *Town Crier*. He was sitting directly behind the opposition's lawyers, looking smug and even amused. I
had not seen him in church since the day Reverend Snover had
given his epic sermon about the curfew.

Suddenly the crowd parted at the doorway, and Mother
Shoe made her entrance. Someone had tried very hard to make
her over into a staid, respectable matron, but human though she
was, all I could think of when I saw her was the great predator
that had appeared to me when I first beheld her. Now the predator was back again, corseted and buttoned to the chin, with a
cinched-up bosom and a crinoline, and fitted sleeves around the
powerful arms. She was all in mauve, with a touch of lace at her
throat, a masterpiece of taste and decorum. Above the blood-
thirsty jaws and terrible eyes of my vision was a frilly bonnet of
matching color, with ruched lining and a posy of flowers. The
pitiful baby, and the cigar, she had apparently left at home.

It seemed clear that someone had provided the funds, and
the conservative taste, for this dramatic overhaul, for it certainly
was not of Mother Shoe's own means, or choosing. Probably
the same person, or organization, that had paid for her team
of clever lawyers. The question remained: Did she really want
Goldilocks so badly? Was it to keep the girl from incriminating
her? If, as the child had indicated, she was not related to Mother
Shoe at all, the woman might face charges of kidnapping,
perhaps with some of the other children as well, not to mention

using them as her own private ring of thieves. Goldilocks must have quite a story to tell, if she ever found the courage to speak. I thought of the day she had spoken up to Gabriel. Would that brave little voice ever be heard again? Then I looked around. Where was Gabriel? Shouldn't he be here? And if he wasn't here, where was he?

38

For the Greater Good

❧

Judge Slugby was announced. A sudden hush fell over the court-room, and he made his entrance, pompous and smug as only the truly inadequate can be. This, then, was the man who held the fragile child's future in his hands. A great barrel-chested human in the requisite black robe and white curled wig, he might have been impressive except that his eyes seemed always to be looking shiftily off to one side, and he had a small, mean mouth above a gelatinous double chin.

"Well, well, what have we here, Mr. Cheater?" Judge Slugby drawled expansively while thumbing through the papers before him. I quickly ascertained that "Cheater" was the actual sur-name of the opposition's barrister, a fact that did nothing to reassure me. A tall, suave human in a pinstripe suit, Mr. Cheater responded with an oily smile, and, rubbing his hands together, said, "A little matter of child custody, Your Worship. Cut-and-dried, really."

"I object!" thundered Mr. Armstrong, the small but

charismatic weasel who was the Vaughns' barrister. "Mr. Cheater has appointed himself judge, and has passed the verdict before the proceedings have even begun! Extraordinary!"

Judge Slugby slammed down the gavel, and turned furiously on Mr. Armstrong. "It is not. Your. Turn. To. Speak!" he pronounced. "Mr. Cheater, please continue."

"Thank you, Your Worship," Mr. Cheater effused. "As I was saying before I was so rudely interrupted, we have here a case of a family broken apart, a mother whose own daughter has been kept from her and so alienated from her that the child refuses to acknowledge her as her parent, or even speak to her. This tears at the very fabric of our society and the sacredness of the family bond. My client looks to the court to correct this grave injustice, and restore this child to her bereft mother."

"Aha!" Judge Slugby exclaimed. "And what do you have to say to *that,* Mr. Armstrong? Speak up!"

Mr. Armstrong, calm in the face of the judge's bullying, answered, "I have a great deal to say, if it please the court. Firstly, my client avers that the child he knows as Goldilocks does not acknowledge the plaintiff as her mother because the plaintiff is not, in fact, the child's mother. Furthermore, he states that the child in question was found abandoned in his own house, hungry, uncared for, little better than a savage. We will show that the child's refusal to speak was in fact the direct result of the most terrifying threats from this woman's son to keep her silent. We will demonstrate that my client has provided for her every need, aiding her transformation into a happy, healthy little girl who is loved and cared for as one of the family, and returns that affection. We will prove that the plaintiff tried to extort a huge sum of money from my client in exchange for giving up her alleged parental rights. Finally, we offer evidence that the plaintiff is an unfit guardian for any—"

"*The court* will determine who is fit or unfit, thank you very much, Mr. Armstrong! Must I remind you of your place? No? Good! Mr. Cheater, you will proceed with your client's story."

Mother Shoe was promptly escorted to the witness-box and sworn in, promising to tell the whole truth, so help her God. What followed was a long, lachrymose melodrama in which Mr. Cheater drew out the tale of the poor (but virtuous!) mother, a mother whose adored golden-haired daughter Mary (her favorite child!) mysteriously disappeared, the little girl so pretty and charming that her mother always suspected that the child had been snatched! Upon further questioning, it was revealed that this tenderhearted mother went immediately into a decline so crippling that she could do little more than weep. As a consequence, she was unable to so much as report the missing child to the constable. A great deal was made of this tragic disability until most of the spectators on the plaintiff's side were crying crocodile tears and emitting theatrical wails. Having managed, without saying so, to imply that the Vaughns or their agents had kidnapped the child, Mr. Cheater left his client to be questioned by Mr. Armstrong.

"Mrs. Shoe," Mr. Armstrong opened, "you say the child currently being cared for by the Vaughns is your natural daughter. When is her birthday?"

"Well . . . um . . . June! She was born in June. Must 'ave been the middle. The fifteenth."

"Can you point out any record of her birth? A church registry, perhaps?"

Mother Shoe's eyes flicked to Mr. Cheater, who made little

hand signals and nodded his encouragement. She grinned slyly and said, "We've moved around so much that I can't even remember what parish we was in when the dear little mite was born."

"Perhaps you could name some of those parishes for the court, as many as you can remember."

Mother Shoe suddenly choked, and cast a desperate glance at Mr. Cheater.

"I object!" cried Mr. Cheater. "Counsel is badgering the witness! She has already stated that she does not remember."

"Mr. Armstrong!" thundered the judge. "You will cease this line of questioning and move on!"

Mr. Armstrong's mouth closed in a straight line, and his eyes narrowed as he rethought his approach. "Is there anyone outside of your immediate family who can attest to her being your daughter or, indeed, to her being under your care? A neighbor? A shopkeeper? A pastor, perhaps?"

She had the answer ready. "Oh my, *yes,* sir! Dozens of 'em!"

Mr. Cheater interrupted. "If it please the court, we have many witnesses ready to testify on my client's behalf."

The judge nodded. "All in good time, Mr. Cheater, all in good time." I was left wondering how they had found even one witness to testify for Mother Shoe. Who could be so deaf, dumb, and blind as to think she belonged anywhere near children?

Mr. Armstrong proceeded to examine her concerning the morning in April, when she arrived at the manor and first saw Mary. When questioned about the child's horrified reaction to her, Mother Shoe pulled out a lace handkerchief and became quite incoherent with sobbing, until Mr. Cheater once again accused Mr. Armstrong of badgering the witness. Changing his line of questioning, the Vaughns' barrister asked her whether she had, in fact, suggested at the conclusion of that meeting that the Vaughns might keep the girl for one thousand pounds.

"Oh, that was only a misunderstandin'!" she declared. "I was just tellin' Mr. Vaughn that my daughter was worth a fortune to me, more than any amount of money. I don't know how he could have got it so mucked up." She smiled sweetly then, but all I could see was the snapping jaws of the great predator.

As the questioning wore on, it became lamentably clear that every challenge Mr. Armstrong offered would be fended off by the plaintiff or her team of lawyers with half-truths, damaging innuendos, and outright lies. And if none of that worked, the judge himself would step in and swat the issue aside. An endless stream of "witnesses" were called to testify on Mother Shoe's behalf, sorry characters with little to commend them except their ability to answer by rote. Each remembered "dear little Mary" with perfect clarity; each proclaimed Mother Shoe's mythical virtues, her unfailing motherly love, and her extreme suffering over the little lost daughter. Mr. Armstrong did his best to debunk their assertions, but they had obviously been very well coached. By the time their final witness had told his memorized story, a halo could almost be seen glowing over Mother Shoe's head. All of their witnesses were whispering in a group behind the lawyers, looking quite friendly with one another, and with Mr. Babcock, and quite pleased with themselves. The only thing that kept me from despair was the knowledge that our side had yet to present its case.

The judge called a recess, it now being midday, and I was greatly relieved to be free from the hot, dusty room and the crush of bodies. With great difficulty the Vaughns and I made our way through the noisy crowd to a nearby hotel, for some tea and refreshments, though we had little appetite. "Where did they come up with all those witnesses?" I asked. "And how could those people lie so?"

"It's not hard to guess," growled Mr. Vaughn. "You saw how neighborly, how *fraternal* they are with one another. They are all members of the same club: the Anthropological Society. They have no doubt convinced themselves that this is for the greater good."

"But they lied! In a court of law! Under oath!"

"Yes, and we're not the only ones who know it. That may give us grounds for an appeal, but it will not help us today."

I looked down at my food, unable to touch it. Taking only a little tea, I gathered my courage for the ordeal still to come.

All too soon, we were back in the stuffy courtroom, the judge glaring sideways at us as he instructed Mr. Armstrong to proceed. Calling Mr. Vaughn to the witness-box, the barrister bade him tell the tale of when and how the child Goldilocks came into their lives. It was a compelling story. Mr. Vaughn held the rapt attention of the onlookers as he described that fateful day. He painted a pathetic portrait of the ragged, dirty little girl, asleep in Teddy's bed, with her thumb in her mouth and a pillowcase full of stolen goods.

Mr. Vaughn went on to tell how they had cared for the wild child, setting her up in her own quarters with Mrs. Van Winkle for a nurse, and providing her with plenty of good food and gentle attention. He reported my own success with the girl in highly complimentary terms. I was touched by this, as I had waited a long time to hear him praise my work. Finally, he spoke eloquently of integrating Goldilocks into their family life. I believed that Mr. Vaughn's well-known and unassailable character must have carried some considerable weight. The audience, at least, attended to his every word.

Mr. Armstrong continued his questioning, asking Mr. Vaughn to describe the events on that April day when Mother Shoe came to the house, ostensibly to claim Goldilocks. He recounted Mother Shoe's insinuation that she would give up the child if he made it worth her while, and her threatening to make his life insupportable when he turned her down.

The judge sat through this entire narrative with an inscrutable expression. Was I only imagining that he might betray some interest, some sympathy for this vulnerable child and her loving foster family? Was there yet a chance?

Now it was Mr. Cheater's turn to question Mr. Vaughn, and he made the most of it. "Concerning this child you claim to have found, was it not true," he asked, "that you, in fact, locked the girl up?"

A ripple of shock traveled the room. Stunned, I wondered who had supplied the opposition with this detail. Only a handful of trusted servants even knew of her presence in the house in those early days. Betsy. James. Cook. Mrs. Van Winkle. And Nurse.

Mr. Vaughn remained calm.

He attempted to explain the situation, but was cut short by Mr. Cheater again and again. In the end the barrister managed to give the impression that the girl had been held prisoner for many months. I felt sick with rage and frustration.

"Now," said Mr. Cheater, "concerning your meeting with Mrs. Shoe, you say that she brought up the matter of money."

"Yes. She stated that her husband sent no money."

"And then *you* asked whether she would accept money in exchange for the child?"

"No! I asked whether *she* was suggesting it!"

"Is it not true, Mr. Vaughn, that it was you—who are so wealthy—who sought to silence this grieving mother with a bribe?"

"No!"

"That it was you who suggested money in exchange for the child?"

"No!"

"And that it was you who named the price?"

"No!"

"And that Mrs. Shoe then told you that her child was beyond price?"

"Certainly not!"

Mr. Cheater turned to the audience with a knowing look, as if *he* had the inside information, and had just caught Mr. Vaughn in a monstrous lie. "That is all," he said with a smirk.

39

Redemption

❧

I knew that my turn could not be far off. Indeed, it took me a moment to realize that Mr. Armstrong was calling my name. I approached the witness-box with my head held high, and was duly sworn in. He examined me at some length, asking me to describe my first encounter with Goldilocks, and my evaluation of her condition at that time, then to provide a description of all the progress she had made thus far. When he asked how I would describe the child's relationships with the various members of the Vaughn family, it gave me great satisfaction to be able to testify to the love and affection she received from each of the Vaughns.

And then we came to the day Teddy and Goldilocks and I had encountered Gabriel and the other Shoe children in the forest. At Mr. Armstrong's bidding, I told of Gabriel's ugly threats against the child, and of his drawing his knife and gesturing with it. Mr. Armstrong questioned me about the next day as well, when Mother Shoe had come to the manor house, supposedly to collect Goldilocks. All these incidents I had firsthand knowledge of, and I felt with some pleasure that with my ready answers I was striking a blow for the helpless child and the Vaughn family.

Then it was Mr. Cheater's turn to examine me. "Miss Brown, how much do the Vaughns pay you?"

"I object!" cried Mr. Armstrong. "That has nothing to do with this case!"

"I propose that it has everything to do with this case," stated Mr. Cheater. "She can hardly be said to be an impartial witness when going against her employer could deprive her of her entire income."

"Answer the question, young lady!" demanded the judge.

"Thirty pounds per year, sir."

"Thirty pounds per year," repeated Mr. Cheater. "And since your father's death, you have no other means of support, is that not true?"

My mouth fell open in surprise. Who would have told them such a thing? Who would have known? I had spoken of this only to Mr. Vaughn, but who might have been listening in at the door, or repeating it in the kitchen—or eavesdropping at the laundry chute? Again, Nurse came to mind. Numbly, I answered, "Yes."

"Come now, Miss Brown, isn't that the motivation behind everything you've said here today?"

I took a deep breath, and said, "It is not! Not for any amount of money would I lie under oath, and neither would Mr. Vaughn ask it of me!"

Mr. Cheater smiled in that repulsive way he had, as if *he*, despite all evidence to the contrary, knew the *true* facts and motives, and would not shrink from the unpleasant task of digging out the dirtiest secrets for all the world to see. I wanted to strike him. I wanted to run away from the courtroom and wash myself of his contemptible insinuations before the miasma of his cynicism could somehow infect me.

"No more questions," Mr. Cheater declared, and my testimony was over. I was trembling as I took my seat. Though Mrs. Vaughn caught my eye and gave me a reassuring smile, I felt as if I must fly into a passion, or do something desperate. I knew that a great many villagers, both human and Enchanted, still remained to testify on the Vaughns' behalf, concerning their sterling characters and their standing in the community, and I could not countenance hearing Mr. Cheater slander them as he had me, but, though I wanted to quit the place immediately, I could not leave. Not without hearing the judge's verdict. I swallowed my wrath, and listened impatiently. The trial went on for hours, as many loyal and true individuals told of their experiences with the Vaughns: stories of Mr. Vaughn's benevolence, his integrity in business; the many stories of Mrs. Vaughn visiting the poor and the sick. Even some of Mrs. Vaughn's estranged friends had come to testify that Mrs. Vaughn was an excellent wife and mother, but Mr. Cheater shamelessly manipulated each witness, smearing them with intimations of payoffs, or other ulterior motives, until their testimonies served his own cause far better than ours.

I fastened my eyes upon the judge's inscrutable visage, reading volumes into his every twitch and flicker of expression. Was there hope? Was it still possible that he would be open-minded and fair? The afternoon stretched on. Tempers flared as patience wore thin, and people began craving their suppers. The assembly could not be restrained from talking among themselves, or even shouting out comments, despite numerous threats from the judge to clear the courtroom.

At last, the final witness had been exhaustively examined and cross-examined, and dragged himself, slope-shouldered and beaten, from the witness-box, and the judge retired to his chamber to consider his verdict. Minutes ticked by with agonizing slowness. A very few minutes. And then the judge resumed his exalted position and demanded silence.

Judge Slugby cleared his throat. "We have before us a case wherein no positive proof can be produced concerning the parentage of the child called by the plaintiff Mary and by the defendant Goldilocks. It is therefore the task of this court to determine what is in the best interest of the child. The plaintiff, Mrs. Shoe, argues that the child was kidnapped, and accuses the defendant, Mr. Vaughn, of locking the child up, a charge that he plainly admits to be true. The plaintiff presents a convincing case for her ability to care for the child, principally that she can provide a loving home for her among her own kind. We find the plaintiff clearly better qualified to raise the child and so rule that Mary be turned over to Mrs. Shoe immediately."

The entire assembly sprang to their feet as one, with a deafening roar—a roar of protest from some, a roar of triumph from others. "No!" I cried into the pandemonium, as in front of me Mrs. Vaughn collapsed into her husband's arms, and our whole team of lawyers gathered round to shield them from the frenzied crowd. I realized that I was myself gasping for breath, and felt an incipient dizziness at the edges of my consciousness. Pushing my way between bodies, I thought only that I must get to the door. I must get out!

I was being pressed further and further toward the opposition's table when, looking frantically about me for an opening, I saw Mother Shoe bang her large, lace-gloved fist on the tabletop and shout, "I want it *now!*" Mr. Cheater hastily put his finger to his lips in a gesture to silence her and, looking mortified, turned behind him to whisper in Mr. Babcock's ear.

"Now!" Mother Shoe roared again, and I watched as Mr. Babcock surreptitiously slipped her a fat purse. Stunned, I tried to make sense of it. Why would Mr. Babcock pay her off when she'd gotten what she wanted? I didn't understand just what had taken place, but the corruption was so thick I could almost smell it, and my desperation to get away was compounded by disgust and rage. Shedding all ladylike restraint, I shoved and shouted people out of my way, and, after a great deal of this, cleared myself a path to the door.

Outside, the crowd was electric with strife. I expected at any moment to see violence breaking out, but the only way to escape the crush was to go through it. I shoved and shouted some more, buffeted on every side by noise and chaos. I pushed ahead, bit by bit, until I had worked free of the worst of the crowd, and then I began to run. I must get home! Though I thought I should not be the one to break the news to the children, I wanted to set my earlier premonitions to rest, and to be with them and comfort them for as long as I could. On I ran, past Reverend Snover's little church, and across the churchyard, taking the shortcut through the woods, gasping for air, and cursing my tight stays and the sadistic dictates of feminine fashion. Reaching the back kitchen door at last, I pounded on it until a startled Cook let me in. She stood, staring at me, along with Betsy and a handful of other female servants, who regarded me as if I carried the fate of the world in my paws.

"We lost," I gasped. "They'll be coming to get her." Then I hurried past them and rushed up the back stairs and through the back hallways to the nursery. I forced myself to pause outside the nursery door to collect myself, feeling I must not break in on them breathless and panic-stricken. Precious minutes went by as I waited for my breathing to calm, then I opened the door and entered the nursery, quiet and empty as an abandoned ruin. Where were the children? Where was Nurse? I called their names, one at a time.

No answer.

No answer.

No answer.

I heard only the slight echo of my own voice reverberating from the high ceiling. I was seized with a sickening dread. Where could they be? Perhaps in the schoolroom? I dashed to the room, just next door, and immediately saw that it was empty. But something was different. The blackboard! A message was written on it, all across the bottom, in a nearly indecipherable hand.

Tha hev run awa I em goin after em. Nurs

Cold panic gripped my insides. The children had run away? Where could they be? How far could they have gotten? How desperate they must be! How utterly mistrustful of the whole adult world. I took a moment to bless the days I had allowed the illiterate Nurse into the schoolroom. Apparently, she had been doing more listening and learning than I would have guessed. My mind began to work feverishly. Gabriel was out there somewhere. What would he do if he found Goldilocks and Teddy alone and unprotected in the woods? I tried to convince myself that it was a huge property and the chances of his finding them were slim, but my every instinct told me to hurry, that time was of the essence. I could track them by smell, but only with a slow process of continually stopping to find their scent. If only I knew which way they'd gone!

I had an idea then, and ran to my own chamber, grabbing the magic mirror and shook him. "Mirror! Mirror! Wake up!"

"Oh! Oh! Oh!" came the startled reply. The carnival mask popped into focus. "What is it? Is the house on fire? Get me out of here!"

"It's the children. They've run away! Please, quickly, tell me where they've gone."

"For Heaven's sake, is that all? Don't even ask me. It's spying! You know I can't spy on anyone! It would violate my spell!"

"Then violate it! This is an emergency. Please, Mirror, you must tell me if they're in danger."

"Hmph. They're probably just hiding somewhere in the house. It's a very big house, you know. Either that or they're out in the forest, going down the path to the waterfall."

"How can you say that so casually? Which is it? Every minute counts!"

"I would only be telling you my opinion."

"What is your opinion based on?"

"Well, nothing. But everyone's entitled to their opinion, don't you agree?"

"Blast your opinion! Tell me the truth, for God's sake! There's no time to lose!"

The carnival face looked mortally offended, but he said, "Oh, very well. Here," and showed me an image of Teddy and

Goldilocks hurrying down a wooded lane, hand in paw in the fading light, while pools of spring flooding encroached on the track on either side of them. Just beyond them lay a large white boulder that I recognized from the path to the waterfall, and in the distant background a voice—Nurse's voice—could be heard calling, "Teddeeeeee! Teddeeeeee!" in a frenzied tone, and a jolt of fear shot through me. Her cries would draw Gabriel to them like a magnet.

"Is there a big brute of a boy chasing them?" I demanded.

"Are you asking for my opinion?" the mirror replied haughtily.

Goaded beyond endurance, I banged the mirror facedown on the bureau and rushed from the room, nearly colliding with Betsy, carrying a tray.

"Oh, miss! What is it, miss?"

"Betsy!" I gasped. "It's the children! They've run away!"

Her pleasant face metamorphosed into a portrait of guilt and anguish. "Oh, miss! I don't know what could have happened! I thought they was all sleeping when I looked in on 'em last, so I didn't want to disturb 'em no more. It's my fault! It's my own fault!"

"Never mind that, Betsy. They're headed for the waterfall. They're in danger, and I'm going after them. You must tell everyone where we've gone, and send help quickly! All the male staff, and anyone else—"

"I will, miss, as fast as I can."

"Tell them to come armed," I said, considering briefly whether to go and get a gun myself, but, unloaded, it would be of little use to me. I chose to listen to my inner voice, which urged me not to delay.

"Quickly, Betsy! I have to go!" I cried.

With that I made my way down the stairs, then ran headlong through the hallway to a little-used side door that was closest to the path to the waterfall. Finding it unlocked and the key lying on the floor, I surmised that the children and perhaps Nurse had come this way. Making straight for the path, I knew that I must pace myself, but the fear that propelled me would not allow anything less than my utmost speed. Soon my breath began to come in ragged gulps, but still I was able to sustain myself and keep on running, my legs pumping harder and harder, automatically now, eating up the ground in front of me as each jolt sent pain into my corseted ribs. I passed the white boulder that I recognized from the first time I had come up this lane. After that one near-disastrous trip, we had never come this way again, and my thoughts of that day were overshadowed by the traumatic memory of Teddy stranded on the cliffside.

What could have possessed him to go there now? My mind refused to consider the question, but my forebodings became more acute with each passing minute. By now my feet were numb, and my lungs were on fire, burning for one deep, cool breath of air. I could no longer deny the dizziness that threatened to overcome me, or the darkness gathering at the edges of my vision. I collapsed against a tree trunk, gasping like a great fish out of water, not knowing whether I would recover or succumb.

One cramped breath at a time, the air flowed back into my lungs and revived me, and as my breath came more easily, I could hear something up ahead. Was I gaining on them? Surely that was Nurse's voice! I could hear it clearly now. "Teddeeeeee! Teddeeeeee!" fading into the distance. With a fresh burst of energy, I forced myself to my feet and lumbered, heavy-legged, down the lane, following the sound. Only a little further, I was sure. And then the cries stopped. What did that mean? Though I was overheated, I shivered with cold. The path finally came to an end at the edge of a large clearing, and I stopped, holding my side and panting. There, at one end of the clearing, was the massive cliff wall that I remembered, the waterfall, swollen with spring runoff, thundering down its rocky face with inexorable force, and filling the air with a fine spray in every direction. The lagoon shimmered with the colors of the setting sun. And there, at the foot of the cliff, stood Teddy and Goldilocks, looking like cornered rabbits. Halfway between the children and me stood Nurse.

"Don't do it, Master Teddy!" she was pleading.

"Don't come any closer!" Teddy warned her. "We're going up, and we won't come down until you all promise she doesn't have to go!"

My heart sank. Would we all survive this day? To think that we had driven these little ones to such a desperate act!

"Teddy! Goldilocks!" I shouted. "Don't do it! Please! You could be hurt, or worse! Come away!"

In answer, Teddy turned and gave Goldilocks a boost up to a low ledge, then pulled himself up. This was the cub I had encouraged to think for himself, to worry less about being perfectly good and obedient. How bitter now was my regret! And yet I had to admire his principles and courage.

"No, Teddy!" Nurse cried, running toward them on her short badger legs.

Goldilocks scrambled up the rough rock as if her life depended on it, and Teddy made his way deliberately after her.

Nurse could not reach the ledge where the children had begun their climb, and so searched the base of the cliff for a way up. I had just reached the rock wall myself, intending to follow the children up, when a voice some distance behind me made my fur stand on end.

"Well, ain't this just prime!"

I had heard this voice, these very words, before. I turned, and looked upon the loathsome physiognomy of Gabriel standing at the edge of the woods, with much the same expression as the great predator I had seen in his mother. His glee at finding such fertile hunting grounds was almost palpable.

"What? Nothin' to say?" he gloated, keeping me pinned in his gaze while he slowly knelt and picked up several large rocks.

A bolt of fear shot down my spine as his intention became clear. I looked all about for shelter, but found none. My back was to the wall. To my right raged the waterfall. To my left a dozen or more yards of exposed rock face extended to the forest. I calculated in an instant that I would stand a better chance dodging his rocks than brawling with him and his truncheon. Though I matched him in size, I feared I was no match for the kind of enraged frenzy I had witnessed in him once before. I could not hope to compete with him in fighting skill, or plain viciousness, and, being Enchanted, I believed I had no more killer instinct than any gently reared young lady. If I ran away, at least he would have to try to hit a moving target, but then nothing would remain between the dangerous brute and the children. No, I did the only thing I could: I knelt and picked up my own rocks. He would not find me an easy opponent. In my tomboy days I had insisted that Papa teach me to throw like the neighborhood boys. This service he had performed admirably, telling me that my skills reflected on his own ability. I would not embarrass him now.

As I scrambled for my own arsenal of rocks, his first missile struck me, grazing my ear with a flash of hot pain, and making me angry. Grabbing a hefty stone, I stood, pulling my arm back, and hurled it with terrific force; it struck him on the forehead and immediately drew blood. His expression was almost comically surprised, but quickly turned to rage. He cast several more stones in rapid succession while advancing steadily toward me, all of them striking me painfully on my head and body, and I retaliated with a large rock, hitting him hard in the stomach. He bent double, and then on he came, implacably shortening the distance between us, no doubt having determined, as I had, that he could beat me in physical combat. Having already resolved that I must not run, I stood my ground and took advantage of the shorter distance between us by throwing much heavier stones, which were plentiful, and aiming at his legs. He dodged them with demonic agility, coming closer and closer to me, and then he stopped, two yards away, in a crouching position, taunting me.

"Wouldn't you just love to wipe this smile off my face?" he said, matching his actions to his words with a smile so evil and exulting that I did take a swipe at him, claws extended, and raked the side of his face as he jumped back. His hand went to his face and came away covered with blood.

"You'll pay for that!" he snarled, his eyes filled with hatred, and we began to circle one another like fighters in a ring as he gripped his truncheon and smiled. I was surprised by a deep growl starting in my throat, and growing to a wild roar as some instinct within me responded to the threat, and was pleased to note that this ruffled his composure considerably. I saw my moment and went for him, teeth bared and claws raking, finding my animal nature at last, but he was fast, and cunning, wielding his truncheon with great strength and efficiency. I believe I might have ripped his throat out if he had not slammed the club down on my sensitive snout with such force that I felt the bone crack and blood fill my nostrils.

I backed away, swaying dizzily, and though he was bleeding from many places, he was laughing at me, and there was something horrible and half mad about his eyes. With obvious effort, he reined himself in and resumed his crouch, one hand turned palm upward and curling toward himself as if to incite me.

"Do it. *Do it!*" He laughed insanely. "You animals, and Rat, and all your fancy airs! So very consid'rate of yous to be all in one place, so's I can fix you all, *one by one*! First you, and then—"

I lunged, throwing all of my weight toward him, intending to knock him down, realizing too late that this was exactly what he had anticipated. In a deft move, he stepped aside, leaving one foot for me to trip over, pulling me off balance by my arm, and using my own weight against me. I slammed to the ground belly-down, and before I could recover myself, he was sitting on top of me, pinning me, and laughing fiendishly. I turned my face to the side just enough to see him raising a great rock high over my head.

ॐ

That was the last thing I remembered for some time. When I fought my way back to consciousness, it was with an awareness of pain in my head and all over my body. Moving experimentally,

I felt that Gabriel must have beaten and kicked me severely as I lay insensible, his craven vengeance exacted at last.

As my awareness increased, my thoughts were all for the children. With extreme difficulty, I pushed myself from the ground and stood, looking up the rock face as the last, dying rays of the sun stained it red. There above me a terrible chase played out. While I had lain unconscious, the children and Nurse had climbed some thirty yards up the cliff. One false move now and the fall would surely be fatal. I saw Goldilocks look down at Gabriel, who had climbed halfway up to them, laughing as he gained on them, and I heard her little scream as she frantically quickened her pace. Teddy, struggling to keep up with her, slipped on some loose stones and sent them flying down the cliffside as he hung on with his claws.

"No!" I cried, cringing as I tried to move too quickly toward the low ledge where the children had started their climb. Realizing that my skirts would be a dangerous impediment to my progress, I bent over to tuck them up, crying out as I did so. Determined that nothing would stop me, I began to climb with all the speed I was capable of, reaching a paw out here, straining for a foothold there, and groaning with pain at each movement. It seemed nearly impossible, but I must do it, and do it faster! Even as these thoughts raced through my mind, I felt that it was hopeless. They were all so far above me! How long could this mad chase go on? We were all one slip away from certain destruction. "Please, God—" I repeated incoherently, my eyes following every move above me.

Teddy and Goldilocks had reached a narrow ledge, and could apparently go no further. They held each other tightly, looking down with horror on Gabriel's progress, as Nurse pulled herself up to join them. Then I saw Gabriel pause. Even from this distance I could tell that he was covered with blood. Could he be weakening? But with a sudden burst of effort, he pulled himself upward again.

"I've got you now! *I've got you now,* you dam'd little buggers!" he crowed. A few more moves and he would have them. I beat against the impervious rock helplessly, my eyes riveted to the scene. Directly above him, Nurse looked down, only for a moment, as if considering. Then she spread her arms out, and with a mighty "YAAAHHHH!" launched her whole body at Gabriel's head, knocking him backward off the cliff. Down they went together, Gabriel's screams ringing through the clearing, and then there was only the roar of the waterfall as it lost itself in the timeless peace of the lagoon.

40

Abide with Me

❧

Here my memories fade in and out like ghosts. Some moments stand out in my mind with lifelike clarity. Some are as insubstantial as dreams, and some are, perhaps mercifully, lost to me.

I remember being surprised by my own great, gulping sobs of grief, mingled with a kind of fierce joy at the magnificence of Nurse's final act, which played over and over again in my mind, then and for years afterward. For the rest of my life I would try to sort out the puzzle of good and evil that was Nurse. Now I blessed her on her way and prayed that her Maker would judge her leniently.

Though I have no memory of what must have been a long and torturous climb, I remember reaching the high ledge at last, and Teddy sobbing, brokenhearted, in my arms as Goldilocks patted his back solicitously. Suddenly he raised his head and looked into my face, crying, "We won't go down! They can't make us! They'll have to promise!" I was well aware by then that descending the cliff in the semidarkness would be madness, even if the children had been quite willing. I knew besides that my battered body had taken all the abuse it could. I felt keenly the damage and swelling on my snout, and I was now barely able to lift a limb. There was no help for it; we must spend the night on this narrow ledge. Looking it over, I saw that it was only about four yards long and about a yard and a half deep, enough space for the three of us to sit safely, with some left over, but we could not lie down. I would have to remain awake and watchful. As my fear of the incipient darkness threatened to overcome me, I tried not to let the children see just how frightened I really was. Already I was imagining a night suspended over a black void, terrified of making one wrong move. And then, before the last of the light faded, I heard the most welcome sound I had ever heard in my life.

"Miss Brown! Miss Brown!" a voice called out. "Are you all right up there?"

There was no mistaking that voice. I crept to the edge of the ledge and peered over. Down at the foot of the cliff stood the one bear in the world I most wanted to see: Mr. Bentley—Jonathan! I didn't know how he came to be there, and I didn't care. All that mattered was his presence.

"Are you all right up there?" he repeated.

My body racked with pain, I hardly knew how to answer him. I took a deep, ragged breath and shouted down, "The children are all right! I'm not so well. I'm afraid we must spend the night up here!"

"Then I'll come up and stay with you!" he called.

I hesitated a moment as relief flooded through me, but then I thought of him making the hazardous ascent in the dim light, and yelled down, "No! It's too dangerous!" to no effect. I was filled once again with the cold dread that had become normal to me in the past few hours, and at first I thought I could not stand to watch. Finding, after a time, that not watching was worse, I looked down and followed his slow progress up the cliff. After watching his every move for what seemed like an eternity, I even came to feel that my vigilance was somehow helping to keep him safe.

As he made his interminable climb, more and more figures came bursting into the clearing. I thought I could make out the faces of Fairchild and Harry, and I saw them take off their coats and lay them over the still forms at the base of the cliff. Mr. and Mrs. Vaughn appeared amid a crowd of others, and several strong bears had to restrain Mr. Vaughn from attempting to climb the cliff himself. I heard someone call for torches and lanterns, and a number of them went away, presumably to fetch them. Constable Murdley was there, telling everyone to keep back, and Reverend Snover stayed close by the Vaughns. It looked as if everyone from both sides of the conflict had followed them home from the courthouse, the curfew ignored, or forgotten, by the Enchanted in numbers too great to be subdued. I could imagine what the outcry must have been when the crowd had reached the manor house only to find Goldilocks and Teddy gone. Probably no force on earth could have stopped them from swarming along on the hunt to find the children. Now they were all gathering here, their attention fixed by the crisis unfolding before them.

On came Mr. Bentley, meanwhile, defying the great stone wall, and the failing light, and gravity itself. When at last he pulled himself over the lip of the ledge, I could not help my foolish tears. I profoundly wished that I could have thrown my arms around him, but instead I only gave him a look full of gratitude and hoped that he could see it in my eyes.

"You came," I said.

"I couldn't leave you alone here in the dark," he answered.

At his words, warmth suffused me. The cold claws of fear that had clutched my heart melted a little, and I suddenly felt that I could face the night to come. The children too seemed calmer in his presence. There was just enough room for him to sit at the opposite end of the ledge. All around us darkness was descending, and the air was turning bitterly cold as the last of the light faded away.

"How did you get here?" I asked.

"I wanted to attend the hearing, but I arrived too late to get into the courthouse. It was packed to overflowing by the time I got there. When word came of the judge's decision, I was caught in the crowd outside, and it was bedlam. I could barely move. I waited for what seemed like an eternity to see the Vaughns coming out, but I must have missed them in the confusion. Finally, I worked my way free of the crowd and came back to the manor. That's when Betsy told me that you and the children had gone, and I followed you here."

"Thank Heaven you did," I replied with a groan.

"Are you hurt? What has happened?"

I described to him the rock fight with Gabriel, and waking up bruised and battered. Teddy told him with tears in his eyes of the savage beating, which the children had witnessed.

"I'll kill him!" was Mr. Bentley's response.

"He's already dead," I assured him. "That was his body at the foot of the cliff."

Teddy and I must have filled him in then, though I don't

recall doing so, on the story of the wild chase up the cliffside, and of Nurse and her heroism. I have a hazy recollection of time passing, and the noise of many distant voices. My gaze was drawn to the masses of torches and lanterns below us, yet even as I marveled at the united show of concern among all the villagers, I couldn't help but wonder if some of those concerned citizens were satisfied now with what they had driven these children to do.

I remember Teddy repeating his ultimatum to Mr. Bentley, explaining with an earnest resolution beyond his years that he and Goldilocks would not come down until they had everyone's promise that Goldilocks would not be forced to go with Mother Shoe. Mr. Bentley listened attentively, then put his paw on the cub's shoulder and told him that he admired him for taking a stand, and would do whatever he could to help. I remember him shouting Teddy's message to the crowd below us, and hearing their cries of dismay.

"Oh, the poor dears!" yelled one.

"Oh, what have we done?" cried many others.

I remember Reverend Snover's voice calling up to us, blessing us, and telling us that everyone down below would be standing together, keeping a vigil with us through the night. Would it be too much to hope, I wondered, that the children's plight could soften some hearts, change some minds? I thought of the tale of Romeo and Juliet, bringing a city to its senses with their deaths, and prayed that it would not require so much as that. Preparing ourselves for the night ahead, Mr. Bentley and I settled the children between us, sitting them with their backs to the rock, and arranged our bodies on either side to shelter them from the sharp wind that had whipped up.

It was some time later, as the first stars were appearing, that I began to hear the music. Softly at first, it blended with the flow of the waterfall in an otherworldly harmony. As it increased in volume, I recognized it as the sound of a multitude of voices raised in song.

> *Abide with me; fast falls the eventide;*
> *The darkness deepens; Lord, with me abide!*

As the familiar strains of the old hymn rose up to us, I thought that surely the whole village must be singing together. The thought brought tears to my eyes. Had the possibility of losing both children been enough, finally, to make them see? I could almost hear Reverend Snover, far below, exhorting his flock to reconsider their priorities, to forgive one another and pray and sing for us together through the ordeal. It was the beginning of a long night of such music—music to comfort, music to pass the time, and, most of all, music to keep us awake, for to fall asleep could mean death.

A crescent moon shone feebly in the dark sky, giving us a point of reference to measure the passage of time. As the wind grew colder still, we huddled closer together, struggling in vain to find comfort on the inhospitable rock. The children soon felt the effects of exhaustion, and despite the cold and tribulation, their eyelids grew heavy. As they were well back from the edge, and we had them wedged tightly between us, Mr. Bentley and I decided to let them sleep.

I too was exhausted, nearly paralyzed by pain and weariness, and filled with fears of what the morning would bring, but Mr. Bentley, sensing my anxiety, reached over and offered me his paw. Throwing propriety to the winds, I took it gratefully, and held it for some time, feeling his strength coursing through me. He made it his special task that night to keep me alert and talking. Though my attention sometimes wavered, I remember him pointing out to me each of the constellations, and telling long, involved stories of the Greek myths behind each. We talked of books we'd both read, and of the story of Robinson Crusoe, which I had read aloud to him in what seemed like another lifetime. Since we had never finished the book, we took turns making up our own endings.

Goldilocks awoke several times, crying with the cold, and I realized that we were all wet through by the mist from the waterfall. I became even more fearful for the child, who had no coat of fur to protect her. The air had become even colder, almost frigid, and we had no shelter. Mr. Bentley and I leaned in toward each other, covering the little ones as best we could with our bodies.

With our faces so near to one another, I was grateful that the darkness hid my damaged face. I wondered how bad it looked, and, if I survived this adventure, how it would heal. Though I was still in great pain, I managed to hold up my end of the conversation. The talk became more personal, with me telling him all about my papa, and, as the moon drifted toward the western horizon, he talked to me of his family, and of the long-standing friendship between his own deceased father and his uncle, Amy's father, that had led to their early betrothal. Though the subject was a torment to me, I was ineluctably drawn to it. As he talked on, I thought how much I wished that he were not so honorable, so chivalrous, so loyal. And yet weren't these all things I loved about him? Could I wish for him to be less than he was? Maybe I could, for just this one night—the only night we could ever spend together. Just for to-night we could sit together in the darkness, and we could hold paws and look up at the beautiful Heavens. Just for tonight he was mine.

Holding tight to each other, we persevered through those fateful hours. Toward morning, I recognized a unique four-part harmony: our friends the Bremen Town Musicians were offering up the sweet refrain of the old ballad they had performed for us one evening at the Snovers'. I felt a surge of gratitude for the villagers, who had sung for us all through the night. But could they, would they, make the promise that Teddy and Goldilocks waited for? Only a little while now until dawn, and I couldn't guess whether the children would agree to descend the cliff at daybreak. It was certain that we could not get them down without their cooperation, and how much more dangerous would the descent be if we delayed, and were all weakened by hunger and thirst? Would my battered body even support me for the long climb down? Somewhere in all my worries I thought I heard Papa's voice reassuring me, telling me that I could do whatever I had to do.

Even die? I wondered.

~

The sky was brightening in the east, stars melting into the rose-tinted radiance. As I watched, a brilliant sliver of light peered above the horizon, touching the opulent clouds with gold, and rousing a world in darkness with a foretaste of Heaven. In the beauty of that dawn, even death did not seem so frightening. If my time came, would I become part of that fiery beauty? Would Mama and Papa be waiting for me?

Goldilocks shivered beside me in her sleep. Mr. Bentley and I had protected the little ones as best we could all through the night, but her clothing was wet and cold from the mist in the air. I felt her forehead and found it cool, but that did not allay my concern.

"We'd best coax her down from here and get her warm and dry before she becomes ill," said Mr. Bentley when I told him of my worries. "The sooner the better."

"But what about the promise?" Teddy asked, crestfallen.

"We'll find out, old man," Mr. Bentley assured him, patting his back. He leaned over the brink of the ledge for a shouted conference with Reverend Snover.

"What's the news?" Mr. Bentley called out.

Reverend Snover's faint voice, barely heard over the waterfall, rose up, saying, "We've had quite a time of it down here! Great things happening!"

"We could use some good tidings!"

"Well, we held a town meeting right here last night, and decided a few things."

"Yes?"

"First, the curfew. We voted it down. The Enchanted were in revolt in numbers too great to arrest!"

"That's good news indeed!"

"And then we voted to impeach Judge Slugby."

"What did you say?"

"He says," cried a stronger voice, "that we impeached Judge Slugby!" I leaned over to see who was talking and was amazed to find that it was Constable Murdley. "That doesn't change the ruling, mind you, but we sent some riders over to the next county to wake up the circuit judge, Judge Newton. He's issued a stay of execution pending your appeal. That means that Judge

Slugby's order won't be carried out unless you lose the appeal. In the meantime, the girl stays with you."

Reverend Snover then shouted, "Mother Shoe has not been seen since late last night! She's nowhere to be found! It appears that she's abandoned her children and run off!"

It required a moment to take this in. It seemed like too much to hope for that she would simply go away, and yet when I thought of the fat purse I had seen her take from Mr. Babcock, I might have guessed she wouldn't share her gains with her pack of hungry children. I felt a surge of anger at the realization that she had never really wanted Goldilocks, or any of them, including the pathetic baby. She had just played the role of the brokenhearted mother for what she could get out of it. Since the Anthropological Society had apparently paid her to put on that act, they must surely have known it was false. Now, if she had really run off, the charade was exposed, and I hoped the whole society choked on their embarrassment.

As I cogitated on these things, Mr. Bentley related the news to Goldilocks and Teddy.

"It's not quite the same as the promise you wanted, children, but I think it's the best we could possibly hope for."

Goldilocks threw her arms around Teddy, tears in her eyes. Disbelief, gratification, and relief rivaled one another on Teddy's expressive face. "Then it's safe to go down?"

"It's safe to go down."

Teddy, who had been the brave little soldier for as long as he possibly could, put his paws to his eyes and cried, "I want my mama and papa!"

"And you shall have them. We will climb down very slowly and carefully, and when you reach the bottom, they will be there for you. Can you do that?"

"Y-yes," said Teddy, drying his tears. For a moment, Goldilocks looked as if she would speak, but she covered her mouth with her hands instead and turned away.

We waited until full light, then Mr. Bentley lectured us sternly about following his route, and testing each pawhold and foothold before putting weight on it. I knew that he too had accepted the awful dangers of the next hour, but he did his best to give the children the confidence they would need.

Mr. Bentley was first to step off the ledge, feeling his way along the cliff face and turning to encourage Teddy to follow him. Goldilocks was next, and I was last. Far below us, the villagers waited and watched, no longer the angry, divided crowd of yesterday, but hushed and anxious, their compassion almost tangible. Mr. Bentley led us in a roughly diagonal route across the rock, taking care to find footholds within the reach of the children's shorter legs, and preventing us from being directly above or below one another. Teddy scrambled nimbly along in Mr. Bentley's wake. Goldilocks was most apprehensive, afraid to look down, but unable to proceed without doing so. I did my best to reassure her, reminding her that she had climbed up this same cliff face the previous day and could surely climb down now. I sounded more confident than I felt. Aching in every limb, I was barely able to force my own body to move, and stretch, and bear my weight.

And then it happened, so quickly that my instincts took over before I fully realized what had occurred: the sound of slipping rocks, and Goldilocks's cry. I grabbed for her, clutching her by the wrist, as first one and then the other of her feet went out from under her. In the space of a moment, she was dangling from my paw over the sheer drop, amid screams from below. I cried out from the terrible pain in my side, not sure how long I could hold her. At once Teddy turned, and, reversing his direction, worked his way back to within an arm's length of his terrified playmate. A few agonizing seconds passed as he reached for her, then I felt a sudden lightening of the burden as the two locked wrists, and Teddy slid her toward him across the rock. Just as her hand slipped from my grasp, she gained a foothold, and found her balance, and the villagers' cheers surrounded us, reverberating against the rock. Had anyone still doubted the love between the cub and the child, they must have surely believed it then.

I called to Mr. Bentley to wait a few minutes while I recovered from the piercing pain and collected my wits, and Teddy comforted the shaken Goldilocks, then we continued our slow, arduous descent. What had seemed nearly impossible to me at first became a tiny bit more possible with each careful movement, until at last we took that final step to the blessed ground. I stood on it for only a moment, long enough to see the children gathered up in loving embraces by Mr. and Mrs. Vaughn, and Mr. Bentley swallowed up by the crowd. I saw Reverend Wright come up to me just as my legs gave way, and I fell into a pair of strong arms. Reverend Wright's arms.

41

The Answer

❧

"Um, do forgive me for the familiarity, Miss Brown," stated Reverend Wright, clearly embarrassed, "but I'm afraid you are injured. I think that I had better carry you back to the manor."

Looking up into his face, I protested that I was much too heavy, and that he mustn't think of such an exertion.

"I'm well over my cold now, Miss Brown, a hale and hearty specimen if ever there was one. And you are really rather light, you know. It's no trouble at all."

As I was actually quite unable to walk back to the manor, I put my arms about his neck, and offered no more argument.

Though I wouldn't have believed it possible, Reverend Wright did indeed carry me all the way back to the Cottage, a herculean act of kindness that seemed no less than heroism to me. I remember very little after that, as I was put to bed and liberally dosed with laudanum. Gabriel's beating had left me with a broken snout, a concussion, two cracked ribs, and numerous bruises. The Vaughns saw to it that I received the best medical care, but there was no help to guide me through the maelstrom of love and guilt that overwhelmed me as I faced the fact that the night I had shared with Mr. Bentley was over now—that he would never be part of my life again. Ahead of me I could see only an endless stretch of loneliness and loss, and in my darkest moments I had no courage to go forward. The days passed, and though my aches and bruises began to heal, I became ever more quiet and lost in my own thoughts. The doctor gave the opinion that it was the shock of the dangerous misadventure that had affected me so adversely, and I let him think it was. He prescribed more laudanum, which acted upon me so that I slept much during the day, but at night I often lay awake. I found that I cared little about the darkness now, perhaps because I had faced such terror in reality that my imagination could not frighten me anymore, or perhaps because it let me imagine that I was back on the cliffside, sharing the dark night with Mr. Bentley.

I remember the Vaughns coming to visit me in my chamber, full of concern, and telling me how grateful they were for all I had done for the children. Mrs. Vaughn described to me the beautiful service that had been held for Nurse's burial, and how the story of her heroic sacrifice had spread far and wide, so that the little church had been packed with mourners. It was not for me, I decided, to tarnish the one shining deed Nurse had done with a postmortem exposure of her many wrongdoings. I chose to consign her transgressions to the past, and her soul to a greater Judge than I.

Mrs. Vaughn also related the news that their home had been burgled while everyone was keeping vigil at the waterfall, with many small but valuable things missing, including her pearl necklace, and that Mother Shoe was wanted for questioning. I did not doubt that the great predator was responsible, though I marveled at the kind of greed that would induce her to risk such an act of burglary when she already had a fat purse to take away with her. No doubt the house sitting empty, and her grudge against the Vaughns, had been too much temptation for her to resist. She was picked up within days, flaunting Mrs. Vaughn's necklace, and inflicted such violence and vituperation on the arresting officer that he resigned from the force shortly thereafter. Mother Shoe was found guilty of felony theft, and was likely transported to a distant land, as such felons are. Of her many children, half were found not to be hers at all. Some were returned to their rightful families, and the rest were made wards of the parish. As proof that many minds had been changed by that night at the waterfall, the children were quietly taken in, one by one, by caring villagers, both human and Enchanted, and no one raised a peep. The appeal would still go forward. We hoped it would be only a formality, with no more legal maneuvering by the Anthropological Society, but in any case the Vaughns had the gratifying task of explaining to Goldilocks that she need never worry about Mother Shoe again.

Teddy and Goldilocks were allowed to visit me, though they had apparently been warned to keep paws and hands carefully folded behind their backs, so as not to unintentionally hurt me with a sudden embrace. I was relieved that they did not react to my altered appearance, and though I had not ventured to view myself in a mirror, I dared hope that my face would not look too bad when the healing was done. Though Teddy was as engaging and ingenuous as ever, there was a discernible difference in him. I saw a seriousness, and a new confidence, the beginnings of the fine grown bear he would one day be, and yet my observations were tinged with a little sadness. Somewhere on that cliff he had left a bit of his cubhood behind forever.

Goldilocks seemed excessively shy at first, as though there were some grave matter that stood between us, and she feared my reaction. Slowly, from behind her back, she brought one trembling fist, which looked to be holding something. Taking my paw, she put the something in it. There I beheld my mother's locket, which had disappeared from my room so long ago—so very long ago that I had given up hope of ever seeing it again. I looked at Goldilocks in wonder, and as I did, she leaned over, cupping her little hand about my ear, and whispered to me, "I'm sorry, Miss Brown."

I enfolded her in my arms then, unheeding of the pain, and whispered back to her my thanks, and that the best gift she could ever give me would be to speak to me again.

When the day of the appeal came, I was unable to attend, but the Vaughns had all their other witnesses ready to testify again if need be. I was all on tenterhooks lest some fresh interference from the Anthropological Society prejudice the new judge against us. The Vaughns returned within the hour. Judge Newton, a wise old soul, having determined that Mother Shoe would never return, had declared the Vaughns to be perfectly fit guardians, and ruled, by default, for Goldilocks to remain with them. That was to be the end of it. There was great celebration from the parlor to the servants' hall, and Mrs. Vaughn reported to me that Goldilocks, perhaps feeling another degree safer, delighted everyone by laughing out loud.

That was the beginning of her road to recovery. When Teddy whispered to her now, she was seen to put her mouth to his ear and whisper back. The rest of us looked on with hope in our hearts, never urging or interfering, but leaving it to the little ones to effect a cure in their own way and time.

Soon I was pronounced well enough to sit up and get dressed. I staunchly refused to wear my corset, at first draping a shawl loosely over my dress so that no one would notice, and set about at once to let out the waists on all my dresses, for I did not intend to ever wear the thing again. I had a brief moment of wondering what Mama would have thought, but I remembered her soft and rounded figure. How did I know that she had actually worn one herself?

And so, comfortably attired, I spent a great many hours sitting in the garden recuperating, taking what pleasure I could in the warm breezes and fragrant blossoms that spring had finally bestowed upon us. The sounds of birds and honeybees lulled me into a healing repose, and there seemed to be a cheerful conspiracy to make sure that I should not be left alone too much. Company came and went much of the day: acquaintances from Reverend Snover's Saturday-night soirees, some members of the men's choir, and even strangers who had spent that extraordinary night singing to us at the foot of the cliff and wanted to come and wish me well.

And then one day Mr. Bentley—or Lord Bentley, as Nurse had once reminded me—came to me in the garden. In a formal manner, he spoke kindly of my courage at the waterfall, and said he was glad to see that I was recovering. I saw again the sadness in his eyes, the stiffness of his demeanor. This Lord Bentley seemed like someone else, someone strange to me, and very far removed. Perhaps he had had time to remember himself and his position, and wanted to distance himself from the very memories I cherished. He said all the proper things, and I managed to say all the proper things in return, but my inner turmoil was so great that I almost wished him gone. Perhaps sensing this, he told me that he would soon have to return to his estate. How far away would he have to go, I wondered, before I could forget our one momentous night on the cliff?

At the same time, Reverend Wright became a regular visitor at the Cottage, sitting with me often in the garden, making attempts at amiable conversation, and reading to me from scholarly tomes that gave me a headache. Nevertheless, there was something about him, after his heroic feat of carrying me home, that appealed to my sense of fairness. He was, after all, a fine specimen of bearhood, even with the thick spectacles, and he did have an admirable character, earnest and idealistic, and what crime was there in trying, a bit too hard, to do the right thing? This was the bear who had offered me my only proposal, after all.

Somewhere in that painful time I began to look on him with new eyes. I saw a bear who had devoted his life to goodness and piety, a bear who strove to improve himself. I even allowed myself to imagine what he might become with a little encouragement, and friendly counsel. Finally, the day came when I asked myself: What if he had been right? What if suitability for marriage was best determined by the intellect and common sense? What had love gotten me but a broken heart? I had prayed for a way out of the desert of guilt and loneliness that I saw stretching out before me. Here was a bear who could provide me with a modest home and cubs of my own, and, if not love, then at least a kindly regard, "till death us do part." Surely, that would be enough to fill up my life and save me from spending the rest of my existence alone, tending other people's cubs, daydreaming about the love I had lost. And though it would nearly break my heart to give up my position as Teddy and Goldilocks's governess, I told myself that my most important work with them was done; that now I must do whatever it took to go on with my life and be at peace again. All of these things I considered as dispassionately as I could, and all the time asking myself what Papa would say if I could unburden myself to him. Though there was no doubt that he and Mama had married for love, I thought that if he knew of my lonely torment, he'd understand how desperate I was to escape it.

While I was so absorbed in these thoughts, I had to admit to myself that I might drown in my own unhappiness if I did not make an effort to rejoin the world, and so it was that I stepped into the schoolroom the next morning, my ribs tightly bound, and my inner turmoil masked with a smile. It was gratifying to see how happy this made the children, though it took some work to restore order. I soon found that there was a new development in our former routine: now when I called on Goldilocks for an answer, she would whisper it into Teddy's ear, and he would relay it to me. I recalled Dr. Ehrlichmann's words that the child might begin to speak when she felt safe and free to do so, and thus I accepted this recent advancement without comment, and behaved as if she had spoken directly to me. And then came the day when I called upon her and heard a little voice say, "My real name is Nellie."

I held my breath in excitement, but thought it important not to make her self-conscious by causing a big fuss. "Would you prefer to be called Nellie?" I asked calmly.

"Maybe sometimes," she answered. "I like Goldilocks too."

"Then I will call you Goldilocks, and keep Nellie as a nick-name."

The golden head nodded, and the lesson went on as usual,

with Teddy and me smiling broadly. Naturally, I reported this earthshaking event to the Vaughns. They greeted it with a mixture of delight and dread. The child had always indicated that Mother Shoe was not her real mother. Here was proof that she remembered a life, an identity, before she lived in the shoe. If Nellie remembered her real family, the Vaughns would be honor-bound to try to find them, and perhaps even return the child to them. It seemed that their troubles were not yet over.

Even with this distraction, Reverend Wright's proposal, which I had formerly rejected, was so much on my mind that I found myself, in unoccupied moments, trying to formulate the right words to approach him on the subject. Surely there was little that needed to be said. I had already told him, after all, that my heart belonged to another, and he had declared it to be no obstacle. I just wanted it to be settled, and quickly, certain that I would experience relief from my suffering once the decision was made.

Accordingly, on Reverend Wright's next visit, when we had talked for a while of inconsequential things, I said, "Reverend Wright, I would like to bring up a subject that may perhaps be painful to you."

"Of course, Miss Brown, you must feel free to bring up any subject that you wish."

"I wish to speak of your proposal to me. Would I be right in assuming you have not since become engaged to another? That you are free?"

"I am free unless you will consent to be my wife, Miss Brown. I have not found another more eligible. Is there a chance that you have reconsidered?"

"Well . . ." I hesitated only for a moment. "I believe I have,

Reverend Wright. But there are some things I should wish to settle. I would like very much to continue my work, at least until our own family demands my attention."

"You'll find that I can be very broad-minded, Miss Brown. You would be quite free to work as long as you see fit. But, Miss Brown, may I ask you something?"

"Yes?"

"Have your feelings changed, then, as regards the 'other' to whom you said your heart belongs? Can you be truly content without your heart's desire?"

"That part of my life is closed, Reverend Wright. I wish to leave it behind me."

"As you will, Miss Brown, but do not hesitate to discuss the subject with me at any time if you feel so moved. As a logical being, I am quite without jealousy."

"Thank you for your concern, Reverend Wright. Are we agreed, then?"

"Agreed."

And so he shook my paw, and the matter was settled. I imparted my plans to the Vaughns. Mrs. Vaughn spent a long afternoon with me expressing her concern that I was still very young for marriage. Because of Papa's passing, they felt some responsibility to advise me in the matter, and they were concerned that I had not been myself since the night on the cliff. Perhaps I was rushing into things. I thanked her sincerely for her interest, but convinced her with much sensible-sounding discussion that I knew my own mind, and since I was willing to continue working, the Vaughns ended by reluctantly approving. The banns were posted, and I waited for the feeling of relief that I had prayed for.

42

A Revelation, and a Wedding

With only fifteen days now until the wedding, I threw myself into my work with the children. It seemed that each day Goldilocks's speech increased, and each day brought new surprises: her favorite color was blue, she liked math, she disliked spelling. She wanted to play outside. Bread and jam was "smashing," and spinach "disgusting." She called Teddy by name at every opportunity. Then Mrs. Vaughn reported to me that she had heard Goldilocks say her bedtime prayers aloud the previous night, giving thanks for her home with Teddy, and asking Heaven to bless each of the Vaughns, and "Nana and Ompah." This created quite a stir with the adults. Clearly, the child remembered these loved ones from her past, however dimly. It was decided that the time had come to try questioning Goldilocks about her history. Because of my rapport with the child, and because she had first spoken to me, I was asked to try to draw her out.

The next morning I held her lovingly on my knee. Reminding her that there was no one left to threaten her now for telling the truth, I asked her whether she would try to answer some questions.

"All right," came the quiet reply.

"Very good, then. Shall we start?"

Goldilocks nodded.

"First, I've been wondering if you have another name, besides Nellie, a last name—like *Vaughn* is Teddy's last name?"

She shook her head.

"Let's see. Can you remember living somewhere else before you lived in the shoe with all the other children?" She cast a frightened look my way, and I assured her again that there was no one left now to harm her. Then I tried a different tack and asked whether there was anyone she missed from that former life, perhaps Nana and Ompah? She nodded again, with a tragic expression on her little face.

"Can you tell me about Nana and Ompah, and how you came to be separated from them? Sometimes it feels better to tell someone about things that make us sad."

Her lower lip trembled, but instead of crying, she began to talk in a small, timid voice. "I used to be little," she said. "Nana and Ompah took care of me."

"Really? No wonder you miss them. What do you miss the most?"

"Nana singing. And Ompah sitting me on his knee. He told me stories."

"And what about your mama and papa? Do you remember anything about them?"

"I don't know. I don't think I had a mama and papa." The lower lip started trembling again.

"Do you remember why you left Nana and Ompah?"

"It was music. The beautifullest music. I followed it. I just had to. All the other children around were following it too, but I was the littlest. It was a man all dressed in funny clothes playing music on a pipe, and all the children ran after him, and so did I."

Thunderstruck, I asked her, "Your town, was it called Hamelin?"

"I don't know. Maybe it was."

"What do you remember next?"

"We went a long, long way, with no dinner, and my legs were so tired, but I didn't want to stop. I wanted the music. I wanted to hold it. But they were all going faster than me, and I couldn't catch up. They wouldn't wait for me!"

"Where did you go?"

"I fell by the side of the road and cried and cried, and they kept going and left me there all by myself." A tear ran down her cheek, and she sniffled into her handkerchief.

"I'm sorry, Nellie. That must have been terrible for you. So you never found your way home again?"

She shook her head, the tears coming freely now. I soothed her as best I could, marveling at the revelation that this was a child the Pied Piper had forgotten. When she had calmed herself, I asked, "And what did you do then?"

She seemed reluctant to talk anymore, but I praised her for being brave enough to tell her story, and promised her that would be my last question. Then her words started flowing like a dam had burst.

"I was lost. A long time. I slept under bushes. I walked and walked. Sometimes people passed me, and I put out my hands to beg for food. They threw coins, but I couldn't eat them. I was so hungry! That's when Gabe found me. He took my coins and sent me back to beg for more and more every time somebody came by. Then he said his ma could use a beggar like me, and he threw me over his shoulder and took me." She buried her face in her hands. "I don't want to talk about anything else!"

I held her close for a long time, until her distress had waned. I told her that she'd done beautifully, and then I sent her off to find Teddy while I went to confer with the Vaughns. They responded to the revelations with dismay, Mr. Vaughn saying gruffly that there was only one right thing to do: they must send someone to Hamelin to try to find Nellie's Nana and Ompah.

He arranged immediately for Mr. Caswell to make the trip, though there wasn't much to go on, only the name *Nellie,* and the fact that she had been separated from her grandparents during the Pied Piper's great theft of Hamelin's children when she was very young. Nevertheless, it took only a few days for the lawyer to return with information, for there was a story known throughout the village of Hamelin of a respected old couple, Hannah and Hiram Chase, who had died of grief shortly after they lost their grandchild Nellie, barely more than a toddler at the time. Mr. and Mrs. Vaughn decided, on hearing this, that Nellie had been through enough, and need not know about the deaths until she was older. They started adoption proceedings the same day.

~

By now the lilacs were in bloom, and preparations were going forward for my wedding. There would be very few guests: just Reverend Wright's sensible parents, and the Vaughns as witnesses. Reverend Snover would officiate. Though sentimental touches like wearing my mother's wedding dress, or carrying a traditional bouquet, or having a flower girl strewing petals seemed somehow silly and inappropriate, I reasoned that I would only be married once, and might appreciate the memories of such things to look back on later in life. Accordingly, I took Mama's dress out of mothballs and set about refurbishing it. Teddy was to be our ring bearer, and Goldilocks was to be the flower girl, and there would be a small wedding breakfast put on by Mrs. Snover afterward. My snout was mostly healed, with a little bump and a scar where it had been struck, and though I was still self-conscious about it, Mrs. Vaughn insisted that it gave me character, and would in no way detract from my appearance as a bride.

Mr. Bentley had stayed on to offer the Vaughns his friendly support during the appeal, and through the investigation into Goldilocks's past, which followed, but now that things had settled down, he planned to take his leave. He came to me to say goodbye one afternoon as the children and I walked in the garden.

"I hear that congratulations are in order," he said kindly but, I thought, with some pain in his voice. I hoped my engagement hadn't hurt him, yet I could see no remedy if it had, other than the solace of his own fiancée's company.

"Yes. Next week Reverend Wright and I will be wed. We didn't want to wait."

"Permit me to wish you every happiness."

"Thank you. We will be happy enough."

"Happy enough?"

"I mean happy. We will be happy." There was a little silence between us, then I said, "I never had the chance to thank you properly for climbing the cliff after us. And for everything you did."

"I don't need thanking," he replied. "I would do it again in a heartbeat."

He took my paw, and bent to kiss it. "Goodbye, then, Miss Brown," he said softly, his words like a caress, and he turned and departed, taking all my happiness with him.

⮾

I found myself counting the days until my wedding, waiting desperately for the feeling of relief, of fullness and guiltlessness, I had thought would come to me once I had made the decision to marry Reverend Wright. Perhaps, I reasoned, it would only come when the marriage was accomplished—when there was no way back to Mr. Bentley.

And so the day arrived. I stood in my room, in my mother's silk wedding dress, the epitome of old-fashioned romance and femininity. It didn't look like the dress of someone who was marrying for plain friendship, though I told myself once again that I only wanted the life of a good wife to a good and virtuous bear. This much I thought I could have, even though my heart would always belong to another. But Mama's gown was no plain dress; it was the embodiment of a romantic dream: a four-tiered skirt, an off-the-shoulder lace collar, long embroidered over-sleeves, and a blue velvet belt, tied in front with a bow. It was a dress to make dreams come true in.

At the church, I waited with Teddy and Goldilocks in the vestibule for the music that would accompany me down the aisle. Mrs. Vaughn arranged my veil with a wreath of wildflowers on my head, and handed me the lush bouquet of lilacs that I was to carry. Goldilocks's eyes widened as she scattered a handful of flower petals in front of me, and said softly, "You're so *beautiful,* Miss Brown." I suddenly felt that to be beautiful in the eyes of a child was to be beauteous indeed. I wondered how Reverend Wright would see me, and decided that for this one special hour, I would feel beautiful, and glory in my mother's precious dress.

The processional music began, and Goldilocks and Teddy started their walk down the aisle. Watching Teddy's erect back as he strode self-consciously in his Sunday suit, I had visions of how my own cubs would look someday. Ahead, I caught a glimpse of the fine bear who was to be my husband, and I thought how happy and full my life might be. Happy enough, and full enough.

Following the path of strewn flower petals, I stepped off toward my future.

43

Mama's Dress

❧

What does happiness consist of? Is it in the fulfillment of a dream, or in the striving after it? Is it conferred on us from without, or generated from within? Perhaps it is all of these. I only know that it is best when shared.

Today is a good day for sharing. It is fall, my favorite time of year. The leaves are red and orange and gold, and two larks have struck up a competition for the most exhilarating song in the garden. I sit at my open window as I write, coming to the end of my story. And what shall I impart to you of myself? That I am at peace? That my life is worthwhile? That I am happy enough? I will tell you.

Six months have passed since Reverend Wright left me standing at the altar.

"I can't do it," he whispered to me after I'd walked up the aisle. "You look so . . . so . . . like . . . a real bride."

"Reverend Wright," I whispered back in consternation, "what is the matter?"

"It's the dress, you know. A veritable confection. You should wear this dress for the love of your life, not for me! I'm suddenly very much afraid, Miss Brown, that I could never make you happy."

"But I wish only to be content and useful, Reverend Wright."

By that time there was a buzzing of whispers in the pews behind us as the few guests perceived that things were not going according to plan, and Reverend Snover, who was officiating, put up his hand and asked them for their patience.

"To be content and useful is enough for me," Reverend Wright whispered thoughtfully, "but not for you. I've been so blind. I should have known it from the beginning. But now, as I see you like this, it seems so clear. Can you ever forgive me?"

In that moment, before God and everyone, I was forced to accept the truth of what he said. It was not enough for me, I finally acknowledged, a single tear making its way down my cheek. This marriage could never be a substitute for my heart's desire. I was filled with warmth toward this fine, well-meaning bear, but it was not enough, would never be enough.

"There is nothing to forgive," I whispered back. "I'm afraid you are quite right in your objection, but if you leave me here now, Reverend Wright, I fear it will ruin your reputation."

He smiled slightly and answered, "Imagine me as a cad, a bounder! I rather think it will do me some good." Giving a little bow, he shook my paw, announced to the witnesses that we had changed our minds, and, with his head erect, walked bravely away down the aisle.

Mr. and Mrs. Vaughn gathered around me and asked if I was all right. Mrs. Vaughn offered me her handkerchief, but I assured them both that I was only slightly discomposed. The

Vaughns, though puzzled by the abrupt cancellation of my wedding, said very little about it, Mrs. Vaughn only observing that it was better to change our minds before rather than after the ceremony. Reverend Snover laid his hand on my head and said, "Let this be a new beginning for you. Live well and fully, and trust your Maker to arrange things as he will."

Such wise and simple words, so difficult to live by! However much I tried each day to summon the strength to set my feelings for Mr. Bentley aside and get on with my life, it remained a grievous trial to me. Instead, I found that I became quieter and more introspective, believing that my sadness was a part of me now, and would always be.

And yet life went on. Out on the grounds, and at the end of the long trail, the waterfall still cascaded down the cliffside, a reminder of that momentous night when Teddy and Goldilocks made their desperate stand—the night when a town grew up. Not all minds were changed, of course, but after that near tragedy, Mr. Babcock's newspaper, the *Town Crier*, which had spread so much ill will, lost most of its subscribers. Mr. Babcock closed up shop and moved on to try to peddle his poison elsewhere. The Anthropological Society lived on, though many turned away from it after the incident at the waterfall. Its few remaining adherents remain as determined as ever. But now the village sees the danger, and watches them closely. History will not be allowed to repeat itself in Bremen Town.

In the wake of the events at the waterfall, I tried to set down on paper an account of my own experience and thoughts of that fateful night. The result was an article that I submitted to Mr. Weatherby, the editor of the *Plain Truth*, hoping nervously that he would print it. To my surprise, my wish was immediately gratified. Not only did he print it, but it was very well received, with many responses in the letters to the editor. I was invited to write more articles to be considered for publication, so I wrote about local events, examined from the viewpoint of the Enchanted. I labored mightily over these essays in my leisure hours, always striving to be objective and honest. When these too met with success, I felt that my career as a writer had really begun. Though the pay was very little, the satisfaction was great, and I looked to the future with a bit more hope.

These were halcyon days for Goldilocks and Teddy. Goldilocks quickly made up for her long period of silence by becoming a veritable chatterbox, her lighthearted prattle interspersed with Teddy's low chuckles. My pride in them threatened to make me vain, especially when Mr. Vaughn himself called me aside one day to tell me how much he respected and lauded the work I had done with the two children.

"*Sophos*, Miss Brown, *sophos*! 'Well done,'" he declared, and how I wished Papa could have heard those words of praise!

Mrs. Vaughn was also generous in her approbation. I had expected that she would no longer seek out my companionship once her social life had returned to normal, but in this I had misjudged her. She was especially kind after my canceled wedding, frequently inviting me to join her for tea in the solarium. With motherly solicitude, she did her best to lighten my depression, even suggesting that when my employment as governess was no longer necessary, she should like me to be her paid companion. Perhaps she anticipated that, having failed to marry, I would now become an old maid. This, she assumed, was the cause of my despondency. In the dark hours of the night when I could not sleep, I felt that it was about time I accepted her notion and planned my life accordingly.

By way of solace, I had the Vaughns' whole great library of

books at my disposal, an escape into so many other worlds that I could never explore them all. When I was lost on my literary travels, all else fell away and I became anyone from Queen Guinevere to the hunchback's Esmeralda to the intrepid Gulliver. With the world of books, and my writing, and the whole great estate to traipse around in, I tried to do battle with my melancholy. Still, my last thoughts before sleep were often of the night Mr. Bentley and I spent on the ledge by the waterfall, high above the rest of the world, pointing out obscure constellations, and making up new endings to *Robinson Crusoe* to pass the fearful time. I sometimes imagined I could see Mr. Bentley coming toward me with a smiling face and open arms. This image appeared to me in odd moments of the day, and in my dreams. I occasionally asked Mrs. Vaughn, quite casually, whether there had been any news from Lord Bentley, but there never was.

I was plagued by my blackest doubts, trying to accept the near certainty that I would never see Mr. Bentley again. And so the summer passed. If our existence had become too calm, too predictable, after the excitement and upheaval of the previous spring, no one complained. Then one day a letter arrived at the house from Mr. Bentley. Mrs. Vaughn shared the news with me at tea, knowing, she said, that I would want to hear about what had become of our own Lord Bentley.

"He tells me he leads a quiet life now, since he broke his engagement. He says he has no taste for entertainments, but has taken a villa by the sea. How very dull that sounds. Do you suppose he suffers from melancholia?"

I barely heard her question, as my mind was reeling over the news that he had broken his engagement. "What?" I asked, wide-eyed, needing to hear it again.

She patiently repeated it, then looked at me strangely. "Are you quite all right, my dear? You look a little peaked."

"When did he break his engagement?"

"Hmm. He doesn't explain much about it. He says that he couldn't go through with it after that night at the waterfall, and Miss Wallingsford released him. I wonder what he means, 'after that night at the waterfall.' What has that to do with it?"

"What else does he say?"

"Hmm. Let me see. He says that he spends a great deal of time reading, and takes a solitary walk on the beach every evening. He's tiring of the villa and plans to move to a more distant destination soon. He bids me give his fond regards to everyone here." At this, I put my head down and burst into tears. Mrs. Vaughn, puzzled but compassionate, put her paw on my shoulder.

"What is the matter, child?" she asked. "You have not seemed yourself for some time. You appear to be carrying a very heavy burden. Whatever it is, you have been like a daughter to me. Surely you can confide in me?"

At her words, I looked into her kind face. Though I had kept my silence for so long, I had come to know and trust her, and her invitation to talk freed up something within me. Before I knew it, I was pouring out my heart to her, and she gently put one arm around me and listened.

Mrs. Vaughn leaned her head to one side thoughtfully and said, "I never guessed. You and Lord Bentley?"

"I know it must seem absurd of me, a governess, to imagine a connection so far above my station," I said, "but it was the plain Mr. Bentley I fell in love with, not the viscount."

"And you believe he loves you too?"

"He told me as much once. He said that I would always have his heart, but now he is a viscount, and I am just a commoner. I believe his feelings may have changed."

"Why is that?"

"He's gone so far away, and now wants to go even farther, and makes no attempt to contact me. What else can I conclude?"

"I don't know, child. Let me think," she said, giving my shoulder a squeeze and getting up to walk the floor. Stroking her chin with her paw, Mrs. Vaughn paced back and forth for some minutes, then stopped suddenly and turned to me.

"Has it occurred to you, my dear, that he still believes you to be married?"

"But . . . ? How could he think . . . ? Didn't you— Didn't anybody . . . ?"

"Mr. Vaughn and I spoke of it to no one. We thought you'd prefer it that way. And who else might he be in contact with here in Bremen Town, unless it would be Reverend Snover? He is a man of the church, and would surely not repeat the story to anyone."

"Oh, this is agonizing!" I said, shaking my head. "How will I ever know whether he realizes that I'm free?"

She smiled warmly at me. "I'm sure you can find a way, my dear. Love does."

"Do you think I could write to him? I'm afraid he'd think me terribly brazen! He'd think I was no lady."

"Aren't you willing to take a risk for your love? Pluck up your courage, dear girl!"

And so I did. I wrote a letter, that very night.

> *Dear Lord Bentley,*
> *I hope you will pardon my boldness in writing to you, but it has been such a very long time since last we met, and I haven't heard from you. We at the Cottage in the Woods are all healthy and doing well, but are anxious to hear news of your return.*
> *I thought of another ending to the story of Robinson Crusoe, and will share it with you if you are interested.*
> *I sign myself,*
> *Miss Brown*
> *(as I never did get married)*

I posted the letter myself, and began the long, agonized wait. All through the days and often into the nights, I tried to calculate the time it would take the letter to reach him, and whether he would send any reply, and how long that might take to reach me. After two weeks of little sleep, I was ready to tear my fur out. Still, there was nothing for it except to go about my daily duties, but even Teddy and Goldilocks were unable to claim my attention, and I found myself spending much of my time staring out the window while they did as they pleased.

One day after school was at last over, I went straight to Mrs. Vaughn to see whether there had been any mail for me, and was disappointed yet again. Possessed of an excess of energy, I had formed the habit of tramping about the pathways of the estate every day after tea, drinking in the sweet fall air. On these excursions, I often returned to the waterfall. Despite all that had happened there, I found great tranquillity in the endless cascade of white water, and the rippling lagoon. This was, after all, the place where I had first met Jonathan, and the place where we had faced that long, dark night together. It seemed easier here to call up his memory, and I did so often. It was as I stood by the waterfall that day, listening to its melodic thunder, that I sensed someone approaching, and turned. There, only a few yards away from me, was my dear Mr. Bentley, not imaginary, but as real and solid as the earth I stood on.

"Mrs. Vaughn told me you would be here," he said.

"Yes," I replied simply, words failing me. How can I express my feelings upon seeing him? I smiled with tears in my eyes, clasped my paws before me, and trembled, all at the same time, while the tender hopes I had tried so hard to throttle tingled with the agonizingly sweet sensation of life returning to a sleeping limb.

"And what is the new ending of *Robinson Crusoe*?" he asked, walking toward me. "I have come all this way to find out."

"Well," I said, gathering my courage, "he is very lonely on his island, but he is found, and makes the long trip home, and there he finds a woman who loves him waiting for him with open arms." I matched my gesture to the words.

"Wait, don't tell me! I know this part," he said, coming to me and enfolding me in a passionate embrace. "He marries her and they live happily ever after!"

"Exactly so," I answered, and that was the last we spoke for some time, lost in a flood of feelings too deep to be expressed with words.

When finally we separated, Mr. Bentley went down on one knee and said, "Miss Brown, Ursula dear, will you do me the honor of becoming my wife?"

"Oh yes, dear Jonathan, with all my heart."

❧

Today, as I said, is a perfect autumn day. The sweet fragrance of fallen leaves permeates the light breeze. The mums are in full bloom, and in the garden in front of my open window I can see my Jonathan waving and waiting for me. In such small, ordinary moments lies my greatest happiness, and it is more than enough.

I only wish Papa were here to see us together. I think of Papa often, and how he would have loved Jonathan. "Love is not for the fainthearted," he told me. Later, not long before he died, he asked me to come close, and whispered, "When you know it's the right one, remember, my dear, that you have my blessing."

Thank you, Papa.

I remember.

Acknowledgments

With a full heart, I would like to thank my faithful adviser, my computer tutor and technician, my grammar and punctuation consultant, my counselor through dark days of writer's block, my first reader and indispensable critic, my personal cheering section, and my one-man encyclopedia, Bruce Coville. *Aeternae gratitudinis.*